THE
SINGLE DAD

USA TODAY BESTSELLING AUTHOR
MARNI MANN

ISBN-13: 979-8835141180

To Nina Grinstead, Nikki Terrill, Kimmi Street, Ratul
Sarah Symonds, Sarah Norris, and Chanpreet Sing
For every SINGLE DAD reason.

PROLOGUE

FORD

I was woken by the sound of an alarm. It took me a few moments to shake the sleep from my head until I realized it was coming from my front gate—a notification that someone was at the call box, trying to get in. The only time the alarm ever went off in the middle of the night was if I invited a woman over. Her presence anticipated, my hands stripping off her clothes the moment she walked through my door, my lips devouring every inch of her skin before she reached my bedroom.

But it was three in the morning, and I hadn't invited anyone over.

I sat up, turning on the bedside light, and grabbed the tablet from my nightstand, the screen showing a woman, wrapped in a dark coat, standing in front of my call box.

I enlarged the camera feed, zooming in on her face.

She was vaguely familiar, not enough that I could recall her name.

"Hello?" I said into the speaker. "Can I help you?"

"Ford ... I need to talk to you."

1

I wasn't surprised she knew my name. She was pressing the button on the metal box on the side of my gate, attempting to gain my attention, so I would hope she knew who I was.

It was the urgency in her voice that startled me.

I ran my hand over my hair. The gel I had put in right before meeting my brothers for drinks caused the strands to be hard, cemented in place. "What do you need to talk to me about?"

"You ... me." She paused. "It's important." Another beat passed and then, "Please, open the gate."

I shook my head even though she couldn't see me.

Our law firm's private plane was flying me to Minneapolis in just a few hours to meet with a client. I needed sleep.

"Can you come back? Let's say, Saturday afternoon at a normal time, and we can—"

"No, Ford, I can't. Please. I'm begging you. We need to talk now."

Goddamn it.

I sighed, "I'll meet you outside."

I pressed the button that would allow her in and forced myself out of bed, throwing on a pair of sweatpants and a sweatshirt, walking through my house toward the front. I flipped on the outside light and opened the door. The woman was standing a few feet from the steps with a face I still only semi-recognized, a body that couldn't be seen in the baggy clothes and long, unbuttoned coat. There was a bag that hung from her shoulder and a strange, misplaced bundle of blankets in her arms.

"I'm sorry, you are?"

"Rebecca."

Rebecca. Rebecca.

My eyes squinted as I took in her stare. "You're the bartender at—"

"Yes."

The night we'd had together was starting to come back to me.

Was it six months ago? Ten months? A year even? I couldn't recall.

But the more I gazed at her, more from the evening we'd spent together began to unfold in my head.

As I'd been sitting at the bar, alone, it had begun as a simple flirtation. That led to us speaking the entire night, and I followed her into the back room once the last patron left. The moment the door was locked, I held her against the wall, slamming my lips against hers.

I'd fingered her while she drove us to my place.

I'd spread her across my kitchen island the minute we got inside.

Even if the whiskey had made the details of that night a bit vague, I could still recount the major parts.

"Why are you here, Rebecca?"

She glanced down at her arms, holding the weightless blankets in an odd way. "I don't know how to tell you this ... but she's yours."

"She?" I walked to the end of the small porch, my bare feet balancing on the edge. "What are you talking about?"

She moved closer, holding the blankets toward me, adjusting her position so she could open one and show me what was inside.

It wasn't a bundle.

It was a baby.

She.

I put my hands up in the air. "Whoa, whoa." I swallowed, my saliva suddenly tasting like acid. "There's no way."

"No way?" she mocked. "You mean, exactly forty weeks

ago, you didn't have sex with me without a condom, not bothering to ask if I was on birth control? By the way, I wasn't."

Forty weeks.

That was a fucking eternity ago.

But did I really not use a condom?

I always used one.

Fucking always.

Had the whiskey made me careless?

It ... was possible.

"I ..."

"I realize you probably sleep with so many women that you can't keep them all straight." Her voice softened. "But that's not the case with me, Ford. There was only you." She looked down again. "And now, because of that night, we created her." As she moved once more, now only a foot separated us, even less as she extended her arms across the open space. "Meet your daughter. She was born three days ago." She lowered the blanket, showing me the baby's round face, eyes closed with long, dark lashes that fluttered against her cheeks, like she was dreaming.

What?

I'm a fucking ...

Father?

A feeling catapulted through my stomach.

A feeling I hadn't been prepared for, a feeling that sucked all the breath out of my body.

"Why didn't you tell me?"

Our eyes locked as she said, "Because, at first, I had no intention of keeping her." A war of emotion was raging inside her eyes. "I made the appointment. I went to the clinic." She took a long, deep inhale. "And I couldn't do it." She glanced down, but not at her daughter. She looked at the ground instead. "I just ... couldn't."

My hands shook; my knees didn't want to hold me up.

"That was months ago, I assume. Yet you waited until now to show up. Why? I don't fucking get it." I took in the baby's face, those chunky cheeks and plump, heart-shaped lips. "Why didn't you tell me the second you found out you were pregnant, Rebecca? Why didn't you tell me once you went to the doctor and had it confirmed? You've had forty weeks"—I sucked in some air—"*forty goddamn weeks*—and you're here now? After?"

Does she want money? Is that why she showed up out of nowhere?

Is it something else?

My thoughts weren't straight.

My head a cloudy mess of questions.

My chest a steady, relentless ache.

Rebecca pressed the baby against my stomach.

I immediately reacted, cupping my arms beneath her, taking the weight of this small, precious bundle, holding her so carefully that I didn't wake her.

Rebecca took a step back and said, "The truth is, I never intended to tell you about her. I was just going to give her up for adoption, and you would have never even known she was born."

I held the baby tighter, tilting her toward my chest. "What made you change your mind?"

"The social worker. I didn't trust her and decided I wanted better for the baby." She nodded toward my arms. "She wrapped her arms around our daughter, and I took her back." Her eyes were getting misty. "It wasn't right."

"I don't understand." My head shook as I tried to process what I was hearing. "What are you saying?"

"I don't want her, Ford. I want you to have her, raise her. Be the parent she needs. The parent I can't be to her." The tears started to well in her eyes. "You'll be so much better than me." She placed the bag on my shoulder and wrapped her arms around her still-swollen belly. "After today, you'll never see me again."

I glanced between Rebecca and the baby. "Let's go inside and talk about this. I'm sure you're just exhausted and—"

"I never wanted her, Ford. My feelings haven't changed now that she's born." She held her hand out as though she was stopping me from coming closer. "Either you take her or I'm calling the social worker in the morning." With her other hand, she reached into her pocket and pulled out a card. "I kept her information." Tears now dripped down her cheeks.

"Rebecca, you need to give me a minute to process this." I looked at the baby again, my brain not computing that I was holding my child in my arms. I tried to connect the pieces of her that resembled me. The eyes? Nose? I couldn't think; I couldn't even breathe. "It's the middle of the night; you woke me out of a dead sleep. You're leaving me with a baby." I swallowed. "My baby." When I looked at Rebecca, the tears were wetting her lips. "I don't know what to do. What to think. How to care for her. I have questions. I have ..."

I wanted to take Rebecca by the arm and bring her into my house and tuck her into the bed in my guest room, giving her the sleep she needed. I would call a therapist in the morning, so we could figure out exactly what was going on here.

But those were just ideas, and all I had in this moment were words. Words that needed to be persuasive enough that I could convince her we could somehow do this—together. So far, it seemed like nothing I'd said was registering. She wasn't hearing me; she certainly wasn't listening.

She was just looking at the baby, crying.

"Rebecca, I'm sure it's been almost impossible to get any sleep. You're tired, your body is recovering from—"

"Don't tell me how I'm feeling." She pulled the sides of her jacket together, the material too small on her to close. "I know exactly what I've gone through and what I want, and my mind is made up."

Our stare broke as she looked at her daughter, using the back of her hand to wipe the newest tears. "I failed you ... I'm sorry." Her voice wasn't any louder than a whisper. "Your father will be everything you ever need."

"What? Wait! Rebecca," I called for her as she turned around and walked toward the gate. "You're her mother. You can't just hand her to me and tell me you don't want her, and she's suddenly my responsibility."

Her stare intensified. "You're her dad. Yes, I can."

I held the baby toward her mother, trying to close the space between us, but at the same time, she was moving in the opposite direction. "Rebecca, we need to talk about this, rationally. We need—"

"Everything you need is in that bag. Birth certificate; a form from the attorney, giving you all parental rights; formula, bottles, and diapers. Notes for what you need for her and when to feed her." She turned her back to me, taking several more steps, but looked over her shoulder to add, "Take care of her, Ford."

She hurried out of the gate, and she was gone.

Fuck.

Me.

As though the little one had heard my thoughts, she started to stir. I instantly froze, having no idea what the fuck to do.

Shit.

Is she going to cry?

Is she hungry?

Does she need to be changed?

"*Waaah!*" the baby wailed.

I didn't know how to make her stop or figure out the reason

she was crying—I'd never been around a baby before—but she was getting louder.

Much, much louder.

"Rebecca!" I yelled, trying to look through the hedges for a flash of headlights. "Rebecca, come back!"

While I waited for her to return, I rocked my arms, hoping the movement would help, establishing a pattern of swinging forward and back.

She didn't calm.

She only cried harder, each sway filling my ears with more, "*Waaah!*"

My eyes shifted between the entrance of the driveway to the baby. But the longer I stood here, expecting Rebecca to round the corner at any second, the more I realized she wasn't coming back.

"What am I going to do?"

I gazed at the baby as she screamed in my arms. Her lips, so miniscule, were curled, showing her bare gums, her cheeks scrunched and red from all the crying.

"I don't know what to do," I told her. "I don't know how to make you feel better. Until I can figure out what time it is and wake your grandma up and have her come over here, I need to somehow care for you." I continued to look at her, hoping the answer would come to me. "Are you cold?" I closed the blanket, bunching it up to her neck. "Hungry?"

I waited for the answer to hit me.

For the realization of what I was actually holding and what my eyes were staring at.

For a picture to form in my head of what my life was now going to look like versus the direction I'd believed it was going in.

I didn't know how long I stood there.

Frozen.

My feet should have been taking us inside, where it was warm, where I could go through the bag and see if there was something in there that could soothe her, see if Rebecca's notes told me how to stop the baby's crying.

But they weren't moving.

For some reason ... I was locked.

My knees didn't want to hold us anymore, and they started to bend until they hit the pavement, the sharp slap of hardness jolting something inside me.

I held the baby up to my chest, patting her back. As I rubbed small circles, my body shifting, swinging, a feeling entered. I didn't understand it. I didn't know what it was, but it made me hold her tighter.

It made my arms build a wall where nothing could get in.

"Hey, hey," I whispered into her face. The heat from her crying thick like steam. "I know you don't know my voice or the feel of my arms, but I'm going to tell you something." I pressed my lips against her forehead, breathing her in, her scent so clean and powdery. "I'm never going to let anything happen to you." I held my lips there, my eyes closing, my heart pounding away. "I promise."

ONE

FORD

I sat on the edge of Everly's fluffy pink bed, holding her heavy, long, freshly washed curls in my hands so she wouldn't feel the tangles as I brushed them. Hair time followed bath time—a ritual we did every night.

"Here I go. Wish me good luck," I said.

She snorted. "Good luck, Daddy."

With her wet hair all combed, I separated it into three sections, starting the painful process of weaving. "I swear, your hair gets thicker and harder to braid every day."

"It's 'posed to be easy. You been doing it *foreveeer*."

I laughed at her remark. "Cut your old man some slack, little one. Hair isn't my specialty."

Braids were something I still couldn't grasp. Even though I applied equal tightness to each layer, maintaining a steady pattern, it always came out fucked up.

Crooked. Partially unbound.

But I tried.

I tied the elastic around the bottom and kissed her cheek. "I survived."

"Barely."

I shook my head. "I think you're going to be a comedian when you grow up."

"No, Daddy. I'm going to be an animal doctor—you know this." She turned around and faced me, wiggling her body until her back was against the pillows. The moment she was settled, she pointed to her right. "Now, their turn since you won't be here to kiss them good night."

The stuffed animals.

All twelve of them, taking up an entire side of her bed, which had to be arranged in a specific order and pecked or she wouldn't go to sleep.

A task, like her hair, that had become one of my favorite parts of the day.

I reached across her to line them up, making sure they were balanced and upright, just how she liked them. I finished by placing the lion in front of the pack and asked, "How's it look, boss?"

"The hippo doesn't go in back. I tell you that *every* night. She needs to be in the front by the giraffe."

"Right, right." I moved the hippo to the side, straightening the pink skirt we'd bought for the animal, and then adjusted the pink tie that hung from the giraffe's neck. "How's that?"

"*Muuuch* better. Now, kiss each one good night."

"Each one?"

"*Daaaddy*, they'll have bad dreams if we don't kiss them and say I love you."

"Whatever you say. You're the boss." I quickly pecked the animals and stopped when I reached my baby's forehead, where I left my lips as I said, "Are you going to be a good girl for Hannah when she watches you tonight?"

"Of course, silly."

12

The words that came out of this four-year-old's mouth constantly made me chuckle.

"I'm the silly one?" I tickled her belly. "I think you hold that title, Miss Eve."

She snorted. "I'm always a good girl, Daddy."

"You are. Most of the time." I tucked a loose strand behind her ear. "You know, I'm going to be with Uncle D and Uncle Jenner tonight."

Dominick and Jenner weren't just my older brothers and best friends; they were like second fathers to my daughter.

She crossed her arms and pouted. "Tell them I'm mad at them."

"Mad?" I smiled. "Why?"

"Uncle D promised me pancakes, and I'm waiting. That was, like, *foreeever* ago."

"I just made you pancakes yesterday for breakfast."

"Not your kinda pancakes, Daddy. The kind Uncle D gets me with gobs of chocolate and whip—" She slapped her hand over her mouth. "Oops. I wasn't 'posed to tell you that part."

She thought she was hiding the biggest secret, that I couldn't tell she was hyped up on sugar and covered in chocolate whenever Dominick brought her home.

"I'll let Uncle D know that you're extremely disappointed in him and that he owes you big." I pushed more loose strands off her forehead. "What about Uncle Jenner? What should I tell him?"

She grinned, her eyes widening, licking her bottom lip. "I want him to take me to the house on the giant mountain, so we can eat all the s'mores outside by the big fire."

"You want to go to his house in Utah, huh?"

Jenner had recently purchased a home in Park City, and it had become one of Everly's most desired places to visit. Mine too. There was nothing like escaping to the mountains, getting to ski on some fresh powder, and unplugging from our busy life in LA.

"Yes, silly."

"I see someone has a new favorite word." I hugged her against my chest. "I'm afraid of the teenage version of you. It's a good thing I have quite a few years before we get there. I need to prep myself."

"Daddy, I'm going to be so sassy."

"That's what I'm afraid of."

We were quiet for a few moments, something unusual for my spunky daughter, and I broke the silence to say, "My little negotiator, I know there's still a few hours left before you have to go to bed, but in the meantime, let's not convince Hannah to let you stay up extra late or let you watch something I wouldn't approve of, okay?"

"Or have a popcorn fight in your bed like last time?"

I leaned back to show her my face. "There most definitely won't be any of that, do you hear me?" I paused. "I think I'm still finding kernels in there."

She giggled. "But it was *sooo* much fun."

"I'm sure." As I moved her against me again, I inhaled the scent from the top of her head, the same smell she'd had since she was born. Even though she now chose her own shampoo and I no longer rubbed her chunky limbs with lotion, her scent, to me, hadn't changed. I missed that baby whose body was the length of my forearm, but I was proud of the girl she was turning into.

"I'm going to be home late tonight, so I won't see you until the morning."

"Is Hannah having a sleepover?"

I hugged her tightly, kissing her nest of hair. "She is. Are you going to let her sleep in the guest room?"

"No way. Cousin Hannah sleeps with me. That's the rule."

It was a good thing my princess now had a queen after quickly transitioning from a toddler bed, or the small mattress wouldn't have held Hannah and all of Everly's animals.

"Just try not to kick her tonight. Last time, she almost went home with a black eye."

She covered her mouth with her hand. "That was the lion's fault, Daddy. He's 'posed to protect her. I can't help I get all wild when I sleep."

I loosened my grip, resting her against the bed, and flattened my palm on her stomach, her large blue eyes gazing back at me. "My beautiful baby girl."

"Baby?" she huffed. "But I'm a big girl."

"Eve, you'll always be my baby. Even when you go off to college and get married someday—"

"*Echhh.*"

"Good. That's the sound I want to hear every time I mention boys—boys who need to stay far, far away from my daughter." I held her cheek, giving her five kisses in a row. Not six. Not four. Five was our number. "I won't be here to say this, so have the sweetest dreams."

"Don't forget to tell Uncle D, I'm *maaad.*"

I winked at her. "I won't."

I pushed myself off her bed, surprised to see Hannah in the doorway.

"Hannah!" Everly yelled from behind me.

"What's up, my little bestie?" Hannah said to her, waving. "I have a present for you downstairs, but I need to talk to your dad for a minute, so I'll bring it up when I'm done. Cool?"

"Cool!" Everly squealed. "Yay!"

I turned toward Eve when I reached the doorway. "I love you."

"More than all the stars in the sky, Daddy."

I held her words in my chest, the same way I did every night when she spoke them.

"I'll be back in a few minutes, Eve," Hannah voiced as I joined her in the hallway.

We were nearing the stairs when she said to me, "My God, you two act like identical twins. You even have the same mannerisms."

"Except she's the cuter one."

Hannah smiled. "There's no doubt about that."

As we descended the long wraparound staircase, I nodded toward my cousin's outfit. "You're dressed a little formal for babysitting. Did Eve ask you to look fancy for her tonight?"

Since Hannah had her own code to my house, she'd come over at some point while Everly and I were upstairs. And knowing my daughter, I wouldn't have been surprised if she'd texted Hannah a slew of emojis this morning from my phone and made that kind of request.

"No, I came here straight from the office."

I checked my watch. "You were working this late?"

She sighed. "He's a relentless asshole, and for some reason, he insists on making my life a living hell."

"Who, Declan—"

"*Shh*," she said, cutting me off. "We don't say that name out loud. The man has ears like a dog, and somehow, miraculously, he'll know we're talking about him, and he'll call me back into the office."

"He's meeting us out for drinks tonight, so he won't be doing that."

"The fact that you hang out with that dickhead makes my skin crawl."

Hannah and her twin brother, Camden, were also on the path to being lawyers. Our fathers were brothers, and we had grown up only a few streets apart, so they'd heard my parents

16

talk nonstop law, molding them like they'd molded us. Camden was in school on the opposite side of the country, but Hannah was here, finishing up her last year and prepping for the bar. She worked part-time at our law firm, under Declan Shaw, one of our top attorneys and one of the most ruthless bastards we'd ever hired.

If you needed a litigator, he was the man you wanted behind you.

He could fight like no one I'd ever seen.

And the motherfucker always won.

"One day, when you've graduated and working with us full-time with a portfolio of clients who'll be earning you millions, your opinion of him will change."

She glared at me as we reached the bottom of the steps. "I promise, that's never going to happen."

"Don't be so sure—" My voice cut off as the smell from the kitchen wafted up my nose, my stomach growling. "You baked? Already?"

"I needed to unwind from that monster"—she held up her finger—"the one we don't name—so I stuck some cookies in the oven. They're probably done by now."

I followed her into the kitchen, where she took a tray out of the oven. At least a dozen chocolate chip cookies were sitting on top.

"Yep. Done." She looked at me. "Want one?"

"One? I want three."

She grabbed a spatula from the drawer and placed the dessert on a napkin. "So you can take them with you," she said, handing me the bundle.

I groaned as the chocolate melted on my tongue. "Man, you make some mean cookies."

"If you find crumbs in her bed tomorrow, don't murder me."

The present she'd referenced.

I should have known.

"You know she already brushed her teeth."

She grinned. "And you know I'm still going to give them to her anyway."

"You're the unruliest part-time nanny in the world."

She leaned against the counter, crossing her arms. "Speaking of that ... Ford, we need to talk."

"Oh shit. It's never a good thing when a woman—even if she's your cousin—wants to talk. Should I pour myself a drink first?"

She went to the fridge and grabbed me a beer.

I gulped down several swallows and said, "All right, hit me with it. I'm ready."

"You need to hire a nanny—not me, not your mom, not your mom's housekeeper. I mean, a real nanny."

"That's what this is about?"

She nodded. "I feel like we had this discussion a few months ago, and I'm still here, so this is your not-so-gentle nudge." She picked up a cookie and chowed down half. "Ford, I'm drowning, and even though I love your daughter like I gave birth to her, I need this gig off my plate before I'm down so deep that I can't find my way up for air."

Hannah and I had talked about this in the past, and I hadn't made the move to hire anyone. Everly just loved being with her cousin, and between Hannah, my mom, and my mom's house-keeper, Eve was constantly watched. But I could see the stress on Hannah's face, and with school and prepping for the bar and her time at the office, life was hell for her.

"She'll be starting kindergarten in the fall. Won't that new schedule make it easier on everyone?"

She shook her head. "Everly needs someone there consis-tently, someone she can really bond with and learn from rather than bouncing between three people. This will be the best thing for her, I promise."

"All right," I agreed. "I'll talk to my assistant. We'll get someone hired soon."

She finished the cookie and grabbed another. "I appreciate it. My waist appreciates it too."

"Stop. With how much you run, you can afford to eat that entire tray." I guzzled down the rest of the beer and set the empty on the counter. "I'm going to head out. You two be good tonight."

"Always."

As I was leaving the kitchen, I said over my shoulder, "She can have one cookie."

"That really means two."

I chuckled and turned around. "You sure you don't want me to give Declan a message from you? Possibly tell him how much you love—"

"You're a dick."

I smiled. "See you in the morning, Hannah."

I hurried out the front door and into the driveway, where my driver was parked and waiting. I climbed into the back of the SUV and wished Stan a good evening before I took out my phone and called my assistant.

"Hi, Ford," my assistant said as she answered.

"Remember that conversation we had a few months back about hiring a nanny, and we did nothing about it?" I stared out the window as Stan pulled onto the road. "Well, it's time we do something about it."

"If I remember correctly, I found an agency that came highly recommended. How about I go that route and place an ad on one of the childcare websites, and I can vet the applicants before I send them to you?"

"I can probably squeeze a few more weeks out of Hannah. Will that give you enough time?"

"It should."

I leaned my shoulder into the door. "Then, that sounds perfect."

"I'll get started first thing in the morning."

I thanked her and hung up, and my phone instantly rang with Jenner's name on the screen.

"I'm on my way," I said after connecting the call.

"I was worried your ass was going to bail."

"Because I'm fifteen minutes late?"

I didn't bother to look at my watch.

I knew exactly how late I was.

"Try thirty," he replied.

"Dude, relax. I get an Everly pass." I felt Stan begin to slow as he approached the entrance of the bar. "You can yell at me in person. I'm about to walk in." I hung up and returned the phone to my pocket.

Stan pulled up to the front. "I'll be in the parking lot on the east side of the building whenever you're ready to leave."

"Thanks, bud."

I hopped out and made my way inside, seeing the crew had taken over the entire back corner. Dominick was the first to approach, man-hugging me the moment I got within reach.

"Thought you weren't going to show," he said as he patted me on the back.

"Jenner bitched about the same thing," I said. "You guys know I wouldn't ever bail. But once you knock up Kendall, you'll learn that it isn't always easy to get out the door on time."

He pulled away and walked with me toward the tables they'd reserved. "Slow your roll. There's no knocking up. We're just getting in a shit-ton of practice."

20

"Then, maybe it's Jenner's turn," I said, moving over to my middle brother, hugging him the same way.

"What are we talking about?" Jenner asked.

"You and Jo having kids," I replied.

"Please don't put that into the universe," he shot back. "We're staying in the engaged phase for a while. If Jo gets the baby bug, we'll steal Everly for a few days."

"According to Eve, she's no longer a baby."

"That's my girl, full of sass," Dominick said.

I shook hands with Brett, one of our best friends, who happened to be the top entertainment agent in the country. I then moved on to his partners, Max and Jack, who were also agents, before finally making my way over to Declan.

"I brought you a little gift," I said to him and took the napkin-wrapped cookie out of my pocket and set it on the table in front of him.

"What the fuck is this?" Declan asked, unwrapping it.

"Hannah made it." I smiled. "You know, the girl you're driving into the fucking grave."

"Jesus Christ." He held up his whiskey. "I need ten more of these just to deal with her. If she wasn't a Dalton, I would have fired her ass a long time ago."

For some reason, I doubted that.

I nodded toward the dessert. "Eat the cookie. Trust me, it's one of the best you'll ever have."

He inspected the top and bottom. "You're sure she didn't poison it?"

"She doesn't know I brought it for you."

If she had, she would have set the whole tray on fire.

I wouldn't tell Declan that. He didn't need the ammunition to make her life even worse.

"Fuck me." He moaned as he chewed. "You weren't kidding. This is exceptional."

"She's good, isn't she?"

"At least she's good at something since it's certainly not law." He took a drink from his tumbler, washing down the sweetness. "Maybe she should become a baker. That sure as hell would save her a lot of headaches—headaches I plan to give her."

"You know she's going to be one of the top litigators at our firm." I squeezed his shoulder. "And the moment she passes the bar, she's going to give your ass a run for your money."

"Bullshit."

I smiled. "Don't underestimate that girl, Declan."

He waved me off. "You don't know what you're talking about, Ford."

When Jack joined us, starting up a conversation with Declan, I took a quick inventory of the tables. All the guys had drinks, and a waitress wasn't anywhere in sight. So, before I took a seat, I decided to head to the bar and place an order.

"What can I get you?" the bartender asked.

"I'll take a—"

"Espresso martini," a woman said, cutting me off.

Her voice was so savory and enticing that I found myself turning around to see what she looked like.

And, *fuck me*, I was taken aback by what I saw.

My hand reached for the edge of the bar, holding on as my eyes dipped all the way down her body.

Slowly.

And rose with no hurry at all, making sure I didn't miss a single detail.

This girl didn't just have a beautiful face; she had it all.

She was absolutely fucking stunning.

With curly, long, dark hair that framed her face like French doors. Icy-blue eyes. Thick, heart-shaped lips, and a dusting of freckles that sat high on her cheeks, light, like whispers.

Our gazes locked.

But I couldn't help myself.

I had to continue viewing her body.

It wasn't often that I got to see one as perfect as hers.

I almost moaned as I studied her—her dips and curves, her arches that were emphasized by her skintight red dress.

Why the hell is it so hard to breathe?

"I'm sorry," she said, her hand gently touching my shoulder. "I'm not the kind of girl who cuts the line, I swear. I just couldn't tell if the bartender was asking you or me. I promise I wasn't being rude."

Her words didn't register.

I was far too lost.

The iciness of her eyes holding me.

The intensity that roared beneath her stare.

But aside from her irises, there was nothing frosty about this girl.

She was all warmth and fire.

Two things I wanted to feel.

Two things I wanted to taste.

Oh fuck.

The only thing that would tone down these impulses was a drink. I looked at the bartender and said, "I'll take a whiskey, neat, and add her order to my tab." I handed him my credit card.

"Oh gosh, you don't have to do that," she said. "Please, let me buy you a drink."

Her hand was suddenly back on my arm—I couldn't remember the moment it had left—and the feeling of her fingers was like a blast that shot right through me. The heat from each fingertip slipping through my shirt and heading straight for my fucking dick.

"Consider it a perk of cutting me off in line."

Even her laugh was captivating.

She repositioned, leaning her back against the bar, now giving me a full view as she faced me. "Thank you. That's very kind of you." She pulled back her hand, covering her mouth while she yawned. "I can't tell you how much I need this espresso. I'm beat."

With her palm gone, I couldn't take my eyes off her lips. "A long day?"

"A long year."

I chuckled. "Shit, maybe you should order two."

Her hair fell into her face, and she instantly pushed it back, exposing both shoulders. Shoulders and a collarbone that showed the tan line of a thin bikini strap.

Damn it, that was sexy.

"One drink should hopefully get me over this jet lag," she said.

"Let me guess ..." My words were only an excuse for me to stare harder, acting as though I could see through her. "Europe?"

Her smile was sensual, beautiful. "London ... how did you know?"

"Call me intuitive."

"*Ohhh,* then you already know I only just got back this afternoon."

"Of course I do. But keep talking."

She laughed. "I was there this time for three months, so to be honest, I'm not sure if it's today or tomorrow or if my feet are on the ground or still in the air." She sucked in a mouthful of air. "But your eyes are telling me I'm very much here ..."

"You're here." I ran my thumb over my lips, wishing they were covered in her scent. "And this isn't a dream ... even if it feels like one."

First, she gave me a smile, then a slow bite of her bottom lip.

"Your espresso martini," the bartender said, placing her drink on the counter.

She reached for it and held it in her hands, her eyes returning to me.

"So, you land in LA and head straight for a bar. I like your style."

She pointed toward a group of girls who were only feet away. "It's my best friend's fault. I've been gone for the last several years—not just in Europe, but all over. She dragged me out with some other friends to celebrate my return."

"A wise decision on your friend's part." My stare dipped once more. "You landed in the right place."

A redness moved across her cheeks that even lowered to her chest.

She said nothing for several seconds, finally voicing, "I'm Sydney." Her fingers extended.

I clasped her soft skin in my hand. "Ford."

"Your whiskey, neat," the bartender said.

Our hands separated, and I clasped my drink and held it in front of hers. "To accidental encounters, Sydney."

Her teeth pierced her lower lip again. "I like that. Cheers."

TWO

SYDNEY

"Are you following me?" I said to the delicious man at my side as we attempted to part from the bar.

Except, apparently, we were going in the same direction, his pace matching mine, our arms almost close enough to touch.

The last few minutes I'd spent with him was a blur of tingles and pulses.

Even now, just walking next to him, I wobbled in my heels, simply from his smile and presence.

I didn't know where he had come from, but, *my God*, I was overtaken by him.

By his handsomeness.

His charm.

His eyes that felt like they could penetrate right through my skin.

"Only if you want me to," he replied, his stare backing up his offer, one that was strong enough to make me shudder. He pointed in the direction where we were headed and added, "My friends and family are over there."

I followed his finger to where a group of guys, dressed

similar to Ford, took up two tables in the back. And of course, the next table over was where my girls sat.

"So are my girlfriends," I told him. "Looks like we're going to be neighbors."

We reached the back of the bar, and he said, "Let me know when you're ready for a refill, Sydney."

He gave me a final look, one that felt like a wave, starting at the top of my head, swishing all the way to my feet, and then he took a seat.

I hurried over to Gabby, where there was an empty chair next to her.

"Um, hello? Who was that hottie you were just talking to?" she asked the second I sat.

"*Shh,*" I whispered. "I don't want him to hear you."

"You do realize we're in the middle of a bar? And the music is loud? And he's surrounded by a ton of friends? I'm positive he can't hear us."

"And he's less than three feet away—yes, I realize all of that."

Because even though three feet separated us, I felt like he was still in front of me, his stare owning me.

Little sparks moved through my body, like I was plugged into an outlet.

"Fine, I'll whisper," she said, only slightly softer than before. "Again, who is that hottie?"

Gabby and I had been best friends since high school, and now, we were roommates. She was also the main culprit for dragging me out, which was exactly how it had looked when she pulled me off the couch and forced me into this dress.

Who is he?

Sigh.

"An accidental encounter." My heart sped up as I said those words—his words. Ones that were so perfect that my pulse continued to rise. "I cut him off in line at the bar. I hadn't meant to, but I can't lie; I'm almost glad I did. That man is *whoa*. Whoa on just every level."

"Agreed, girl, but *daaamn*, I can't figure out why you're here when you should be three feet over there, sitting on his lap."

I stole a quick glance in his direction. His profile faced me, giving me a view of that incredibly sexy beard and those full lips and that square jaw and those broad, muscular shoulders.

My God.

He must have felt my gaze because he turned toward me, causing me to look away before I got caught.

I did everything in my power to keep my eyes on Gabs while I said, "We met. We exchanged names. He bought me a drink." I took a deep breath. "That's it, nothing more. Definitely no lap sitting."

Sadly.

But just like I wasn't the girl who would rudely cut ahead of him, I also wasn't the kind to straddle him in the middle of a bar.

And even if I was feeling aggressively out of character, I was in no position to straddle anything other than dreamland tonight.

I hadn't even been back in LA for twelve hours. My clothes still hadn't arrived from the boxes I'd shipped, and I currently didn't even have a bed. I would be sleeping with Gabby or on the couch for the foreseeable future.

"Well, I have to disagree," she said. "It looked like he was about to ravish you." She waved her hand in front of her face, like she was hot. "The chemistry, girl. Oh my God, the chemistry."

I sipped my martini. "Really?"

"His eyes were on the verge of knocking you up."

I laughed. My best friend was so over the top sometimes. "Ford is extra swoony—I can't deny that. But I assure you, the only thing growing inside me is a heavy case of jet lag and a wicked need to take off these heels and find myself a pillow."

"*His* pillow." She put her arm around my shoulders and turned me toward him, saying in my ear, "Even his name is sexy."

My eyes briefly closed. "I know."

"Do you know what I see when I look at him?"

"I can't wait to hear this."

She squeezed my shoulder. "Handcuffs. Dirty sex. Waking up in the morning with his face between your legs." She lowered her voice, finally whispering, "That man has dominance written all over him."

I wondered if she could sense how sweaty I was getting.

How it only added to the hotness Ford had already built.

"You can tell that just by looking at him?"

"I possess that talent. You should know this by now."

I'd only seen my best friend a handful of times over the last four years. All of our conversations had taken place over the phone—through text or FaceTime. Even then, our schedules made our time limited, so we had to squeeze in all the important details in just a few minutes.

Therefore, I'd almost forgotten she had this talent and how she came with zero filter.

"Gabs, what are you trying to tell me?"

"You need to go jump that man before he goes home with someone else."

I looked away from him, scanning the rest of the room so I wouldn't be so obvious. But after a few seconds, I returned to his profile, watching his lips puff out as he took a drink. That mouth had certainly been made for kissing. Surrounding his lips were short, thick, dark, well-groomed hairs that continued up his cheeks and over his chin. Even though his almond-shaped hazel eyes weren't on me, they were striking.

The moment the glass left his mouth, his hand brushed away the wetness from his lips.

A hand with fingers that were long, thin.

Perfect.

Yum.

"I'm starting to think this time difference is messing with your ability to see how scrumptious he is."

"Oh, I see." As I filled my lungs, more tingles burst through my chest. I turned, now looking at my best friend. "But I'm half dead, I'm here with my girls tonight, and my life is"—I took another breath, bringing myself back down to reality—"in this weird, in-between phase, giving me no position to really get my flirt on."

She patted my cheek like a baby's butt. "You're sexy as fuck. You haven't been laid in what ... years? You have every reason to get your flirt on, especially now that you're back for good and you can once again appreciate what LA has to offer, starting with that man over there."

"You're relentless."

"No, I'm your voice of reason."

"And you're relentless," I repeated. I took a moment to soak in this conversation, the fact that it was happening here, in person, and not over the phone. That I was at this popular, well-known bar—a place I'd never been before because the last time I'd really had a chance to hang in Los Angeles, I wasn't of legal age. "Regardless, it just feels really good to be home."

She tucked one of my big curls behind my ear as she said, "I was worried that wasn't ever going to happen. That once you left your job, you were going to stay in New York."

I had spent months debating on where I wanted to live. Even though I'd been traveling the world, New York was where

I'd come back to at the end of each trip, a city I'd become familiar with.

But a city where my best friend and family didn't live.

"I made the right choice," I admitted, smiling.

"Yes, you did, and now, we're going to celebrate with shots." She looped her arm through mine and then said to Carrie and Natasha, friends who were deep in their own conversation, "Shots, shots, shots!"

Why was I not surprised that there were already eight shot glasses on the table?

Glasses I hadn't noticed when I sat down because I hadn't been able to keep my eyes off Ford.

"What's in those?" I groaned.

"Tequila," Gabby replied, "two for each of us." With our arms still hooked, she raised her glass into the air and said to the group, "To Sydney, who's going to see stars tonight."

"No." I shook my head but still held my tequila into the air, and we clinked all our shots together. "That's a terrible idea."

"Remember, I'm never wrong," Gabs replied, air-kissing me before she downed her shot.

My throat burned as I swallowed the liquor, and I immediately reached for the lime that hung on the rim of the glass, my eyes watering as I sucked on the tartness.

"One more," Gabby ordered, grabbing a full shot. "Come on, girls."

"We have all night," I told her. "Shouldn't we be pacing ourselves?"

"Don't worry, my little lovebug." She twirled a piece of my hair around her finger before we downed our second shot. "I'm going to make sure this is a night you'll never forget."

I had no idea how she planned to make that happen, but just as my chest was starting to settle from the tequila, I heard in a gritty, tantalizing voice, "Need another martini?"

I hadn't seen Ford change seats, sitting in the one on the other side of me.

And for some shocking reason, I hadn't felt him.

But as I turned, meeting those hauntingly beautiful hazel eyes, my body instantly responded. "No." I tried to find my breath, his new position sucking all the air out of me. "I've barely recovered from those shots." I nodded toward the empty glasses.

His stare dipped, but not to the table. It lowered down my face, focusing on my mouth. "Shots aren't your thing?"

"I'm more of a sipper than a chugger."

He laughed. "That's cute."

Hearing those words from his mouth, in that deep, dark voice, was far from cute. It was like a moan vibrating across me.

His gaze, like a set of hands wrapping around me, was more intense than I'd ever felt.

"Interesting ..." His eyes narrowed. "That earned me a smile. Why?"

The combination of the martini and shots was slowly dropping my inhibitions, especially as I glanced toward Gabby, who had moved to the other side of the table, closer to Natasha and Carrie, her facial expression urging me on.

"I don't know." I glanced down; all of this was too much. "I guess I like the way you sound."

"My voice?"

I nodded as I was fixed on him again. "Yes."

"No one's ever commented on that before."

I took a drink even though I didn't need it. "It matches you —I mean, it fits your face, your ..." I couldn't think of what I wanted to say. Nothing was coming to me. I didn't even feel like I was breathing. "Exterior."

The corner of his lips lifted, a half-smile so devilishly attractive. "Exterior, huh?"

"If power had a sound, it's you."

He was sitting between both tables but chose to lean his elbow on the one closest to me. "My voice isn't where I hold my power, Sydney. At least, not in my personal life. But I'll tell you, it wasn't a bad guess."

My brain was spiraling.

My legs were already feeling weak.

"No?" I swallowed. "Then, where?"

He licked across his bottom lip and said, "Here."

His mouth.

Because of the things he could do with it. The way he could use it to make a woman feel.

I'm dying.

"And here," he said, holding his hands on the table.

I'd noticed his fingers long before this, and I didn't doubt their strength.

Their talent.

Their ability.

"A refill," one of the guys said to Ford, breaking our contact, placing a drink in one of his hands.

"Thanks, buddy," Ford replied.

I almost gasped when his eyes found mine again, the feeling so overwhelming.

"Are you sure you don't want another one?"

I shook my head. "I'm sure." My martini was still half-full, and I brought it up to my lips. "It's already working. I'm not tired anymore."

In fact, I couldn't feel anything.

Except him.

"That didn't take much to get over your jet lag."

I huffed out a mouthful of air, not knowing how to say he'd made it disappear. But I had to say something, so I glanced around the bar. "It must be the energy in here."

"Or it's me."

I felt my eyes go wide as they connected with his.

He reached forward, and I held in my breath, expecting his hand to land on me but it didn't; it just tugged on the hair that was stuck to my lip, moving it out of my face.

"What's your last name, Sydney?"

"My ... last name?"

He smiled. "I've now bought you a drink, and I've shown you the sources of my power." He winked. "It seems only fair that I know a little more about you."

"Summers."

"Sydney Summers," he said, his tone the grittiest it had been so far. "I like that." He took a sip of his new drink, sucking one of the ice cubes into his mouth. "I'm Ford Dalton."

"Ford Dalton," I repeated. "That's like the perfect celebrity name."

"No interest in being one of those." He paused. "I like right where I am at."

"In life or ..."

"Right now."

Oh.

Gabby was right.

This man was dominant.

I let his response simmer, my chest pounding, my hands steamy even though they were wrapped around the chilly martini glass.

"You know how I ended up here tonight." I glanced behind him at his friends. "What's your story?"

He shrugged. "The guys were going out, and I was craving a drink."

I would have needed the break and looked around the bar. Not Ford. He stayed glued to me.

"This is one of our favorite spots. The rest ... you've witnessed."

Because he'd spent that time with me.

First at the bar.

Now here.

Where I swam through his gaze.

Had it been seconds?

Minutes?

I had no idea.

"I have this feeling about you, Sydney. This hunch that won't go away."

"Yeah?"

He moved a little closer, our faces now aligned, to the point where I could even see his eyelashes. "You're really not the kind of girl who cuts off people in line. Something tells me you're a healer, not a fighter."

I nodded and said, "You're right." I exhaled. "I don't know how you know that."

He shifted just a few inches, the movement causing his coat to part, showing more of the button-down he wore beneath. With the collar open, I could see there was a hint of muscle and a light dusting of hair. "I'm reading you, Sydney."

"If that's true, then what else do you know about me?"

"Do you really want to know?"

My heart was on the verge of exploding.

My lungs couldn't take in any more air.

There was shaking happening from somewhere inside me, but I couldn't place it, and I couldn't stop it.

"Yes."

"Your breath hitches every time my eyes land on you. The longer I stare, the harder you breathe." His voice lowered again as he continued, "Your skin is heating. There are goose bumps slowly rising over your arms."

I could feel them.

The sweatiness too.

He was right.

About everything.

His mouth moved even closer. "There's a tingle inside your body. You've been trying to repeal it, dismiss it. But you can't."

The tingle had been replaced with fire.

One that was so strong that it owned me.

And I was completely, utterly lost.

"Do you have the same ability, Sydney?" He waited. "Are you able to read me?"

I shook my head, unable to form any words.

This time, when he reached forward, his hand landed on me. It held my cheek as his thumb pulled at my lip—I hadn't even realized I had been chewing on it—and he freed it from my teeth.

"What I'm thinking about is your mouth." He ran his thumb over my bottom lip and then the top. "What it would taste like. What it would feel like." His gaze was there, on the spot he was speaking about, making those same lips part. "And I don't know how much longer I can wait to find out."

THREE

FORD

"You want to kiss me"—her voice was soft, breathless—"in the middle of the bar?"

With my hand still on her cheek, I aimed her mouth up to mine. "It's not just that I want to." I lowered my face until we were only inches apart. "It's that I have to." The feeling inside me was so brutally overwhelming that I couldn't leave this bar until I had her taste on my tongue. Until I was satisfied with the feel of her lips. That was why I'd moved my seat next to hers. To have this moment between us, to re-create the fire that I'd felt before. "If you don't want this, Sydney, tell me to stop."

I waited.

And just as I was about to close the space between us, she whispered, "Ford ..." She swallowed. "I want this."

My mouth crashed against hers, my tongue slipping between her lips, a tropical coconut scent filling my nose.

Fuck.

She tasted even better than I'd anticipated. A sweetness that hadn't just come from the liquor she'd been drinking or her perfume. A sensuality that dripped from her body that she seemed unaware of.

This woman wasn't just sexy.

She was breathtaking.

As I pulled her closer, moving her to the end of her chair, her back arched. I ran my fingers up and down her spine, taking in the temperature of her skin. There was a thin bra strap, lacy material holding her tits in place. Her nipples hard and poking, dying for me to lick.

Bite.

My cock fucking throbbed.

I widened my legs to move her in between them and held her face, devouring her lips, memorizing their feel, flavor.

When I finally came up for air, every bit of her flesh was flushed.

I was sure mine was, too, and I couldn't catch my breath.

All I knew—what I was absolutely positive about—was, that kiss wasn't enough.

She touched her mouth, blinking several times as her fingers traced across it. "Ford ..." Her hand flattened against her chest, pushing as though she were trying to move air through her lungs. "God, you can kiss." She lifted her hair off her neck.

That was because it hadn't just been a kiss.

It was a promise.

But, fuck, I wasn't the same man I had been four years ago, when I would have taken her by the hand and brought her back to my place. It wasn't just my house anymore; it was Everly's, and my daughter came first. That meant random hookups and one-night stands were all sacrifices I had given up when she was placed in my arms.

Sydney's fingers were on my stomach, rubbing the outline of my abs, causing my cock to fucking pound against my zipper. I would do anything to be inside her pussy right now, to feel her naked body pressed against mine, to have her moans filling my ears.

To give her so many fucking orgasms that she lost her voice from screaming.

My lips touched her cheek, skin that was soft, delicate. I dragged them to her ear, inhaling her scent that reminded me of a piña colada, hair that tickled my face.

"Your friends are standing at the bar. Go to them," I whispered in her ear.

Her chest stopped rising as she moved to look at me.

"Go," I added, "before I toss you over my shoulder and carry you out of here." I took a breath, only smelling her. "One more second, and I won't be able to stop myself." I ground my teeth into my lip, her gaze taunting me, building this tease. "Sydney ... go."

Her smile made my dick even harder, especially as she swiped a finger across my lips, like she was wiping herself off me, before she walked over to her friends. I watched every step she took, the back of her just as gorgeous as the front. An ass that was the perfect shape with just the right amount of thickness, toned legs that made me groan as I thought about wrapping them around my face, hips that only accentuated her curves.

Goddamn it.

There wasn't a girl in this bar who compared to her.

I had to force myself not to follow her, to look away, to focus on the guys who were sitting around both tables in front of me.

"Jesus Christ," Jenner said, taking the empty seat next to mine, moving it closer before he sat. "Who the hell was that?"

"A girl I can't get enough of." I put my back toward the bar, so I wouldn't keep staring at her.

"She must feel the same way because she keeps looking over here," Dominick said.

"Oh, hell yes, that girl has it bad for you," Declan said.

I shook my head. "It doesn't matter. She's not coming home with me. You guys know I don't play like that anymore."

I downed my drink and set the empty on the table.

Dominick handed me his and said, "Ford, you're only thirty years old. You're not dead. You need to fucking live a little. There's nothing wrong with being a father and getting your dick wet once in a while."

"You say that like I'm celibate. We all know that I'm not."

The guys knew I'd dated a little since Everly had been born. None of those relationships had lasted more than a few months, and none of those girls had stepped foot inside my house.

I didn't know balance.

I didn't know how to make anyone a priority other than my daughter.

And that was the demise with each girl I'd gone out with.

"Celibate, no. Semi-celibate, unfortunately, yes," Jenner said.

"Listen to me, brother," Dominick started. "It doesn't make you a bad father to take a little time for yourself." He squeezed my shoulder, shaking me. "And if you don't jump on that fucking girl, then you're a damn fool."

"Even if I was going to consider it—which I'm not—Hannah and Everly are at my house. It's not like Eve is staying at Mom and Dad's for the night and I'm free."

"More Hannah talk," Declan groaned. "I still can't believe you let her watch your daughter."

"Ignore him," Jenner said, referring to Declan. "Everly is being well taken care of tonight, so you do have all the freedom to do whatever you want—and I know that girl is exactly what you want."

"You guys don't get it," I told them. "This is one of the sacrifices you have to make when you have a kid, and being a single dad makes it even harder. I'm responsible for that little girl, and every move I make affects her." I looked at my brothers. "When you guys were single, you could fuck whomever you wanted and never feel guilty about it. You could jump on a plane and leave at any time. You could stay out all night and not give a shit." I chomped on the ice from Dominick's glass and set the empty on the table. "My life isn't like that."

"But you can go to her house," Jenner said. "What's stopping you from doing that?" Just as I was about to respond, he added, "Hannah's at your place, and she'll stay there until you get back in the morning—whatever time that might be." I attempted to reply again, and he continued, "You've traveled for work; you've traveled for pleasure. Both instances, you've left Everly with Hannah or our parents. How would tonight be any different?" He smiled. "Try to fight me on that. I dare you."

My mouth opened, but I closed it as I thought about what he'd said.

Go to her house.

Something so simple that surely should have crossed my mind, but I hadn't even considered it. Hannah would stay until I got home; that certainly wasn't a problem. I could come back in the morning before Everly woke up.

In less than an hour, Sydney's legs could be wrapped around me, her nipples in my mouth while I buried my cock inside her.

My hard-on returned.

"Now, that's a possibility," I told the group.

"Then, what the fuck are you waiting for?" Jenner asked,

giving me his drink too. "You're starting to act like a fucking dinosaur, and it's scaring the shit out of me."

"I'm not *that* bad."

"No," Dominick replied. "You're worse. Now, go think with your dick"—he nodded toward the bar—"and go buy them a round of drinks."

Jenner pushed my shoulder. "Giddyup."

Declan added, "And for one goddamn night, stop being the nice guy."

"All right, all right." I pushed myself off the stool. "You guys win."

"Nah," Dominick said. "You win."

I walked to the bar, moving in behind Sydney, gently clasping her waist, my mouth not far from her ear, where I whispered, "I can't stay away from you."

She'd stiffened from my touch, loosening once she realized it was me. "I'm surprised it took you this long to come over."

I liked that answer.

And from her profile, I could see her smile.

I handed the bartender my credit card. "Whatever the girls want, it's on me."

"Ford ..." She looked at me over her shoulder. "You really don't have to do that—again."

One of her friends grabbed Sydney's arm and said, "Speak for yourself, woman. I'm a poor college graduate. If that man wants to buy me a drink, I'm going to say hell yes."

I laughed as the bartender swiped my card and handed it back to me. "It's my pleasure. Get whatever you want." I tightened my grip on Sydney's waist, my hands scorching from the heat that was coming off her hips. I got closer, wanting to feel more, to soak in her scent.

She pressed her back against my chest and said, "My best friend is much needier than I am."

"I can handle it." My mouth moved to the edge of her ear this time, and her exhales matched mine, like our bodies were building together.

"Tequila for all of us," Gabby said to the bartender.

"None for me," I replied.

I wanted to remember this.

Every fucking second of it.

"Or for me," Sydney added.

"What's wrong with you two?" Gabby asked.

When Sydney turned around, facing me, my stare dipped down her body, slowly taking in those perfect-sized tits and her slim waist, the way the dress hugged the outside of her thighs.

"I have all I need right here."

Sydney smiled.

A sight so fucking beautiful that it was almost painful.

"Okay, that was the dreamiest answer," Gabby said. "Please marry that man. Immediately."

Marriage.

A word that made me shiver.

As Gabby walked toward the other girls, leaving us alone, I closed the space between Sydney and me, holding the back of her head.

Several seconds of silence passed before I said, "I'm going to do something that I never do."

"What's that?"

"Ask you to leave with me."

Her teeth were back, grazing her lip. "Please, that's something I never, ever do."

She was a good girl.

An innocent girl.

I'd felt that long before she said it.

My hand lowered to her stomach, the flatness as sexy as the dip of her curves. "Let's get out of here." When she didn't argue, I added, "Tell your friends, so they don't worry about you."

While she went over to where the three of her friends had moved, I turned toward Dominick. Once his eyes caught mine, I nodded and mouthed, *I'm out.*

I know, he mouthed back.

By the time I faced Sydney again, she was joining me.

My hand went to her lower back, and I brought her outside to where my SUV was waiting. I opened the door for her, and once she was in, I climbed in after and wrapped an arm around her back, pulling her toward me.

As soon as Stan had us out of the lot and onto the main road, I kissed across her cheek and whispered, "Give my driver your address."

She quickly glanced at me. "We can't go to my apartment."

"We ... can't?"

She shook her head. "I just moved here, like, hours ago, remember? I don't have a bed yet, so I'm going to be sleeping with Gabby. I can't kick her out and have her crash on the couch. That would make me the worst bestie ever."

Fuck me.

That wrecked every one of my plans.

"Can't we go to your place?" she asked.

My place—a detail I didn't want to get into.

I glanced out the window, trying to come up with a plan.

I could take her to a hotel; I just didn't know how that idea would come across. I could sneak us into Dominick's guest-house, but Kendall was probably home, and I didn't want to alarm her.

"Sydney—" My voice cut off as our eyes connected.

The hunger, the need. I didn't know if I was gazing at my own reflection in her stare or if she felt the same way as me.

Either way, I hauled her body up against me and kissed her.

The warmth from her mouth, the taste of her tongue, like silent promises of what was waiting for me between her legs.

I pulled my lips away and said, "Stan, we'll be going to my house."

"No problem," he replied.

I didn't know what the hell I was doing, what I was saying, what the fuck I was thinking, but I certainly couldn't walk into my house with Sydney unless I gave Hannah a heads-up.

"I just have to send a quick text. Give me a second," I said to Sydney and pulled out my phone.

Me: On my way home, and I'm not alone. Make sure Everly stays in her room and doesn't try to come into mine. It's been her thing lately—and that can't happen tonight.
Hannah: Easy solution: lock your door. Now, I'm going back to bed, and I'm going to try not to have nightmares over this conversation. Because gag.
Me: I'll lock it, but make sure to distract her if she gets up. Please, Hannah, this is important.
Hannah: You know you can count on me.

I slipped the phone back into my jacket just as Sydney said, "Is everything all right?"

"Yes. Sorry about that."

She cuffed her arm around mine. "Where do you live?"

"Hollywood Hills." I kissed down her neck, the coconut becoming even stronger as I reached her collarbone. "Not far."

Thank God for that.

The fifteen-minute drive would be torturous enough. Anything longer, and I didn't think I'd be able to wait, and I'd have to tear this dress off in the backseat.

"That's my favorite area," she said and giggled as I kissed

up to her ear, taking her lobe into my mouth. "Why do I get the feeling, Mr. Dalton, that you're completely relentless?"

"I go after what I want." My fingers traveled up her chest, slowly moving between her tits until I reached her throat, holding it to keep her face straight. "And right now, that's you."

"Ford ..." She sucked in her lip.

I growled as I glanced out the window, needing to know exactly how many seconds it would be until we were at my place.

"In less than three minutes, I'm going to taste how wet you are."

"Oh God."

I took in her mouth one last time, giving her my tongue until I felt the SUV come to a stop. A peek through the windshield showed me we had reached my driveway. Without waiting for Stan, I opened the backseat door and helped Sydney out, waving good-bye to Stan as I brought us in through the garage—the quieter of the two entrances.

"Do you want anything to drink?" I asked as we passed the row of cars.

"No. I'm good."

Once inside the main house, I silently shut the door and led her into the kitchen. Everly was a hard sleeper, but I didn't want to cause any excess noise and risk the chance of her waking up.

With the pendants over the island fully illuminated, the glow was just enough that I didn't have to turn on any other lights.

We were halfway through the kitchen, just passing the pantry, when Sydney stopped. "Do you bake?"

"Fuck no."

She appeared to be glancing around. "All I can smell is chocolate chip cookies. It's making my stomach growl."

I chuckled as I got a whiff of Hannah's dessert. "Do you want one?"

"I don't know." She smiled. "I don't think so."

"Then, you're coming with me."

I hurried us through the open space of the living room and toward the master wing. The moment I had her through my bedroom door, I locked it behind us—something I never did—and pinned her against the wall.

"You have no idea how gorgeous you are." I traced the side of her cheek, her hair framing a face that was far past beautiful. In fact, Sydney was the most breathtaking woman I had ever kissed. "Positively stunning."

As the cool iciness of her eyes stared back at me, there was such innocence inside. Generosity. Submission.

"When you say those words, I feel them."

My thumb crossed her mouth. "You should. They're true."

Her lips were almost equally as plump, the bottom only slightly larger. I tugged on the bigger of the two. Something about that one made me want to bite it.

"Do you know what I want right now?"

Her head pressed against the wall as my hand lowered to her neck. "I can't read you like you can read me, but I can feel …"

Our bodies were aligned. Of course she could feel my hard-on; it was practically bursting through my pants.

"I want to devour you."

"Ford, you have my permission."

I reached down even farther and gripped her ass. The dress had made it look perfect when I was staring at it in the bar, but nothing compared to the way it felt as I circled my hands around her incredibly full, round cheeks. And just thick enough that I could pull her against my body.

When that wasn't enough, when I needed her even closer, I

lifted her into the air. She wrapped her legs around me while I pressed her against the wall. As I kissed her, her small, sensual moans filled my ears.

Even her sounds were taunting.

"You taste so good." I licked her off my lips.

"That's all the alcohol."

"No, Sydney, that's you."

I walked her down the hallway toward my bed, placing her on the floor, only inches from the edge of the mattress. I wasted no time in getting her naked, instantly reaching for the zipper of her dress, lowering it enough so the material fell to her heels.

She stood before me in only her bra and panties, both light pink.

And lace.

Fuck me.

I backed up a few inches, needing to take in this view.

"Man"—I shook my head—"I'm one lucky motherfucker."

The dress had looked exquisite on her, but what was underneath was even better. Sydney in just her skin was a whole different level of sexy. All curves and dips and muscle. The gap between her thighs just as pronounced as I'd dreamed about at the bar.

My stare dipped to her feet and slowly rose, and I moaned, "Magnificent," as I reached her face.

"You're too much."

"Nah." I paused, my cock fucking throbbing. "My words barely do you justice."

A flushness moved across her cheeks as she said, "Get over here."

Once I was within reach, she began to unbutton my shirt, working her way down my chest. My sports coat and shirt dropped at the same time. She didn't stop until the only thing covering me was my boxer briefs. That was when her move-ments slowed, peeling the shorts down my legs until they fell.

"Good God," she whispered, gradually looking down, viewing my chest, abs. Lastly my fucking cock. "I'd say you're the one who's perfect."

I backed up until I reached my nightstand, grabbing a condom from inside. "Do you want to know what I want to hear?" I waited for that question to set in. "The orgasm that's soon going to be screaming from your mouth." I lifted her again, resting her on top of the bed, where I hovered over her.

"You're going to make me scream?"

I kissed down her chest, unhooking her bra, her tits falling loose. With the lace covering them, I hadn't been able to see the sexiness of her nipples. But now, I captured one in my mouth, grazing my teeth across the tip.

As I glanced up at her face, I promised, "Endlessly."

"*Mmm.*"

I switched to the other side, and as I gave it more pressure, her back arched, and her fingers clutched the blanket.

She liked that.

So, I did it again, sucking the whole nipple into my mouth, flicking just the end with my tongue, like it was her clit.

I didn't hurry.

There was nothing about this moment that I wanted to end. I wanted to continue tasting this girl until the goddamn sun was rising.

She pulled at my hair as I tugged on her nipple. I was careful not to cause her any pain; I just wanted her to teeter on that ledge. I wanted her to feel the difference between my teeth and tongue. I wanted her to yearn for them equally.

And she did.

Her sounds got louder as I alternated between the two.

Her body moved, wriggling, like my cock was inside her.

"*Yesss,*" she breathed as I kissed down to her navel.

I halted just below her belly button and removed her panties, slipping them down her legs, showing me the sight I'd been saving for last.

"Sydney ... fuck."

I didn't touch her.

I just stared, fantasizing about what I was going to do to her pussy.

But before my cock went anywhere near it, I continued to kiss her until my nose reached her clit, staying there, inhaling.

"Sydney ..." I breathed her in again, savoring the scent. "You smell like a fucking dream."

Her legs parted, giving me the access I needed.

That I wanted.

And my fingers found their way down her pussy, circling her wetness.

"Ford," she sighed, her knees bending, toes grinding into the bed.

I spread some of the wetness to the top, giving her clit enough friction that she moaned. I then lowered, going in as far as my knuckles before I turned my wrist. I based my movements on her breathing, increasing my speed as she got louder.

Screams.

That was what I was after.

And I didn't stop until I heard my first one.

"*Ahhh!*"

"That's it," I whispered against her clit. "Let me fucking hear you."

My bedroom was like a cave, so I didn't worry about the sound traveling—that was why I encouraged her. Why, when her voice went high again, I brushed my thumb over her clit, adding a third finger, getting that pussy ready for my cock.

"I need you."

I gazed up, covered in her wetness. "Tell me." I narrowed my stare. "Tell me how bad you need me."

She lost herself in moans, my hand still moving, my thumb still brushing over that sensitive spot. And then she cried, "I want your dick." Her teeth gnawed her lip. "Please. Now. I can't wait another second."

I pulled my hand away and ripped off the corner of the foil, taking out the rubber to roll it over my shaft. I pumped my cock a few times, and once I was covered in latex, I positioned her legs over my shoulders, my hand returning to her clit as I plunged inside.

"*Fuuuck*," I groaned, my head leaning back. "You're so goddamn tight."

I'd suspected that when I was fingering her, but I'd had no idea it would feel this good.

Her pussy was so wet, so fucking hot.

So ready for me.

"Oh God!" She swallowed. "Ford!"

Each of her reactions only encouraged me to go harder, gripping her thigh, using it as leverage to plow into her. A space so narrow that she was practically keeping me locked in.

"Do you know what you're about to do to me?"

I knew.

I could feel it.

I flicked her clit back and forth. "I'm going to make you come."

I watched the moment it happened.

Her stomach shuddered, her calves tightened over my shoulders, her mouth opened, and, "Ford," came bursting through those sexy lips.

I fucking loved that sound.

There was nothing hotter than making a woman feel so good that she couldn't hold it in.

And there was no better feeling than giving her that kind of pleasure.

The ripples moved through her navel, and when she stilled, I picked right up again, sliding through her wetness, rubbing across her clit. I worked this angle for a few more thrusts before I pulled her to the end of the bed. I flipped her over, lifting her onto her knees, placing her in doggy style.

My cock teased her as I moved the tip around her opening. "Look at me." I waited until she glanced over her shoulder before I gave her my crown. Just the head, nothing more. "You're going to come again, Sydney."

"I've never ..."

She's never had two orgasms in one night?

"I'm going to change that."

I rocked my hips forward, giving her my entire shaft. She was closing in on me, tightening.

"But if you keep feeling that good, you're going to make me come."

She began to meet me in the middle, arching her hips up, adding pressure to my cock.

"You like this position, don't you?" I growled.

"*Yesss.*"

I could guess why.

From here, I could reach even deeper.

I could rub her clit at the same time, like I was doing now, and hit her G-spot.

And every time I brushed across it, she gave me a reward.

Her sounds.

Fuck me, it was like music.

My head leaned back as my balls tightened, and her hips began to buck against me.

"Fuck, Sydney, you're getting me far too close."

She glanced over her shoulder again, her teeth teasing that lip I loved. "I want to feel you come."

Not before her.

She owed me another orgasm first.

And I wanted a front-row view to watch it happen.

I pulled out, my cock instantly missing her pussy, and I moved directly in front of her, backing up until I hit the headboard. That was where I took a seat, stretching my legs out, and said, "Come ride my dick."

She crawled toward me, her nipples so fucking hard as she straddled my waist, gradually lowering onto my shaft.

"Fuck," I hissed as her pussy took ahold of me.

While her nipples bounced in my face, I licked them as she rose and gave them a quick nibble as she lowered.

She gripped my shoulders, her speed intensifying, her breathing increasing, especially as she moaned, "Ford ... yes."

She was getting close.

I would bring her even closer.

I clamped her nipple between my teeth and thrust my hips forward, giving her more of my cock each time she sank over me.

"Oh God," she gasped.

As I flicked her with my tongue, I pressed the pads of my fingers over her clit, and I ground over it.

She went wild.

That was when I knew I had full control. When I could get her body to do anything I wanted.

And what I wanted at this moment was for her to, "Come!"

It was instant, like she'd been waiting for the command.

"Ford! Fuck!"

Shudders moved through her body, creating what felt like a vibration over my dick. While the intensity wrapped around her, I showed no mercy, taking over the movements, pounding into her, making sure each wave left an impression.

"Don't stop!"

Goddamn, those words were fucking erotic.

But she didn't have to worry; I was far from stopping.

With this girl, I didn't need fuel.

Her moans and pleasure were my only concerns.

Both simmered inside me, causing me to go deeper, harder. My strokes turned relentless, my need for her screams an intoxicating combination.

"Oh my God!"

I wasn't sure who had breathed those words. I just knew I was overwhelmed by her tightness, wetness. Sydney's pussy was swallowing me, and I never wanted out.

Her arms wrapped around my neck, and she hugged me against her, and while she kissed me, she began to buck.

"Sydney, fuck," I roared.

"It's your turn."

I ran my hands across her back, holding her to me, feeling her incredible body as we moved together.

"Now," she begged.

There was something about the neediness in her voice, the way she was pulling at my hair, the way her cunt was sucking me that made me lose it.

The feeling started in my balls, the spike blasting through my stomach, erupting like an explosion. "Fuck yes!" I gripped her as tightly as I could, and she took that opportunity to take over, stroking my cock, milking the cum out of me.

"More," she urged, biting my earlobe.

Damn it, this one was naughty.

And I fucking loved it.

I held on, waiting for the peak to pass, shooting stream after stream into the condom. Once she emptied me, I surrounded her face with my hands, staring into her eyes as the calm took over.

We were frozen.

Breathless.

An unexpected satisfaction hummed through my body.

I grazed my lips across hers, taking in her coconut scent, trying to fill my lungs with air.

As our eyes locked, a smile passed over her mouth, and she whispered, "Who are you?"

It was as though I'd voiced those words, the very same thought in my head.

Who is this girl ... and what the fuck is she going to do to me?

FOUR

SYDNEY

I was still on London time. No matter how hard I'd tried to sleep, just a few hours after Ford and I finally went to bed, I was now wide awake.

What I'd learned in the short time that I'd been in this bedroom was that Ford couldn't be satiated.

He wanted more of me.

More kissing.

More touching.

More tasting.

I soaked up every second because no man had ever treated my body like him. Had ever made me come so hard. Had ever given me two orgasms in one night.

But Ford hadn't stopped at two.

He'd given me a third in the shower.

A fourth, fifth, and sixth before I fell asleep.

Oh God.

And to even think, I had almost convinced myself that the timing of last evening was all wrong, that my life was too unsettled to even consider pursuing him.

Gabby had been right, of course.

Had I shut myself off, which I'd been leaning toward, I wouldn't have woken to his arm wrapped around me like a seat belt.

He was even incredibly handsome when he slept. His expression so honest. His core so dominant, his hands so experienced, his mouth so pleasurable.

How could only the lightest graze of his fingers, the subtlest exhale of his air cause me to quiver?

But I did.

In the last four years, I hadn't had the time to explore the possibility of dating. Even if the opportunity had presented itself, I would have been in no position to act on it, far too tied up with my job.

Back in LA for less than twenty-four hours, and this had already happened.

Blanketed by this incredible man's heat.

As I stared at his face, I couldn't help but wonder where this was going to take me and what this was going to look like.

So many unknowns.

What I did know was that I needed to fill myself with caffeine, or he would open his eyes to a side of me that was wickedly devilish.

He was far too adorable to wake up, so I carefully lifted his arm a few inches and squeezed my way out, sneaking soundlessly off his bed.

Rather than putting my dress on, I found his button-down on the floor and slipped my arms through the large holes, buttoning the middle as I tiptoed to his door. When I turned the handle, I realized it was locked and twisted the lever in the center. I shut the door behind me, my feet hitting the cold hardwood floor as I made my way through the living room.

Halfway to the kitchen, I immediately halted my steps

when I noticed a woman sitting at the counter. With her back to me, I could see her long, dark hair, which was twisted into a messy bun; she was wearing a T-shirt and shorts with several textbooks spread out in front of her. The silent house was filled with the sound of her pen tapping.

Why is there a woman in Ford's kitchen?

Is this not his home?

Is it hers?

Or ... is it one they share as a couple?

Oh fuck.

I slapped my hand over my mouth as I felt myself gasp, the noise causing her to turn around.

The youthfulness of her face told me we were close in age.

That only caused more questions to fill my head.

"I'm sorry." I took a few steps back, not exactly sure what to say, where to go. "I didn't realize anyone else was here."

"Oh no, you're fine." She waved me over. "Please come in."

"Are you sure?"

She smiled. "Yes, of course."

"Are you Ford's roommate or something?"

She laughed, shaking her head. "I'm his cousin. I spent the night to babysit his daughter."

Daughter?

That was something Ford hadn't mentioned.

I wondered why he'd left out that detail.

The more I thought about it, he'd left out almost all the details. I knew nothing about this man, aside from the facts that he was ridiculously handsome, he dressed well, and he lived in the Hollywood Hills.

And he knew my body like he'd spent his lifetime studying it.

I had been a little too drunk last night to take in his home, but as this girl's words were fresh in my head, I glanced around the large, open space, looking for those clues.

There was a small pink chair by the fireplace, an *E* sewn across the back cushion. Dolls were in baskets along the far wall. Pink bound books were in a pile on the coffee table, right next to a stack of adult hardcovers.

He had a little girl.

My heart began to pound.

"Is she here?" I asked, looking into the kitchen, where she could have been eating.

I knew the challenges of children and strangers. I didn't want to take the chance of causing any confusion.

"She's sleeping."

"So, it's safe to grab some coffee?"

She nodded. "I appreciate you asking."

She turned toward her books, and as I passed the counter on my way to the island, I asked, "What are you studying?"

"Law." She sighed. "One day, I'll be a lawyer at Ford's firm. In the meantime"—she banged her fist against her notebook—"I'm in complete hell."

So, Ford was a lawyer.

Maybe that was why he could read me so easily.

"I'm about to start college," I told her. "I'll soon be in hell, too, so I get it." I stood in front of the coffee machine, looking for a mug stand, like Gabby had in our apartment. There wasn't a cup in sight. "Mugs are where?"

She pointed at one of the cabinets. "And creamer is in the fridge. Sugar and sweetener in the pantry."

"Thank you."

I opened the cabinet, and the first thing I saw was a cup with *Best Dad Ever* across the front, a photo of Ford and his little girl underneath the words. The picture was small, detailed just enough that I saw curly pigtails and a smile that was identical to Ford's—genuine, beautiful.

Absolutely adorable.

My heart was melting.

I chose a standard white ceramic mug and stuck it under the spout of the Nespresso machine. While I waited for it to finish pouring, I grabbed the creamer from the fridge, shook the bottle, and added some to the top of the coffee.

"Where are you going to school?" his cousin asked.

I surrounded the cup with both hands and brought it up to my mouth. "UCLA." I took my first sip, savoring the warmth. "I start in a few weeks, at the beginning of spring semester. Just gen ed, but I'm taking them online. Hopefully, that'll make them a little more tolerable."

"That's the way to go, trust me. I'd rather pause a lecture on my laptop than get caught snoozing in front of the professor."

I laughed. "Good point."

"So, did you just graduate high school?"

There was concern in her expression.

I assumed she was worried an eighteen-year-old had just stayed the night with her much older cousin.

"No, no." I shook my head. "I took a job right after gradua-tion, and I've traveled the world for the last four years. College has always been on my radar, but the timing was just never right. When it became possible, I made the move."

"But what an experience that must have been."

I tucked my unruly hair behind my ears. "I don't regret it for a second."

"Good luck with school. I have a feeling it's going to go great for you."

I grinned. "Thank you—and for you too. Wear that crown and show those boys at the law firm what it looks like when a girl kicks ass."

"*Ohhh*, yes. I plan to."

I waved good-bye and returned to Ford's room, bringing the coffee into bed. Even though I'd been quiet, the movement of the mattress caused him to stir, his eyes gradually opening, meeting mine.

God.

He was perfection in the morning. Hair completely messy, beard a little thicker than it had been last night, a stare that was lusty and feral.

I was ready for whatever he wanted to do to me.

"Good morning," I said softly.

He eyed the cup, pulling the comforter up to his abs as he sat up and leaned his back against the headboard. "Morning."

"I met your cousin. She told me where I could find a mug." I smiled. "She's really lovely."

He lifted a remote off the nightstand and held it toward the windows, the blinds suddenly opening. "Was she out there alone?"

"Yes." I took a deep breath. "Your daughter is still asleep."

He ran his hand over his hair, attempting to tame it. "I probably should have told you." He paused. "She's the reason I didn't want to come back here last night."

"I understand." I looked down at the cup. "This is ... I don't know what this is, but you don't owe me an explanation."

"I still want to give you one." He continued to drag his palm over his hair, but now, I had a feeling it was for a different reason. "I'm a single dad, and I've never brought a woman I'm dating around my daughter. It's not that I'm against the idea; I just haven't been in a long-term, committed relationship since she was born. It's never felt right, and dating is hard when I have a daughter."

I put my hand on his stomach. "I really do understand, Ford."

Before he could ask why or say another word, we were interrupted by his phone.

He looked away to lift it off his nightstand. "One second. This is my assistant." He held his cell to his ear and said, "Good morning." He was quiet for several seconds. "I want you to vet them. If they pass your test, send me their résumés, and if I like what I see, we'll set up interviews." He paused again. "Thank you."

I waited until he hung up to ask, "Are you hiring another assistant?"

He shook his head. "A nanny." He stole my coffee and took a sip. "Hannah, my cousin whom you met, can't do it anymore. She's gotten too busy."

"But she's going to kick ass at your law firm."

He laughed. "I see you two talked." He took another drink from the cup. "Yes, she most certainly will. But that still leaves me in a predicament since I can't exactly leave Everly alone."

The *E* that was sewn on the little pink chair.

"Everly," I whispered. "That's beautiful."

He handed the coffee back to me. "That was my choosing ... not her mother's."

His tone told me there was a story there. One that was complicated, and his mention of being a single dad only emphasized that, but I decided not to ask.

If and when he wanted to talk about it, he would.

His hand went to my cheek, his thumb brushing across my lips in a way that he'd done many times last night. Each time stirring so many sensations in my body. "I don't want to rush you out, but Everly typically gets up in about forty-five minutes. That'll give me just enough time to drive you home, assuming you don't live too far from here, and come back to make her breakfast."

"That's cute."

His brows rose. "Breakfast is?"

"That you want to be here when she wakes, that you cook for her—all the things."

He took my coffee again, this time setting it by his phone, and he caged me in his arms, moving me flat on his bed so he could climb on top of me.

I was completely full of Ford.

The heat of his skin, the citrus tones of his cologne. The scratchiness of his beard as he dragged it across me.

Everything tickled.

And fluttered.

"Do you know how sexy you look in my shirt?" He was kissing around the collar, and my head moved from side to side to give him more access. "How I want nothing more than to rip it off you and fucking devour you again."

But he couldn't.

Because of Everly.

I could accept that.

He hovered over my face, and I held his cheek and said, "I can feel ..."

He was naked, his hard-on pressing against the button-down, the thin material the only thing separating us.

"Last night was amazing," I continued.

His eyes closed, and he kissed my cheek. "I had a great time too." He said nothing for a few seconds and then, "I'd like to see you again."

A tingle erupted between my legs. "You would?"

His lips were only inches from mine. "Why are you questioning that?" He shifted to my neck, tasting me, like he was discovering new skin.

"It just sounded like you don't date much, so ... I don't know. I just assumed."

"I don't, but it sounded like you understood my circumstances."

I nodded. "That's true."

He returned to that same spot on my neck. Kissing. Caressing. "Then, yes, I most definitely would like to see you again."

He was holding himself up with his arms, and I skimmed them, feeling the muscles bulge on each side. "Give me your phone. I'll save my number."

He unlocked the screen and handed it to me, and I went into his Contacts and added my information.

Rather than setting a date, this felt like the option that put the least amount of pressure on him.

Still, the thought of him calling sent that tingle afire, and the thought of him not calling made my heart start to ache.

I set his phone down and wrapped my arms around his neck, holding him against me. My nose went into his hair, smelling, my mind memorizing.

Just in case.

And once a few beats passed, I respected his wishes and whispered, "Let's go."

He gave me a quick kiss, his eyes holding mine as our mouths parted, and we climbed out of bed. He went into his closet, and I tossed his button-down on the bench in front of his bed and worked the tight dress up my body.

When he walked out, he was in a pair of gray sweatpants, a T-shirt, a baseball hat, and sneakers.

If he moved just right, the sweatpants showed the outline of his crown.

I almost felt guilty for looking.

But I couldn't help myself.

Good God.

He was so incredibly sexy.

"Are you ready ..." He shook his head as his voice died out, his eyes consuming me. "Damn it, it fucking pains me to ask you that."

I grabbed my coffee from the nightstand and gulped down a few sips. "Ready."

On the way out, I slipped on my heels and picked up my clutch from the floor and then followed him into the living room.

"Morning, Hannah," he said as we passed the counter where she was still sitting. "Was Eve good last night?"

"A little whiny when it was time to go to bed. She wanted to play, take another bath, have a popcorn fight in your bed—you know, all the excuses." There was a container sitting on one of her books, and she handed it to me. "Aside from that, she was perfect."

Inside the Tupperware was cookies. Ones that looked homemade.

That would explain what I'd smelled last night in Ford's kitchen.

"Have one," Hannah urged.

I grabbed two and moaned behind my hand as I chewed. "Wow. This is excellent."

"Take another. I made three dozen, so there's plenty."

"Two is more than enough. Thank you." As I tried to taste the ingredient that she'd used to make the dough extra rich and fluffy, I held the container toward Ford.

He shook his head, and he said to Hannah, "I'm going to take Sydney home. I should be back before Eve wakes up, and then you can bounce."

"Works for me," Hannah replied.

I handed the Tupperware back to Hannah, and as Ford and I were walking past the fridge, I heard, "*Daaaddy!*"

"Fuck," Ford whispered, freezing mid-step.

We turned at the same time, seeing his daughter bouncing down the steps that wrapped around the living room.

"*Daaaddy*, is it pancake time?"

He glanced at me, and I instantly saw the worry on his face.

I didn't know what to do.

Where to go.

What to even say.

But as I looked toward the staircase, there was a flash of pink descending so fast, curls like loose springs on top of her head, that I knew it was too late to try and hide.

The second she hit the bottom landing, she came running for her father.

My heart clenched as he picked her up in his arms, hugging her against him.

"Good morning, my baby girl." He rubbed circles across her back, her body so tiny against Ford's tall, muscular frame. "How did you sleep?"

"I woke up with the giraffe in my face." She rubbed her fists over her eyes. "He was hungry and thought I was leaves. Silly giraffe."

"Well, I woke up with your feet in my face," Hannah said. "Were your toes hungry for my nose?"

Everly snorted, which made everyone in the kitchen laugh.

I had no reason to be biased, but she was one of the cutest kids I had ever seen. She had bright, giant, round blue eyes, a hooked nose, puffy lips, and little freckles that sat high on her cheeks. Her hair was golden brown and all curls.

"I'm glad you slept well, baby. I missed you last night."

I'd melted when I saw the *Best Dad Ever* mug. That was nothing compared to this. Watching the two of them together—their love and interaction, the way they gazed at each other—was the most beautiful sight.

Everly played with the keys in her father's hand. "Where

are you going, Daddy?" When she finished speaking, she turned in his arms, facing me. "Who are you?"

I didn't want to say the wrong thing. I didn't even want to address his daughter unless Ford was comfortable with it, especially because he'd told me he sheltered her from the women he dated, and even though I wasn't in that category, this gray area was just as complicated.

My gut told me to stay silent, so I looked at Ford and then at Hannah, hoping one of them answered her.

"That's my friend," Hannah said. "She came over to have some cookies with me."

Ford shifted his stance, holding Everly toward me so she didn't have to turn around. "Everly, this is Hannah's friend Sydney. Can you introduce yourself to Miss Sydney?"

Still holding one of the cookies, I switched the dessert to my other hand, extending my dominant one to his daughter. "Hi."

"Hi, Miss Sydney. I'm Everly Dalton. Daddy calls me Eve. You can call me Eve or Everly."

I smiled. "It's very nice to meet you, Everly." Her hand was so warm against mine. "You can call me Syd, if that's easier. That's what my friends call me sometimes."

She had a dimple on her right cheek when she grinned. "Really? That's *sooo* pretty."

"Thank you. I think your name is very pretty too. Do you know what else we have in common?"

Her eyes went wide. "What?"

"We both love the color pink."

"You *dooo*? Is it your fave, like mine?"

I nodded. "My absolute fave." There was a smudge of chocolate on her cheek, telling me Hannah had probably given her a cookie before bed. "You know what else is my fave?" I held up my free hand. "Hannah's cookies."

"Cookies for breakfast!" she shouted.

I laughed, pulling back both hands. "That's what I had for breakfast, but it sounds like you're going to have pancakes, and that's just as yummy."

"You like pancakes too?"

"Of course." I winked. "Who doesn't love pancakes? They're the best when they have loads of chocolate chips."

"Daddy, you have to make some pancakes for Syd. She likes them like I do." She glanced at me again. "Did you get pretty to have pancakes with us?"

I realized she was talking about my dress and heels—an outfit that felt outrageous at the moment.

When I didn't respond, she gasped and said, "Daddy, we need to have a pancake party. I need to go put on my pink dress!"

"No party, baby." Ford held the side of Everly's face and kissed her. "Sydney only came over for cookies, but now that she's had some, she and Hannah are going to leave." He looked at Hannah, and I could tell from his profile he was silently asking her to take me home.

"No, Daddy!" Everly leaned away from him and crossed her arms, pouting. "I want to have a pancake party."

"Look at me, baby." He waited until Everly did as he'd asked. "Hannah and Miss Sydney have to get going. Maybe one day, Miss Sydney will come back and have pancakes with us, but it's not going to be today."

"*Daaaddy,*" she whined.

He set her on the counter and handed her a mixing spoon. "Are you going to be my sous-chef, or are we going to pout and ruin our breakfast?"

She huffed a few times until she muttered, "*Okaaay.*"

I was impressed with the way he'd handled her, how he

hadn't given in, how he'd calmed her before a tantrum took over.

"Okay," Ford repeated. "Now, say good-bye to Hannah."

Hannah quickly gathered her books and placed them in her bag and went over to Everly. "I'll see you tomorrow, bestie."

I could tell they had a special bond, and by the way Everly looked at Hannah, I knew she was a significant role model in Everly's life.

Everly wrapped her small arms around Hannah's neck and hugged her. "I wanna go hiking. Then, we can get those fruit things. You know, the mixed-up kind."

"Hiking and smoothies, huh?" She tickled Everly's belly. "You just like to torture me and race me up the hills, don't you?"

Everly snorted. A sound that was so sweet and pure.

Once they separated, Ford said, "Can you say good-bye to Miss Sydney?"

I waved my hand in the air. "See ya, Eve. It was really wonderful to meet you."

Everly mirrored my wave with her short fingers. "Can you come hiking tomorrow?"

"*Awww.*" I shrugged. "Probably not, but maybe someday soon."

Ford had left Everly on the counter and returned from the pantry with a glass canister in his hand. He opened the lid and stuck his finger inside, dabbing what looked like flour onto Everly's nose. "Are you ready, little lady? We've got some stirring and flipping to do."

He'd already distracted her in such an adoring way, so I turned around and followed Hannah. Before I rounded the corner, cutting off my view of them, I took a quick glance toward the kitchen.

Ford was watching me.

Words didn't have to be spoken between us, nor did he have to lift his hand and wave.

That was because I could feel his stare throughout my entire body.

His needs.

His wants.

And a heat started to move through my chest and slowly lower.

I gave him a quick smile, one he wouldn't forget, and I walked out to Hannah's car.

"Thank you," I said once we both climbed in. "I know you didn't sign up for this. I'm happy to take an Uber."

"It's no problem at all." She started the engine. "Just show me the way. I'm really horrible with directions."

I hadn't looked at my phone since the bar and pulled it out of my clutch. There were a few texts from Gabby, asking for updates, and an explosion of notifications from every social media site. I'd posted a picture of us before we went out last night, letting the world know I was back in LA, and there were hundreds of reactions.

Instead of reading all the comments, I typed the address of our apartment into Maps, and the app pulled up the directions. I turned up the volume and said, "This'll take us there much better than I can."

While waiting for Ford's gate to open, she tightened her bun and gave me a brief glance. "So ... you met Eve." She winced. "Oops."

I exhaled loudly. "I know that wasn't supposed to happen, but I'm glad it went well."

"I'd say it went well. You should go to school to become a teacher; you're freaking amazing with kids."

I laughed. "I am."

"No?"

"Really, I am. I've been an au pair for the last four years, and now—"

She slammed on her brakes halfway through the gate. "Shut up. You're a nanny?"

I nodded. "I was, yes. That's why I've been all over the world. The family I worked for homeschooled their three kids, and their dad traveled almost every week for his job. He had a private plane and took us with him."

She began to drive again, moving us onto the main road. "That's why you looked like such a professional with Eve."

"I don't know about that, but I have a lot of experience with children. I understand their needs and what it takes to raise them." My voice softened when I said, "It's not easy, being a single parent. I give Ford a lot of credit."

"He's so good with her. He has been since the very beginning."

I wanted so desperately to pick her brain, but I knew how inappropriate that was, so I said, "It sounds like they're lucky to have each other."

She was silent for a few moments while listening to the app give the next instruction and then asked, "Now that you're starting school, will you be working as well or just focusing on classes?"

"Oh, no. I need a job." I traced my fingers against the glass, staring at the palm trees that lined the street. "I haven't begun looking for one, but it's on the agenda along with getting a bed and furniture—I have nothing." We connected eyes as she slowed for the stop sign. "I have so much to do. I'm what I call a hot mess."

"I can take one thing off your plate. I have the perfect job for you. You could be Eve's nanny."

My hand immediately went to my chest. "Me?"

"If you helped homeschool three children and you're going

to UCLA to become a teacher, there isn't a person more suited than you."

"I don't know ..."

"Everly is a doll. I mean, sure, she gets cranky at times and throws fits—all kids do, as we know—but she's already so smitten with you. Ford is looking for a live-in, so you wouldn't have to buy furniture. You need a job, and he needs a nanny; it's a match made in childcare heaven."

I swallowed, almost choking on my spit. "So ... a few things." I took a deep breath, trying to process this. "I don't mean to get overly graphic, but I slept with Ford last night, and he mentioned something this morning about going out again." I paused. "I don't know if what we have will turn into anything, but it seems like sleeping with the boss isn't the best way to apply for the job."

"Listen, I despise my boss. I'm talking, I loathe him in the worst way. I'd much rather be in your shoes than mine, wouldn't you?"

"Fair enough, but ..." My voice faded out as I thought about the opportunity Hannah was suggesting.

Working as a nanny wasn't something I had even considered when I pondered ways to make money in LA. The truth was, I hadn't really given the topic much thought at all. With the savings I'd banked over the years, I'd paid for the entire semester up front, and I still had enough to pay my rent for the rest of the year while I figured things out.

But by taking my classes online, that would leave me with lots of extra time, and I wanted to fill those hours with a job. Nannying Everly would certainly put me in the environment that I was seeking. I just didn't know how that would affect things with Ford. I knew he didn't want to bring women around his daughter, but would things be different with me due to my experience with kids? Or maybe because I'd already met her?

"What are you thinking about?" she asked.

I was still staring out my window, but I looked at her profile as I replied, "Hannah, I just don't know. It's a lot to consider."

The app told her to turn at the upcoming light, so she did and said, "How about this? Email me your résumé, and I'll pass it along to Ford's assistant. If she likes your experience, she'll reach out and set up an interview. Just see how it goes. If things are meant to be, they'll work out." She made another quick turn. "I know I would be relieved to have Everly in your care. You two really connected, and I sense you're more than qualified—that's for sure."

"You're kind to say that."

"It's true."

I loved my interaction with Everly. She was definitely a sweet kid, adorable from top to bottom. Curious. Inquisitive. Extremely loving. She'd responded to Ford's voice when he turned a little stern, and she'd calmed down when he prompted her to.

"I know I'm only judging this on a few minutes of conversation, but you have an incredible talent, Sydney. And I know it's probably extremely selfish to say this, but I want my little Everly to reap the benefits of your talent."

"Wow." I wrapped my hands around my clutch, holding it against my stomach. "You have a lot of faith in me."

"You know when your gut is telling you it's a good thing?" She briefly faced me. "That's happening to me now."

"Oh, I sure do."

"*Sooo*, is that a yes?"

I laughed. "You're going to make an excellent attorney." My phone was resting on my lap, and I lifted it into my hands and exited out of the navigation screen to open my email. "What's your email? I'm going to send you my résumé." Out of boredom, I'd worked on it during my flight home from London, not even thinking I was going to need it this soon.

She rambled off her email, and I attached the document I'd saved in my inbox. A few seconds after I hit Send, a ding came through the speaker of her phone.

"Got it." She pulled up to a stop sign only a few blocks from my building and looked at me. "Hey, for the time being, let's keep this job thing between us. If you mention it to Ford, that'll just complicate things."

"And if he asks how I heard of the job, assuming I get that far in the process?"

Her smile didn't fade when she said, "Get creative."

FIVE

FORD

"Daddy, what are we doing today?"

Everly's voice pulled me from my dream, and I slowly opened my eyes, seeing my little girl's head resting on my chest. She'd come in at some point in the middle of the night, waking me almost every hour with her feet. But this position, the way she looked up at me, soft and snuggly, made up for the lack of sleep.

"What do you want to do today, baby?"

"*Hmm.*" She rubbed my prickly beard, her fingers getting lost in my whiskers.

"We can do anything you want."

She sat up, resting one of her legs across me, her eyes wide and lit. "*Anythiiing?*"

"Well, within reason." I pushed her curls out of her face. "I know, given the opportunity, you'd pick Disney, which wouldn't be practical today, or to go to Uncle Jenner's house in Utah—also not an option."

"I want to have pancakes with the girls."

"What girls, baby?" The braid I'd put in her hair last night had fallen so loose, and her hair was a wild nest. I pulled the elastic out of the bottom and tried to form it all into a ponytail, tying it together.

"Hannah and Syd."

I chuckled, trying to think of a way around this.

"Daddy, I'm going to help you make a big batch of chocolate chip pancakes. And wear my sparkly pink dress. And they can come over and eat them. *Okaaay?*"

"Eve, I don't think Hannah is available today—"

"Just call her. *Pleeease.*"

I glanced at the tablet on my nightstand to check the time. My cousin was certainly awake at this hour. She barely slept. Hell, when I had been her age, in law school, I hadn't either.

"You want me to call her right now and ask her?"

She nodded so furiously that the ends of her long curls hit her eyes.

I grabbed my phone next to the tablet and found Hannah's number, holding my cell to my ear.

"Put it on speaker, Daddy."

This child was far too smart. Soon, it would be impossible to get anything past her.

I hit the button for the speakerphone and set my cell on my chest.

"Ford," Hannah started as she answered, "if you're calling me to babysit—"

"Hannah!" Everly shouted. "Come over. I wanna have a pancake party." Her sparkly pink nails were now playing with my fingers. "I will be the flipper. We can make them super gooey with a whole bunch of chocolate chips."

"Oh, my little bestie, that sounds amazing," Hannah replied.

"They will be so yummy. Because chocolate is our *faaave*. Besides, Daddy doesn't make the gooey ones right. You have to come. *Pleeease*."

"How can I turn down an offer like that?"

"Yay!" She clapped her hands together, her dimple so pronounced that I had to lean forward and kiss it. "Will Syd come?"

"Who?" Hannah asked.

"Your cookie friend," Everly responded.

"The friend you gave a ride home to," I added, reminding her of the clusterfuck she'd helped me get out of. "Isn't she going out of town to visit family today?"

"*Ohhh*," Hannah groaned. "Yes, you're right; she is."

Everly's bottom lip stuck out. "She can't come to my party?"

"No, bestie, but I'll be there. Won't that make up for it?"

"What about Uncle D and Uncle Jenner? Can they come?" Eve asked us. "And Mimi and Papa?"

"Mimi and Papa are in San Diego this weekend," I said. "They won't be able to come."

"But I think you should call Dominick and Jenner," Hannah suggested. "If they're free, I bet they'd love some of your pancakes."

"Can I call them, Daddy?"

I chuckled.

Only my daughter could put together a breakfast party at eight in the morning. But if this was what she chose to do—to spend time with her family over everything else—I knew I had one special kid.

"We'll hang up with Hannah and give them a call, baby. How does that sound?"

"The bestest!" Eve sang.

"Good." I took the phone off speaker mode and held it to my ear. "Hannah, you're also the bestest."

"You owe me. Again. I'm thinking a new car sounds like the perfect—"

"See you soon," I said, laughing, and I hung up.

"*Daaaddy*, I need to go put on my dress." She wiggled her leg off me and pushed her little butt to the end of the bed, jumping onto the floor.

"Don't you think we should call your uncles first to make sure they can come over?"

"You call." Her tiny, bare feet started to run. "I have to go get ready."

"Don't run!" I yelled as she rushed out of my room. "Be careful on the stairs. One at a time, and use the railing."

"I *knooow*."

That girl, I thought, shaking my head.

I didn't want to call the boys in case they were still sleeping, so I pulled up the group text we constantly had going between the three of us and started typing.

Me: Your niece would like to cordially invite you to the breakfast party she's having this morning. She's in her room right now, putting on her party dress. She'll be terribly disappointed if you can't attend. No pressure.

Dominick: Is she doing the cooking?

Jenner: Because if it's you making those pancakes and not her, I'm not coming.

Me: Dicks.

Dominick: Chef Craig is due at my place around 9. I'll text him and send him to your house instead, letting him know we're switching days.

Me: It's just pancakes. I think I can handle it.

Jenner: Dom, send him over. Ignore Ford.

Dominick: Done.

Me: Does that mean you're all coming? Say around ten?

Dominick: Kendall and I will be there.

Jenner: Jo and I will too.

Dominick: What's going on with the girl from the bar? Is she joining in on this morning's family feast?

Me: Eve wanted to invite her, but I shot that down before it could become a thing. They met—by accident. Fuck me.

Jenner: Oh fuck, how'd that introduction go?

Me: Shockingly ... perfect.

Jenner: Then, what the hell are you waiting for? Invite the girl for breakfast.

Me: Don't start.

Dominick: Brother, you know we haven't really even gotten started.

Me: It's too early for this shit. I'm not going there with you two.

Jenner: Pussy.

Me: See you bitches in a couple hours.

After Hannah had taken Sydney home yesterday morning, whenever there was a slow second in the day, when Everly wasn't occupying my every move, my brain was filled with memories of Sydney.

Of the night we'd spent together.

I couldn't get her out of my head.

And even though I had her number, I hadn't reached out.

I needed more time to think this through.

I needed distance to do that.

And I probably needed to stay far, far away from her.

Because that woman was fucking dangerous.

I'd felt that the second I touched her.

But my hands were aching to run up and down her body. My lips yearning to kiss her. My cock fucking throbbing to be inside her.

What the hell is happening to me?

Texting would start a dialogue; it would open something that surely needed to stay closed. And despite telling her that I wanted to see her again, I wasn't sure if that was really the best idea.

Not when things with Eve were in such a good rhythm.

But as my heart pounded away, my fingers found Sydney's name in my Contacts, and I pulled up a message. My thumbs pressed the letters, typing a text, and I hit Send before I could stop myself.

Me: Everly asked if you were coming to breakfast this morning. I thought you'd find that cute.

Me: It's Ford, by the way.

Sydney: Hi! Awww. She's adorable. I really, really loved meeting her—and hanging out with you, of course.

Me: It was certainly a good night.

I waited for the bubbles to appear, telling me she was replying.

But they didn't.

Maybe I needed to write more, to engage her.

Fuck me. Why was I even contemplating this?

But I was.

And just as I was about to send another message, I heard, "*Daaaddy*, I can't find my pink tutu. Where did Linda put it?"

Her pink tutu.

That my housekeeper had washed and hung in her closet—I was positive of that, so I shouted back, "Check your dress rack!"

"I already looked. I need it for the pancake party. Can you find it?"

My thumbs hovered over the screen, and as I was about to type another message, Eve shouted, "Hurry, Daddy. We have to fix my hair. I want extra braids today. And lipstick."

"You're not wearing lipstick. You're four."

"I'm almost five!"

I glanced toward the doorway and yelled back, "That doesn't change my opinion!"

"But it's pink and sparkly, like my tutu."

I looked back at my phone, not even remembering what I was going to write to her.

"Daddy!"

Damn it.

I set the phone on my nightstand and climbed out of bed, heading upstairs to help Eve.

"To one delicious pancake party, my little one," Dominick said as he held Everly in his arms, clinking his Bloody Mary against Everly's lidded plastic cup of orange juice.

Since Jo, Kendall, and Hannah were drinking mimosas, she wanted to be just like the girls—even if orange juice wasn't her favorite.

"Uncle D, you didn't hit my cup hard enough. I wanna feel the slosh inside."

"Let me fix that," Dominick replied, making a new attempt, which caused a few drops of his Bloody Mary to splash on the lid of Everly's cup.

"Maybe that was a little too hard." Eve giggled.

Our breakfast had been perfect. Everyone had shown up when they'd promised, even Craig, our chef—giving me a chance to hang with my family rather than spend the whole morning in the kitchen.

The smile on Eve's face told me how happy she was.

"Eve, your uncle is hogging you," Kendall said as she sat next to Dominick on the couch. She held out her arms and added, "When is it my turn to snuggle with you?"

"Now," Eve sang, climbing onto Kendall's lap. "Yippee!"

Kendall straightened the bottom of Everly's skirt, fluffing it even higher. "I'm obsessed with your tutu."

Man, I was so lucky to have Kendall, Jo, and Hannah in my family; they were such amazing motherly figures in Everly's life.

"Hannah gave it to me. Isn't it the bestest thing ever?"

"It sure is," Kendall agreed.

My family spoiled her rotten. I couldn't keep track of all the gifts and purchases. Even today, Dominick had bought Everly pink roses—her favorite. Jenner had brought some fancy hot chocolate to go with her pancakes that had colorful marshmallows and sprinkles. I had no idea where he'd found that shit before ten in the morning, but leave it to my brothers.

My daughter relished in the role as the only kid in our family. But I would make sure, as she got older, that this position didn't affect her personality. That she didn't just expect everything to be handed to her, that she appreciated what came her way instead.

Above anything, my child was going to be humble.

And even now, as she got almost everything she wanted, there was such kindness inside her, such generosity when it came to the people she cared about. The way she gazed at Kendall, how she hugged her with all the strength in her tiny body, how she played with Kendall's hair.

That was the way Eve showed love.

And when she loved, she loved hard.

"So ..." I heard Jenner whisper behind me, pulling my attention away from Eve. "Did you ever invite her over?"

I turned around to face him. "Who?"

"You know exactly who the fuck I'm talking about."

My hand went into my hair as I sighed loud enough for him to hear. "Yeah. I texted her."

"And?"

"Jesus, you're really starting with me? Again?"

"If roles were reversed—and they were—you'd be doing the same thing. For what you put me through with Jo, I owe you a lifetime of shit, so, yes, I'm starting, and I don't plan to stop."

I shook my head, remembering, preparing myself for the amount of pressure he was about to lay on. "We exchanged a few texts, but I didn't invite her over."

"She's already met Everly, so what's the problem?"

"What's the problem?" I mocked. "Have you lost your fucking mind?" I didn't wait for him to respond before I continued, "If anything, I'll take her out on a date, but our second time together isn't going to be a family gathering with my daughter."

"You're wasting time, Ford." He glanced at Everly and then back to me. "When I suggested inviting that girl over, it wasn't just for your benefit, but for Eve's too. I'm looking out for the both of you."

"And the best thing for us is Sydney?" I tested.

He finished his Bloody Mary just as Craig brought us another round, and he took a bite of the celery, swallowing before he said, "What are you afraid of? Things not working out?"

My hands began to shake as my memory brought me back to a day I didn't like to revisit. "What would I tell her then?

Another woman had left her life?" I took a long drink. "Do you think that's easy for me?"

"You can't compare the two situations."

"But I can." I took a deep breath. "And I will."

Anger pulsed through my chest.

Jenner didn't get it.

Neither did Dominick.

They could love Everly endlessly, they could put her first, they could protect her with their lives, but they didn't carry my pain. They also wouldn't have to live with the guilt of intentionally bringing someone around Everly and dealing with the ramifications when the relationship didn't work out.

The questions.

The sadness.

No one was ever going to hurt my daughter again—at least, not if I could help it.

And in this situation, I had all the power.

"You can't compare every woman who comes into her life to your baby mama—"

"Jenner," I practically fucking growled, "we don't talk about her, especially not near Everly. Ever." I handed him my cocktail, knowing I needed something much stiffer, and I announced to the group, "I'm going to go grab a drink. I'll be back."

I stopped at the bar in my man cave and poured myself some whiskey. Rather than rejoining my family, I went outside onto the patio and walked to the edge of the pool deck, taking in the view that overlooked the Hills.

I knew Jenner hadn't intentionally pissed me off, but Rebecca was a topic I didn't discuss.

Listening to the boys push me about women was a hard fucking limit for me.

They acted as though I didn't want one in my life.

As though I wanted to be single forever.

That wasn't the case.

I just wouldn't put myself first.

Those days were long over.

The vibration in my pocket pulled me from my thoughts. I took out my phone, and my assistant's name was on the screen.

I held it up to my ear and said, "Morning. I hope you have good news for me."

"I have three interviews lined up. All of the nannies look extremely impressive on paper. Each not only met my criteria, but exceeded it as well."

"Excellent."

"If I'm as pleased with them in person, I'll set up a time for you to interview them. Would you like that to take place at the office or at home so they're able to interact with Everly?"

"We'll start at the office. If I like what I see, I'll have them meet my girl."

"No problem." She paused. "You know, I was reviewing your schedule this morning, and I saw that you have a weeklong work trip at the end of the month. Your parents are going to be in New York. I just want to make sure you've booked someone else to stay with her. Hannah perhaps?"

As I held on to the gate that surrounded the edge of my property, my head dropped, and I filled my lungs with air.

I'd known about my parents' trip because I'd already asked them to watch Eve. I was hoping Hannah could fill in, my brothers alternating nights if they had to, but those questions were something I'd been avoiding.

Even though they loved spending time with my daughter, they had their own lives, and I fucking hated putting my responsibility on them.

"I don't know what I'm going to do with her," I admitted.

"Well, this will be a great time for the nanny to start, then.

This'll give her a few weeks to get acclimated before she's completely on her own with Everly."

"A week alone with my daughter? That sounds like a big step."

"For you, Ford. I assure you, these girls—at least on paper, like I said—can most definitely handle it."

My assistant had been with me since the beginning of my career.

She knew the circumstances and how protective I was. And in many ways, she helped guide me. Having three children of her own, all in their twenties, she'd been through this before.

I trusted her navigation skills.

I just couldn't ask her to babysit. I had to draw the line somewhere.

"*Ughhh*," I groaned. "I just don't know."

"Let's not stress about this now. Let's first see how the interviews go. I'm positive one of the nannies is going to be perfect for you and little Everly. If my assumption is correct, then things will be just fine, Ford."

She was right.

Hell, if I was being honest, she was always right.

"I like that plan," I replied.

I thanked her, and we hung up.

Before I put my phone away, I scanned the messages and notifications that had come in over the last few hours.

Not a single one was from Sydney.

Why did that feel like a letdown?

Is Jenner right? Am I wasting time?

Fuck.

Not only was she owning my goddamn thoughts, but now, I was questioning our conversation from earlier and whether I had been warm enough.

Did it matter?

Not if things were going to end there.

But if I was going to follow through with more, then I needed to text her again.

More.

My dick fucking hardened at the thought of that, and my hands clenched. I licked across my lips, wishing it were her skin I was kissing.

What the fuck is happening to me?

Was there a reason to avoid having dinner with her? To take this slow? So slow that a crawl would feel like a sprint?

Still staring at my phone, I returned to our last message and began to type.

> *Me: What do you have going on tomorrow night?*
> *Sydney: Why? Do you have something in mind?*
> *Me: I'd like to see you. Dinner?*
> *Sydney: I think I can make that happen.*
> *Me: Does 7 work for you? We can start with drinks.*
> *Sydney: Yes, and I'm already looking forward to it.*
> *Me: Send me your address. I'll pick you up.*

As I was shoving my phone into my pocket, I turned around, and Jenner was walking toward me.

"You fucking texted her, didn't you?" He laughed, shaking his head. "That's why you have that grin on your face."

"Asshole."

"But I'm right, aren't I?"

I said nothing as I passed him.

"I'm fucking right," he added as I made my way to the door. "All of that fight for what? Absolutely nothing because you texted her and you're probably seeing her tonight."

"Tomorrow," I said over my shoulder.

"Tomorrow. That's my boy." He joined me at the sliding

glass door, his hand on my shoulder as I reached for the handle. "You've made me hella happy."

I looked at my brother, waiting for the words. When they didn't come, I asked, "Aren't you going to say *I told you so?*"

He smiled. "There's no need. We both knew it was going to play out this way."

SIX

SYDNEY

"What are you going to wear?" Gabby asked as she stood with me in her office, the room we'd converted into my semi-bedroom, both of us looking inside the closet.

I'd filled a small side with the clothes that had fit in my suitcase; the rest still hadn't arrived from New York.

"Sigh." I crossed my arms over my stomach. "I have no idea. He didn't say where we're going, so I don't know if I should lean toward fancy and wear a dress or put on jeans and a tank top and assume sports bar-ish." I looked at my best friend. "Help."

She turned me toward her, holding the sides of my head. "Honestly, you could show up in a hazmat suit, and his eyes would drop from his head. You look hot as fuck in everything you put on."

I rolled my eyes. "I love you, but you're not helping."

"*Fiiine.*" She reached inside the closet and pulled out a black dress. "This." The material was extremely form-fitting, the bottom ending just above my knee, with spaghetti straps that hugged my shoulders. "Wear a jean jacket over it with wedges. This way, you'll fit in, no matter where he takes you."

"You're a genius."

"I know." She smiled and handed me the hanger. "What does Ford think of your upcoming interview with his assistant?"

My eyes widened as I processed her question. "*Ummm ...*"

"Oh fuck." She paused, staring at my face. "He doesn't know, does he?"

I shook my head. "His cousin Hannah told me not to tell him."

"Why?"

"I have no idea." I swallowed, the dishonesty causing my throat to tighten. "She must have a reason, but I don't like it. You know lying is not my thing."

"Do you think she's trying to sabotage you?"

"No." I took a breath. "I mean, you should have heard the way she was praising me. She kept saying she wanted me to be Everly's nanny and how she would benefit from having me around."

"Well, she's right about that."

"Stop."

"It's true." She shrugged. "She must have her reasoning— whatever it might be."

"Gabs"—I grinned as I thought of Everly—"she's seriously so freaking cute. She reminds me so much of Lilac."

When Lilac, the youngest of the three, had been Everly's age, she had been just as smart and sassy. Her little dimples made it impossible for her father to say no to anything.

I had a feeling Everly's dimple was one of Ford's biggest weaknesses.

"Of course the hottest man in LA made the cutest kid in the world. But, Syd, what's going to happen when you pass the assistant's interview and you walk into Ford's house and he doesn't know it's you who got the job?"

"Let me focus on tonight's date. Once I get through that, we can stress about the nanny part." I placed my hand on my heart, trying to calm the racing. "However, I have to believe that whatever is supposed to happen will."

"That's the strategy you're going with? *Okaaay*."

"Think about it. Isn't that the way my life has gone so far?" I folded the dress over my arm and leaned my back against her tall bookcase. "I wasn't ready for college, and the job with the Turners fell into my lap. I wanted more than anything to travel the world, and that's exactly what happened. I was ready to return to LA and got accepted to college. And you wanted to drag me out the first night I was home, and I met Ford. See? It all unfolded just the way it was supposed to." I pushed hard against my chest as the images from that night, at his house, caused the pounding to turn to flutters. "Whatever happens, whether I get the job or not, hopefully, Ford will be in my life some way or another."

She twirled a lock of my hair around her finger. "You're so mature; I can't stand it."

"Truth: I'm pushing on my heart, so it doesn't pop out of my chest."

"I was just trying to make you feel better. We both know this is a fucking implosion waiting to happen. We also know you're getting laid tonight, so we'll focus on that for now. But I do have a suggestion ..."

I wanted to laugh but couldn't. Things were far too tight in there. "What's that?"

"Make it a night he'll never forget."

"Jesus," Ford said as I climbed into his car, his stare covering the whole length of me. Each inch he rose, starting at my feet, caused tingles to burst in my chest. "You look stunning, Sydney."

"You're sweet."

The intensity in his eyes, the hungriness in his lips told me Gabby had chosen the right outfit.

Even after I put on my seat belt, he stayed double-parked along the curb.

Unmoving.

Except for his eyes, still traveling, still taking me in like I was a feast.

"Damn it," he said, shaking his head, a slight moan coming from his throat before he leaned across the middle of the car. Rather than go for my lips, he went for my cheek. He kissed it softly, keeping his lips there, breathing me in.

I didn't mind.

I was doing the same to him.

Refreshing my memory with the scent of his cologne. The citrus tones I remembered from the morning after the bar, the way it had lingered on his shirt when I put on his button-down.

"Thank you for coming out with me tonight." He whispered those words against my cheek, sending a shiver through me.

One that made my skin turn hot. One that made me quiver.

My body felt like a rose, each petal opening, the layers peeling back until I was bare.

Ready.

Oh God.

As he moved back, his eyes finding me, not letting me go, I replied, "You make it pretty easy to say yes."

A smile crossed his lips, and he shifted into first, pulling onto the road.

I took a deep breath, waiting for the nerves to settle. "Where are we going?"

"A favorite place of mine."

"Oh yeah?"

"I promise I wasn't only thinking of myself when I booked it." He glanced at me while he approached the light, his tongue skimming his bottom lip. "You're going to love it there."

"Do you go to this magical foodie place often?"

He laughed. "If I'm being honest, I don't get out as often as I'd like. Normally, my brothers and friends drag me to a meal or drinks, like the night we met."

Because of Everly.

That made perfect sense.

When I'd been in Manhattan with the Turners, they had been the same. Most of our meals eaten at home. But when we were traveling, all we did was eat out. During the four years I'd worked for them, we'd been in LA several times, always dining at the best restaurants. One meal in particular was a dinner I'd never forget.

I closed my eyes, recalling their meatballs as I said, "The best food I've ever had here was at—"

"Origin's," we both said at the same time.

I felt a warmth come across my cheeks. "Sounds like we have similar taste in food."

His fingers brushed against the outside of my hand, where it was resting on my thigh. "That's where we're going tonight."

"You've got me excited." *In more ways than just food*, I thought. "Admittedly, I was never a foodie until four years ago," I told him. "I learned to try new things, challenge my taste buds. Now, I crave things that I never would have dreamed of eating before."

"Oh yeah?" He looked at me again before he changed

lanes. "Tell me about your family. Were you born and raised in LA?"

"I was, which seems so rare nowadays."

"Seems we have that in common too."

I grinned even though he couldn't see me. "My parents are both CPAs and own their own accounting firm. I have an older brother who lives in Denver. We're a small but close family. My parents wish my brother and I—or at least one of us—loved numbers as much as them. Sadly, we didn't inherit that gene. In fact, numbers loathe me."

He laughed. "So, if numbers aren't your thing, what is?"

"Education."

"You're a teacher?"

I sighed. "I will be."

Words that made our age difference and place in life even more apparent.

"I realize I don't know you that well, but the way you were with my daughter tells me you're going to be an exceptional teacher."

"Thank you." I folded the sleeves of my jean jacket, my hands busy, fidgety, as I continued, "It's funny; my parents do the books and taxes for so many wealthy people in this city. They never say names at the dinner table, just numbers and their earnings. I have no desire to make that kind of money. I just want to be around kids and make a difference in their lives." I glanced out the passenger window, recalling the feeling in my heart when I'd submitted my UCLA application, bringing me one step closer to my dream job. "I want to help mold them into wonderful little humans. I think it's often forgotten that kids are the most important people in our world. They're our future. I just wish education got more credit and had more resources, so kids had every chance to succeed with endless opportunities at their disposal." I stopped, realizing I was going on a mini rant. "Sorry. Clearly, I'm extremely passionate about this."

"Can Everly be in your class? For the rest of her education?" He gazed at me again, his stare honest and genuine. "I'm serious."

"I appreciate that." My fingers halted but immediately started right back up, now playing with the end of the sleeve. "Except I have no classroom. I'm working on that part. You know, once I finish the next four years of college."

His eyes widened. "Does that mean you just graduated high school?"

"No, no." I giggled a little, realizing he thought I was only eighteen. "I'm twenty-two years old. High school was four years ago."

I saw the relief and felt it when his hand moved on top of mine, squeezing my fingers. I could feel the sweat forming on my palm.

"Something tells me you're going to work your ass off and get that degree much faster than you think."

"I hope so." I didn't want to continue dwelling on me in case we ventured further into the topic of employment—something I certainly didn't want to lie about if it came up. So, I said, "What about you? Hannah told me you're a lawyer. I'm assuming the guys you were with at the bar were friends? Colleagues?"

"Yes, but more importantly, they're family." He turned at the light, taking his hand back to shift. "I have two older brothers—Jenner and Dominick—who were there that night, and we more or less run the law firm even though my parents are technically in charge."

"And Hannah will be working for you?"

"With us, yes."

"How nice that your family works together and that you all wanted to be lawyers."

"Where your brain revolted against numbers, the dinner table conversations did quite the opposite for my brothers and me. Our parents' chatter ended up fueling us. We each concentrate on a different type of law. Mine's estate planning, which means I deal with nothing but numbers."

"That sounds like hell."

He laughed. "So does education."

I held myself back from snorting. "Fair enough." I watched the headlights flash across his face, reading his expression even if it was just his profile. "I get the sense that you love it."

"I do. My brothers are in entertainment and real estate law —areas that require them to be on the road much more often than me. Estate planning is perfect for my lifestyle and my daughter."

"She's adorable, Ford. You two seem very close."

"We are." He exhaled loudly. "And we always have been, even during the days when I had no idea what I was doing."

I placed my hand on his arm, surprised by the jolt of sensations that instantly moved through me. "No one does. It's all a giant guessing game, especially when they're born. How old were you when she was born?"

He was silent for a few seconds before he answered, "Twenty-four. I hadn't given children much thought. I was far more concerned with partying and making money than being responsible for someone other than myself." When our eyes connected, there was emotion in his. Emotion I couldn't quite pinpoint. "But Everly came into my life and exploded everything I'd thought to be true. It's just been her and me ever since."

My questions were accumulating.

Where is Everly's mom? Does she have a role in her life?

What happened to the relationship between Ford and her?

What is the cause of the emotion I'm seeing?

Instead of asking any of those, I softly said, "She's lucky to have you."

"Nah, Sydney." He stilled, his voice so coarse. "I'm the lucky one to have her."

I melted.

My heart, my body—all combining together into a puddle of goo in this seat.

I'd witnessed many conversations during my time as an au pair—talks between the Turners, their friends, and their neighbors. There were things parents said about their children, obligatory responses. And then there were replies that came from the rawest part of their soul. An admission from the most beautiful, unfiltered place.

That was what I'd just heard.

A side of Ford that he kept protected.

That was extremely vulnerable.

I would cherish this moment.

"I believe that," I whispered. "But I believe that to be true for both of you."

He said nothing as he pulled into the restaurant, and we got out of the car, his hand moving to my lower back as we walked inside.

The silence finally broke when he said, "Should we start in the bar?"

I wanted the evening to last as long as possible.

So, I nodded, and he led us into that section, where there were two barstools along the far side of the bar. He stood behind me while I sat, making sure the seat didn't shift as I got comfortable.

Before he left that position and got onto his own stool, he

breathed, "That dress, Sydney ..." His tone turned hoarse, gritty. "Fuck."

The air from each of his syllables swished against my neck, like it was being carried off a lake, the echoes hitting the walls inside my chest, sending goose bumps down my back.

"I'm glad you like it."

He sat on his stool and turned the base of the seat toward me, our knees brushing. "Do you drink wine? They have quite an extensive list here."

"I do, and I prefer red." I smiled. "I don't peg you as a white wine drinker."

He chuckled. "You're right about that." He took the leather-bound menu the bartender handed to him and continued, "Do you have a preference, or should I choose one for us?"

"Surprise me."

I hadn't been in a relationship since high school. The few dates I'd been on since were with guys closer to my age. They took initiative without asking my opinion. They just assumed and dealt with the consequences.

Ford was different.

He was older.

Thoughtful, considerate.

And when the bartender approached, Ford requested two glasses of a Cab I didn't recognize and turned back toward me. His eyes filled the silence, speaking so loudly as they roamed across my face that I found it almost hard to breathe.

"You're getting into education," he said, his stare dipping to my lips, his hand following with the gentlest touch as he grazed my chin. "You come from a family of numbers. You have an older brother. What else should I know about you, Sydney?"

My heart began to race even faster.

I felt like I was keeping a vital piece of information from him by not mentioning my upcoming interview with his assistant. The last four years were such an important milestone in my life, so it seemed disingenuous to not discuss it.

But I didn't want to go against Hannah, so I reluctantly steered him toward my other hobbies by saying, "I love to bake. Run. Work out. Travel—that's a big one. And swim in all oceans and seas—I don't have a preference, although the Dead Sea was incredibly badass." My breath hitched as his thumb pulled at my bottom lip. "And I have the most fabulous best friend, who you've met. *Hmm*, what else ..."

"You bake."

"Out of all things, that's what you focused on?"

"I have a sweet tooth."

I got the sense that he was talking about something other than chocolate.

And it made me wiggle, recrossing my legs, my knee hitting his in the process. I didn't move it away. I kept it locked against him. "Yes, I do."

The Turners had had a personal chef. Meals that she mastered for their entire family and me, but desserts were her weakness, so I'd learned how to bake to give the family something sweet after every dinner.

Details Ford didn't need to know.

But details that had been such a big part of my job since the kids often helped me in the kitchen.

"Here's your wine," the bartender said, pulling my attention away from Ford as two glasses were set in front of us.

I lifted mine and held it toward Ford.

"To new memories, starting with this ..." He leaned forward and pressed his lips against mine.

The kiss was unexpected, like a fire that had erupted out of nowhere, the flames quickly moving through my body.

I wasn't just breathless.

I was wet.

And neither sensation faded when he pulled his mouth away and took a sip.

I took a drink as well, trying to cool myself off, tasting the rich, bold red.

"Tell me what you bake."

What I bake, I repeated in my head, forcing my brain to register his question.

"What, are you wondering if my cookies will trump Hannah's?"

"The thought might have crossed my mind."

I twirled the stem of the glass between my fingers, watching the dark wine slosh against the sides. "I'm not one to boast, but I'm pretty good. I can make just about anything."

"You're tempting me to take you home."

I laughed. "To wrap an apron around my waist and make you cookies that will rival anything you've ever tasted?"

"Sydney ..." His hand returned to my mouth. This time swiping across my lip. Slowly. "I said nothing about putting you in my kitchen."

SEVEN

FORD

Goddamn it, I couldn't get enough of her.

Our time together in the bar hadn't satisfied me. Neither had dinner.

And, now, as we sat in my car outside the restaurant, the last fucking thing I wanted was to take her home. And then drive back to my place without getting the chance to touch her.

Taste her.

To leave without her scent on my body.

But that was the circumstance I was facing as my hand rested on her thigh instead of the gear shift, my car still in Park.

"Hannah is at my house, watching Everly."

"I know. I mean, I figured."

That didn't make up for the fact that I wanted to tear her fucking clothes off.

That I wanted her in my bed.

That I wanted my lips on her skin, eating, licking. Devouring her until morning.

But my conscience was stopping me, reminding me that it had been a close call last time, and I didn't want to risk it again.

"Sydney ..." *Fuck me*, she was breathtakingly beautiful. "It just doesn't feel right to bring you back to my place."

"I get it; you don't have to explain yourself." She sucked in a mouthful of air loud enough for me to hear. "But our evening doesn't have to end ... if you don't want it to." Her expression was timid as she said, "Gabby is out for the night."

It fucking pained me to reply, "I want that. But I can't stay over."

Her throat bobbed as she swallowed. "You don't have to."

"Then, let's get the hell out of here." There was no hesitation when I took back my hand, which had been resting on her thigh, and shifted into first gear, quickly maneuvering my way out of the parking lot.

I was just pulling onto the road when she patted her stomach and said, "That was delicious. Better than I remember." I could feel her gaze on me when she added, "Even the dessert."

"It's hard to beat Oreo cheesecake."

"Wait until you try mine."

I turned toward her when I reached the light. "Oh yeah?"

"I add a layer of Oreo on top. That way, if your fork doesn't reach all the way to the bottom, you get a piece of cookie with each mouthful."

"Jesus."

"Have I enticed you?" She laughed.

"Sydney, Sydney ..." I reached across the space between us, knowing I had little time because I'd need to shift again soon. I just wanted to feel her. My fingers circled under her chin, swiping that bottom lip, the one that was begging for my teeth. "I was enticed long before I knew you could make my favorite kind of cheesecake."

"But it helps?"

Now, it was my turn to laugh. "It certainly doesn't hurt."

Silence returned to the car, and I broke it with, "What do you have going on tomorrow?"

"It's probably time to buy myself a bed. I'm still sleeping with Gabby, and she hasn't complained, but I'm just starting to feel bad."

"That's all the furniture you need?"

"And a dresser and a couple of nightstands. But Gabby and I have this problem where we head out to go shopping and end up at brunch with bottomless mimosas, and all of our plans go to shit."

"She sounds like my kind of friend." I turned at the light, weaving my way through the traffic. "How long have you known her?"

"Since high school. She moved in a few houses down from where I grew up. I could see her bedroom window from mine, and in the mornings, before school, we would stand in front of them and show each other our outfits. Because, you know, that was one of the most important parts of high school—clothes."

"My daughter would agree, and thank God, we're nowhere close to high school yet."

"See? So, you get it." She went quiet for a moment. "We've been through everything together, and now, we're roommates. It feels very full circle." As I pulled up to the curb, the car coming to a stop, she glanced out the passenger window. "We're here."

I waited for her to look at me again before I nodded.

"Have you changed your mind about coming up?"

I lifted her hand off her lap and moved it over to mine, resting her fingers on top of my hard-on. "This is what you do to me. All through dinner. The entire ride here." My gaze lowered to her mouth. "I can't stop thinking about you. So, fuck no, I haven't changed my mind."

"This is what you do to me." With our hands still linked,

she brought my palm to her face and pressed it flat against her cheek.

Her skin was scorching.

Some women would have slipped me up their dress.

Some would have rubbed their nipples.

Not Sydney.

Her innocence was one of the things I liked most about her.

I pulled my fingers away and reached past her body, opening her door. "After you."

She climbed out, and I turned off the engine, locking the car behind me as I joined her on the sidewalk. My hand instantly went to her lower back, and I followed her through the front entrance and into the elevator. While we rose to her floor, I couldn't stop myself.

I needed a taste even if it was going to be a quick one.

I backed her up against the wall and surrounded her face with my grip, my lips pressing to hers. My tongue parted her mouth, moving in with urgency, and I didn't pull away until I heard the chime of the elevator, signaling we had arrived at her floor.

Her cheeks were flushed, her breath coming out in pants.

"God, Sydney, you're so fucking sweet."

As my words resonated, more redness moved across her flesh, adding to the crimson that had already been there.

But what was new was her smile.

"Come on," she whispered.

The moment her door was unlocked, I grabbed her waist and turned her toward me. It had only been seconds since I'd kissed her, and already, I missed the warmth of her mouth.

Fuck.

"What is it about you that I can't get enough of?" My thumb was back, grazing across those lips. Right, left. Again. "Why do you keep finding your way into my mind?"

THE SINGLE DAD

I didn't wait for her to respond.

I slammed our mouths together instead, resuming what had started in the elevator. She had far too many layers on, and I began to strip them off. Her jacket was the first thing that hit the floor before I lowered the straps of her dress, peeling the tight material down her body.

"Ford," she moaned.

I moved to her neck.

Licking.

Biting.

Taking in that flavor that I'd been thinking about non-fucking-stop.

Once the dress was in a place where it would fall, I unhooked her bra and lowered her panties down her thighs until she was wearing nothing but heels.

"Remember, no bed," she reminded me.

I held her hips, taking in her gorgeous body, my stare on her tits and that fucking pussy that I knew would be soaked the second I touched it. When our eyes finally connected, I replied, "There are plenty of surfaces in here. I see no need for a bed."

And now that I had her in my arms, my lips back on her skin, I wanted to try out each spot to see how I made her feel. To test how far I could bend her body. To please her in even more ways than I already had.

I lifted her legs around me, kissing her as I held her against the wall.

Her thighs tightened on my waist. Her arms circled my neck.

The bareness of her pussy rubbed against the hardness of my cock.

Goading me.

Each shift told me how much she wanted me, and so did her exhales that ended in more moans.

With her hips rocking against me, I growled, "Do you want this?"

"*Yesss.*"

"Show me."

The moment I finished speaking, she began taking off my clothes, rushing to get to my skin. She shed my shirt and pants —the only items she could reach with the way I was holding her.

I kicked off my shoes, letting everything but my boxer briefs drop, and I brought her to the back of the couch, setting her on top of the cushion.

"Don't move," I warned.

I picked up my pants from the floor, grabbing a condom from inside my wallet.

As I returned to her, ripping the top of the foil off and rolling it over my dick, I heard, "And you say I'm the gorgeous one?"

I glanced up, meeting her eyes.

"You're perfect." She shook her head, her stare rising from my cock, to my abs, and slowly up my chest. "Beyond anything I've ever seen."

I spread her legs around me. "It's yours. All of it."

I didn't immediately enter.

I rubbed her clit, getting her ready.

Her head fell back. "Oh God." Her feet pressed against my ass, urging me inside her. "Please, Ford."

The sound of her begging was fucking music to my ears.

But I didn't give in. I rubbed her clit back and forth, the wetness coating my finger.

"How badly do you want me, Sydney?"

I went lower, teasing the warmth of her pussy, the wetness even thicker down there. I gave her just the tip of my finger, inserting it into that tight, dripping cunt.

Fuuuck.

I went as far as my knuckle, and that was when I turned my wrist, giving her pressure from both angles, my thumb on her clit, so she could feel the combination.

"How badly?" I repeated.

Her nails stabbed my shoulders, her heels driving into the backs of my thighs.

It felt impossible not to plunge inside her.

But I didn't.

I wanted the build.

I wanted to be so worked up that my cock was fucking throbbing for her pussy.

"I can't," she breathed. "I can't wait."

"But you're going to have to because I'm not done."

She cupped my face, keeping our mouths pressed closely. "I need you." She sucked on my lip, releasing it to add, "I need you right now."

Fuel.

That was what her reactions did to me.

But I also knew I couldn't stay the night, waking her after a few hours to have her again. I couldn't carry her into the shower in the morning, holding her against the cold wall while the hot water washed our bodies.

This was it.

So, I was going to savor every second.

I went in deeper, to the end of my finger, twisting my wrist, circling, arching to reach that spot.

The one that would make her fucking howl.

And she did.

She went wild.

"Ford! Oh God! Yes!"

When her head tilted back this time, I kissed up her throat, hissing, "I want you to come."

That was my goal tonight.

To see how many times I could get her off.

To see how loud I could make her scream.

To see how hard I could make her body shudder.

When I left this apartment tonight, I wanted her to feel a sweet ache every time she squeezed her legs together, remembering what it felt like when I was inside her.

I added a second finger, overlapping the two. The deeper I got, the more she bucked.

She wasn't just holding my face.

She was gripping it. Kissing me like I was her air, her nails now like claws.

"You like when I'm finger-fucking your pussy ..."

Every time I pulled out, her walls clenched me; her sounds made me believe she was yearning for more.

But I wanted words.

Her words.

"More than anything," she sighed, exposing her neck again. "You have no idea how good this feels."

But I did.

Because watching her unravel made me feel even better.

"I need you."

Hearing that simple statement made my goddamn dick pound.

"I fucking need you, Ford."

Her arms dropped from around my neck, and she reached between us, fisting my cock.

Pumping me.

Leading me toward her.

"I want you to come the second I enter you."

She was tightening around my fingers.

"I want to feel the orgasm pulse through you."

She was getting even wetter, her moans becoming louder.

She was close.

I gave her several more thrusts, and the second I pulled out, replacing my fingers with my cock, she fucking screamed.

I swore I could feel the vibration of her throat across my shaft.

And how soaked she was.

And how fucking narrow.

"Sydney," I growled into her neck, holding the couch to leverage my movements, giving her more power and speed as I drove into her. "You feel so fucking good."

"Ford!"

She was on the verge.

I reared my hips back and glided into her, my thumb now on her clit to give her that added friction. But my thumb didn't move; it stayed still until I knew she was seconds away. That was when I flicked it across her, circling, sending her over that edge.

"Oh fuck!"

She was clutching me—her hands, her pussy.

"Oh my God!"

I surrounded her nipple, sucking it into my mouth, grazing the end with my teeth. It was that moment that I felt the first wave of ripples move through her, pounding across her stomach.

Her heels pressed into me; her arms caged me in.

I didn't let up.

I went harder.

Faster.

My teeth added more pain to her nipple.

"Ford! *Ahhh!*"

She was lost.

But I had her.

And while her pussy hugged my cock, shudders tearing through her, I stroked through her wetness.

Her stare turned feral.

Animalistic.

"*Yesss*," she cried, pulling me closer. "You are"—she panted, searching for her breath—"incredible."

Now that she had stilled, I held her face, taking in her lips. "No." I slid my tongue through the opening, sampling, wanting to know if the orgasm changed the way she tasted. "You're fucking incredible."

I lifted her off the back of the couch and carried her to the table, moving the place mat to set her directly on top of the wood.

"I want you to think of this moment every time you sit down for breakfast," I said and plunged inside her. "I want you to think of my fucking cock when you're drinking coffee here."

I didn't know how it was possible, but she was even wetter, her pussy sucking me in like I'd never left.

"Oh!" she shouted. "Yes!"

I captured her clit between two of my fingers, rubbing both sides like a coin. "Remember how loudly you just screamed?" I gave her a quick pump, doing it again before I started to slow. "This time, I want you even louder."

Her knees bent, her feet rounding over the table, giving me all the access I needed while her arms reached behind her, holding her weight.

Her tits bounced with each thrust, her legs trying to cave in. She was lost again, unaware of her movements, unable to stop what was happening inside her body.

But I was in control.

And this was my pussy.

And I wasn't going to halt until we both came.

But, *fuck me*, she was getting tighter, making it harder for me to hold off.

"Jesus, your fucking pussy."

I took her nipple into my mouth, the little bud already red from what I had done to it earlier, and I licked the end, sucking it. Flicking. And with my fingers still on her clit, I squeezed, rubbing the top back and forth.

"Ford!"

She lifted her ass off the table, meeting me, pausing in the center, where I circled my hips. Each rotation caused a different sensation. One that made it hard for me to fucking breathe. One that made it almost impossible for my balls not to explode.

"Sydney," I moaned back. "Damn it." I held her hip, increasing my speed. "I need you to come with me."

"I'm already there."

I didn't hold back.

I didn't go gently.

I added pressure, friction, driving into her cunt, each draw causing her roars to get louder.

As my balls started to constrict, she wrapped her arms around my shoulders, connecting our chests.

Our mouths.

Keeping me tightly inside her.

And after only a few dives, the eruption began.

Together.

"Sydney," I demanded, my tone an order as my release started to tear through me. "Fucking Sydney."

She was moaning even louder, giving me exactly what I wanted.

And just as her voice cut off, the shudders ripped through her stomach. Her pussy clenched, her wetness like a fucking hose as it coated me.

"Goddamn it."

I let go.

The moment I did, a burst moved through my balls and across my stomach, the intensity so overwhelming that my fingers bit her.

"Fuck," I growled.

"Ford!"

The first load shot into the condom.

"Oh my God!" she belted out, holding me even tighter.

I pulled back and drove in. "You're fucking milking me."

She was taking every drop, suctioning it from me, working the peak of my orgasm through my body.

"*Yesss!*"

I sucked her lip into my mouth, waiting for the intensity to slow from within us, easing the power behind my strokes until I was still. My thumb left her clit, and I surrounded her face, keeping her steady as I studied her eyes.

"Your pussy ..." I shook my head. "Fuck, Sydney." I pressed our foreheads together, our breaths mixing. "What I wouldn't give to taste you again in the morning."

"*Mmm.*" She smiled. "Sounds like you're promising a second date."

I kissed her.

I needed it.

The heat from her lips, the feel of them.

"I can do that."

"I'm already looking forward to seeing you again." She pecked my mouth, loosening her grip around my neck. "I know you have to go, but I have something for you to take home."

"A present?" I ground my lip with my teeth. "You mean, you have more for me?"

She nodded. "I made homemade brownies."

I was deep into my emails, finally having a few minutes to respond to my clients and their questions, when my phone rang. I reluctantly pulled my eyes away from the computer screen, and the caller ID showed it was my assistant, phoning from her desk on the other side of the wall.

I held the receiver to my face and said, "Morning, or is it"— I glanced at the monitor again, seeing that it was after three— "afternoon? Sorry. Hell, it's been a day. What do you have for me?"

"The nanny is here for her interview. The final candidate."

"Is she a good one? Because I've got to tell you, I haven't loved the personalities of the last two. Excellent on paper, incredibly qualified, but too stern. I don't need someone dripping in warmth, but I need someone Everly can connect with on some level."

I'd expected professionalism, but I'd been met with icy exteriors. Middle-aged women, certainly well suited but more interested in education than athletics. I didn't know how they would keep up with my constantly moving daughter, who preferred hiking over spelling and playing outside over coloring.

I also couldn't picture either of them living in my house.

"This is my favorite of the three," my assistant said. "She's not the most qualified of the group; however, something tells me you're really going to like her."

"Excellent. Send her in." I lifted my coffee cup to take a drink, realizing it was empty. "Any way you can grab me a coffee?"

"Of course."

I hung up and returned to my emails, eventually hearing a knock at the door.

MARNI MANN

"Come in," I announced.

The door opened as I was typing. But I didn't glance up. I needed to get this whole thought out before I focused on anything else, especially given that the client I was responding to was paying me by the minute.

I hit Send and finally looked up.

It took a moment for my eyes to adjust, for me to realize what I was looking at.

Or better, *who* I was looking at.

"Sydney?"

"Hi." The warmth on her face was contagious. "Your assistant told me to give you this."

She smiled as she set the coffee cup on my desk and backed up to the set of chairs that were in front of me, taking a seat in one of them.

She looked stunning.

Her hair was down and curled around her face, and she was wearing a bright blue dress that flowed well past her knees, the color making her eyes pop. She had little makeup on, aside from a strong swipe of gloss across her lips.

A mouth I'd never seen glossy before.

A mouth that already owned my attention, and now, I couldn't look away.

"What are you doing here?" I leaned my elbows on the desk, surrounding the cup with both hands. "Bringing me more dessert?" I glanced toward the closed door, hoping my assistant wouldn't send in the nanny until after Sydney left. Since I hadn't seen her in a couple days, I needed time with her, time to hear why she'd come to my office—something that seemed extremely out of character for her.

"No dessert." She laughed, almost bashfully. "I'm here to be interviewed." Her hands rested on her lap as she added, "Looks like I applied to be Everly's nanny."

EIGHT

SYDNEY

"You did ... *what?*" Ford asked, shock and confusion filling his handsome face. "How?"

This was exactly what I hadn't wanted. To have a conversation like the one that had just started.

To base this on lies.

I just wanted to tell him about the talk I'd had with Hannah when she dropped me off at my apartment, how she had told me about the position and persuaded me to apply.

But I kept telling myself there was a reason she had wanted me to go this route.

That coincidences could happen.

That this, somehow, could be one.

"I saw the ad and applied," I told him. "I'd been looking for a nanny position in LA before I even left Europe."

"You didn't know the job was for me? And Everly?"

I'd never seen the ad, but I was positive it wouldn't have listed Ford's information. I was sure it would have only had his assistant's info. It also wouldn't have given Everly's name.

I shook my head. "I had no idea."

As I took a breath, trying to calm my nerves, I couldn't get over how sexy he looked in this big office. His broad, muscular frame in the high-back leather seat. Framed accolades all over the walls and a view of LA's skyline out the window.

"I'm sorry." I glanced down at my lap, the heat from his gaze becoming too much. "You, in that navy suit, in this setting, is just a vision I was not prepared for."

I couldn't believe I had said that out loud.

But those words were more honest than anything I'd said so far.

Ford Dalton screamed power.

And remembering just how much power he'd given me on the back of Gabby's couch and again on her wooden table was making my entire body blush.

A topic I'd much rather ponder than the lies.

When I finally glanced up, there was hunger in his stare.

A hunger I recognized. I'd seen the same look while we were at the bar and again when we were eating dinner.

"I'm shocked as hell right now."

"Me too," I whispered.

"I just assumed you worked in the education field. I realize now that I never asked."

I reached inside my bag and pulled out my résumé, setting it on his desk. "I'm not sure if you've already seen this."

"I haven't."

"Then, take a look. My background is all on there, detailed. The last four years, I was employed by the Turner family as an au pair for their three children. I homeschooled them, baked for them. Raised them, if I'm being honest."

"An au pair," he said as he looked at the sheet.

Without his eyes, I couldn't get a read on what he was thinking.

I wondered if he could feel the panic that was blasting through me.

"As you know, I'm going to school for education, a degree I'll be starting in a few weeks at UCLA." He finally looked up as I added, "It's an online program. I'll have plenty of time to work and fulfill all my obligations."

"You're qualified—there's no question about that—and I've seen you with my daughter ..." His voice faded out. "What made you become an au pair?"

This was where the honesty came in. Where I could look him in the eyes and give him a part of myself.

"When I graduated high school, I wasn't ready for college. I just didn't know what I wanted to do, what I wanted to study, where I wanted to be in life. What I did know was that I wanted to see the world, so I applied to be a flight attendant and an au pair, not expecting to get either job at eighteen years old. Ironically, I got both." I glanced past his chair, at the framed degrees that hung on the walls, looking forward to the day when I had my own to use as decor. "I've always loved children. I babysat every kid in my neighborhood, and when the Turners told me the job required an immense amount of travel, I was sold." I smiled as I thought of my littles, the texts we'd exchanged just a few days ago when I told them how much I missed them. "Four years later, there was no question as to what I wanted to do. I just needed my degree." I shrugged. "So, now, I'm here, going after that degree."

"And you'd be comfortable in a nanny role again?"

"Ford, it's a role I know very well." I repositioned my legs, recrossing them, trying my hardest not to fidget. "I'm paying for my own schooling, my apartment. I fully support myself. And although I do have a nice chunk in savings, I don't want to deplete it. I have to work. It feels wrong not to." I wrapped an arm around my stomach. "I know, not typical information that's shared during an interview, but this"—I shook my head—"isn't your typical situation."

He was quiet for a moment before he said, "This job requires you to move into my home."

I nodded. "That was in the ad. But now that I see it's you, I realize that probably changes things a bit." I tried not to wince. "Makes things a bit ... messy."

The moving-in had also been mentioned by Ford's assistant, something I hadn't dwelled on since I didn't know what was going to happen when he realized it was me.

He looked down at his coffee, taking his time to eventually gaze up at me. "Do you really think this could work?" His teeth grazed his lip, reminding me of what that had felt like when he did the same thing to my nipple. "We've slept together, Sydney. I don't know how you could be Everly's nanny at this point."

I took a deep breath—something that wasn't easy to do. "Things are a little complicated now, yes."

"A little?" He laughed. "I've made it clear that I'm overly protective of my daughter and the people I bring into her life. If things don't work out between us and you're her nanny, that's another woman abandoning her, and I won't stand for that."

Another woman.

I assumed the first—and only—was her mother.

My stomach hurt for that sweet, precious girl.

And it just added to the questions I already had.

"But there's another side to this," he continued. "And that is, you're perfect for her—everything I want and need in a nanny." He looked down at his coffee again, this time taking a drink. "You're young, you're fit, you'll be able to keep up with her energy." He ran his hand over his beard, wiping the sides of his mouth. "You'll be able to teach her and mold her and give her all the tools she needs to start kindergarten in the fall. And once she starts school, you'll only enhance what she's already learning there." His voice lowered when he said, "She fell for you the moment she met you. She even still asks for you."

"I fell for her." That was also the truth. "She appeared so mature for her age with such an old soul."

"She had no choice. I've only ever treated her like an adult."

"I appreciate that parenting style, to be honest." She took a breath. "Ford, it would be an honor to take care of your little girl."

Ford leaned back in his chair, adjusting his tie, like the knot was too tight. "What the fuck am I supposed to do, Sydney?" He paused. "I'm in a position where I need to hire someone immediately. Hannah is at her wit's end. Tops, I can squeeze a few more weeks out of her."

"And here comes the *but*."

He exhaled loudly. "The *but* is that I've been inside your body. I've made you come." He glanced down my body, making me feel as though I were completely naked, as though he were inside me again. "I'm doing everything I can not to reach across this desk and make you come again."

My legs tightened, the fluttering instantly sparking between them.

The tingling making it hard for me to process the reality of this situation.

"What are you saying, Ford?"

He was silent as he stared at me. "I don't see a way around this."

"I'm not sure I understand."

"I can't have both, Sydney."

Both.

And then it hit me.

It was either the job or the start of this relationship—or whatever direction we were moving in, together.

But I couldn't have both.

I was slowly inhaling, trying to convince my heart to settle, as he asked, "Which do you want more?"

I pulled my hair to one side, holding it in my slick hand, my heart increasing instead of calming. "You can't ask me that. It's not fair."

"But it's the only way I'm going to decide."

I released the strands of hair, my head dropping, my hand now holding my forehead. I needed the pressure; my brain felt like it was going to explode.

Which do you want more?

The one thing I knew, the one thing Ford had emphasized, was that he didn't bring women into her life. Even in this office, he'd reminded me of that.

Up until this point, things had been going well between us. We'd had an excellent time on our first date. Before he'd left my apartment, there had been talk of seeing each other again.

But I got the sense that relationships weren't easy for him, that there hadn't been many since Everly had been born—if there had even been any at all.

Oh God, I liked this man.

My accidental encounter, who constantly found his way into my mind. A set of eyes that, every time I stared into them, I wanted to see more.

To see deeper.

To see ... a future with him.

But Ford had his reservations about women, and something told me that was because of what had happened with Everly's mother.

I didn't know if he would ever take the next step with me.

If we would get to the place where he allowed me around his daughter.

If he kept those two parts of his life separate, why would it be any different with me?

I'd finally met someone I really liked.

Now, I was here, in this emotional place, forced to make this decision.

All I knew was that if Ford was the person I was supposed to be with, one day, this would all work out.

And maybe I would never be more than Everly's nanny, but at least I would be spending time doing what I loved with the little person Ford loved the most in this world.

"What's your answer, Sydney?" He folded his hands together, waiting for my response, his eyes fixed with mine.

"I choose ..." I held in my breath, unable to stop my brain from spiraling.

Am I making a mistake?

Am I going about this all wrong?

Will I regret this decision?

Will he see right through me?

He would always put her first, but showing Ford that I would do the same had to mean something.

"Everly," I finished.

A reaction came across his face like a wave, one that I couldn't quite read before he said, "That's what you want, then? To be her nanny?"

There was no doubt in my mind that I could give Everly exactly what she needed. If there was one thing I was extremely confident about, it was that.

At the same time, I could apply the skills I would be learning at school into the lesson plans I designed for her.

The only thing I wasn't sure about was what it would be like, living in his home. How it would put us in close quarters every single day, showing vulnerabilities, especially considering my attraction to him was so strong.

But I wasn't afraid.

If anything, the thought excited me.

"Yes," I answered. "That's what I want."

"You know what that means, don't you?"

I tightened the grip I already had around my stomach. "It means that whatever was happening between us is now over."

He nodded. Slowly. "And nothing can ever happen between us again." His stare intensified. "We can't date. We can't fuck. You're there for Everly ... not me."

Am I making a mistake?

Those words were on repeat.

Again, I heard them.

"I understand," I told him.

"And you can accept that?"

He wasn't testing me. He wasn't being derogatory.

He was being Everly's father.

"Yes."

He reached across the desk, holding out his hand for me to grab. The moment we linked fingers, his voice softened as he said, "Are you sure?"

I knew what he was doing.

And there was no question; I felt the energy between our hands. The promise in his grip. The heat in his skin.

All of it made the tingle inside my body beat like techno.

But I had to stay focused on Everly.

I broke our connection, returning my hand to my thigh, my palm even slicker than before. "Yes, Ford, I'm sure."

He pulled his arm back and hugged his coffee, allowing plenty of silence to pass before he said, "I need some time. I want to think this through. Sleep on it. Make my final decision in the morning."

"No problem."

His thumb traced the rim of the mug. "You know, you've

been very patient since I met you. Understanding in a way I couldn't quite comprehend, given your age—I don't mean that in any disrespect; it's just not a trait I see often." He glanced down at my résumé. "Now that I see you on paper, it all makes sense."

"Four years is a long time to be with a family. I might not have seen everything, but I saw enough to know the things you go through as a parent. Therefore, I can only imagine how difficult it has been for you to do it all on your own."

His brows narrowed. "It would be full transparency if you moved into my home. I'm not perfect, Sydney, but I try my hardest to be everything Everly needs." His voice turned a little quieter as he added, "She deserves that."

I didn't want him to know how that admission made me feel.

That I could, so easily, wrap my arms around him and bury my face in his chest and tell him he could make any woman's ovaries combust.

But I stayed on course instead and replied, "I'm far from perfect. I'm going to make mistakes—I made mistakes with the Turners. We're human. All we can do is try our best when it comes to raising children."

"Truth." He sipped his coffee. "What about your friend Gabby? Would she be all right with you moving out?"

I smiled. "More than all right. I'm sure she's dying to get her office back that I've completely hijacked."

He slipped my résumé into a folder and placed it into his drawer. "I'll give you a call in the morning."

The interview was over.

I just hoped it had been enough. That I'd given him answers he wanted to hear.

Maybe even ones he hadn't considered.

As I stood with my bag, he said, "I want you to know, you're an incredible woman to sacrifice the possibility of us—all for my daughter."

My lungs tightened, my throat, too, as I held the back of the chair I'd been sitting in. "This might sound simple and overused, but I've always believed that things in my life happen for a reason. I didn't want to go to the bar that night. I was exhausted, jet-lagged. Grouchy, if I'm being honest. But there, I met you, and then Everly the next morning, and that could quite possibly be the best thing that's ever happened to me."

He continued to stare at me until he replied, "I'll be in touch, Sydney."

I smiled and gave him a quick wave, and then I walked out the door, thanking his assistant.

"Sydney," I heard when I was halfway down the hallway, realizing the sound had come from one of the offices I'd already passed.

I backed up to the closest doorway, where Hannah was inside, sitting behind a desk. "Hey," I said to her.

"How did things go?"

I shrugged. "Good, I think. He's going to let me know in the morning."

She got up and walked toward me. "I hope this doesn't affect you two. I mean, he's been in such a good mood since he met you."

"It will. I had to choose."

The crushing blow moved across her face. "Oh God, no."

I nodded. "I picked Everly."

She sighed, her hand going to my shoulder. "I just wanted what's best for her, and I know that's you." She stalled, looking at me. "I remember when I started working here at the firm, and one of the very first things Ford ever told me was that I needed to listen to my gut. When it came to law, life, lessons, it would never steer me wrong. That's what I did when I met you."

We certainly had that in common.

But I was curious and said, "Is your gut telling you that I'm going to get the job?"

"I think you're going to get a lot more than that."

I didn't know why she thought that. Ford had made it very clear that I would never have both.

Maybe her gut was telling her otherwise.

Maybe it was how well she knew Ford.

Maybe it was something else I couldn't pinpoint.

But then she pulled me in for a hug and whispered, "Don't let me down, girl."

NINE
FORD

I headed straight for Jenner's office, walking toward the back, where he'd built a wet bar, and grabbed a bottle of scotch and three glasses, carrying it all to his desk. I filled the tumblers with several fingers' worth and handed one to each of my brothers, who happened to be sitting there, in the middle of a meeting.

They'd said nothing when I walked in.

And still didn't as they accepted the glass I gave them and stared at me.

"Drink," I ordered and raised the scotch to my lips, swallowing.

"Yes, sir," Dominick replied. "Even though it's not five yet … and I have a meeting in an hour."

"Cancel it," I said. "I need your help." I looked at Jenner. "And yours."

"What's going on?" Jenner asked.

"Oh shit," Dominick said. "Something tells me this is going to be good."

I downed the liquor and poured myself more.

"Yep," Jenner responded to Dominick. "I think you're right."

I waited for the burn to subside and lifted the glass off his desk, squeezing it between my fingers. "I had three nannies come in today to interview. Guess who the last one was."

Jenner shook his head. "Dude, I have no idea. An ex? One of my exes? If that's the case, fuck."

"Sydney," I told them.

"You mean, the girl from the bar?" Dominick inquired.

I nodded. "Yes. That one." I downed another mouthful. "The girl I've been balls deep in—twice." I drained more from my glass. "Why does this shit happen to me? I finally find a girl I would like to get to know better, and she ends up interviewing to be Everly's fucking nanny."

"Dude, I don't know. But it's fucked up."

I wasn't sure who had said that, but I agreed and nodded again.

"Seems she's doubling her duties, huh?" Dominick joked.

"Fucker." I punched his arm. "It's not funny. I'm in a fucking situation, and I don't know what to do." I glanced at Jenner. "You used to bitch about Jo's age." I stopped and glared at Dominick. "And you didn't want to date a client when you first got with Kendall. Well, none of that compares to this." I took another sip. "She's twenty-two. After graduating high school, she went straight to work as an au pair, traveled the world with the family she worked for, basically raising their three kids. Four years later, she decided she wanted to be a teacher, moved back to LA, enrolled in college, and I met her on her first night back."

"How'd she find out you were hiring?" Jenner asked. "I assume that's why she applied, right?"

"No. It's a coincidence. When she applied, she had no idea

it was me." Still looking at him, I said, "Yours was just graduating. Mine is just starting."

"Notice how he called her *mine*," Dominick said.

"It means nothing."

"Bullshit," Dominick shot back. "But we'll go with it, for shits and giggles."

I sighed, annoyed with my brother. "She needs a job to support her while she's in school." I quieted for a moment. "Since she'd be so good for the job, I gave her an ultimatum. My daughter or me."

"That's very lawyerly of you," Dominick said.

"Listen, it can't be both. It wouldn't work. There's far too much crossover and—no. If things ended between us and Eve lost her and—no, again."

"Which did she pick?" Dom asked.

"Everly," I told them.

"Of course she did," Jenner said. "Because how the hell could she pick you? You don't run toward relationships; you sprint the fuck away from them. You don't think Sydney can tell that by now?"

"No," I snapped. "And that's not true."

"It's not?" Dominick pushed. "I can think of three chicks from the past who would have given up their implants to have more with you."

"You're such a dick."

"It's true," Dominick said.

"It is," Jenner agreed.

"I didn't come in here to talk about the problems you think I have." I swallowed the rest of the scotch and filled my glass again. "I came in because, damn it, she'd make the perfect nanny and I don't know what the hell to do."

"You hire her," both of them said.

I ran my hand over the top of my hair, digging in to tug at

the roots. "Just like that? Ignoring the fact that we've been together? And I have her move into my house, like I'm not going to picture her naked every time I see her bent over?"

Dominick smiled, recrossing his legs. "Can you stop yourself from sticking it in when she's in that position?"

My head dropped as I tried to get that perfect image out of my mind. "No." I glanced up. "Yes." I took a long, deep inhale. "I'm asking for fucking trouble, aren't I?"

Silence ticked between us until Jenner rested his arms on his desk and said, "Kids are her passion, obviously. She has experience. She's going to be a teacher. Hell, there isn't anyone better suited than that. And if I remember correctly, you said Everly really liked her when they met."

"She did."

"Then, what's the problem?" Jenner said. "Because you always put Eve first, you'll keep your dick in your pants. You'll have the perfect nanny for your daughter. Life will be all good."

Me.

I'm the goddamn problem.

There was something about this girl that I couldn't get enough of. That I wanted more of. That was different than the dates I'd gone on in the past.

But every time I started talking to a woman, things would fizzle out when I couldn't give her more of myself.

I was sure this would be no different.

That, somehow, I would fuck shit up between us.

It was better that things had ended before they even began.

"Maybe you're right," I said. "Maybe there is no problem."

Dominick's hand went to my back, patting just below my shoulder. "There's no law that says she has to move in right away. See how things go for a few weeks. Make sure you don't have to take ten cold showers a day. Then, make the transition."

I nodded. "I can do that."

But could I?

Goddamn it, yes. Of course I could.

Jenner held out his glass in front of me. "Congratulations, brother. You've finally got yourself a nanny. Now, we can drag your ass out whenever we want."

"Hardly." I laughed as I clinked glasses with him and then Dominick. "She's going to relieve Hannah's duties, not mine. Nothing's going to change with my availability."

"That's right; he's going to stay home, but now, he'll be cuddling with Sydney," Dominick teased.

"Such a dickhead," I groaned.

"I've got a question for you," Jenner said, pausing. "When you last saw her and went back to her place, did you schedule another date with her?"

The morning following my meetup with Sydney, I'd texted my brothers, telling them how it had gone since one of them had asked.

I was wondering if my honesty had been a mistake.

"We didn't set a date, but I was definitely going to see her again."

Jenner looked at Dominick and then back at me. "Now, I know why you're sucking down that scotch like it's water."

"Right ... fuck me," I sighed.

"My advice," Jenner said, "skip the glass and just start drinking from the fucking bottle."

———

Me: I'd like you to come over and hang with Everly for a bit. I want to see how she interacts with you under normal, expected circumstances. I know this is last minute, but are you available tonight?

Sydney: Hi! Yes, I can make it tonight. What time?

Me: Would 6 work?
Sydney: That works. Usually, I lesson-plan, carving out time for
learning, fun, outdoor activity, and exercise. With me, it's not all
play time. Would it be okay if I planned something for Everly
and me to do? I realize it'll be dinnertime, followed by a bath
and reading her a story in bed. I promise I'll account for all of
that.

I stared at her text, blown away by what I was seeing, and it wasn't because there was a hell of a lot of scotch flowing through my veins.

Granted, I'd never had a nanny before, but I was positive Hannah did none of those things. Her time with my daughter was all about fun. But that was what Hannah was there for.

This—Sydney—was different.

Me: You can do whatever you want. My plan is to sit back and
observe you two together.
Sydney: Perfect. Thank you. See you tonight.

There was no question that Eve was going to immediately connect with Sydney. My daughter wasn't shy. She didn't lack for personality. She found a way to charm everyone she encountered. And the moment Sydney walked into my house, surprising Everly, I saw my little one in action.

She flew off the couch, running straight toward Sydney. "Syd!" She hugged Sydney's waist. "You came back!" She glanced up at her, smiling. "And you brought presents!"

Since I was nearby, Sydney handed me everything she was holding and reached down to pick up Everly.

Fuck me.

The two of them couldn't be any more beautiful together, and her having my baby in her arms was certainly a sight I could get used to.

She was dressed casual in loose-fitting jeans and an off-the-shoulder top—not even the oversize clothes could hide the perfection of her body. She had put her hair in a ponytail and had little makeup on.

She looked stunning.

"I don't know if I'd call them presents, but I brought lots of stuff," Sydney said. Although I'd never doubted her strength, she lifted Eve with ease, like she was an infant. "I've missed you, Miss Everly." She hugged my girl and then pulled back, so she could look at her face. "Your dad invited me over to hang with you for a little while. Does that sound cool?"

"*Sooo* cool." She brushed her hand back and forth over Sydney's bare shoulder. "I wanted you to come to my pancake party. Daddy said you were busy. Chef Craig made the pancakes, but mine are better. Next time, I am going to make the pancakes, and you *haaave* to come."

Sydney gave me a quick glance, and my dick instantly fucking throbbed. "I'll do my best to be there."

Eve held out her pinkie. "Promise?"

"Promise."

Sydney carried Eve into the kitchen, setting her on a stool, away from where Craig was working. Since I wasn't far behind, I placed her things right next to her, the closeness giving me a whiff of her coconut scent that I loved so much.

Damn it.

I needed to put distance between us, so I took a seat behind the bar, and now had a perfect view of the girls.

"I made us a little plan for tonight," Sydney told her.

Eve's face lit up, her large eyes going wide. "You did?"

Sydney nodded. "You and Dad are going to have dinner—"

"Not to interrupt," Craig said, his salad chopping coming to a stop, "but I'm preparing dinner for the three of you."

"You are?" Sydney asked.

She glanced at me as I said, "Did you think we'd eat without you?" I shook my head. "Not going to happen, not at my house."

"I had a snack before I came. I'm—"

"Going to join us," I said. "Please, Sydney. Eve and I both would like you to."

She looked back at my daughter and said, "Well, I guess I'll be having dinner with you and your dad, and then guess what we're going to do."

"What?" my baby asked.

"We're going to bake some cookies and decorate them."

Eve gasped. "We are? What kind? And do you have pink frosting? Because pink frosting is the best."

A few hours after I had invited Sydney over, she'd sent another text, asking if she could make dessert with my daughter —a lesson on measurements would be their focus for the night. She wanted to know if I had rules about her eating sugar, whether I only allowed organic products in my house, if she had any allergies, or if I had concerns about Eve being near an oven—all questions I appreciated being asked.

Except now, I would have all these extra cookies at my house, and every time I reached for one, each bite would make me think of her.

I didn't need the reminder.

Sydney was already far too deep into my head.

"I think we can whip up some pink frosting," Sydney replied.

Eve bounced on top of the counter. "Can we have cookies for dessert?"

"Of course we can, and after we bake and eat, it's going to

be bath time and story time and bedtime. How does that sound?"

"Like the best night ever," Everly sang.

"Perfect." Sydney reached into her pocket and grabbed what looked to be an elastic, bunching Everly's hair together on top of her head, tying it high. "But like all good chefs, we have to make sure our hair doesn't get in the food." She looked at Craig. "Chef Craig doesn't have that problem."

Eve giggled. "Chef Craig is bald, silly."

Craig ran his hand over his shaved head. "Because the ladies love it like this," he said quietly, so little Eve wouldn't hear.

"Since it looks like Chef Craig is almost done with dinner," Sydney said to Everly, "let's go wash our hands and get ready to eat. Then, you can show me where everyone sits at the table. Sound good?"

"But I'm clean." Everly held out her hands to show Sydney, a coy smile on her face. "See?"

"You know what? Mine are all dirty from driving over here," Sydney said, "so, maybe you can show me where the bathroom is, and we can wash our hands together, just to make sure they're extra clean."

"Okay!" She stretched her arms out to Sydney. "Get me down."

"Everly," I said, "use your manners when you're speaking to Sydney."

"Please help me down," Everly corrected.

Sydney lifted her off the counter and set her on the floor, and Everly instantly linked their fingers.

"Come on, Syd. I'm going to show you the bestest bathroom in the whole house, where there's pink everything, even the soap." She laughed again. "Even the seat on the potty. It's so cute."

"Let me guess. This bathroom is in ... your room?"

"Yep!"

As the two of them disappeared upstairs, the break from looking at Sydney—even if it was short-lived—was appreciated.

I went to the fridge and grabbed a beer, twisting off the top as I said, "Things going well with you, Craig?"

He gave the pot a few more stirs and turned toward me. "All is good, my man. Looks like things are moving along nicely with you too. Getting a new nanny in your life?"

I nodded. "Hannah is tapping out. She's got too much on her plate."

Hannah had been such a staple around here, and the two of them knew each other well.

"This one seems to be great with Everly, and I've got to say, she's pretty easy on the eyes."

He'd noticed.

Fuck, it was impossible not to.

"I'm not going to deny that," I admitted.

"She single?"

I guzzled the rest of my beer and walked back to the fridge to grab another. "Why? You interested?" I asked from over my shoulder.

"Hey, man"—he put his hands in the air—"it's not a bad thing to know since there are two single men in this room."

I shut the fridge door, tossed the metal top into the trash, and glanced toward the stairs. "I don't know."

But one thing I did know was that if Sydney went on a date with Craig, she wouldn't be working for me anymore.

Fuck, I thought, shaking my head.

What the hell is wrong with me?

I couldn't control who she dated, nor should I care who she went out with.

But for some reason, at this moment, I did.

"There's a good chance she'll be moving in here at some point soon," I told him, leaning against the counter, "so you'll be seeing a lot more of Sydney, giving you plenty of time to ask her."

"Can't say I hate the thought of her being around here more." He sliced several roasted vegetables and tossed them into the pot. "There's nothing hotter than feeding a woman as sexy as Sydney."

And watching her eat.

Something I'd enjoyed immensely when I took her to dinner.

The way her lips surrounded the fork. How they parted over the rim of her wineglass. Her tongue licking the spoon when we shared dessert.

I needed her out of my head.

I needed to focus on something besides my future employee.

The girl whose pussy had fucking clutched me when she was coming.

I chugged several sips' worth and said, "What are you making for dinner?" I tried to take a deep breath, but all I could smell was coconut even though she wasn't in the room. "I know I approved the menu. I'm just drawing a blank."

He moved back to the stove and grabbed a set of tongs from the drawer. "Eve asked for spaghetti, so I loaded the sauce with vegetables—she won't even taste them—and I added in some ground turkey and sausage for you. I made a homemade bread that I'll serve with truffle oil and a Caesar salad."

"Delicious."

"If Sydney moves in, I assume I'll be meal prepping for her as well?" He used the tongs to take out the pasta, twirling the noodles around the center of the plate.

"Yes."

The thought fucking burned through my brain.

"If you don't mind, I'm going to check with her regarding any dietary restrictions, her likes, and loves."

I nodded as he glanced up.

Craig didn't just prepare our dinners. Every three days, he came over and prepared breakfast and lunch, packaging the meals, labeling and dating them. He also organized the snacks and did all the food shopping.

When Hannah was here, he did the same for her.

And if Sydney was hired, it would be no different.

That was, if I hired her.

If I could wash away these fucking fantasies and remind myself that she wasn't here for me, that Hannah needed a break, that my daughter needed her, and that Sydney would truly be the best thing for her.

"Tonight is a tryout," I told him. "If she gets the job, I'll let you know, and, yes, I'd like you to make sure her favorites are all stocked."

"By the looks of it, she's already nailed the Everly side of the interview."

I said nothing, finishing off the rest of the beer.

"I mean, hell, look at them." He nodded toward the stairs that the two girls were descending, hand in hand, their laughter drifting into the kitchen. "If that's not a perfect sight, shit, I don't know what is."

He wasn't wrong.

I could tell Sydney had a protective way about her, keeping Eve on the inside of the stairwell, far from the banister, how she watched my daughter take each step.

I tried to look away, but my eyes followed them the entire way until they were walking into the kitchen.

"Daddy, we're all clean," Everly said, holding up her hands. "*Seee.*"

"Did you show Sydney your bedroom and bathroom? And the explosion of pink you've got going on in there?"

"Yep. She even sat on the sparkly toilet seat." She giggled. "Not to pee, Daddy, just to see how the sparkles tickle your bum. It made Syd laugh. It was *sooo* funny." She glanced at the island, where Craig was plating all the dishes. "Oh, dinner's done. Come on. You *haaave* to sit next to me." She grabbed Sydney's hand and led her over to the table and pointed at the head. "Daddy sits there. I'm here," she said, holding the chair to the right of mine, "and you're next to me."

"Whatever you're making smells delicious," Sydney called out to Craig.

"Wait until you taste it," he responded.

I ignored the way he was looking at her and returned to the fridge for more beer. When I joined them at the table, I asked Sydney, "Would you like one?" and I held up the bottle.

"No, thank you, not while I'm hanging with your girl."

She'd given the right answer.

Maybe she wasn't plagued with the same thoughts as me.

Maybe this was easier on her.

Maybe she had cleared me from her head when she chose Everly.

Can I do that?

Can I make it happen right now?

"All right, Eve, here's your giant plate of spaghetti, just like you asked for." Craig set the pasta in front of her along with a small salad and piece of bread.

"*Mmm.* Yay!" She already had her fork in her hand and dived it into the noodles, freezing mid-twirl. "Oops, I forgot." She looked at Sydney and added, "I'm 'posed to wait till everyone has food. It's polite."

"You're right; it is the polite thing to do. That's so mature of you, Everly."

Eve smiled, waving her head so the ponytail bounced. "When Daddy takes me to fancy restaurants, there're so many forks, and I don't know which one to use, but I know to wait. Daddy says that's the important part."

Sydney glanced at me, and my dick pounded through the jeans I'd changed into when I ditched my suit. "Your daddy gives you good advice."

Daddy.

That fucking word.

From Sydney's mouth.

Jesus.

I looked away from her and started to guzzle.

"Here you go, Sydney," Craig said, delivering her plate next. "Enjoy."

"I appreciate it. Thank you."

"Craig makes the bestest s'getti ever. Like, *eveeer.*"

"Oh yeah?" Sydney leaned closer to her plate, her eyes closing as she inhaled. "My mouth is watering." When her lids opened, she pointed at Eve's salad. "I'm proud of you for eating vegetables. Which is your favorite one?"

"Cukes! But only if Chef Craig takes off the peel. That part is *ewww.* Daddy made me try it though. He makes me try everything. That's the rule."

Craig placed my dinner in front of me and said, "I find creative ways for Everly to eat her veggies. There's some she hates pretty hard, but we're making headway, aren't we, Eve?"

"Yep." My daughter looked around the table, making sure everyone was served, and instantly dug in. "Those long green things. I *haaate* those."

"Asparagus," Craig told Sydney.

"*Ahhh,*" Sydney said. "Those."

"Can I get you guys anything else?" Craig asked.

As the sounds of eating filled the silence, I said, "I think we're good. Thank you, Craig."

Except we weren't good.

My dick was hard, and this meal was the last thing I wanted to be eating right now.

What I wanted ...

What I craved ...

What I needed ...

Was Sydney's pussy.

TEN

SYDNEY

"Look at how pretty you've made this cookie," I said, checking out Everly's design. The sprinkles she had added to the middle. The tiny butterflies and flowers, made of fondant, that she'd pasted around the rim. "You've done such a good job."

"Thank you." She squirted more frosting on, adding another pile of sprinkles. "Done!" She held it up to view. "It's so perfect."

I pointed at the frosting and asked, "What color is this again?"

She picked a piece of it off the side and put it in her mouth. "Turquoise."

"Nailed it." I gave her a high five. "For only four years old, you're so smart."

"Daddy says I'm his little girl, but I'm really his big girl."

"You most definitely act like a big girl."

The purpose of this lesson was for Everly to help measure the ingredients for the cookies, to work on her hand and eye coordination when making each ball the same size, to watch the clock and grasp the concept of patience while we waited for them to bake. And as they were cooking, we worked on the frosting, using food dye to create turquoise and magenta, pumpkin and mint—colors that were beyond the primary shades.

And the whole time, Ford had been watching.

He kept his distance, sitting in the next room, his open floor plan giving him a direct view of everything we were doing. The lesson wasn't what made me nervous or the fact that I had an audience—I'd anticipated him observing every move, deciding whether I'd be a good fit for his daughter.

It was his stare that made my breath hitch.

My body constantly reminded of his presence.

His hands.

His mouth.

His tongue.

The effect he had on me.

But I couldn't let that show, so I piped out some pumpkin-colored frosting onto one of the cookies and used the gel icing to draw eyes and teeth, a stem across the top. "Can you guess what this is?"

She wiggled in her seat—a sign that she knew the answer. "He-he. A punkin. Like Halloween!"

"Everly, can you say pu*mp*kin instead?" I sounded out the entire word, emphasizing the letters she had missed.

"Punkin. That's what I said. *Puuunkiiin.*"

I couldn't help but laugh.

And I could hear Ford do the same.

"How about this one?" This time, I spread mint-colored frosting across a different cookie and used the gel to draw a long trunk, the leaves at the top making a very specific pattern. I added a small sun in the corner and aimed it toward her. "Can you tell what it is?"

"A tree."

"And what kind of tree?" I broke a turquoise cookie in half and handed her a piece.

"*Mmm.*"

The second the frosting hit her lips, it stained them.

Which meant it was doing the same to mine.

Oh God.

"These cookies are the *bessst.*"

I put my arm around her. "I'm glad you like them." I used my other hand to point toward the tree, repeating my question.

"Like the trees behind our house," she said, her hand going to her eye, rubbing over her lid in a circle.

I knew she was getting tired.

We were minutes from bedtime.

I continued to hold the cookie up and said, "Is it an elm tree?"

She shrugged.

"How about a weeping willow tree?"

She shook her head. "That's a silly name."

"*Hmm.*" I added a small bee, made of fondant, just underneath the sun and said, "A palm tree?"

"Yes! Silly me. I forgot what they were called."

"Great job, Everly." I set the cookie down and collected all the gel icing. "You were so helpful tonight, counting out all the measurements and helping me keep an eye on the timer and decorating these cookies with me. You've done the most fantastic job."

Her blue lips opened wide. "Can I have another cookie?"

"Last one," I said even though she'd only eaten half of one. "And then it's time to brush your teeth and get ready for bed."

Her smile dropped, and she shook her head. "But I'm not

tired. I don't want to go to bed. I want to stay up and hang out with you."

"I know, honey." I set my hand on her shoulder. "The cookies taste so delicious, and we don't want this fun to end, do we? But do you know what will happen if you go to bed?" I handed her the magenta one she had decorated.

"Yummers." She took a bite, her teeth now covered in pink. "What?"

"It means, tomorrow will be here even sooner, and do you know what happens then?"

Ford had discussed Everly's plans over dinner, so I knew exactly what was in store for her.

"No," she said with a full mouth, more sprinkles falling onto the counter with each bite.

"Hannah comes, and you two are going hiking, remember?"

Her face lit up. "Hiking!" Tiny bits of cookie sprayed from her lips. "With Hannah!"

I pushed some of the baby hairs off her forehead and tucked them into the top of her ponytail. "So, there's no reason to dread going to sleep. You're going to have such a blast with Hannah tomorrow."

"Can you come hiking too?"

Ford entered the kitchen, and the moment he reached us, he stole a cookie from the counter.

"I can't tomorrow, Everly." I scooped some of the fallen sprinkles into my hand. "But maybe we can go hiking someday very soon."

"Daddy, you just ate Syd's palm tree."

I laughed. "That's all right. Your dad is more than welcome to have it." I looked at Ford, smiling. "You can have as many as you'd like."

"This cookie," he groaned. "It's phenomenal."

I bunched the end of Everly's ponytail in my hand, the

curls springing right back. "Miss Eve is the star. She did all the baking tonight."

"Daddy, I make the bestest pancakes, but my cookies are 'nomenal."

He laughed. "Yes, baby, they are." He scooped her into his arms, holding her while she finished her pink cookie. "You are the best." He kissed her cheek, not caring that she was covered in frosting and stickiness and glittery sprinkles. "And now, it's time for this princess chef to go to bed."

Today wasn't the first time I'd seen them together, but it was the first time I really studied them. Their smiles so similar, their love for each other so present.

The way he looked at her took my breath away.

But it was the way she looked at him that completely stole my heart.

When her arms wrapped around him, her head leaning against his neck, I saw that she wasn't just half of him. She trusted him more than anyone in this world.

It was just the two of them.

And their bond wasn't just apparent; it was beautiful.

"*Okaaay*, but I'm not happy 'bout it," she told him, taking the last bite of her cookie. She finished chewing, her eyes getting heavier. "Daddy, Syd's fun."

My cheeks blushed as his gaze moved to me.

"She likes you," he said, his voice a little gritty.

I rubbed her back, the warmth of her body coming through her shirt. "I like her. A lot."

She sucked the frosting off her finger. "We eat blueberry muffins for breakfast when we hike, and Chef Craig cuts my strawberries into little hearts. Can we make muffins and hearts sometime?"

"I would like that, Everly."

145

"Can you give Miss Sydney a hug and thank her for the good time you guys had tonight?"

She released his neck and held her arms out to me, letting me take her from her father. The moment she was in my grasp, she clung to me. A hug that wasn't forced. That wasn't weak. That came from a girl who knew how to love.

"Thank you, Syd. I had the bestest time."

"Me too, honey."

She didn't release me. She squeezed even harder and said, "I can't wait to cook something else with you. And take you hiking. And show you all my animals." She gasped and turned toward her dad. "I forgot to show Syd my animals."

"You will next time, baby. You can give her a whole tour, even show her the pink skirt we got for your hippo."

"Wait till you see, Syd. It's so cute."

I leaned back, so I could take in her adorable face. "I can't wait to see it—all of it. But what I'm looking forward to most is spending more time with you."

"We are going to have the bestest time ever."

Ford clasped Everly's chin and said, "All right, my girl, it's time for Sydney to go home and for you to get some sleep."

"Okay, Daddy."

I gave her a smile and whispered, "Bye, Everly. Sweet dreams."

"Bye, Syd."

I handed her back, and as she transitioned to his arms, Ford mouthed, *Give me five minutes.*

As he carried her through the living room, on the way to the stairs, I began to clean up the kitchen. Since Everly had helped with the dishes once we put the cookies in the oven, I only had to gather the frosting bowls, wipe down the counter and floor, and collect the decorations. The leftover cookies went into Tupperware, and I stuck the container on the counter, so they could munch on them for the rest of the week.

With nothing left to do, I found my phone in one of the bags I'd brought, seeing a text from Gabby on the screen.

Gabby: How's it going?

Me: I think good. Everly just went to bed. I'm waiting for Ford to come down and talk to me.

Gabby: He's going to offer you the job. Obviously. I mean, you made cookies with his daughter. It doesn't get cuter than that.

Me: Um, hello? There're a million reasons why he won't offer me the job, but I do think Everly had a good time, and she was so much fun. Gabs, he's the best dad. Sigh.

Me: Oh shit, I hear him coming down the stairs. Got to go. Wish me luck. XO

Gabby: You've got this. Love your ass. See ya at home.

"Sorry," I said, sliding the phone back into my bag as Ford took a seat in one of the barstools across from me. "That was Gabby. She was just checking on me."

"You don't have to apologize. You're allowed to use your phone." He glanced around the kitchen. "You didn't have to clean up, Sydney."

I waved my hand, showing him it was nothing. "If I make the mess, I'm certainly going to clean it. That's part of my job."

"But you weren't here tonight as an employee, which reminds me"—he reached into the pocket of his jeans and pulled out his wallet—"how much do I owe you?"

"For what?"

"The baking supplies, frosting, those little crunchy things you put on the cookies. I want to reimburse you for everything."

I shook my head. "You're not giving me a dime. I had all this stuff—I bake at home." My voice quieted as I added, "You know that." Since he was sitting across from me, I would have put my hand on his, but I refrained. "Please put your money away."

I could tell he was reluctant, but he did what I'd asked, adding, "If you become her nanny, you will have a credit card, and all purchases will go on that card. You won't be paying for anything, understood?"

I smiled. "Yes."

"Good." He took a deep breath. "She loved you, Sydney. I think you know that."

I nodded. "She's a pretty fabulous kid, Ford. She was receptive to my instructions, she followed directions, and she stayed on task, needing very little encouragement. Tonight went great."

I didn't want to sell myself.

I didn't want to list the reasons I wanted this job.

I hoped, after this evening, it was obvious to him.

We were now at the point where he was either comfortable with having me here or not.

"I'm going to be completely honest with you, Sydney."

As he paused, my stomach started to bubble, as I had no idea where he was headed with this, unable to read the expression on his face.

"I knew you were going to be perfect for her—I never questioned that. What worried me was how I was going to feel about having you here."

As he halted, the churning rose to my chest, a tightness forming.

"Seeing you with my daughter"—his gaze dropped, like the intensity was too much—"it was more than I expected."

What's more?

His attraction to me?

His concern?

When he eventually looked up, his eyes glued to mine, his mouth slowly parting. "She needs you." His hand ran across his beard. "Hannah's wonderful—I don't mean she isn't—but what you taught her in the little time you two were together was so impressive. You were patient with her, and you tested her, pushed her. She had no idea she was in the middle of a lesson; she thought she was just having fun, and that was the best part about it."

As his hands folded on top of the counter, his thumbs rubbing together, my heart wanted to calm.

But couldn't.

I sucked in a mouthful of air and said, "But ..."

He didn't answer immediately. He just stared at me, the seconds building between us.

The tension.

The memories—at least in my head—were exploding, one after the other.

"But then there's us."

I had known that was the underlying factor. The reason he wasn't sliding a contract with an NDA across the counter.

"Can you handle the close quarters?" he asked. "The time we're going to be spending together?" His voice lowered while he said, "The idea of living in this house?" He pushed up the sleeves of his shirt, showing muscular forearms and dark hair.

Arms I remembered wrapping around me, the feelings and sensations they had given me.

The security.

But then the thought of Everly popped into my head.

How I'd enjoyed every moment I spent with her.

There was no question that I would love this job.

I could ignore the beating in my heart.

The desire to close the distance between Ford and me.

The gasp in my throat if he ever got near.

I could.

For Everly.

"Yes," I answered, "I can handle it." I inhaled again, holding in the air as I said, "Can you?"

He broke eye contact to look down, his face expressionless.

Is he struggling as badly as I am with this?

Does he want to reach across the counter and take me into his arms?

I waited for an answer.

The silence simmering.

And then, finally, he voiced, "Yes," and gradually glanced up. "I'd like to offer you the job. I realize we haven't discussed a salary or benefits. I assure you, you'll be well compensated."

"It's not something I'm stressing about," I admitted.

There were far too many other things on my mind.

Like his mouth.

"As for Eve," he went on, "she'd like to know the exact date she's going to see you again—a request she made before falling asleep."

He chuckled, and the mood instantly lightened.

I smiled. "I can start whenever."

"Before you do, I just want to make one thing clear." He pushed his sleeves higher again, the movement sending me his cologne. A scent that I tried to ignore as he continued, "I need someone who's in it for the long haul. I understand you're going to school and you'll eventually become a teacher, but that's years away. I want to know I have you until then."

His words hit me. Whether he'd chosen them on purpose or they were merely a coincidence, I felt the power behind each one.

"I'm not going anywhere, Ford." I swallowed. "You have me."

"Then, my assistant will send over the necessary paper-work. I'm sure you're familiar with an NDA."

"I've signed one before, yes."

He exhaled, a sound that was more like a sigh. "Now, as for moving in, I've given that some thought, and I don't want to rush it. Let's take our time, see how things go the next week or so. Are you okay with that?"

A sense of relief passed through me.

One I hadn't expected.

"Yes, of course," I replied.

His hands had been moving but froze. "I want you to get comfortable with Everly, and I want to get used to having you here all the time."

"An important part of the process, I agree." As he nodded, I asked, "When would you like me to start?"

He pulled out his phone, tapping the screen, his eyes going back and forth, like he was reading. "I can draw up the contract and NDA tomorrow. You're welcome to counter my offer. If that doesn't hold us up, then maybe within a few days?"

"That shouldn't be a problem. And, you know, even when I start school, like I already told you, the classes are online, so I can get all my work done once my day here ends." My chest constricted again. "If I do move in, would that be into one of the guest rooms upstairs? We passed a few on our way to Everly's room."

"No." He shook his head, as though I needed the emphasis. "I had an apartment built over the garage. It has its own kitchen and bathroom, small living room and bedroom. You'll have your own entrance, giving you all the privacy you need, where you can come and go as you please. To access the house, you'll just walk through the garage and come in through the back. I just ask one thing ..." He cleared his throat, quickly glancing down. "It's your own apartment, and I would like you to treat it as such. I just want you to be respectful with who you invite over."

"Ford, I would never—"

"You don't have to say any more."

I quieted.

I wasn't surprised he didn't want to talk about it. The topic couldn't have been more awkward.

But even if the apartment was technically mine, I would never disrespect him.

I wouldn't even bring Gabby over.

As though he sensed I needed another break from his eyes, he got up and went to the fridge, returning with two bottles of water, one which he placed in front of me.

"As for the minor details," he said, "like I mentioned before, you'll be given a credit card. I want you to use it when you're out with Everly—if you stop for ice cream, lunch, shopping. I will cover all expenses for the both of you, no exceptions. That also goes for anything you need for projects, lessons, whatever —just charge it." He took a drink of his water. "I'm also going to give you a car to use, so you'll no longer need yours. I'm sure the one you drive is fine, but keeping the both of you safe is my top priority; therefore, I need you driving something I've chosen personally."

My hand went to his arm, a reaction that I immediately regretted but I still didn't pull away. "I've gone through this all before. I understand how it works. If my daughter were in your care, I'd want to choose the car too." My fingers left, grabbing the water bottle and untwisting the cap. "However, if Everly's not with me and I'm going somewhere personally, I'll pay for the gas."

"No, you won't." He laughed. "I won't allow it."

"Ford—"

"Listen to me. Your sole responsibility is my daughter.

Teaching her. Molding her. Giving her everything she needs without turning her into a spoiled brat—that, I won't stand for." He wiped his lips and continued, "Above all else, my daughter is going to learn the meaning of hard work and humility. She needs a foundation that's concrete. That, Sydney, is where you come in. Everything else, like money, let me worry about."

I took a deep breath, squeezing the bottle with both hands. "I promise ... I'll give you and Everly everything I can."

ELEVEN

FORD

"One drink," I said to my brothers, who were sitting across from me at the corner table at the bar. "One," I emphasized, holding up my finger in case their goddamn ears were clogged.

They needed the reminder because on the rare opportunities that they dragged me out after work, like tonight, one almost always turned into ten.

And this evening wasn't going to be a bender.

Not with Sydney at the house, who had agreed to watch Everly after the twelve hours she already spent with my daughter today. She'd only been employed for two weeks. I certainly didn't want to push it at this point.

"Yeah, yeah," Jenner groaned. "We get it. We've only got you for ..."

"One drink," they both repeated.

"Just so you know, when my baby girl, Eve, is eighteen and off to college, you won't be able to use the kid excuse anymore," Dominick said, clinking his glass against mine.

"Maybe not," I replied. "But by that point, the two of you

will have so many little ones running around, you'll be too busy to go out." I felt a vibration in my pocket and pulled out my phone, making sure the message wasn't from Sydney. Once I saw that it wasn't, I put my phone away.

"Which is why you need yourself a woman," Jenner said. "So you won't get lonely when Dom and I have a million fucking kids."

That was enough to make me drink more.

I raised my glass to my lips and chugged. "Was this your plan tonight? To give me the woman talk? Hold some type of single-dude intervention?"

They looked at each other.

And then Dominick said, "No. But since you brought it up, yes."

"Jesus—"

"Don't *Jesus* us, Ford," Jenner barked. "You gave us plenty of shit during our bachelor days, encouraging us when we needed it, giving us a firm spanking when we needed that too. Did you honestly think your situation would be any different?"

I laughed.

Because every word that had come out of that bastard's mouth was fucking hilarious.

"What situation, Jenner?" I adjusted my position to get a better look at him. "I'm not in a relationship. I don't have any prospects. It's me and my daughter—that's it."

"Did our brother wake up this morning with amnesia?" Dominick asked Jenner. "Or is the motherfucker suffering from a concussion from getting hit over the head with a two-by-four?" Dominick's stare left Jenner, and he looked at me. "In case you need the reminder, her name is Sydney. You know, your goddamn nanny."

I laughed again. "That's exactly it. She's my nanny. Nothing more."

Jenner leaned his elbows on the table to get closer to me. "Really? That's all she is—your nanny?"

"Yes, my nanny. Who the fuck do you think is watching my kid right now?" I checked my phone, making sure there was nothing from Sydney. I wasn't sure why I had this nagging anticipation that she was going to text a question or a picture out of the blue, but every few minutes, I found myself reaching inside my pocket. "So, yes, guys, that's all she is. Someone to take care of Eve, not me."

"No reason she can't be there for you as well."

I sighed, shaking my head. "We're not going there again."

Dominick called over the waitress and ordered another round, ignoring my only request.

I wasn't the least bit surprised.

"How are things going with her and Eve anyway?" Jenner asked. "Everyone happy?"

They couldn't be any more obvious.

They were forgetting they'd asked me the same question almost every day since Sydney had started. I could see right through their constant inquiries. Even though they were protective over Everly, I knew this had nothing to do with that.

They wanted more.

And they weren't going to get it.

"Things are no different than when you asked yesterday or the day before or even the day before that." I rolled my goddamn eyes. "But in case you need to hear it again, Everly loves her. She couldn't be in a better place."

"And you, dickhead?" Dominick asked. "Are you happy?"

I pointed at my chest. "I'm the dick here? Because I'm tired of answering the same question over and over?" I shook my head. "I don't think so. The two of you have a motive, and I see right through it."

"I'm genuinely curious how things are going between her

and my niece and what it's like, having her around all the time," Jenner said. "There's no motive here."

"You're a riot." As I held the glass, I turned it around in a circle, the ice banging against the sides. "But since you asked so nicely"—I huffed out some air, the sarcasm dripping from my mouth—"I'll say that things couldn't be better. They're perfect in fact."

And they were.

Everly woke up every morning, asking for Sydney—when she was coming, what they were going to do that day. Sydney would arrive while Everly was eating breakfast, and she would go over their schedule. She provided structure. Goals. In the short time Sydney had been with us, I had seen a difference. Everly's vocabulary was expanding, her knowledge growing.

Hannah was a babysitter.

Sydney was an educator.

"In what way?" Dominick asked.

They weren't going to give up. That much was apparent.

"In every way," I replied. "You guys haven't seen Eve since I hired Sydney. Just wait. You'll notice the change in her. You'll see it. Hear it."

"Don't even tell me we're getting close to her not being my little girl anymore," Dominick said. "I won't be able to handle it."

"Not yet, but we're not far away," I told him. "She's getting old, man. I fucking hate it. I want to keep her this age forever, where she still needs me and isn't fighting me on every goddamn thing, like her curfew, boys—fuck that."

"What about you and Sydney?" Jenner asked.

I checked my phone again, deciding to leave it on the table so I didn't have to keep reaching into my pocket. Once I placed it down, I took a drink and shrugged. "Fine."

"No issues with her being around all the time?" Jenner continued.

That depended on what he considered as issues.

If he counted a constant fucking hard-on. My head filled with fantasies of every place I wanted to fuck her in my house and not being able to take my eyes off her. Then, yes, I had issues.

"None at all," I fibbed. "It's like nothing happened between us. And when you think about it—I mean, really think about it —not much did. Two hookups. That's nothing."

But in my mind, the opposite was true.

Each of the hours we'd spent together had left an impression that echoed constantly. That relentless vibration of memories wouldn't let me forget the taste of her skin, the feel of her body, the wetness that had coated me.

"When is she moving in?" Dominick asked.

I was going there again—deep into the remembering phase.

My dick already hardening.

I shook my head, pulling myself out, and responded, "I haven't asked her." I glanced toward my phone. Still nothing. "I have a business trip coming up that I've mentioned to her, but we haven't even discussed those logistics. I need to figure that out and then talk to her about moving in."

"If she can't cover the nights you're gone, you know one of us will," Dominick said.

"I know."

The waitress delivered the second round, placing a scotch in front of me.

"Drink it," Jenner ordered.

There wasn't much left in my original glass, so I combined the two and handed the empty to the waitress. "I can't go anywhere with you two assholes. You never listen to a fucking thing I say."

Dominick chuckled and gripped my shoulder. "That's why we're good lawyers, brother. We always win."

I was just bringing the glass up to my lips when Jenner said, "You've got a nanny now. Stop stressing about getting back home. You haven't come out with us in weeks."

Before I took another drink, I needed to know if this was all right with Sydney. I didn't want to just assume she would stay longer.

I lifted the phone into my hands and typed out a message.

Me: Do you mind staying a little later?
Sydney: Ford, have fun. Don't worry about us. I'm heating up
the dinner Craig left, and then we're going to make cupcakes.
Since we made bath bombs yesterday, Eve is pretty excited about
testing one out tonight. Take your time. I'll stay as late as you
need me to.
Me: What's a bath bomb?
Me: Or maybe I don't want to know?
Me: And, shit, am I screwing up all your plans tonight? I didn't
even ask if you had something going on.
Sydney: Gabby and I were supposed to have a girls' night. She
spent all day cooking for it. :(
Me: Fuck ...
Sydney: I'm kidding. I had no plans. Stop worrying. All is good.
Sydney: Also, come home hungry. There will be tons of extra
cupcakes.
Me: I appreciate you doing this.

"He's texting with Sydney," Dominick said. "There's no one else, aside from Everly, who can make him smile that hard."

I glanced up from my phone.

Jenner said, "Is that true? Are you texting with Sydney?"

"Yeah, but—"

"Oh hell, he's in it hard."

"Stop it," I told them. "We were talking about fucking cupcakes, and since Hannah started baking at my house, I've developed a sweet tooth. That's what you saw—an excitement for the dessert, nothing else."

"But Hannah isn't the one baking. It's Sydney." Dominick paused. "Am I right?"

I nodded.

"And it's more than just her cupcake you want to eat," Jenner added.

I flipped him off and returned to my phone.

> Me: *Just out of curiosity, what flavor?*
> Sydney: *Your favorite, of course.*

I laughed.

She knew.

She'd learned during her first week when she made a cake with Everly and she watched me pick around the vanilla cake and only eat the chocolate frosting.

Since there was no reason to reply, I set the phone on the table and gazed up at the guys.

Both were staring at me.

"What?" I asked.

"What?" Dominick mocked, laughing. He raised his hand and called over the waitress, saying to her, "Can you bring two rounds of tequila shots, please?"

"No," I said before she left our table. "You can bring two rounds for them, and I'll take a water."

"Don't listen to him," Jenner instructed. "He'll take the two rounds *and* a water." Then, he looked at me the moment she was gone and said, "We're getting shit-faced tonight."

My phone showed it was well after one in the morning when I tiptoed into my house. Sydney had known I was going to be this late; we'd shared a few more text exchanges since discussing the flavor of cupcakes, so I wasn't filled with guilt as I made my way into the kitchen.

The smell instantly hit me, the chocolate in the air making my goddamn stomach grumble.

"*Fuuuck*," I moaned as I searched for where she had put them.

And then I found the adorable display—the cupcakes shaped like a mountain with a glass dome over them.

I lifted the lid, checking out the decoration that had undoubtedly been done by my daughter. Although, I had to admit, she was getting much better. The frosting was mostly swirled, the rainbow sprinkles evenly distributed. She'd even attempted to write a *D* for Daddy across several. I could tell the ones Sydney had assisted with—the squiggly letters much straighter, smoother.

"You're home."

I looked up as Sydney was rising from the couch, a blanket wrapped around her shoulders.

God, she was beautiful.

Her hair was down and a little wild, her clothes clinging to her, outlining a body I hadn't been able to stop thinking about.

Lips pouty, like they needed to be ravished. Eyes heavy, as though I'd just given her three orgasms.

"What are you doing down here?" I asked. "I told you to crash in one of the guest rooms if you got tired."

"I figured I'd drive home once you got back." She tightened the blanket around her, cutting off my view, and waddled into the kitchen as the blanket hung well past her feet. "I didn't want to get too cozy, but I guess I failed because I fell asleep."

I checked the time on my phone again. "You're not driving home tonight. It's too late."

Shit.

I'd fucking fathered her.

Not my intention.

Still, my opinion didn't change.

"I just don't want you on the road at this hour," I clarified. "And I'm sure, by now, my driver is halfway to his house."

She set the blanket on the back of a chair and went to the fridge, grabbing a carton of milk. She poured some in two glasses and handed me one. "You're going to need this. They're rich." She placed a cupcake on a napkin that she set in front of me and grabbed one for herself. "And it's fine, by the way. I probably shouldn't drive this late; you're right."

I could hear the tiredness in her voice and felt like hell because I'd woken her up. "I'm sorry, Sydney. Go upstairs and get some sleep. I've got this."

Whatever this was.

I wasn't sure.

I just knew there were cupcakes in front of me, and at least one was going to get eaten.

"I can't. I'm hungry now." She raised the dessert to her lips and took a bite. "And, damn, they're good."

I couldn't fucking wait.

I took almost half of it into my mouth, the chocolate melting the second it hit my tongue.

"You weren't kidding," I groaned, pointing at the mountain of cupcakes. "That'll be gone by tomorrow."

"That quick?"

I popped the rest in and chewed, reaching for another. "Yep."

She laughed. "You should have seen Everly decorating them. She was covered in glittery sprinkles. They were even in her eyebrows. And then the bath bomb turned her hair blue." Her hand went to my arm as she giggled. "Don't worry; we got it all out, but oh my God, it was a sight."

Her fingers felt like a wave of heat that went straight to my cock.

I did my best to ignore it, asking, "Did you ever tell me what a bath bomb was?"

She traced around the rim of the cupcake and then licked the frosting off her finger.

I couldn't look away.

I could think of nothing but her tongue circling my cock, her lips surrounding the head, her throat taking in my shaft.

Fuck.

"I didn't, I don't think." She took a drink of her milk. "But it's a little bath accessory that dissolves in the water, full of vitamins and skin conditioner and lots of goodies. We made a bunch, all in different colors. I didn't realize the dye that I used was so strong." Her eyes went wide. "Oops."

"That's all I'll hear about over breakfast tomorrow." I pulled the wrapper off my second cupcake. "How much fun she had. How her hair turned blue. How she won't be able to bathe without a bomb ever again."

"Oh boy, have I created a monster?" She took a bite, her tongue swiping across my favorite lip to get the chocolate off.

Jesus.

She'd asked a question.

I was sure of it.

But I couldn't think of anything but her mouth.

"Say that again," I voiced.

Her lips went thin as she smiled. "Did I create a monster?"

"A baking monster, for sure." I glanced down, needing the

break, and shoved more sweetness into my mouth. "Sydney, this is delicious. Fuck, I'm sure I already said that."

She snorted. "I'm jealous of your buzz right now."

I glanced up, struck by that breathtaking face. "I'm that obvious?"

"Maybe not to just anyone, but your voice changes when you drink." She quieted as she said, "I know that tone by now and how it gets grittier with each glass of red wine—or in tonight's case, scotch." She paused, staring at me. "I can smell it." She licked across her lips again, this time for no reason, just out of habit. Or because she knew it drove me fucking mad. "Did you have fun at the bar?"

Not only had she been learning about me, but she had also been paying attention.

I didn't know what to think about that.

"Yeah." I took a deep breath. "It's always a good time with my brothers."

She took the final bite of her cupcake. "You know, when I was with the Turners, I insisted they had a date night at least once a week. It's important, Ford. So, that's what I'm going to propose to you." Her skin flushed, her chest rising as her breathing sped up. "To go out with your brothers, I mean. That's what I'm proposing. I want you to make it a priority. And I'll be here, so you don't have to worry."

I shook my head, taking her in.

That soft voice with an erotic edge.

That mouth.

Those fucking hands that wouldn't stop moving.

"Sydney ... I don't know how they let you go."

"They didn't want to. They tried everything to keep me."

She leaned her elbows onto the counter, bending to accommodate the new position. As she did, her top fell lower, showing the humps of her tits.

What a fucking sight.

I couldn't look away even if I tried.

"But it wasn't about the extra money they were offering," she continued, "or the additional time off or the less responsibilities. I loved my job—that's not what made me leave. I just knew it was time for me to come back and start school and be planted in one place for a while."

And meet me.

My head dropped as the truth settled in.

But I didn't say it out loud.

Instead, I said, "You needed a different life."

"Yes."

"And now, it's much quieter."

She laughed. "Isn't that the truth?" She rubbed her thumbs together, her hands folding, fingers intertwining. "Three kids make for an extremely loud household."

"What are you going to do to fill the silence?"

"That's an interesting question."

"Why?"

She tucked a chunk of dark hair behind her ear. "Because now that I've begun school and I have an amazing job, I've been asking myself the same question." She exhaled. "What am I going to do for me?"

I took a long drink of my milk, wishing it were scotch. "I know one thing you can do ..."

"What's that?"

There were so many ways I could answer that. Replies that were much easier to say because liquor was running through my body.

But words I would regret the second I sobered up.

My mouth opened; I wasn't sure I trusted what was going to come out of it.

And then the perfect response hit me.

"You can move in here."

"A cure to the silence, huh? Fill it with Everly's squeals." She grinned.

I shifted my stance, considering another cupcake. "If you're open to it."

"I am." As though she were inside my head, she placed a cupcake in front of me. "I would actually really like to move in."

She was already here all the time.

Now, she would only be a quick walk across the garage.

Have I lost my fucking mind?

To keep her this close? This accessible? When all I can think about is being inside her?

Tasting her.

Licking her.

I swallowed, staring at the cupcake. "It's good timing because I know we've talked about the business trip I have coming up. If you were living here, I wouldn't have to worry about Everly shuffling from Dom's place to Jenner's. You could be with her the whole time I'm gone—as long as that works for you."

"Of course." She finished the rest of her milk. "It can be a test of sorts, and if things feel right for the both of us, then I'll move the rest of my stuff in when you get back." She glanced toward the garage. "Admittedly, I've never even seen the space. Would it be all right if I went and took a peek?"

I took a bite of the cupcake. "Now?"

"If that's okay with you."

I lifted the cupcake off the counter. "Come on. I'll take you up."

She followed me to the back door and into the garage, where my four vehicles were parked. On the far side was a set of steps, and after climbing them, I turned around to face her at the top.

"The door over there"—I pointed just below—"is where you'll come and go whenever you want to leave. The code is the same as the front door. And like I said before, you'll have full privacy." I opened the door to the apartment and walked in, flipping on the light. "The kitchen is here." I stood in the center. "Obviously, living room is over there." I took my time moving between rooms. "Bedroom and bathroom are in the back."

She stood only a pace away, looking at the walls and furniture. "Did you decorate yourself?"

I laughed. "Hell no." There was only a bite of cupcake left, and I took it down, wishing I had brought my milk. "I used a decorator. The same one who did the main house."

"Ford, it's stunning."

The colors in here were much different than in my place. The apartment was all white and tan, airy and light. The decorator had chosen the scheme intentionally, knowing I preferred a woman watching my daughter over a man.

"I'm glad you like it."

"Love it," she said, our eyes connecting. "Not like." Her stare moved to the ceiling, where beams ran across the entire length. "She thought of everything. Important accents that make this small space feel giant and these little touches that soften it."

"Check out in here." I walked to the bedroom door, turning on the light, and a chandelier over the bed set the whole room aglow.

"Wow."

I turned toward her. "Cozy?"

"And, quite honestly, a little romantic." She headed for the en suite, frozen in the doorway. "You put in a tub? Oh my God, look at the size of it."

I chuckled.

The designer had promised that would be a huge selling point.

I wouldn't know. I fucking hated baths.

But I could envision Sydney inside it.

Naked.

Bubbles all around her, floating over her body, her hair splayed out in the water.

"Is this a steam shower?"

I blinked.

Hard.

"Yes," I replied. "And, listen, feel free to bring whatever you want when you move in. This is your place. Change it, move things around, whatever—just make it yours. I want you to feel comfortable."

She came out of the bathroom and stopped a few feet away.

Close enough that I could smell the coconut.

The scent that haunted me.

That I couldn't get enough of.

That I had licked off her skin.

"It's perfect, Ford."

Her neck tilted back, exposing her whole throat, and she turned in a circle to do a final scan. As she moved, a swish of her shirt whipped across my arm, a cushion so velvety, like her fingers.

A memory immediately filled my head of what her hands had felt like.

The pressure she had used to touch me.

The way it had caused my dick to react.

Fuck.

Something was wrong with me, something that continuously made my brain go there.

But I knew better.

I knew how wrong it was.

This was just the booze talking, bringing me to a place I needed to stay far away from.

"I can definitely see myself living here," she said once she stopped moving.

I backed up, adding distance between us, and leaned against the nearest wall, searching for a reply.

My daughter. The topic I needed to keep my mind solely focused on.

"When I travel," I said, "I'd like you to stay in the main house, so you won't be far from Everly."

"Absolutely. I'll shack up in the guest room. But something tells me Everly is going to try to persuade me to stay in her room." She smiled. "She tried tonight."

"You're right about that. She did the same to Hannah. She also convinced her to have a popcorn fight in my bed. Let's steer away from the latter."

A new thought entered.

Of Sydney's dark hair fanned across my pillow.

Her laughter filling the quietness in my room.

Her body, in low-cut shorts and a tank top, spread across my California king.

My dick was fucking throbbing.

"Don't worry; I don't plan on us spending any time in your room."

I glanced down at my feet, trying to fill my mind with something other than Sydney. But every time I reached a new fork in my brain, the path always led me straight back to her.

What made it worse was when my stare lifted and our eyes fixed.

My hands wanted to reach for her.

My arms wanted to wrap around her.

My lips wanted to press against hers.

But I couldn't.

I couldn't ruin this.

Everly needed her.

And I needed space, or something was going to happen—something I would regret.

"It's late," I whispered.

She nodded. "Let's go to bed."

Why did that feel like an invitation for us to go to bed together?

And why did my body immediately fail me the moment her words resonated?

I forced myself to turn away from her and leave the apartment, heading back down the stairs, across the garage, and into the main part of the house. Once I was in the kitchen, I grabbed a bottle of water from the fridge and chugged down half.

"I'm going to crash on the couch," she said from behind me.

I shut the door to the fridge and faced her. "The guest room would be much more comfortable."

And farther from my bedroom.

Much farther.

She was holding the edge of the island, her hair framing her cheeks, her eyes filled with a seductive glare.

My fucking God.

"No, it's okay. It'll only be a few hours anyway. I'm going to get up extra early, run home, shower, change, and come right back, so I'll be here before you leave for work."

"I'm working from home tomorrow." I screwed on the cap to the water, squeezing the bottle between my hands. "That gives you an extra hour since my first meeting isn't until eight."

Her head tilted to the side as she analyzed me. "I didn't

know that was ever an option." She laughed. "I just mean, I had no idea you worked from home."

That smile, that sound.

They hit my chest.

So fucking hard.

"I do on occasion, but I try not to make a habit of it. As you can imagine, it's hard to get a lot done here."

"I'll keep Everly busy, so you don't have to worry about her bothering you." She took a step back and another, her hands falling at her sides until she grabbed the blanket from the back of the chair. "I'll see you in the morning, Ford."

She went over to the couch and found a spot between two oversize pillows. Her head nuzzled into one, her feet resting across the other, and the blanket covered her to where I could only see her hair.

Go to fucking bed, Ford.

I listened to the voice inside me and went over to where the switches were located, turning off the lights. The only ones I kept on were the pendants in the kitchen. I dimmed those, so if she got up, the glow would be enough that she wouldn't run into anything.

When I reached the hallway to my bedroom, I didn't say good night to her. I didn't even pause. I just instantly closed the door behind me, my back resting against the wood the moment it was shut.

I filled my lungs and released a long, deep exhale.

When I tried to move, to walk down the hallway toward my bed, my feet wouldn't lift. My hands wouldn't release the door.

So, I slid down the flatness until my ass hit the hardwood beneath me.

And that was where I stayed.

TWELVE
SYDNEY

I sat on the side of Everly's bed, watching her stir until those big, beautiful eyes opened wide, a smile coming across her adorable face. "How'd you sleep, Miss Everly?"

"Syd!" She rubbed her eyes and pouted. "I woke up in the night, and you were gone."

"I wanted to talk to your dad when he got home, so I went downstairs and"—I tickled her tummy—"fell asleep on the couch by accident." I switched from tickles to rubs, my palm moving around in a slow circle. "And guess what. Your dad ate three cupcakes. Three! Can you believe it?"

"He's a cupcake monster. Like a cookie monster, but with cupcakes."

"Yes, he is." I pushed her hair back, away from her face, the braid loosening overnight. Without the little wisps covering her cheeks, her freckles popped against her pale skin. "Has anyone ever told you that you have the prettiest freckles in the whole wide world?"

"Daddy has. He loves my freckles. He says a face with no

freckles is like a sky without stars." She grinned, wiggling until she sat up. "He says Mommy has freckles too."

My heart began to pound.

This was the first time Everly had ever mentioned her mother. From Everly's description, it sounded like she'd never seen her mother's freckles in person.

Or maybe she just didn't remember seeing them.

I didn't want to push the subject, but I was so curious that I couldn't help myself.

"Where's Mommy now?"

She kicked off the blanket and looked at her hot-pink toes from the pedicure we'd gotten a few days ago.

"She wasn't ready to be a mommy." Her voice was quiet, solemn.

Where my heart had been beating so rapidly only moments ago, now, it was completely shattered.

I didn't want to judge. I didn't want to assume.

But what I did know was that her mother wasn't here and she had no part in Everly's current life.

And that made me so sad for Everly.

I held her little arm, massaging up to her shoulder, and when I reached her face, I cupped her tiny cheek. "Are you hungry, precious girl? How about we get dressed and have some breakfast?"

She nodded, her curls bouncing.

Before she'd woken up, I'd already picked out an outfit for her to wear, making it easy to change from her pajamas. After a quick brush of her hair and teeth, we walked downstairs, where her father was sitting in the kitchen with a giant cup of coffee in front of him.

"*Daaaddy!*"

The moment she reached the bottom of the staircase, she went running and climbed his leg until she was on his lap.

"Good morning, baby girl." He kissed the top of her head. "Your dad is pretty tired this morning, so that's why Sydney got you dressed."

"Is it from eating all the cupcakes?" She pointed to the counter. "You messy cupcake monster."

"Wow," Ford exhaled. "I guess I created quite the disaster, didn't I?"

I hadn't noticed the crumbs when I came in early this morning, but they were all over the island, where we'd been eating last night, bits of chocolate and sprinkles everywhere.

I grabbed the sponge and cleaned it off, and Ford mouthed, *Thank you*, when my eyes eventually connected with his.

Last night ... *oh God.*

An evening that had triggered more than just a dirty counter.

There had been several moments in this kitchen and in the apartment over the garage when I was positive he was going to kiss me.

But the whole time, I stayed cool. I didn't instigate.

I just acted like myself despite the war happening inside my body.

A war that was causing part of me to silently beg for his lips, the other part knowing it would make things look exactly like his crumb-covered island.

But that hadn't stopped me from wishing.

Dreaming.

Envisioning.

"Can we have cupcakes for breakfast, Daddy?"

"I know you would love that," he said into the top of her head, "and I would too, but no." He took a drink of his coffee. "I'm sure Craig left us something. Hold tight. I'll grab it—"

"I've got it," I told him. "Don't get up." I set the sponge by the sink and went to the fridge to see what Craig had labeled for this morning.

A quick glance through the glass containers told me it was fruit, yogurt, granola, and a muffin.

Deliciously healthy. Nothing I would be craving if I was hungover. And I knew he was. His groan this morning when I'd first arrived and the way he was holding on to the coffeemaker for dear life told me he was feeling like shit.

I glanced over my shoulder. Their bodies were cuddled together. With Ford's so much larger and broader than hers, he made her look even smaller than she was. And while his head was probably pounding, she was talking his ear off, showing him her pink nails and toes, describing the glitter they had used during the pedicure.

That was love.

I took a deep breath and said, "How about I whip up something super yummy?"

Ford slowly glanced at me. "Craig didn't leave anything?"

"He did ... but are you really in the mood for yogurt?"

He shook his head and winced. "No."

I moved over to where they were sitting. The second I reached them, Everly took off my baseball hat, revealing my wet hair underneath, and put it on her head.

"What are you guys craving?" I asked.

"Pancakes!"

I laughed. "Why does that not surprise me?" I winked at her and looked at Ford. "How about you?"

He rubbed the side of his head. "Pancakes work for me."

"And how about something greasy, like bacon? And hash browns?"

"Yes," Ford said, "and yes."

"Then, I've got an idea." I stole my hat back from her and held out my arms to Everly. "You come with me, Miss Eve. We have lots of cooking to do, and your dad will head into his office, so he can get some work done. Once we're finished, we'll bring him a giant breakfast. How does that sound?"

"I canceled my meeting this morning," he said. "I'm going to sit here and nurse this coffee for a little while longer."

"Woof," I joked.

He nodded. "Yep. That."

"Well, that changes nothing," I said. "It only means Everly and I will have an audience while we're cooking all the things."

"I wanna cook the bacon," Eve said.

She climbed into my arms, and I carried her to the fridge.

"You can lay it out on the pan, okay?" I handed her the packet of bacon and took out the eggs. "And while I'm flipping the bacon, you can tell me when it's done. We're shooting for extra crispy."

"What's extra crispy?"

"When the bacon turns brown at the ends and the texture wrinkles up a bit, like your fingers last night because you were in the bath for so long."

"Ohhh." She laughed. "I 'member now."

Once I set the eggs on the counter, I found her step stool in the pantry and placed it on the floor near a large section of countertop and balanced her on top of it. I then found a fry pan and put it in front of her.

"Align the pieces in stripes," I instructed. "Like a zebra."

"A zebra!" She looked at her dad. "Daddy, we need a zebra for my animal family. One with extra stripes. And I wanna dye her tail blue, like my hair was last night."

He circled his fingers over his temples. "A zebra. Check."

I giggled to myself and gathered everything else I needed for the pancakes and potatoes and started measuring and mixing. "Eve, I'm going to need your pancake-flipping exper-tise. Are you up for the task?"

"Oh boy."

I laughed at her response. Words she'd most definitely learned from me. "What's wrong? Not feeling it this morning?"

"The last time I made 'em with you, they were a gooey mess, Syd."

That had been a couple days ago when she reached inside the fishbowl I now kept in her room and fished out the letter *P*. This was an activity we did every morning, incorporating that letter into our day's adventure.

Of course, she'd immediately announced we were making pancakes the second she saw the letter.

As she flipped the first batch, some had ended up on the backsplash.

Some on the floor.

But the survivors had been edible, and that was all that mattered.

"That's not true at all." I moved over to where she was standing. "You did a fabulous job, and we had so much fun, didn't we?"

"Syd ..."

I put my hand on her shoulder and said softly, "Who says pancakes have to be round? They all taste the same, whether they're oblong or octagon."

"Or a scrambly mess."

I grinned. "Or a scrambly mess." I gently shook her, urging her on. "We're going to try again. I'll be right next to you to assist if you need it, but I don't think you will."

"*Okaaay.*"

I combined all the ingredients and added butter to the skillet, waiting for it to melt. In the meantime, Everly finished aligning the bacon, and that was starting to crisp up while the potatoes were browning on the stovetop.

I poured small amounts of batter onto the pan and waited for the bubbles to appear.

"Eve, you're almost up." I handed her the spatula and moved her stool a little closer to the stove, so she wouldn't have to reach. "Remember, you're going to try to get the spatula all the way under the pancake before you flip."

"Bubbles!"

"It's ready. Work your magic, girl."

She bit her tiny lip as she moved the metal tip under the batter. My hand was in place, ready, if she needed me. But she didn't. She wedged the whole blade beneath the pancake and gradually lifted it before she turned her wrist, and it landed with very little smear.

"You did it," I sang. "And look how pretty it is."

"I did it!" she shouted back. "Daddy, I did it!"

"Great job, baby," he said from the other side of the kitchen.

I was sure he was dying over all the noise we were making even though I was trying to be as quiet as I could.

"Can you do another one?" I asked since there were several more that needed flipping.

She started the same way, and as she shimmied the spatula under the pancake, I stole a quick peek at Ford.

His eyes were on us.

More specifically, me.

I could feel the heat from his gaze, and it made a sweat break out over my body.

Good Lord, that man looked sexy, even in his current state. He had on the gray sweatpants that I loved so much, a T-shirt that hugged his back, showing a ripple of muscle, and hair that wasn't tamed or gelled but wild, like I'd just run my fingers through it.

"Syd! Look!"

I glanced away from Ford, my stare returning to Everly as the second pancake landed even better than the first.

"You're doing the best job. Now, can you do the remaining ones too?"

"Yep!"

I kept my eyes on her, but I could still feel Ford's on me.

I wouldn't look at him.

I couldn't.

I was positive he'd see right through me, and then he'd know exactly how I was feeling. How last night had taken every ounce of restraint I had. How this morning, watching the two of them together, feeling the intensity of his eyes, was more than I could handle.

I couldn't shut off the tingles in my body.

I couldn't stop the desire from pulsing.

The need.

The want.

Both owning me with a strength I couldn't fight.

Maybe he had been born with a switch that made him forget, but the time we'd spent together was still so fresh in my head.

And time with him was something I wanted more of.

"Come on, little pancake. Be nice," Everly said as she moved on to the last one, so focused on what she needed to do. "Don't be mean, little pancake."

I held my breath until it hit the pan, and we jumped in celebration.

"You nailed it," I told her. "Look at that perfect flip."

"Daddy, I nailed it!"

I gave her a high five, and then I handed her the spoon, so she could mix the potatoes. "Be careful with those. If any oil splatters and hits your skin, it'll hurt."

"I'm careful."

I stayed in charge of the bacon, the oil in that pan a little too unpredictable for Everly to manage, and as I watched her, I said, "You're doing such a good job."

"That's 'cause I'm a chef."

I put my arm around her now that everything on the stove was settled for the moment. "You are, huh?"

"The bestest."

"Well then, Chef Craig had better watch out. It sounds like you might be the new cook in this house."

She tried tucking her wisps away while she stirred. "Do you think Daddy would get sick of pancakes for breakfast, lunch, and dinner?"

"I think if you threw in some cupcakes, that would make it a fair balance." I glanced toward Ford as he was looking up from his phone. There was no question where his stare landed —I could feel it on every part of my body. "Chocolate cupcakes, that is."

"He'd love that a whole lotskies."

It took everything I had to glance away from him. "Miss Chef, do you think the pancakes are done?"

She shrugged.

"Do you know how to check?"

"Nope."

I led her hand toward the pan and helped her lift the edge of a pancake. "You're looking to see if it's the right color. Too light—you risk the chance of the middle still being raw. Too dark—that means it's burned or on the verge." I lifted another one to compare. "How do these look to you?"

"*Yuuummy.*"

I laughed. "You're right about that. Are they done?"

"Yes!"

And they were, so I plated them and held her hand while she stepped off the stool. "How about you go grab your dad's coffee cup, so we can give him a refill? And then we'll sit down to eat."

"Okay!"

I set the pancakes on the table, placed the potatoes and bacon on a small platter, and added silverware and napkins to the place mats. When Everly returned with Ford's mug, I made him another cup and one for myself, water for the little one, and grabbed syrup and ketchup and butter from the fridge.

Ford was still on his phone—working, I assumed. But as I moved around the kitchen, I still felt his eyes on me. With the help from my hat, I was able to mostly hide mine. That didn't stop the tightness in my chest every time I neared where he was sitting, nor did it stop the flutters that seemed to be constant whenever I was in his presence.

After being here for weeks, I would have thought they would have died down.

But they were getting worse.

Stronger.

Moving even faster through my body.

And this time, when I circled the kitchen, making sure everything was the way I wanted it, my lungs were having a hard time taking in air.

I knew why.

I'd gotten a whiff of his cologne.

There was something about that scent that brought me back to the nights we'd spent together, the memories pouring in.

Oh God.

"Syd, I want blueberries on my pancakes."

Fruit.

Pancakes.

What am I even doing right now?

"Everly," Ford said with a warning, "use your manners."

"Please," she added.

I picked up the strawberry and blueberry containers from the refrigerator and set those on the table before I announced, "We're ready. I hope everyone's hungry."

"I am!" Eve shouted.

"Me too," I agreed, and I helped Everly get situated in her seat, taking the spot directly beside her.

Ford was the last to join, sitting at the head.

"Do you need anything?" I asked him.

He lifted the mug I had refilled and said, "Thank you for this." He paused. "This breakfast looks amazing."

"Yummy for my tummy," Everly sang as she chewed a piece of bacon.

"Even better than Craig's," Ford added.

I froze, my knife deep in the butter, to gaze up at Ford. "I doubt that."

"It's true."

The intensity in which he looked at me was like a fierce grip. One that moved around my throat. One that shackled both hands and feet.

There were too many tingles.

Too many sensations.

"Daddy, we're going hiking today."

Our eyes were still locked as he said, "Oh yeah?"

"Come with us."

My back straightened as the words left Everly's mouth, and I immediately looked down, pulling my knife out and spreading the butter over the pancake. It seemed far too sweet for me this morning, so I focused on the potatoes. I tried lifting them off the plate, but my stomach wasn't ready.

I couldn't eat.

I wasn't even hungry anymore—at least, not for food.

"Come with you," he said, as though he was debating.

I sucked in my breath, moving the bacon to the other side, trying to act busy.

"But, baby, I have to work today."

"Tell Papa you have a bellyache."

He laughed. "Papa's not my boss."

I tried to imagine what a morning of hiking with Ford would feel like. The two of us on the trail, Everly several paces ahead. Sweat running down our faces. Sun hitting our eyes.

How we'd have to move close together when we passed other hikers on the narrow path.

His scent.

His hand on my lower back.

"Runyon Canyon?" he asked.

Since I didn't hear Everly respond, I nodded.

Was he really considering?

Was a morning with Ford now a real possibility?

Could I call in sick?

Fuck.

When I'd taken this job, I'd thought it was going to be so straightforward. I would take care of Everly and go to school.

There was nothing simpler than that.

My feelings for Ford would stay separate. They would dull over time until there was absolutely nothing left to our spark.

Except just the opposite was happening.

Now, all I thought about was him.

And each day, those thoughts became more consuming.

I would arrive at his house, hoping, somehow, his arms would find their way around me.

His lips would press against mine.

His voice would whisper, *I want to be with you.*

But that wasn't going to happen.

He'd made that clear.

Even when he was drunk, his filter and inhibitions gone, he didn't want me.

That was my fault.

He'd given me a choice, and I'd picked Everly.

For the first time, a part of me was regretting that decision.

But it was too late. I couldn't go back; I couldn't pick differently.

I had to live with this.

I had to accept that Ford Dalton would never be mine.

"Sorry, Eve. I have too many calls today. I can't go." He gazed at his daughter. "But you two are going to have so much fun."

"*Daaaddy*." She pouted.

"I'll take you this weekend, baby, when I have all morning and afternoon to dedicate to just you."

THIRTEEN

FORD

As I sat in my home office, catching up on some final last-minute work, I heard Sydney's bare feet coming down the hallway. There was a difference in sound between her and my daughter—the speed being the main one. Since the hallway was long, that gave me several seconds to prepare for her presence.

I needed each one.

And I needed to try to fucking breathe.

That girl had power over me, and she didn't even realize it.

As she came closer, nearing the doorway, I shifted my gaze away from my computer screen, anticipating that face I couldn't get enough of.

Waiting.

She paused the second she stilled, smiling. "Do you need anything? Or can I help with anything?"

Goddamn it.

Several weeks into her employment, and she looked more beautiful every day.

She'd braided her hair, the long tail falling across her left shoulder, which was bare due to the angle of her shirt. She wore almost no makeup, aside from glossy lips that were making my dick hard and darkened eyelashes that were long and blinking as she stared at me.

From her looks alone, there would be another cold shower in my very near future. Since the start of Sydney's employment, my dick had seen much more of my palm than usual.

I pulled my hands off the keyboard, my palms falling onto a pile of folders of the accounts I would be visiting during this weeklong trip.

The one I was leaving for tomorrow morning.

A trip I was almost grateful to be going on because it would give me a break from being around her. Not that I wanted the distance, but resisting Sydney Summers was becoming a job of its own.

"Thank you for offering," I said. "That's sweet of you."

"But ..." She laughed.

"I think I have everything mostly wrapped up for the night." I placed the folders I'd been resting on inside my brief-case and closed the top.

"Good. Now, you can relax." As she adjusted her position, leaning her back against the frame, she crossed her arms at her stomach, showing the narrowness of her waist. "And don't worry; she's dead asleep. I just checked on her."

I'd taken a brief break to tuck in my little girl and kiss her good night. That had given Sydney the heavy lifting of giving her a bath and braiding her hair and reading her a story, so I could finish up my work and be able to get to bed at a decent hour.

"What time is it?" I checked the clock on my computer. "It's ten already. Shit."

Two hours had passed since I'd kissed my daughter's cheek. I hadn't realized I'd been in here that long.

"I know, and I'm beat." She tucked some loose strands behind her ear. "Just an FYI, once Eve went to bed, I unpacked my things into your guest room upstairs. And when you get back, I'll just bring them to the apartment over the garage, assuming you want me to move in."

Where she would be staying every night.

A ten-second walk from my bedroom.

Fuck.

"Yes ... I do," I told her.

My brain couldn't stop creating a fantasy where I captured her from the doorway, carried her to my desk, and spread her across it.

Burying my face between her legs.

Why the hell is this becoming such a tease? Why is it becoming harder to control my thoughts?

Why am I not stronger than this?

Why can't I accept the fact that Sydney is Everly's nanny and she won't ever be anything more?

"Perfect," she said. Her cheeks changed to a deep red. "That'll make things much easier when I can just walk across the garage to go to bed."

I laughed.

I couldn't even hold it in.

Because nothing about her moving onto my property would make things easier on my dick.

In fact, if I were smart, I would end her employment.

I would have my assistant start looking for a new nanny, so I wouldn't feel so guilty about the things I wanted to do to this one.

But Everly was in love with Sydney.

Things were going so well with her.

I couldn't fuck that up, and I certainly couldn't find someone who would be as good with my daughter as her.

Sydney is irreplaceable.

That was what I kept repeating in my head as I stared at her.

"I have to tell you something ..." She bent her knee, placing her bare foot on the molding. "It actually happened a little while ago. Part of me sort of forgot about it, and part of me didn't want to mention it to you. But it feels only right to say something."

I leaned back in my chair, folding my arms, trying to prepare myself for whatever she was about to say. "All right."

"Everly never talks about her mom. I don't bring up the topic. I don't know anything about her. But she did on this rare occasion, and I think it's important that you know."

I exhaled as the heaviness moved into my chest. "What did she say?"

"She said that they have the same freckles, inferring that it was something you told her, not something she observed herself."

"They do ... and you're right."

She shifted again, tightening her grip around her stomach, her breathing speeding up. "She also told me that her mom wasn't ready to be a mommy."

My head dropped, my hands going into my hair, rubbing the sides of my skull. "It's a hard topic to discuss with a four-year-old." When I glanced up at her, her eyes were full of emotion. "I don't like to talk about Rebecca."

"Ford, you don't have to."

But I did because Sydney was responsible for my daughter. Therefore, she had to know at least a little of the circumstances that had surrounded that night.

"Rebecca and I had a one-night stand. We never bothered exchanging numbers; we made no attempt to go out again. Forty weeks later, when Everly was three days old, Rebecca showed up on my doorstep in the middle of the night. She told me she was going to abort her and couldn't follow through. She was then going to put her up for adoption and didn't do that either." I took a breath, the pain in my chest so present. "She handed the baby to me and told me she wanted nothing to do with our child, and that was the last time she ever saw her daughter in person."

"Oh my God." Her hand was flat on her heart, her voice not any louder than a whisper. "I don't ... know what to say."

I was silent for a few seconds. "Everly doesn't know. One day, she will, but not until I'm positive it won't destroy her."

She took a moment to respond, finally saying in a shaky voice, "She'll think it's her fault. That she had done something to cause her mother to abandon her."

As she announced my fear, it was as though she'd turned the knife that was already stabbed in my chest.

"And it's far from her fault," I confessed. "But it'll take time and probably some therapy for Everly to understand that."

Hell, it had been four years, and I still couldn't understand it.

I crossed my hands, feeling the warmth on the inside of my palms, a sickness churning away in my stomach. "Rebecca did what she thought was best for her child, and despite my not agreeing with most of her decisions, she made one that I will be grateful for, for the rest of my life." I paused, swallowing. "She placed that baby in my arms."

"Ford ..." She shook her head from side to side. "You're an incredible father." She wiped the bottoms of her eyes. "I'll never say anything to Everly about this; you don't have to worry."

I looked away, needing a break, staring at my briefcase instead.

It had been a long time since I'd talked about Rebecca. I

wouldn't let my brothers or my parents discuss her. I kept my feelings inside, where, at times, they ate away at me. Where they often became too much.

Maybe it was a relief that Sydney now knew more of the story.

That I'd gotten some of this off my chest … even if that meant I was letting Sydney in a little deeper.

A level that no woman had ever reached before since this was a conversation I'd never had with any of them.

"Fuck, I could use a drink."

"I brought a bottle of wine with me. We can open it, if you'd like." As I looked at her, her eyes went wide. "Oh God, please don't think I was going to drink on the job. I just thought, maybe, long after Eve went to bed one night—"

"Sydney, it's fine. Don't worry. There are plenty of nights I have a drink once she goes to bed."

"Should I go open it?"

I turned off the screen to my computer and stood from the chair. "Yes."

She walked down the hallway, and I flipped off the light to my office, following her into the kitchen. Each step she took, my eyes were glued to her ass.

Fuck me, it was perfect.

A sight I could never grow tired of, and in those jeans, it looked as good as I remembered when my hands had been holding it. Squeezing it. Fantasizing about when my cock was going to slide into it.

But, shit, that had been before she became my nanny.

Now, she was making her way into the pantry, grabbing the bottle she must have brought with her. She didn't need to ask where the wine opener was—she knew.

With all the baking she had done here, she'd probably used gadgets in this kitchen that I didn't even know I owned.

She took the cork out and grabbed two glasses from the bar, filling them halfway.

"I recognize that bottle," I said, reaching for it after I wrapped my fingers around the stem of the glass.

A blush came across her cheeks, not as red as they had been in my office, but certainly darker than normal. "That's because it's the wine we had on our date. At Origin's."

"*Ahhh*. Yes ..."

She took a breath. "I really enjoyed it, so I bought a case."

Our date.

That had ended in her apartment.

With her ass bare on the fucking table, her legs straddling me, my dick thrusting in and out of her.

I didn't give a toast.

I didn't clink our glasses.

I just brought the wine up to my lips and took a long, hard sip.

"Are you in the mood for something sweet?" She reached for the display that now permanently held desserts in the center of my island, lifting the glass top. "Everly and I made mini pies today."

"Have I ever said no to anything you made?"

She laughed. "I suppose not."

She lifted one out of the case and put the top back on. "This one is for me. Yours are in here"—she walked to the fridge and took out a separate container that she placed in front of me—"because they have to be kept cold."

Several pies were sitting inside the Tupperware.

I brought one up to my nose, smelling it. "Chocolate?"

"Chocolate cream."

"You didn't?"

Her eyes went wide as she nodded. "But I did. Do you want a fork?"

"Nah." I took the pie out of the small foil dish and bit into it. "Damn it, Sydney."

She did the same, holding it with her hands, chewing as she answered, "Right? It's beyond."

"You keep this up, and I'm going to have to start running ten miles every morning." I moaned as I took in another mouthful. "But, shit, it's so worth it."

She laughed. "Thank God your daughter likes to hike; it's the only thing that's saving me from all these treats. That, and the gym in my apartment building, which I'm really going to miss."

"You're welcome to use the gym here, and I'm not saying that because you need to use it—that's hardly the case at all. I'm saying it because I can see how much you work out, and it sounds like you enjoy it."

I didn't know if I should have said any of that.

But every word was the truth.

Sydney had a hell of a body, and it was obvious she did far more than just run trails. The muscles I could see—that I had touched—told me she spent plenty of time lifting weights as well.

She moved to the other side of the counter to get a napkin and handed me one. "You really don't mind if I use your gym?"

"That's why I had it built—to use it. Help yourself, anytime you want." I finished the first pie, deciding it wasn't enough. I needed another.

"I took a quick peek inside when I first started here." She wiped the corners of her mouth. "You've built quite the masterpiece. You have everything—free weights, cables, every machine I can think of."

"Did you go all the way back?"

She shook her head.

"There's a sauna and whirlpool in there too. Both are pretty easy to operate, but if you need any help while I'm gone, just give me a ring. I can talk you through it."

"Thank you." She looked at the top of her wine, twirling the glass in her fingers. "What's this trip going to look like for you?"

I sighed and drained half my wine. "Busy. Stressful. I think I'm hitting four states and meeting with twenty-something clients. It's taken my assistant almost three weeks to coordinate all the logistics."

"Will you be going anywhere fun?"

I laughed. "I'll only be seeing the inside of my hotel rooms and the homes and offices where I'll be meeting my clients and probably some restaurants. Unfortunately, aside from that, there won't be time for any fun."

"I hate that for you." She brought the glass close to her lips but didn't drink from it. "Travel, somehow, someway, should always be enjoyed."

I broke the second pie in half, the cream oozing out the middle. "There will be good food involved, I'm sure. Scotch that'll rock my world. And some of the clients I'm meeting I've known my entire career, so hanging with them is never a bad time."

She wiped her crumbs away now that she'd finished and returned to her wine. "Speaking of food, I wanted to talk to you about that."

I finished swallowing and said, "Food. All right, hit me."

"Craig doesn't need to stop by while you're gone. Since Everly likes cooking so much, I'd like it to be something she and I can do together."

My brows rose. "What about the grocery shopping?"

She nodded. "I'll handle that too." As if she could sense my hesitation, she added, "I know what Eve likes to eat, and it would be a great lesson to take her to the store and talk about

193

ingredients, teaching her about healthy options and foods from different cultures."

Something I didn't have time for in my life.

But I could picture the two of them, holding hands as they walked the aisles.

Everly's loud, contagious laugh.

Sydney's patience.

"So, you want me to give Craig the week off, huh?"

"If that's all right." She reached across the open space, her fingers gently touching my arm. "You're going to have to trust me. I know you already do on some level. I mean, you're leaving your daughter in my care, but food is something I can easily tackle. I promise."

"Our conversation in my office should prove how much I trust you. I don't tell anyone about Rebecca, only my brothers, parents—that's it. But I wanted you to know, maybe even needed you to know."

Her expression warmed, her hand tightening on my skin.

"As for the food, I didn't want to burden you with the weight of having to do all the cooking and shopping. But if it's something you want, then I'll cancel Craig."

She pulled her fingers back. "Thank you."

My arm tingled where she had touched me.

Fuck, I wished she hadn't let go.

In fact, I wished she would lift the bottom of my shirt over my head and undo the button of my jeans and let me lift her onto the island.

Jesus Christ.

I need to fucking stop.

As our stares locked, silence passed between us, my brain spiraling even further out of control.

As though she could read my face, hear my thoughts, she said, "I should probably go to bed. It's getting late."

"Yeah ... I should do the same."

Except I wanted her under my covers.

I wanted to kiss her in the morning before I left for the plane, tucking the blanket around her since I was no longer in there to keep her warm.

She made no effort to leave and go upstairs.

And I knew I couldn't move—my feet would only lead me to her—so I reached for the bottle. "I hope you don't mind if I have more?"

"No, please. Have all you want."

The second I set the bottle on the island, my glass now refilled, I realized I needed to put more distance between us, and I backed up a few paces until the range hit my ass.

It was only two feet.

Maybe three.

Still, I wasn't sure it was enough.

Since, once again, my stare found hers.

And within the quietness that passed, so many words were spoken.

Needs.

Emotions.

If Sydney didn't know what I was feeling, she had to be fucking blind.

But ...

Goddamn it, she's your fucking nanny, Ford.

Everly needs her.

You push every woman away because you fear they're going to abandon your daughter. Sydney's different. She's here for Everly—that's who she chose.

She's the first non-family member who Everly's fallen for.

You can't afford to fuck that up.

Her eyes broke away from me, and she whispered, "I'm going to go to bed ... unless you want me to stay."

The war inside my head halted.

She was giving me an invitation.

One that involved spending more time with her, one that would allow me to continue gazing at her.

Did I want her to stay?

Of course I fucking did.

I also wanted to fight these urges.

I wanted to tell her to go to bed and lock the door.

I wanted ...

Her.

"Don't go," I ordered. "Don't move a fucking inch."

As I took a deep breath, I smelled her in the air.

A coconut breeze that made every part of my body hard.

"Sydney ..."

Her arms moved behind her, and she gripped the edge of the island, her hair framing her cheeks, her eyes filled with a seductive glare.

The new pose, with her shoulders pushed back, caused my eyes to dip to her tits.

My fucking God.

That smile.

The way her breathing was speeding up, her chest rising and falling so fast.

The way her eyes were luring me in.

Urging me.

Goading me.

I needed to calm myself down.

I needed to push these thoughts out of my head.

I couldn't have this woman.

I couldn't kiss her.

I couldn't put my hands on her.

I couldn't ...

I took in a mouthful of air, my hand clenching at my sides.

This wasn't a need that was pulsing through me.

Nor was it a want.

Those were far too simple words.

This was deeper.

This was at my core.

This was ingrained.

This was too strong to fight anymore.

My feet were suddenly moving, my heart ignoring the warning signs that were blaring inside my gut, the feeling that I was about to make the biggest mistake.

Because no matter what, I couldn't stop.

I couldn't even pause midway.

I could only close the space between us.

The second she was within reach, I pulled her against me, my lips instantly crashing against hers.

The heat from her body scorched my skin, enveloping me, my body responding like I was already inside her.

"I can't wait another second. I need you, Sydney."

She moaned, "Ford," as my hands went down her sides, rubbing those dips that I'd been staring at for so long, the way her back arched into that incredible heart-shaped ass.

Perfection.

That was what she was.

And I needed more.

While my tongue slid between her lips, I searched for that spot that would make her scream.

That was what I wanted.

That sound.

Those screams.

"I need to feel how fucking tight you are."

I tugged at the button of her jeans and moved her zipper down, burying my fingers under her panties.

"That pussy," I moaned.

Fuck.

The bareness.

The fucking tightness that I knew was waiting for me.

The wetness that would be coating my fingers.

I dived in.

Straight to my goddamn knuckle and heard, "Oh my God. Yes!"

This girl was ready for me.

Dripping.

Gripping my arm to move me deeper inside her.

I twisted my wrist when I got all the way in and halted. I wanted to relish this moment. One that I'd been thinking about for fucking weeks. And as I stilled, she pulsed.

Clenched.

"Tight ..." I hissed against her mouth. "That doesn't come close to describing what I'm feeling right now."

Her hands moved to my shoulders, piercing me, urging me to go in farther.

And that was what I wanted, but first, I needed something else.

I needed the taste that I'd been after.

I quickly pulled out and rubbed my finger across my mouth. "Holy fucking hell." I licked her off me, savoring her. "Sydney ... that flavor. My God." I swallowed. "I want more."

But before I allowed myself more, I needed to see what the wetness would look like on her lips. "Your turn." I swiped my finger across her mouth and commanded, "Taste yourself. Tell me how good it is."

This was new to her.

I could tell by her timidness.

By the way her eyes followed my hand.

But she licked.

She swallowed.

And she quivered, saying, "Oh fuck," before she slammed her mouth onto mine.

I returned to that spot I loved, two fingers sliding right in, my thumb against her clit, and I plunged in and out of her pussy.

"Ford!"

I knew it felt good.

I could hear it in her breaths.

I could taste it on her tongue.

I moved faster, deeper, her hips meeting me, my thumb grinding against the highest point.

Circling.

Flicking.

Over and fucking over.

She squeezed my arm, tensing, bucking. "I'm going to come." She said it against my mouth as though she was warning me.

But I knew.

Her clit was hardening. Her wetness was thickening.

Her sounds were getting even louder.

"Let me hear it," I demanded. "Let me fucking feel it."

That was all it took before she was shuddering against me, her pussy contracting, her moans filling my ears.

"That's it, Sydney." I gripped the back of her head, bunching her hair into my fist. "That's fucking it." I mashed our lips together. "Yes!"

The second she stilled, our eyes connected.

Our mouths separated.

Our breathing mixed.

My dick was so goddamn hard that all I could think about was lifting her onto the counter, spreading her legs, plunging inside her pussy, and fucking coming.

"My God," she whispered. "No one has ever made me feel like you." Her hands went to my face. "Ford, I ..."

The feeling came out of nowhere.

Straight through my chest.

Like a thick fog that moved around me, preventing me from feeling anything other than guilt.

A regret so strong that everything began to sting.

"Don't." My spit felt like acid, going down my throat. I couldn't stand myself. I couldn't believe what the hell I had done. What I'd jeopardized. What I'd probably fucking ruined. "I'm sorry."

Her hands left my face.

"Sydney, I'm so fucking sorry I did this to us."

She shook her head. "No, I'm the one who's sorry."

"I fucked this all up. I told myself I shouldn't do this, and I ..." I couldn't get my thoughts straight. I couldn't even think. Breathe. "I couldn't stop myself. I wasn't thinking of Everly. I don't know what the fuck is wrong with me, but this can't happen again. It just ... can't." I slid my fingers out of her pussy, but I didn't move. I stayed close, caging her against the counter. "Forgive me, Sydney. Please forgive me."

"It's not your fault."

There was emotion in her eyes.

I couldn't take it—the pain, the hurt.

The sadness.

I cupped her cheek.

It was just for the briefest of seconds, but she needed to feel me.

To know I cared.

To know how goddamn sorry I was.

"Forgive me," I whispered.

"I ..." She held in her breath, staring, blinking. Waiting. "I should go to bed."

I couldn't say anything.

I didn't trust myself.

I moved my arms back, giving her enough room to get by.

"Good night, Ford," she said in the softest voice as she disappeared from the kitchen.

I watched her entire journey through the living room, her bare feet climbing the stairs until she was too far up to see.

I heard the click of the guest room door as it closed.

And I stayed right where I was, holding the wine to my mouth, doing everything I could to calm down my body.

To not climb those stairs.

To not knock on her door.

To not make another mistake that I wouldn't ever be able to come back from.

If I didn't get off, if I didn't have an orgasm right this fucking second, that mistake was undoubtedly going to happen.

I downed the wine and headed for my room, locking the door behind me. Once I got to my bathroom, I turned on the water in the shower and stripped off my clothes, not even waiting for the temperature to warm before I stepped in.

I squirted some soap onto my hand and wrapped my fingers around my cock.

Tightly.

Like it was her fucking pussy.

And as the steam started to fill the large walk-in space, my fist rode down my shaft toward my balls and glided back toward my crown.

Pumping.

As I envisioned that tight, wet cunt.

The one I had tasted tonight.

The one that had come on my fingers.

The softness of the soap, the bubbles, just like Sydney's

wetness. The hold of my fist, like the narrowness as I plunged inside her.

My eyes closed, and I saw that gorgeous body.

That beautiful face.

Those long, lean, toned legs spread wide.

Just for me.

My balls were tingling, the sensation moving through them and into my shaft.

But I didn't slow.

I sped up, and I increased my grip, moving as if I were thrusting into her pussy.

Until it was too much.

Until I couldn't hold off a second longer.

"Fuck," I breathed as I shot my first load. "Sydney ..." I moaned, my wrist twisting up and down my dick, closing in as I neared my tip.

The second stream came bursting out.

But I kept up the same speed, like her pussy was fucking milking me.

The third shot came, and I was drained.

My eyes finally opened, showing me the hard, ugly truth ...

I was in the shower.

The water scalding.

The reality of tonight, the pain I had caused, all unfolding in front of me.

I lifted my hand to my nose, hoping her smell would still be there.

But all I smelled was soap.

The scent of Sydney long gone.

FOURTEEN

SYDNEY

Ford: Everything going all right?

As I sat with Everly in the kitchen, rereading Ford's text, positioned almost in the exact spot as the scene of last night's crime, everything inside me began to warm.

A scene Ford now regretted.

A scene I couldn't stop replaying in my head.

Oh God.

He'd briefly spoken to me this morning before he headed to the airport, reminding me of a few things he didn't want me to forget while he was gone. The conversation was pointless; they were things we'd already discussed days prior. I was positive he was just testing my reaction, to see if I was angry or upset.

To see where we stood.

To see if I was going to walk out the door and never come back.

Things I would never do because I cared about him and his daughter, those feelings growing stronger each day.

What happened between us last night wasn't all his fault.

I knew I was inviting myself to stay in the kitchen rather than go right to bed.

And I had known how risky that was, how out of character that was, what kind of challenges that would create for us.

But unlike Ford, I didn't regret a thing.

And maybe—just maybe—he would realize that he shouldn't either.

Me: We're in the middle of making paper flowers and clay vases. Your island is covered in construction paper and glittery pens and stardust. She's having a blast.

Ford: I'm going to have the smartest kid in LA because of you.

Me: Her intelligence has nothing to do with me, but thank you for saying that. Seriously, she's doing fab. After going through one of my cookbooks, she's decided she wants this fancy egg salad with pickled onions on a brioche bun for lunch. We're very busy over here.

Ford: I don't have the peanut-butter-and-jelly kid.

Me: I can't tell you how happy that makes me. How's the trip going?

Ford: That was a really cute picture you sent earlier of Eve on the hiking trail. Seeing her face makes the time go by faster. Keep sending more.

Me: You sound ... stressed?

Ford: One state down already, three to go. I'm headed to a meeting now and then jumping back on the plane. It's all good.

Me: Take photos. This way, Everly and I can follow your trip and have a little geography lesson while living vicariously through you.

Ford: Everly would love that. Did you document your travels?

Me: Hold. I'll show you.

I could feel the tension in his messages. I didn't know the

cause, but I wanted to try to lighten his mood even if it was with my silly, nonsensical photos. So, I opened my Photos app and flipped through the more recent shots, sending him three different ones from the Turners' private plane. The monitor behind our seats had tracked our location, so I'd always known our whereabouts and which country I was photographing from the sky.

Me: First was in Switzerland. That's the Alps beneath us. The second, Germany—somewhere around Munich. The third, Finland. I remember how badly I wanted us to land, so I could go explore.
Me: And so I could have all the wine.

Just as I was setting my phone down, Ford texted a picture. The shot could have been any downtown city, but there was no question in my mind that it was Manhattan. Of course, I could have looked at the itinerary his assistant had sent, each of his stops broken down along with the hotels he was staying in. But I didn't need to. New York had a certain feel, and he'd captured that in the photo—a slight blur of buildings, followed by more prominent tall ones. A yellow cab in the next lane. Smoke billowing from the subway grate ahead.

I could close my eyes and smell that city.

Me: Oh God, I miss New York so much.
Ford: You'd better not miss her too much ... you can't leave me.

A heat whipped across my face, my skin warming to the point of sweat.

I knew he was talking about my employment, but I couldn't stop my mind from thinking he meant it in a personal way.

That he was replaying what had happened in the kitchen.

That he wanted it to happen again.

> *Me: I'm not going anywhere; don't worry.*
> *Me: Have a good meeting.*

> *Ford: Good morning. How'd she do last night?*
> *Me: Aside from kicking me in the face, she did fantastic.*
> *Ford: Wait ... I thought you weren't going to be persuaded to sleep in Eve's bed? Isn't that what you said last night on the phone before she went to sleep?*
> *Me: Your kid has expert negotiating skills. I'm talking EXPERT LEVEL.*
> *Ford: Her father is a lawyer, so this shouldn't surprise you.*
> *Me: The only thing that made up for the fat lip she almost gave me was that I woke up to her asleep on my chest. So freaking cute. I took a pic ... if you want to see it.*
> *Ford: Of course I do.*
> *Me: Okay ... incoming.*
> *Ford: Look at you two. Her little leg wrapped around you. Sydney, you guys are adorable.*
> *Me: She's a great cuddler. She definitely kept me warm.*
> *Me: P.S. Today's agenda: getting your little lady to like asparagus.*
> *Ford: Good luck with that. Craig has tried and tried.*
> *Me: Ford, don't doubt my skills. I'm not saying Craig isn't good. He's superb, but he's not me. Look what she ate for breakfast ...*

I sent a second photo, this one of Everly eating an omelet that had mushrooms, onions, and roasted tomatoes inside.

> *Ford: Are those mushrooms?*

*Me: She loves them now. She wants them on her homemade
pizza that we're making for dinner.
Ford: All right, you win that round. Damn ...
Me: :)
Me: How are your meetings going?
Ford: I'm in Vegas this morning. Check out this view.*

A picture came through after his message, showing the skyline of the Strip. The sun was peeking out from the top of the mountains in the distance, the glass of the hotels glistening from the early morning rays.

*Me: Absolutely gorgeous. Everly is going to love this one.
Ford: Kiss her for me.
Me: Always.*

---

*Me: Don't panic, but Everly has a fever. I promise she's fine. I
have everything under control. I'm watching her like a hawk. I
just wanted you to know.*

Since we'd spoken this afternoon, I knew he was at dinner with a client, so I'd debated about sending that message. I also knew the moment he got out of the restaurant and checked his phone, he'd see my text and call right away.

I just hated to alarm him, but telling him was the only thing that felt right.

Less than a minute after I hit Send, my phone was ringing, Ford's name on the screen.

I held my cell to my face and said, "Ford—"

"Is she all right?"

"One sec," I whispered.

Not wanting my voice to wake her, I carefully climbed off her bed and tiptoed into the hallway, closing the door most of the way so the sound wouldn't travel.

"She's okay. I was just lying with her in bed, and she fell asleep. Her temp was at 102.2. Since I knew you were with a client, I called your mom, just to be on the safe side, and she agreed that I should give her some Motrin. I gave her some about forty-five minutes ago."

"I'll come home." There was movement in the background. "I'll call the pilot and get the plane on the tarmac in less than an hour."

"Ford, no. You don't have to do that. You know kids get sick all the time. This could be nothing. Let's see how she feels in a couple hours or maybe even the morning." When he didn't respond, I added, "I promise I have this handled. I'm not going to let anything happen to her."

"I've never been away from her when she's sick." His voice was so quiet. Grittier than normal.

I couldn't just hear the struggle; I could sense it.

"Her stomach seems to be fine," I said, giving him more reassurance. "She's not coughing or sneezing, and she doesn't have a runny nose. She was rubbing her ear a bit and complaining that her head hurt, and that's what triggered me to take her temp." I paused, waiting for a reaction, but all I heard was his breathing. "I made some soup that I found in the pantry, and she ate a little in bed. We were cuddling, and she fell asleep."

"Fuck." A one-worded response that dripped with so much concern. "She gets ear infections. She has since she was a baby. They don't happen as often as they used to, but she averages a few a year."

I paced the hallway, and with each pass, I looked into Eve's bedroom to make sure she hadn't stirred. "Don't worry; she's not leaving my sight. If I sense things are getting even the tiniest bit worse, I'll call the doctor."

"Sydney ..." He exhaled. "This isn't easy for me."

I knew that.

And I had known the moment he read my text, he was going to react this way.

If I were a parent, I was positive I'd do the same.

But the amount of vulnerability in his voice was making my heart ache. I couldn't imagine what it would feel like to have half my soul in a different state and know she was sick.

I couldn't fix this.

But I could try to make him feel a little better.

"I'm going to call you on FaceTime, so you can see her."

I hit the button to FaceTime him, and as soon as the video connected, the scenery behind his head told me he was outside, that he'd left the restaurant to talk to me. Even with little backlight, as I stared at him, something was still so apparent.

And each time he'd FaceTimed with Everly since he'd left LA, I'd seen the same look on him.

He appeared beat, agitated.

Completely drained.

But this was the first time Everly wasn't in the room.

The first time we'd been alone and I could bring it up.

"Ford, you look so tired."

"I am."

Something was bothering him that went beyond his concern for Everly.

"Are you all right?"

He ran his hand through his hair, glancing away from the phone. "It's been a long ... day."

"Are you sure that's it?"

I'd seen his long days. The moment he walked through the

door and set his eyes on Everly, the stress would evaporate. But none of those days had ever looked like this.

This was different.

This was deeper.

He didn't respond to my question, so I got more specific and asked, "Is it your clients? The traveling? Something else?"

He continued to stay silent.

"Ford, tell me how I can help."

He finally looked at the screen again, his gaze covering my entire face while he said absolutely nothing. "Sydney ..." He shook his head, like the words were on the verge of coming out but he just wasn't ready to voice them.

Was this about us?

What had happened that night?

Was it eating at him? Causing more guilt? Triggering something else?

I watched him take several deep breaths, the angst in his expression building until I heard, "I just need to see her."

I was wrong.

This was all about Everly.

Before the disappointment came crashing into me, I held my finger to my lips. "Okay, but *shh*. I don't want to wake her."

As I walked into her bedroom, I flipped the camera around, so he could view her. She was in the same position as when I'd left—sleeping on her side, the blanket pulled up to her neck, her little wisps covering her cheek. The cutest sounds still coming through her parted lips.

I kept the phone pointed at her for several seconds, giving him plenty of time to see her, and then I turned it back toward me, and I returned to the hallway.

"See? She's all cozy and comfortable. There's nothing to worry about." I could tell he wasn't convinced. "I will call you the second something changes even if that means I have to stay up all night."

"I don't want you to stay up all night, Sydney."

"But I will."

He sighed. "I know."

He was still outside and made no attempt to get off the phone and return to his client. I didn't want to leave him feeling like this. If I were there, I'd pour him a drink. But I was here, and all I had were words.

"Do you want to talk about it? Or do you want to go back inside and drink your face off, pretending to listen to your client blab when you're really not hearing a word they say?"

He chuckled.

It was short, but that noise was better than any he'd made so far tonight.

"I want to hear about your day."

"My day?" I smiled. My God, he was beautiful. "Let's see ..." I moved several paces away from the door, making sure my voice wouldn't carry. "We made muffins with fresh blueberries that we'd picked up from the store today—where she loves going, by the way." I paused, looking to see if there was a change in his eyes but there wasn't. "We made three dozen, so we brought some over to your next-door neighbor, who's really lovely. She was planting flowers outside her gate when we went on our walk, and Eve asked her if she would like some. Your daughter's quite the social butterfly."

He smiled.

And the movement made me remember just how his lips had felt when he kissed me.

The strength of them.

The way they had tasted just like wine.

"In exchange for the muffins, your neighbor gave us some lemons from her tree, so we came home and made fresh lemonade. It was around that time that her ear started bothering her. I popped some soup into the microwave, and now, she's in bed. Surrounded by all her animals." I smiled, hoping it would lighten things a little. "Yesterday was a bit more interesting."

"Yeah?"

I took a quick peek inside her room and hurried back to the wall I'd been leaning against before. "She's all good; don't worry." I cleared my throat, getting lost in the way he was licking his lips. "Should I tell you about yesterday, or are you sick of hearing me talk?"

"No, far from that." Now, he was rubbing his fingers over his mouth, drying it. "Tell me everything."

"Hold on a sec. I'll show you. I snapped a pic of her." I exited out of FaceTime and pulled up my Photos app, searching for the one I'd taken at the nail salon, and sent it to him. When I returned to FaceTime, I said, "Check your messages."

I waited, anticipating his face to disappear from the screen.

But he didn't go anywhere, nor did he look at my text.

In fact, he didn't move at all; he just stayed staring at me.

"Anyway, I took Eve to get her nails done. The photo I sent is of her in the massage chair. There's a girl giving her a manicure, another girl doing her toes. She had my sunglasses on. It was cuteness overload." I paused. "Should I keep going?"

"Yes."

He was acting stranger by the second, but I wasn't going to try to figure this out.

I was just going to do what he asked.

"We learned all about the different spots that her daddy has visited during this trip. We even printed the pictures you've sent so far and glued them to a map." I winced, chewing the corner of my nail. "Don't kill me, but she might be asking for a Vegas vacation when you get back."

"Is that right?" His gaze was so intense that I swore he was looking right through me.

I didn't know if it was his stare or the way he was so focused on me, but my body was pulsing. My limbs becoming weak. Tingles exploding everywhere.

I slid down the wall until my butt hit the hardwood floor, and I sucked in a breath before I said, "She also wants to go to Colorado, after seeing that picture you sent of Denver."

"I'm sure I can make that happen."

A piece of hair was stuck to my lip, and as I moved it away and tucked it behind my ear, his eyes narrowed.

"She would love that," I said softly.

"Would you?"

"Would I?" I repeated, unprepared for his question. "What do you mean?"

"If we go, I would like you to come with us."

"Oh."

I swallowed, trying to envision what that would look like.

When I'd worked for the Turners, all we had done was travel.

Things were so much different with Ford.

Because we'd slept together.

Because only a few days ago, he had fingered me in his kitchen.

Because I wanted so badly to be with him.

The thought of going to Vegas and Colorado, being with him every hour of every day, was an overwhelming feeling.

But this was what I'd agreed to.

There was no way I could refuse.

I hid the anxiety from my face.

The worry.

The hope.

And I said, "Yes, I'll go."

He glanced away from the camera, giving me his profile and the thickness of his beard. "I'll plan it when I get home."

"You're so good to her."

His stare returned, making it almost hard for me to breathe. "Don't let anything happen to her."

"You know I won't." I found my lip, chewing the top. "I hope my rambling made you forget—you know, about the stressful parts of today."

Even though I wish I could do more, that I could take away whatever is bothering you.

Because I would do anything for you.

"No, Sydney ... you certainly didn't make me forget." He quieted. "Talking to you ... I can't stop remembering."

My chest tightened.

I rested the phone on my bent knee when the screen started to shake.

"But you gave me exactly what I needed for right now." He was moving, the background changing, and I could tell he was inside the restaurant. "I'll call when this dinner's over."

FIFTEEN

FORD

"We'll take a round of tequila," Dominick said as the waitress approached our table. "Actually, make that two rounds."

"Starting tonight with a punch," Jenner said to him. "I like it."

"My cousins don't fuck around when it comes to drinking—that's what I like," Camden said.

Hannah's twin was in town for the week, and it was good as hell to see him.

Brett pounded fists with Camden and then clasped Dominick's shoulder. "Your brother's got a reason to celebrate. We just closed the highest-grossing deal in Dalton family history."

"Fuck yes!" I clapped.

The table erupted in applause.

While sitting next to Dominick, I punched his arm, clamping my fingers around the same place I'd hit. "Proud of you, brother." I then reached around Dominick to shake Brett's hand. "You too, Brett." As he released my grip, I continued, "I love how you guys are fucking killing it."

Dominick had texted Jenner and me earlier, telling us about the deal and that it involved Brett's fiancée, James, so I added, "James is taking over Hollywood. There isn't anyone more deserving. It's impressive to watch this all go down and the work you guys have done behind the scenes."

"My girl's kicking ass," Brett said. "Now, it's up to you, Ford, to shelter that money from the tax gods, so it doesn't all go to Uncle Sam."

I laughed.

James had become one of my largest clients. As her earnings increased, so did the workload.

"You know I'm on it," I told him.

"For what she's paying you, you'd better be." He clinked his glass against mine.

"Listen," I said to him, "if you two start having some kids, it'll make things a lot easier on me. I can set up—"

"You're preaching to the choir, my man." Brett took a drink of his scotch. "I've told her this countless times. I'm ready. I'm just waiting on her."

James was young. At the peak of her career.

I understood why she wanted to wait.

"Maybe, during your next meeting, you can talk to her about pulling the goalie," Brett said. "Tell her it's for tax purposes."

I chuckled. "Now, that's a topic I'm staying far away from."

"I know a topic I'm going to harp on tonight," Declan said.

I groaned and nursed my drink. "If it's Hannah, I don't want to hear it."

"Neither do I," Camden growled.

"Hannah? Who the hell wants to talk about Hannah? That girl is a fucking mess." He leaned far away from Camden in case Hannah's brother decided to give him a right hook. "Who I want to talk about is Sydney, your goddamn nanny."

"I second this," Jenner said, raising his glass.

"Fuck yeah, I third this," Dominick said.

"Sorry, buddy," Brett said, clinking his tumbler against all the others'. "I'm with them."

"Same," Camden said.

"Jesus." I ran my hand through my hair, keeping my fingers locked on my head to dull the throbbing in my skull. A throb that had started the moment Sydney and I had hooked up in my kitchen and had gotten progressively worse. "You guys need to lay off."

"You mean to tell me you're not banging the nanny yet?" Declan asked.

"No"—I swallowed—"I'm not."

And I was angry as hell about it.

Angry the entire time I had been traveling—her texts, when we FaceTimed, nothing but a fucking tease.

Angry when I'd returned home and she wasn't running into my arms.

Angry when I'd watched her cuddle Everly as she recovered from an ear infection because I wasn't on the other side of Sydney, my face on her chest, like my daughter's was.

But all of that was my fault.

I'd pushed her away.

I'd stopped us from doing more.

I'd told her nothing could ever happen again.

"But you should be banging her," Dominick said.

I'd been home for two weeks.

And it had been two weeks of fucking torture.

"Except you know I can't," I replied to Dominick. "Do you have any idea how hard it is to find someone you can trust to take care of your kid?"

"Can't be that hard," Declan said. "You had Hannah watch her, and I wouldn't trust her babysitting my fucking fish."

"Watch it," Camden warned.

"This guy," I said, pointing at Declan, shaking my head.

"You need to convince me why you and Sydney would be a bad idea because I'm still not buying any of your excuses," Jenner voiced, leaning onto the table to get closer to me. "She works for you—I don't see that as an issue. She's Everly's nanny —I don't see why she would have to stop being her nanny, so there's no problem there. What else you got, brother?"

I drained my scotch, hoping like hell the waitress would hurry up with our shots. Once the burn finally subsided, I replied, "The issue is, if things didn't work out between us, then I'd have no nanny, and Everly would lose another woman in her life. That's what I tell you guys every time we discuss this. It hasn't changed. It's still a problem."

"Ford, relationships don't always last. We're human. Not a single thing in life is guaranteed. I could wake up tomorrow, and Kendall might not want anything to do with me. Jenner could return home tonight and find Jo had moved all her shit out. James could come to her fucking senses and leave Brett's ass—"

"Don't even put that into the universe," Brett said.

Dominick chuckled. "What I'm saying is, women will come and go from Everly's life regardless of if you try and stop it."

"Sydney isn't the only constant in Eve's life," Jenner voiced. "There's Hannah and Mom. Jo and Kendall too."

I understood their points.

There had been times over the last few weeks when I almost told Sydney how I felt about her. That I was positive I couldn't let another second pass without her knowing that I wanted her.

That I couldn't stop thinking about her.

That I'd been doing everything in my power not to wrap my arms around her.

But, goddamn it, I just couldn't say those words.

Maybe it was weakness.

Maybe I just couldn't cave when it came to my daughter's needs, protecting her to the point that I would sacrifice my happiness.

Maybe, in some way, I was protecting myself.

"Trust me, there are millions of other nannies out there," Brett said. "In fact, if you need me to, I can steal one of Angelina Jolie's." He pulled out his phone. "You know that woman's got a busload of kids and a house full of help. I've got her number. Give me ten minutes. I'll have one of her nannies drive here for an interview."

I shook my head. "You're fucking wild ..."

"Nah, I'm just tired of you being the single dad when there's a girl in your house right now who's fucking dying to be with you."

"How do you know that?" I challenged Brett.

"We all do," Jenner said.

I looked at Dominick, and he was nodding.

"How?" I asked. "How could you possibly know *that*?"

"I stopped by your place while you were on your work trip," Dominick said. "I had a few things I wanted to give to Eve, and while I was there, I happened to mention your name to Sydney." He smiled. "That girl's face lit up like a fucking Christmas tree."

"She has it bad for him, doesn't she?" Declan said.

"You have no idea," Dominick replied, like I wasn't sitting at the fucking table with them, hearing every word of this.

"Dude, I saw the same thing last week," Jenner said, his eyes now on me. "When she stopped by the office with Everly and I came in to talk to you. The way she was looking at you"—

he sighed—"man, there's no question in my mind. That girl has feelings, and they're strong."

She had feelings.

I could sense that the night in my kitchen.

The way she had tried to take care of me over FaceTime.

But what the hell am I supposed to do?

Put myself first and Everly second?

"There's more," Brett said.

"More?" I wrapped my hand around my empty glass, squeezing it in my palm. "How could there be more?"

Brett rested his arms on the table, folding his hands together. "When you gave her the ultimatum, she knew better than to choose you."

"What do you mean?" I asked.

"With your track record, she'd lose you to Everly. I'm sure she figured that out. Did she go in through the back door? Maybe. If I were in her shoes, that's what I would have done. But does it matter? Hell no. Because while she's been falling for your daughter, you've been falling for her." He moved in closer. "Look me in the face and deny it."

I shook my head, exhaling.

"You can't, can you?" Brett tested.

I stayed silent.

Brett crossed his arms against his chest. "We all knew this was going to happen. It just took you a little while to come to terms with it." He took a drink. "All I can say is, thank fuck you finally did. Your boys here"—he pointed around the table—"have been worried it might be time to stage an intervention."

I flipped them all off. "Really? You fuckers."

"You've been a damn fool about this entire situation," Jenner said.

"We've been trying to call you out on it, and for some fucking reason, you haven't been listening, so we were on the verge of doing something outrageous." I went to respond, and Dominick cut me off with, "Fortunately, we won't have to. It appears like you're actually hearing us—and before you say anything, don't act like you wouldn't do the same for one of us."

"Listen, I'm not saying things are going to change between Sydney and me." I glanced around the table, at each of their faces. "But I hear you. I'm listening. And I don't necessarily disagree with the things you said."

"You've been looking for reasons not to date her, and they're all bullshit," Declan said. "It's time to stop."

"Not you too." I put my hands in the air, surrendering. "All right, all right. I get it. Enough."

"Do you?" Jenner challenged. "Because I sense you're about to waste more time, and I'm not having it."

Dominick pounded my shoulder. "Take it from someone who wasted plenty of time—it's not worth it, my man."

"Same," Jenner agreed.

Brett pointed at his chest. "Guilty of it too."

"Don't look at me, fellas," Declan boasted. "I'm single and proud of it."

"That makes two of us," Camden said.

My cousin was the ultimate bachelor who bragged about his one-night stands.

But Declan was different.

Not that he wasn't a player; he certainly was.

But I had a feeling about him, so I nodded toward him and said, "You know that bastard is going to get married before any of us."

"I'll take that bet," Dominick said. He pulled out his wallet and slapped a hundred on the table.

"I'm in," Jenner replied, matching his wager.

Brett and I added our money.

"It's on," I said.

"Fuck all of you," Declan said to us. "That pile of cash is going to be mine—I promise you that."

Before anyone could say anything else, the waitress appeared at our table, her tray filled with two rounds of tequila shots.

"Now that Ford has his goddamn head on straight," Declan said, holding his shot glass in the air, "let's get fucking drunk."

"Thanks for staying out late tonight, Stan," I said to my driver as he pulled up to the front gate of my property.

"Ford, you know it's always my pleasure."

The second the wrought iron gate swung open, a set of headlights immediately shone through the windshield of the SUV, blinding me in the backseat.

"Looks like someone else is here," he said.

I held my hand above my eyes, like a visor, trying to see who was parked in my driveway, who had breached the security and managed to get through my gate without me knowing.

"It's Sydney," Stan added, as though he could read my thoughts. "A rideshare is dropping her off."

After a bit of squinting, I saw exactly what he had described.

Sydney was shutting the backseat door, her purse wedged under her arm, tugging at the bottom of her dress to lengthen it.

A dress that was so fucking tight that I could see every curve of her body.

Every dip.

Every inch that my hands had once grazed.

Goddamn it.

"I'll get out right here," I told Stan, not needing him to pull all the way up to my front door. I climbed out of the back and continued, "Thanks again, buddy. See you Monday."

The moment my feet were on the ground, Sydney started heading for me. Stan's headlights, as he turned the SUV around, illuminating her.

Her beauty.

More of her body.

And I was in fucking heaven.

"Ford," she gasped, "who's with Everly? I didn't realize you were out. Oh my God, I hope ..." Her voice drifted to nothing as fear filled her face.

Today was Sydney's day off. I hadn't seen her since yesterday, and fuck me, I'd missed her. There had been so many times this morning and afternoon that Everly asked if we could go knock on Sydney's apartment door, my daughter wanting to hang out with her.

But I wouldn't let her even though I wanted to do the same.

"She's with my parents."

Sydney's hand went to her chest, as though she could finally breathe. "I just had a heart attack."

I smiled.

"Don't laugh at me, Ford. I did." She fanned her face with her purse. "All I could picture was that little muffin all alone in your house and—I can't."

"It's all good. Don't worry."

She glanced toward the ground.

Since she was no longer looking at me, I took my time, taking her in. The dress was one I hadn't seen her wear before, fitting her the same as the night we had met at the bar. The top hugged her tits, revealing a sexy amount of cleavage, the sides showing those achingly beautiful curves. The bottom landed far above her knees, her gorgeous, long, lean legs ending in a pair of sky-high heels.

I wasn't just hard.

I was fucking throbbing.

"Except I think I just lost years of my life." She patted her chest, like she was pushing air back into her lungs. "Anyway, I'm sorry I'm coming home so late. Gabby and I were at a bar, and"—she shrugged—"I don't know ... having too much fun, I guess."

At a bar.

Where every motherfucker in there had been staring at her body in that sexy dress.

My fucking body.

Jesus, Ford, what the hell is wrong with you?

I shoved my hands in my pockets so I wouldn't reach for her and said, "Are you really apologizing for going out and coming home late? This is your home. You can come and go at whatever time you want. You never have to explain yourself."

"I'm just not used to that. When I worked for the Turners, I never went out."

"You deserve it. Go out. Have fun with your best friend."

Her hands went to her hips. "Looks like you went out too. With your brothers or ..."

"My brothers and a few friends."

She closed her eyes for just a second. "I can smell the tequila."

"Those boys and their fucking shots," I groaned. "They're relentless when it comes to celebrating."

She shifted her stance. "Oh yeah?"

The movement made her wobble.

I was worried that she was going to fall, so I grabbed her, holding her steady. Once she gained her balance, my arms stayed around her, locking her in place.

She didn't leave my grip.

She remained close.

Far too fucking close.

In fact, she even leaned into me.

And then she slowly gazed up at me. "Thank you ... for not letting me fall." A beat passed, her lips drawing an even bigger smile. "I have a favor-ish to ask."

The light from the front door showed me her eyes and how they were focused on my lips.

"Anything, Sydney."

"Good. Then, will you hopefully not kill me if another car shows up here tonight?"

Another car?

That meant someone was coming over.

At this hour, that could only mean one thing ...

A fucking dude.

My stomach dropped.

I'd lost her.

I'd lost her before I even had her.

And it was my fucking fault—I'd waited too long; I'd pushed her away.

I'd sent her right into the arms of someone else.

My body stung at the thought.

At the goddamn realization.

I hated myself for it.

My hands dropped to my sides, and I added space between us. "Your house, remember? You can do anything you want."

She smiled. "Thank God because I'm starving, and I'm going to order some food to be delivered." She laughed. "My fridge is so empty."

That's what this is about?

Food?

Relief flooded my chest, and I practically fucking growled, "You don't have to order anything. You can raid my fridge."

Her face tilted up as she studied me, positioned perfectly

for me to kiss her. "Does that mean you're going to cook for me?" Her hand pressed against my chest. I wasn't sure if she was holding herself up or if she needed the feel of me against her fingertips. "Or are you just giving me access to your food?"

My fucking God, she was hot.

"Sydney ... it means I'm going to feed you."

"*Mmm*," she moaned, biting that lip I loved. "Hurry, I'm about to eat my arm."

That sound.

That mouth.

Fuck me.

"Come on."

My hand went to her lower back, and the moment we got into the kitchen, she stopped at the island, reaching under the glass lid to grab a cupcake.

"I forgot I made these."

I waved my fingers at her. "Hand one over."

"Chocolate for you." She set one on my palm. "Pumpkin spice for me." She pulled off the bottom wrapper and took a large bite, her upper lip covered in frosting. "God, I can bake."

Sydney was the epitome of humble.

Timid even when it came to her sexuality.

With alcohol flowing through her veins, there was a confidence inside her that I didn't normally see. A flirtatious side that she usually kept reserved.

I wanted more.

"Yes, you're incredible at it." I took a bite, the chocolate melting on my tongue. "In ways I can't even describe."

She held hers out to me. "Try this."

"Nah. Pumpkin isn't my thing."

"Try it, Ford." She licked her finger, where a gob of frosting had fallen. "It has a brown butter and maple cream cheese frosting that's"—her head fell back, exposing a neck that I wanted to kiss—"all kinds of *mmm*."

Whether I liked pumpkin or not, it didn't matter. She could demand anything from me at this point.

My hands just needed to touch her.

My lips just had to be on her.

I fucking needed this girl.

And I couldn't wait. I couldn't hold off. I couldn't stop what was already in motion.

Nor did I want to.

With her head still tilted back, she was unaware that I'd closed the distance between us until my mouth surrounded the same finger she had just sucked.

"Ah!" she gasped the second I dipped to her knuckle, licking the remainder of the sweetness she had left behind. "Ford ..."

My tongue swirled around her skin, and once it was clean, I pulled her finger out and went in for the cupcake, taking a bite. "Delicious." I chewed, swallowed. "But not as delicious as you."

She smiled, glancing away. "What are you doing to me?"

"What I should have done a long time ago."

My hands gripped her sides, and I was overtaken by the coconut—a scent that now drove me fucking mad.

"But, Ford, you're going to regret this again." Her eyes were on me, her voice a whisper.

Her back was against the island. She was unable to move. That was exactly where I wanted her—caged in by me.

"The only thing I'll regret is not telling you how much I want you."

She sucked in a huge breath. "Don't." She paused. "Don't do this to me again. My emotions can't take it. Not if you come and go like last time."

I surrounded her face, pointing her eyes up at me. "Have your feelings changed?"

"No." Her lips stayed parted, exhaling, inhaling. "They've gotten stronger. That's why I can't handle it, Ford. I can't handle hearing those words and seeing that expression on your face, knowing I'm the one who caused it. It's ... too much."

"Do you know that I've wanted you from the very beginning? That I've fought these feelings because I thought that was the right thing for my family?"

"You were trying to protect Everly—I get that—but, my God, that hasn't made it any easier on me."

"I know." My stare hardened. "Sydney, I'm not good at this. I push women away, so they can't hurt Everly like Rebecca did. It's all I know. All I've ever done. When you came along, I wasn't ready. Even though my feelings were different after spending time with you, I expected to push you away like all the others. But you've been here, every day. Caring for her. Loving her. And every day, I want you to be doing the same for me."

"Ford ..." She glanced down, as though my stare was too much. "The last time we were in this kitchen together, I understood. It made sense. But have you considered what I want?" The pain deepened in her eyes. "How badly your decisions affect me?"

"No, and that's where I fucked up." I held her tighter, kissing above each of her eyes. "I only thought about myself. I've been the selfish one here, where you've been there for me this whole time. You've given me everything I needed."

"Because I have feelings for you. Because there isn't anything I wouldn't do for you."

I pressed my nose against hers, breathing her in. "You need to believe me when I say this, Sydney: there isn't anything I wouldn't do for you."

"But still ... you hurt me." She squeezed the back of my hands. "How do I know you're not going to do it again? How do I know this time is different? How do I know you're not going to change your mind tomorrow morning?"

I made sure her eyes didn't move from mine, and I said, "Do you want to be with me?"

She filled her lungs. "Yes."

"Then, you're going to have to trust me."

"Ford—"

"Do you remember when Eve was sick and I wanted to come home from Vegas? But you wouldn't let me. You wanted me to trust you. And I did. I put all my faith in you." I rubbed my thumb across her lips. "That's what you're going to have to do now, Sydney. Trust me. Believe me when I say, I'm not going to hurt you again."

She was silent.

Staring at me.

I swore I could see her brain processing these revelations.

But I had no idea what she was thinking.

What she was going to decide.

If this time ... she would choose me.

And then, suddenly, "Why now? Why, after all these weeks since we've been in this kitchen together, do you want things to change between us? Why is now ... different?"

This wasn't a multiple choice. There was no easy answer.

My feelings couldn't fit into a box that needed to be checked off.

I lifted her onto the counter, and the moment she was settled, my hands went to her thighs, and our eyes locked. "You're looking to hear about the moment when it all hit me. This defining second when I snapped my fingers and thought, *Sydney is the woman I want to be with.*"

I rubbed my hands over her legs, searching for the right words.

"That didn't happen. Because, honestly, I've always known you were right for me. I felt that in the bar the night I met you, when I couldn't stay the hell away from you. I knew it again the next morning when I saw you with Everly. And again when we went to dinner and I couldn't take my eyes off you. Each day that followed, especially when you became Everly's nanny, those feelings built."

I glanced down at the disappointment that hit my chest. "Did I fuck up? Yes. Did it take me too long to confess this to you? Yes." I fixed my eyes to hers again. "Will I make more mistakes in the future? I can promise you, yes."

I reached for her cheek, holding it, caressing it. "But when I was out at the bar tonight and the guys were giving me a boatload of shit for not being with you, they were putting the fear of God into me that I'd waited too long, and I knew they were right. You were going to find someone else, and that would be my fault. I pushed you away, and I'd deserve that. But"—I held her so steady, getting lost in those icy-blue eyes—"I'm not going to let that happen. You are going to be mine."

I leaned across the space and kissed her forehead. "I made you choose, and you picked right. I never should have given you that ultimatum. I'm sorry. I'm so fucking sorry, Sydney. But you don't have to choose now. You can have both of us ... if that's what you want."

There was so much emotion in her eyes. Not the kind that dripped, but the kind that stirred, that swirled. And she stayed silent while she gazed at me.

"Ford ..." Her head dropped, her chest rising and falling so fast.

My breathing matched as I waited.

Every tick, every fucking beat excruciating.

When she finally glanced up again, there was a new kind of emotion in her stare.

One I was positive I recognized.

Her arms wrapped around my shoulders, her hands diving into my hair. "I would pick her over and over again. Everly means everything to me." She took a breath. "But I want you both, and the truth is, I always have."

I couldn't wait.

My lips slammed against hers, and I held our faces together.

My tongue couldn't wait either, slowly sliding into her mouth, tasting her.

That flavor.

That heat.

It wasn't enough.

I needed more.

I reached behind her back, lowering the zipper until it hit the counter and I couldn't go any farther. The space was enough to slip off the tiny straps from her arms. I tugged the material down her torso and thighs until it was well past her knees and on the floor. Her bra came off next, followed by her panties.

Her shoes fell.

She was finally naked.

The way I'd been dreaming about.

I glanced down her body, sighing as I took in this gorgeous sight. "Do you know how long I've wanted to do this?" I didn't rush as I gazed back up. "How long I've waited?"

"Ford ..." Her voice was as soft as her skin.

But I didn't wait for a complete answer.

I just bent my knees and dived my face in between her legs, licking across her clit, my nose pressed against the top of her so

I could breathe her in. "Fuck ... that scent, that taste. It's so fucking good."

"Ford!" She shivered, and I caught her. "Oh my God!"

I wanted to savor her.

But I didn't have the patience to take my time tonight.

I needed her wetness covering my face.

Her screams filling my ears.

I flicked my tongue back and forth across her clit, two of my fingers sliding into her pussy. "So fucking tight," I growled. I pulled back and slipped in, repeating that pattern.

Over and over.

Her hand was in my hair, yanking the strands, holding on like she was about to fall.

"Yes!" She arched her hips forward. "*Yesss!*"

I focused on the top, licking that sensitive spot, sucking it into my mouth while my hand picked up speed. She was tightening, closing in around me.

That was what I wanted.

For the orgasm to pound through her.

"I want to feel it, Sydney." I pointed my tongue, using just the tip to swipe, giving her the pressure she needed. "I want to taste your fucking cum."

Her legs were caving in toward my face, her knees bent, toes clinging to the edge of the counter.

I held her thighs apart.

I rubbed my beard against the inside of them, letting that bit of pain help her get there.

The second she really felt it, when she connected the roughness to pleasure, she jerked her hips forward and shouted, "Oh! Yes!"

She was seconds away.

I knew by the way her wetness was thickening, by the sound of her breaths.

By the way she was narrowing around me.

"Come," I demanded. "Fucking come on my face."

That was all it took.

"Ford!" she screamed. "Fuck!"

While she shuddered against my lips, her motion showed me the wave of pleasure as it moved through her stomach and up her chest. Her sounds told me how intense it was.

My hard-on banged against my goddamn jeans as I gazed up from between her legs, watching.

Listening.

Fucking relishing it.

She gripped my hair, her legs falling. "*Ahhh!*"

This time, I didn't push her thighs apart.

I let the momentum take her wherever she wanted to go.

And I didn't stop licking.

I didn't stop sucking.

I didn't stop fingering her.

Not until she completely stilled.

That was when my face left her pussy, and I unbuttoned the top of my shirt, giving me just enough room to pull it over my head.

"Get over here," she demanded the second it dropped to the ground.

Her mouth found mine.

And right before our lips touched, I ordered, "Taste yourself." While I mashed our mouths together, I unhooked my belt and loosened my pants and boxer briefs. "Tell me how fucking good it is, how good you are."

"Ford," she moaned.

I stepped out of the clothes that were around my feet and kicked off my shoes and socks, finally dragging my mouth away. "One second. I have a condom somewhere in my wallet."

"Ford, no."

I paused, looking at her.

"If we're together, then you don't need one," she said. "I'm on the pill. We're both safe ... right?"

I nodded. "But, Sydney—"

"Do you trust me? You know I'm not Rebecca."

She could tell I had hesitation.

She assumed where that hesitation had come from.

"Yes," I replied. "Of course I do."

"Then, get over here."

"This demanding side of you," I growled as our lips aligned, "I like it."

But right now, it was going to end.

Because I was the one in control here.

And I let her know that the moment my crown circled her pussy, spreading her wetness over me before I plunged straight in.

"Oh ... my ... God." Her head tilted back.

I kissed up her neck—a spot I had been dreaming about—starting again at the very bottom, slowly working my way up her throat.

As I plunged in and out, I breathed, "You're so fucking wet."

Without a condom, I could really feel it.

She was dripping.

Clenching.

"Fuck, Sydney."

I repositioned her, moving her ass to the lip of the counter, and I held those perfect fucking cheeks while I thrust in. With her knees bent, I had full access.

I could pound.

I could twist.

I could reach the deepest part of her.

And I was—a section of her body that was the tightest.

That made her moan the loudest.

I stayed in, grinding my hips, circling within her.

She was holding our bodies together, her arms around my shoulders, her mouth on mine. I could taste her groans; I could feel them vibrating against my tongue.

"Ford ..." She swallowed and gasped in more air. "I'm so close."

I reached down and rubbed my thumb over her clit.

It was already drenched from my tongue, and now, it was hard as her body began to build.

"*Ohhh.*" Her nails stabbed me, her hips moving with me. "Yes!"

As she tightened, her pussy started to suck my cock, like it was trying to pull the cum out of me.

"Fuck," I hissed, doing everything I could to hold off my orgasm.

To give her more speed.

More power.

The second I heard her scream, I felt the orgasm rush through her, changing the way her wetness coated my shaft.

"Ford!" She arched her back, moving with me. "Ah!"

"Yes," I barked. "Give me that fucking orgasm."

Her quivers turned to tremors, rocking across her navel.

The moment her throbbing began to weaken, when her movements died and her noises quieted, I pulled my thumb off her clit, and I lifted her into the air.

I carried her to the nearest wall.

My pumps were slow at first, allowing her to get used to me again.

"Oh God." She tried to catch her breath. "That was—"

"I'm not done," I roared.

The moment I felt like she was ready, the gentleness was gone.

So was the slowness.

I reared my hips back and stroked into that fucking heat.

That sopping closeness that was holding me in.

I used my strength.

I used the feelings I had for this girl, the ones that had been building each day, and I gave her everything I had.

Her legs squeezed around me; her arms braced on my shoulders.

Her nails dug into my skin.

But the only thing I felt was her pussy.

The way it responded when I buried myself, the way it clenched when I pulled back.

"Fuck, Sydney." I kissed her. I gave her my tongue. "You feel so fucking good."

I was close.

So, I held her even harder against the wall, and I reached down between us, finding that spot again.

The one that was hardening under my thumb.

That one that was so fucking wet.

And I rubbed it back and forth as I sank into her.

"Sydney ..."

She kissed me back; she took in my air.

My pleasure.

And she gave me everything I needed.

"I'm going to come," I howled against her mouth.

I knew she wasn't far behind, but I also knew how to speed her up, how to get her to that place even faster. So, I rubbed her clit even quicker. I gave her all the energy and power I had left, circling, hammering into her cunt, and when I felt myself start to fall, I ordered, "Come."

Her pussy squeezed me, and I lost it, the two of us coming together.

"Ford!"

The burst moved through my balls and into my shaft.

"Fuck!" I bit her lip, sucking it into my mouth, emptying myself inside her. "Sydney!"

She was screaming, giving me the sound I wanted, clamping down around me.

With each dip, I gave her more of me.

Filling her.

Until there was nothing left but silence.

But even then, I didn't move.

I waited until her hands settled on my face, until her lips pressed to mine.

Until our breaths tamed.

"That was ..."

"Just the beginning," I told her.

I could taste her smile, and I opened my eyes from our kiss to see it.

Her grin widened as she said, "You mean, there's more?"

"I'm going to carry you to the shower, and then, yes, Sydney, there will be a lot more."

SIXTEEN

SYDNEY

"Gabs ... we had sex." As I held the phone to my ear, sitting on one of the lounge chairs on Ford's patio, I tucked my legs against my braless chest and stared out into the Hollywood Hills, waiting for my best friend to respond. "Hello?" I inquired when several seconds of silence passed. "Are you even there?"

"Oh, I'm here ... barely. You woke me out of hangover-land, and she's retaliating with a vengeance." She yawned. "Also, I'm trying to decide if I should start screaming in celebration or if I should drive my ass over there and slap that man for taking so long to come to his senses."

"God, I love you."

"I'm not kidding."

I twirled my hair into a bun. Since I didn't have an elastic, I held the long strands on the top of my head. "You're perfectly allowed to do either—or both. But how about you hold off on the slap and maybe just give him a jab in the ribs?"

"Sounds like he fucked the hangover right out of you. I'm jealous as fuck."

I laughed, waiting for my head to hurt.

But only one thing on my body ached at this hour.

And I only felt it when I squeezed my legs together.

"Oh, Gabs, he did."

"That's the only reason I'm forgiving you for calling me this early." Her voice rose as she added, "Because I couldn't be happier for you right now." There was movement in the background and then, "Ouch. Gabby cannot talk too loud or sit up too fast; she's slowly dying."

"You realize you're talking about yourself in third person, right?"

"I hardly even know I'm a person right now, never mind what I'm actually saying." She cleared her throat. "But now, I'm flat, in darkness, buried under the blanket—and much better." She paused. "Tell me the details. Was there talking or just humping?"

"We started with talking, which then led to humping."

"And?"

"The guilt was gone. He wants this." I sucked in a breath. "He wants us."

Gabby sighed. "Thank fuck. I was starting to worry about that man and his ability to see what was right in front of him."

"He saw." I remembered the words he had said. The way they hit me. The way they made me question. The way they settled every bit of apprehension I'd been feeling. "It just took him time to admit to himself that I'm what he wants. He knew all along, like I knew I wanted him, but coming to terms with that isn't easy, not when you have a child to protect."

"You're the queen of understanding, you know that?"

The sun was just starting to rise in the sky, a sight that made me smile. "I don't know about that. I just get the dynamics of family because kids are all I know."

"But you're harmless, Syd. You're like a yellow Lab. Who protects their kids from yellow Labs?"

I giggled. "I'm not perfect. Maybe things wouldn't have worked out. Maybe they still won't. Who knows?"

"I know. And I know they will. And I know you wouldn't hurt that child, no matter what." A bit of quietness passed until she said, "*Sooo*, how was it? Why aren't you spilling all the epic details?"

My eyes closed, my body clenching as the memories from last night filled my head. "It was intense. Passionate. Wickedly amazing." A heat moved across my cheeks. "Beyond anything I've ever had—and ever experienced. He knows my body in ways"—I sighed—"in ways I don't even know myself."

"Then, why aren't you in bed with him right now? Doing it all over again? Getting laid for the both of us? Girl, things are dry as a well over here. I need to live vicariously through you."

My legs dropped onto the lounge chair, and I crossed my feet at the bottom, the light from the sun just starting to spread across my face. "I can't sleep, so I figured I'd call you and then make us some breakfast. Eve is at her grandparents' house. I assume she'll be back late this morning. That gives us time to talk."

"You mean, plan how many children the two of you are going to have."

I laughed so hard that a boob almost popped out of the top of Ford's button-down. I adjusted the shirt and replied, "Calm down, Gabs. There won't be any babies for a long time. We're at the kissing stage, not the kid stage."

"Mark my words: it's going to happen."

"I have a lot of college to get through first and then job hunting and teaching—things I want to accomplish before I even think of starting a family."

"Stop being so driven. It's the worst trait ever. I don't know how I can be friends with someone as inspiring as you."

Her sarcasm made me grin, and I sat up, my feet falling to the deck. "Dinner tonight?"

"Obviously." She groaned, "And you're buying. Consider it payback for waking me up so early."

"Deal." I pushed myself off the chair and headed for the sliding glass door. "See ya tonight."

We hung up, and the moment I opened the door, I froze, shocked by what was unfolding in front of me.

Music was playing lightly through the speakers.

Mixing bowls were on the counter in the kitchen.

Coffee was brewing, the smell immediately hitting me.

"*Mmm.*" I closed my eyes, realizing how badly I needed some caffeine.

As my lids opened, Ford was smiling from the island.

Shirtless.

His hair messy, his beard untamed.

His eyes primal.

"Hungry?" he growled.

My body was suddenly on fire, the ache between my legs now a rapid, beating pulse.

"Yes," I replied. "Starving." I took several steps closer, taking inventory of everything on the counter, trying to figure out what he was making. "You're cooking?"

"For you." He cracked a few eggs into a bowl. "I woke up, and you were gone. I came out to look for you and saw you on the patio, on the phone. Figured I'd make good use of my time since I was up."

"I was talking to Gabby. You know ... girl stuff."

As I sat on one of the barstools, the placement gave me the perfect view of him.

The muscles that protruded from his shoulders, the definition in his chest, the way his abs were etched across his stomach. The line of hair that disappeared below his mesh shorts.

Good God.

I took a breath, trying to focus. "I didn't think you knew how to make anything, aside from pancakes."

He laughed. "Listen, I'm no Craig—or you—in the kitchen. There're only a few meals I can conquer. Eggs, bacon, and biscuits happen to be one."

"Biscuits?" I wiped the corners of my mouth. "I might have just drooled."

"I just popped them in the oven."

He came over to my side of the counter, bringing me a cup of coffee that he placed in front of me. As soon as his hands were free, he didn't return to the eggs that needed whisking. He cupped my face and slowly kissed me.

Part of me had expected to wake up this morning, thinking last night had all been just a dream.

But his lips told me that wasn't the case.

His eyes confirmed it.

He stayed close, holding me even tighter. "Everything all right with Gabby?"

I nodded. "Yep."

He traced my bottom lip. "I can't stop thinking about last night." He closed the distance between us again. This time, his kiss was gradual, savoring. A brief swipe of his tongue followed before he pulled away. "I can't stop thinking about you."

His expression was raw.

Emotional but sensual at the same time.

"Sydney, if I'm being honest, I barely slept last night."

"Same." I swallowed. "My thoughts were ... all over the place."

He scanned my eyes, back and forth. "What happened between us, it wasn't a mistake." His thumbs pressed into the sides of my mouth. "It was perfect, and every word I said was the truth." He paused. "I want you."

My heart was bursting.

"I want you to know something, Ford." I gripped the back of his hand, holding our fingers together. "No matter what happens between us, Everly will always have me." I lifted my cell off the counter and pulled up a text box. "Do you see this?" I pointed the screen at him. "It's a group text with the kids I used to nanny. Well, two of them—the youngest doesn't have a cell yet, but she texts me from her brother's phone."

I returned my cell to the counter, my hand back on his.

"Even though I no longer work for their family, I will be in their lives forever. I love those kids. Nothing will ever change that." I gazed into his eyes, trying to read them—something I'd never really been able to do with Ford. "Regardless of what happens between us, I will always be here for Everly. I know that's one of the things that worries you, and I'm telling you, you don't have to worry."

His eyes closed for the briefest of seconds, like he was processing this news. "What about your job? Do you still want to be her nanny?"

"Of course." I took a breath. "Absolutely."

"You think you'll be able to do both?" His hand lowered to my neck, tilting my face up a bit more to meet him. "Date me and nanny her?"

My stomach fluttered at the thought.

That was what I'd wanted since my interview.

What I'd thought about every night when I crawled into the other side of Gabby's bed, trying to tire my mind enough to fall asleep, and now, as I slept above the garage.

It was what I thought of every morning on my way into Ford's house.

"Yes." I smiled. "There's no question in my mind." I

wrapped my arms around his neck. "Being with you and caring for Everly are all I want. Choosing between you two was one of the hardest things I've ever done, but I knew that if things were meant to be, they would happen." I locked my hands behind his neck. "Where you were filled with what-ifs. *What if we don't work out? What if she abandons Everly? What if a twenty-two-year-old can't handle this type of life?* Because, let's face it, most probably can't. I never considered any of that. I didn't fear what would happen. I feared it would never happen."

"Maybe I need to be more like you and less like me."

"I think you're good just the way you are." I softened my voice, feeling the need to repeat, "I'm not going anywhere, Ford." I ran my fingers across his lips—a move that had previously belonged solely to him. "I've wanted to say this for a long time, and I finally can." My chest pounded as I took in his eyes. My whole body tingled. "I'm yours."

He lifted me from the stool, holding me in his arms, and my legs wrapped around his waist. He held the back of my head, positioning our mouths only inches apart. "Say that again, Sydney."

"I'm yours—"

He slammed our mouths together.

And in that moment, I knew something else to be true.

Ford Dalton was mine.

SEVENTEEN

FORD

"Today's my birthday," Everly said as she twirled in front of Sydney and me, the layers of her tutu fluttering with each circle. "My birthday, my birthday, my *birthdaaay*."

She was covered in pink. An explosion of color that started with fake pieces of pink hair tucked into her curls, a glittery gloss on her lips, paint on her nails, matching socks, shoes—all courtesy of Sydney.

Her nanny wasn't dressed in pink, but, fuck, she looked gorgeous.

And she was all mine.

"And how old are you today?" Sydney teased, as though she'd forgotten.

A game the two of them had been playing for the last week, counting down until her big party, which was starting as soon as our family arrived. A countdown that included a secret handshake and hip wiggles and some song they had made up.

Everly held up her palm, her five fingers spread wide. "This many." The living room light picked up the shimmer on her nails, her goddamn hands like little mirrors. "I'm not a baby no more." She twirled again, shook her hips. "No, no, *nooo*." Her arms lifted, moving from side to side, her hips matching the motion.

Sydney was doing the identical dance, singing the same song.

When she connected eyes with me, I said, "Here I am, ready to lose it over Eve turning five, and you're celebrating with her." As she flopped onto the couch beside me, I put my arm around her shoulders. "How dare you," I growled.

Her cheeks flushed, as though she could read my mind.

A quick glance at Everly told me she wasn't paying attention, giving me a few seconds to lower my hand and rub between Sydney's ass, whispering, "I should punish you for that."

A part of her body I hadn't taken yet.

But I planned to.

Soon.

Just like I planned to tell my daughter that Sydney and I were together.

I wanted to make sure this was going to work between Sydney and me before we sat Everly down and talked to her about us.

A month into our relationship, and things couldn't be better.

So, that talk was going to happen shortly.

"Age is a battle you're not going to win," Sydney said, laughing. "So, you need to get used to the idea that your little girl is getting older, whether you like it or not."

"I don't like it."

She smiled. "I think you should dance with Everly and let her know exactly how you feel."

"Dance, Daddy! Dance!"

Sydney rose from the couch and grabbed Eve's hand, the two of them picking up right where they had left off.

"No, no, *nooo*. I'm not a baby no more. No, no, *nooo*."

I joined in.

I couldn't help myself; they were too fucking cute.

I moved in between them, linking hands with both, the three of us dancing in a circle, singing their new song until I heard, "Now, this is a sight I never thought I'd walk in on."

I glanced toward the kitchen, where Dominick and Kendall were making their way into the family room.

"Where's my birthday girl?" my older brother said as he knelt on the floor, opening his arms, waiting for Everly to run to him.

Which happened seconds later.

"Uncle D!"

He lifted her into the air, kissing her cheek.

"It's my birthday, Uncle D. I'm not a baby no more. No, no, *nooo*."

He laughed. "Have you told your father that? Because I think he'd disagree."

"Uncle D, Daddy knows I'm this many years old." She held up her hand.

"Is that right?" He paused. "So, if you're not our baby anymore, then what are you?"

Everly smiled and bounced. "A big girl."

"I don't approve," Dominick said, kissing her forehead. "I remember when you were so small that you fit in both my hands. Now"—he shook his head—"you're almost as tall as me."

Everly snorted. "You're a giant, like Daddy."

"You know what else I am?"

Everly's eyes went wide. "No?"

"I'm a tickle monster."

"Auntie Kendall," Everly screamed as Dominick tickled

her, her laughter filling my entire house. "*Ahhh!* Auntie Kendall, *saaave meee.*"

"Dominick, give me our girl," Kendall said, holding out her arms. The moment she scooped Everly from Dominick, she added, "I've missed you like crazy. Why haven't I seen you in a few weeks?" She fixed Everly's tutu and moved some hair off her forehead.

"I've been *sooo* busy," Everly replied, breathless.

Kendall laughed. "Can we have a sleepover soon?"

Eve played with the side of Kendall's hair and replied, "Yes!"

"I want a sleepover too," Jenner said as he joined the party, his hands full of gifts. "Because I believe it's our turn to have Eve for the weekend."

"Uncle Jenner!"

"Did you leave any pink at the store?" I asked him.

Jo was right beside Jenner, her hands also full of pink bags.

"There's another load still in the car that we weren't able to carry in," Jo responded, smiling.

"Jesus, you guys," I groaned. "You're spoiling her."

Everyone looked at me and laughed.

"Whatever you say, Daddy," Jenner mocked, rolling his eyes. He dropped the bags and held out his hands. "Give me my girl."

He took Everly from Kendall and danced around the living room with her while Jo went back outside to get the rest of the gifts.

"She loves them so much," Sydney said to me as we watched Everly in Jenner's arms, beaming from all the attention.

"She lives for them," I agreed, my gaze turning to Sydney. "And she lives for you." I ground my teeth together. "Fuck, I want to kiss you right now."

My brothers knew.

My parents knew.

Hannah, of course, knew.

We weren't a secret.

But today was all about Everly, and until we talked to my daughter about what was going on, I wasn't going to kiss Sydney in front of her, filling Eve with questions.

"You have no idea how badly I want that," Sydney whispered back.

"Look who I found," Jo said.

Her announcement caused my focus to break away from Sydney, and I glanced toward the entrance of the living room, where my parents were walking in.

More gifts weren't just overflowing from Jo's hands, but my parents' too.

"Mimi! Papa!"

"Look at my beautiful birthday girl," my mother said, crouching onto her knees so she could hug Everly.

My family was going to keep my daughter occupied for the next several minutes. That meant, for the short time being, I could do what I wanted.

I could do what had been on my goddamn mind since Sydney and Everly had walked downstairs after Eve finished getting ready.

I put my hand on Sydney's back and growled, "Come with me."

The kitchen wasn't safe.

Neither was the powder room or my bedroom or any of the rooms near the living room.

Therefore, I led her into the garage. Once the door was shut, I pressed her back against it, holding her neck, tilting her face up to me.

I stared into those gorgeous eyes, at those plump fucking lips. "Finally."

I didn't wait.

I slammed our mouths together, slipping my fingers down her side until I reached her ass, squeezing it into my palm.

"*Mmm*," she moaned. Her eyes opened as I pulled my mouth away. "Don't stop."

There was nothing hotter than hearing her demand more.

I devoured her lips again, brushing our bodies together, grinding my hard-on against her pussy.

Fuck, she felt so good.

My tongue slowly slithered between her lips, tasting her.

Savoring.

But it wasn't enough.

Even though I'd eaten her pussy just last night, even though she'd ridden my cock and I'd filled her with cum.

It was never enough when it came to Sydney.

The time in between made me miss her.

Like this morning, when she'd been upstairs, helping Everly get ready.

And again, now, as she separated us and said, "We have to get back to the party."

"You sure?" I nuzzled into her neck, inhaling her, kissing up to her ear. "I need just one more minute."

She laughed, gently tapping my erection. "Down, boy. It's Everly's day. We're not missing a second of it."

"Fuck ... you're right." I adjusted myself to hide how hard I was. "But do you have any idea what I'm going to do to you tonight?" I left her neck to graze my thumb across her mouth, my stare following the pad of my finger as I fantasized about those fucking lips.

"I think I can guess." Her teeth pierced her bottom lip. "And I can't wait."

"Sydney ..." I pulled it loose, rubbing, tugging it. "You're fucking teasing me."

"Not teasing. Promising." She kissed me and wiped her gloss off my lips, and then she turned around and reached for the doorknob.

I gave her ass a quick slap and followed her inside.

Craig was in the kitchen when we entered and said, "I took the cake out of the fridge, Sydney. I want it to get to room temperature before anyone eats it."

"Perfect. Thank you," she replied.

He wiped his hands on his apron. "You did a hell of a job on it." He reached for a bowl and began dumping some hummus into it. "Everly's going to flip out when she sees it."

Sydney smiled. "That's my hope."

I hadn't seen the cake. Sydney wanted it to be a surprise, but she'd asked if she could make it rather than having me order one, like I usually did. Of course, I had agreed. There was nothing sweeter than my girl wanting to bake for my daughter.

"I'm going to bring out another wave of appetizers in about five," Craig said to me.

"Sounds good, buddy."

Sydney and I left the kitchen, and as we were coming into the living room, Hannah approached.

"There you are," she said. "I've been looking for you."

"We were hiding." I laughed.

"I noticed," she replied. "Can I talk to you for a second?"

"Now?"

Hannah nodded.

I looked at Sydney and said, "I'll be right back," and I followed Hannah outside onto the patio.

We stayed close to the sliding door, giving me a view of everything that was happening inside. But I wasn't looking through the glass. I was focused on my cousin, the concern building on her face as she paced from the pool to the table, where I was standing.

"I know Everly's birthday isn't the right place to discuss this," she said, stopping a few feet away. "But I can't wait any longer. I need to know."

This wasn't typical Hannah behavior.

Something was up, and I needed to get to the bottom of it.

"Need to know what?" I inquired.

She'd been avoiding my eyes, but she finally gazed at me. "Are you upset with me?"

"Upset with you?" I repeated. "Why would I be?"

She filled her lungs. "Because of Sydney. What I told her to do." She took in more air. "You know ... about the job."

"The job?" I shook my head, bewildered. "Hannah, I have no idea what you're talking about."

"Wait ..." She continued to stare at me, like she was analyzing my response. "I can't tell if you're lawyering me right now or really clueless about what I'm talking about."

"What job?"

"The nanny position."

I repeated her words in my head, trying to figure out what the hell this all meant.

"You really are clueless, Ford ... aren't you?" Her eyes widened. "Sydney didn't tell you?"

"Tell me what?"

"Oh dear God." She pulled back one of the chairs and sat at the table, pointing at the one next to her so I would join her. Once I was seated, she started, "Please don't kill me. It's Eve's birthday after all, and the whole fam is here. They'd kinda notice if I suddenly ended up floating lifelessly on top of the pool."

"Hannah, what the fuck are you talking about?"

Her stare moved to the tabletop, her hands clenching, her

knuckles cracking. "When I gave Sydney a ride home after the night you guys met, she told me she was going to school to become a teacher and that she had been an au pair in her previous job." She swallowed, her hands no longer fidgeting. "Once I heard all of that, I told her to apply to be Everly's nanny."

I was trying to work this out in my head, piece it all together. "Go on."

"She sent me her résumé, and I forwarded it to your assistant, and then I asked Sydney not to tell you what I—or we —had done."

"Hold on a second." The points were sliding into place, but I needed to make sure I had this straight. "You're telling me that when Sydney walked into my office to be interviewed, she knew that the job she had applied for was to be Everly's nanny?"

She nodded. "And it's my fault she didn't confess that to you." Her hand clamped down on my arm. "All my fault, not hers, which is why I thought you were mad at me and just waiting for the right time to talk to me." Her head dropped. "Since you guys started dating, I just assumed she'd told you. I can't believe she didn't—I mean, I'm happy that she didn't, I think. I'm just shocked."

Sydney had told me she'd found the job posting online.

To this day, she'd never mentioned anything about having a conversation with Hannah.

She'd ... lied?

What the fuck?

"Hannah, I—"

"If you're going to be mad at anyone, please be mad at me. This is all my fault. I'm the one who told her not to tell you."

I glanced toward the Hills, processing, attempting to ratio-nalize this news in my head. "I don't know how I feel."

Her fingers squeezed me, drawing my attention back to her. "I remember the day I started working at the law firm and the very first thing you told me was that I needed to listen to my gut. Ford, that's something I've been practicing ever since, and when something feels right, when it looks right, when it sounds right, I get this feeling in my stomach." Her brows lowered, the furrow between them gone. "That's what happened when I met Sydney and when I saw her interact with Eve. They instantly took to one another. So, when I heard she needed a job and you needed a nanny—it was a home run, in my opinion."

"Except I wouldn't date a woman who was caring for my child. Did you ever think about that?"

"I know you better than you know yourself, Ford Dalton. Obviously, I thought about that." A smile came across her lips.

"You intentionally kept us apart ..."

"No." Her smile grew. "I put you guys together."

I searched her eyes. "Explain yourself. I'm fucking lost."

She pulled her hand back and crossed her fingers over the table. "You suck with women. I'm sorry, but it's true. Maybe things with Sydney would have worked out had she not become Everly's nanny. But what I did know at the time was that things would most definitely work out if she did become her nanny."

I rubbed my temples as a Hannah-headache worked its way through my brain. "How in the hell would you know that?"

"Have you listened to anything I've said today?"

She waited for a response. I didn't give her one.

So, she continued, "I know you. I know how you operate. I know the second something turns slightly serious with a girl, you go all AWOL, and you bail because you don't want to bring them into Eve's life." She turned her head, peeking through the glass. "There's one way to your heart"—she nodded toward the living room—"and it's through that little girl right there." She gazed back at me. "If you had any feelings for Sydney, which I kind of assumed you did, then having her around all the time would only emphasize them. And, eventually, you two would be together ... like you are." She raised her arms in the air, like she was cheering. "Who's the genius here? Me."

"I don't even know what the fuck to say right now."

Her arms dropped. "You can tell your little coz how much you love her since I am the rock star of this equation."

"Hannah ..."

She leaned into the table to get closer. "Okay, so I might have gone about it in a shitty way. I might have told Sydney to lie to you—which is all kinds of fucked up, I agree, and I'm sorry again—but it was only out of your best interest and hers. Because, let's face it, had you known she was going to interview, you wouldn't have let her, and then who knows if we'd all be here right now?"

The things she'd said weren't far from the truth.

Had I known Sydney wanted to apply for the job, I wouldn't have let her.

In fact, I wouldn't have even considered her for the position.

And Hannah was right about my dating record. Although I wanted to think things would have been different with Sydney, I didn't know if that was true.

So, my cousin had intentionally put us together. That wasn't such a bad thing.

It had worked, and I was happy as hell.

The only thing that really bothered me was that Sydney hadn't told me. Even now, a month into our relationship, she'd kept her word to Hannah.

Was that a huge deal?

I didn't know. I just feared there were other things she was keeping from me.

"Tell me what I'm looking at," she said as she stared into my eyes. "A wicked, pissed off Ford? Semi-pissed? Ready to hug me and call me a goddess matchmaker?"

I sighed. "I'm not mad. It all worked out—that's really what matters."

"Your tone isn't convincing me."

I glanced through the glass, seeing Sydney on the floor, playing some kind of game with Everly. "I just wish she had told me." I looked back at Hannah. "That would have made me feel a lot better."

"Would it have though? Because she still chose your daughter over you, am I right?" She let that simmer. "And if she only wanted you, she wouldn't have wanted to interview for the job."

"What are you saying?"

"I'm saying, it doesn't matter that you knew or not. Her heart was always in the right place—she has been there for Everly, and she's proven that to you every single day." She broke eye contact to gaze inside. "Look at her, Ford. Is there anyone in this world who's better for you and your daughter than Sydney Summers?"

At a party full of her favorite people, Everly was on the floor with Sydney.

Laughing.

Smiling.

Hugging her.

Fuck, Hannah was right.

And when I looked at Hannah to respond, she was smiling again.

"I know; I'm going to make the best lawyer ever."

I laughed. "You really are."

"Don't be angry with her." Her voice softened as she said, "She's one of the good ones, Ford."

I said nothing more, knowing the person I needed to talk to about this was Sydney, not Hannah.

And since there wasn't anything left to say, we stood.

As we were walking to the door, I couldn't help but add, "By the way, little cousin, you do have a serious set of fucking balls on you."

She had reached the door and glanced over her shoulder at me. "And that's why I'm going to be the highest earner at your firm."

"Is that so?"

"Really?" She laughed. "You're doubting me? After I just pulled off the biggest dating scandal the Daltons have ever seen?" She patted my shoulder as she slid the door open. "Come on. Let's go spoil your daughter some more."

As I walked inside, Sydney got up from the floor and joined me.

"Is everything all right?" she asked. "Things looked like they were getting a little heated out there."

I briefly put my hand on her back, just long enough that she could feel my fingers. "It's all good."

"Daddy!" Everly screamed, rushing over and clinging to my leg. "Daddy, Daddy! Uncle D says it's present time. I wanna open presents!"

"And she's opening mine first," Dominick said from the couch.

I chuckled, rubbing the back of my little girl's head. "Tell Uncle D you're opening mine first. He's going to have to wait." I lifted her into my arms and carried her over to the couch, setting her on the large ottoman. "Stay right there," I told her.

I went into the area of the living room where all the presents had been placed, finding mine among the massive stack. I grabbed the small bag and handed it to her.

By the time I sat, everyone had found a place on the couch, Sydney directly next to me.

"Open it," I said to Everly, who normally needed no prompting, but I was sure the small bag was puzzling since my gifts typically came in larger packaging.

She pulled out the small bundle and tore off the tissue paper, holding the book in her hands.

"Do you know what it is?" I asked.

The book was made entirely of photos.

She opened to the first page, her curls bouncing as she wiggled on the cushion. "Photos! From your trip!"

"That's right." I looked at Sydney, smiling.

The gift had been my idea, but the way I was presenting it had been Sydney's. She'd also helped put the booklet together, downloading each of the pictures I had sent during my time on the road and arranging them in order.

"Do you know why I'm giving this to you?" I asked Everly.

She shook her head.

"Because we're going to make our own book, just like this one." I moved to the end of the couch to get closer to her and pointed at the shot of the Las Vegas Strip, the picture she had just arrived at. "We're going to fly there, and you're going to see all the lights and have all the adventures, just like you asked for."

Her mouth opened so wide. "We are?"

"How nice," my mother said. "Everly, your daddy got you such a wonderful gift."

"And we spoil her," Dominick huffed.

I ignored my brother, flipping back a few pages to show her the mountain shots. "And we're also going there, to Colorado, so you can see those mountains and ride some horses."

"I am?"

"You're going to love the horses," my father said to her.

I lifted her off the ottoman and set her on my lap. "We're leaving in this many days." I held two hands in the air, spreading my fingers wide—the same way she had all morning.

Her face lit up even more. "Yay!"

Sydney reached for Everly's hand, swinging it so gently. "What do you say, Miss Everly?"

"Thank you, Daddy." She threw her tiny arms around my neck and squeezed me.

"You're welcome, baby." I rubbed circles across her back. "Can you guess who's coming with us?"

She leaned away, looking at my face. A second passed, and she shrugged.

"I am, sweetheart," Sydney said.

"Wahoo! I wanna leave now!" She jumped off my lap and landed on Sydney's, giving her a hug. When she pulled away, she asked, "Did you get me a present?"

Sydney laughed. "I made you a present. Would you like to see it?"

"Yes!"

She carried Everly off the couch and set her down in the kitchen, leading her into the pantry.

I followed behind, wanting to see Everly's face when Sydney showed her the surprise.

The cake was sitting on a table that Craig had set up, so no one would see the dessert until it was time for Everly to blow out her candles.

But Everly rushed right up to it, her eyes so wide, her mouth open. "My animals!" she screeched. "All of them!"

Three layers tall, the cake had taken Sydney two days to make. She hand-carved each of the animals, matching their faces and coloring to the ones that slept on Everly's bed. She'd even remembered the pink skirt that went around the hippo's waist and the pink tie that hung from the giraffe's neck. Since

Sydney knew how much Everly loved the mountains, that was the design of each layer, the animals grazing, climbing, resting in different sections and along the base.

This wasn't just a cake.

This was a masterpiece that had been baked and designed straight from Sydney's heart.

But I wasn't sure my daughter understood that part.

I rubbed the back of Everly's neck and said to her, "Do you know that Sydney made this cake just for you?"

"Like when we bake?" Everly asked her.

Sydney nodded. "Yes, like when we make cupcakes, but this was a bit bigger of a project."

"I love it, Syd." She wrapped around Sydney's waist, holding on to her, not letting go. "*Sooo* much."

While Sydney held Everly's head, she looked at me, her face filled with something I recognized.

Something I felt as I glanced between both my girls.

EIGHTEEN
SYDNEY

The first three days in Las Vegas had been an absolute dream. Ford spared no expense, and that didn't surprise me one bit. He wanted memories, adventures, and he gave us both. We took Everly on the High Roller Ferris wheel, so she could see the lights of the Strip. He even rented a helicopter to fly us to the Grand Canyon for the day with a huge picnic set up the moment we landed. We had gone to the best restaurants and had the most delicious wine, and every evening, we went to a show that he'd chosen just for Everly.

And then we boarded Ford's private plane and went to our second stop.

The one I was most excited about.

Colorado.

It was as though the sky had opened and sliced out a piece of heaven.

That was Vail.

The mountain ranges, the little rivers nestled in between—it was all perfection.

And I loved watching Everly take it all in.

Especially when Ford announced that she was going horse-back riding. It was scheduled through a kids' club—a camp that was run by the hotel—and it included an entire day of activities. Ford had brought up the idea on the plane, and Everly couldn't wait to go.

She gripped my hand so tightly, dragging us to the entrance of the club—a small room on the first floor of the hotel. The counselor met us in the doorway and introduced herself.

Ford knelt down, so he could speak to his daughter. "You're going to do everything the counselor says, right?" He fixed her shirt and made sure her hiking boots were tied tightly.

"Yes, like a big girl."

"I don't want there to be any accidents, Eve."

She shook her head. "No accidents."

It didn't matter how often I saw the two of them together or what they were actually talking about; my ovaries still threatened to explode each time.

He was so good with her.

Patient.

Understanding.

So fatherly in a productive, not overwhelming way.

"And you're going to listen to the counselor?" he asked her.

Everly gave him a big nod.

He hugged her and kissed her forehead. "All right, go have fun. I love you."

"I'll be good, Syd," she said as she came over to me, hugging my waist. "Don't let Daddy get in trouble today."

I slid my fingers through her hair, tightening her ponytail, holding back a giggle. "I'll make sure he stays far away from trouble."

She waved. "Bye, Syd. Bye, Daddy." She linked hands with the counselor and disappeared inside the room.

There had only been a few moments during this trip when

we were able to sneak away and have some time alone together. Each of those occasions was after Everly went to bed, and he'd come into my room of the two-bedroom suite he had rented. We didn't want to take any chances—we were worried that she'd wake up and come in—so we hadn't done more than just kiss. Now, with an entire day to ourselves, I suspected I was going to get more than just his lips.

But before we went anywhere, I needed to make sure of something.

I turned toward him, waiting for his eyes to leave the door of the kids' club, and said, "Are you all right? I know it's not easy to hand her over to a stranger who's going to take her hiking and horseback riding and ..." I paused, deciding not to add any more fuel. "It's just a lot."

"Jo and her father own this hotel, and the kids' club was her idea. I trust them implicitly."

"Good."

His hands went to my lower back, and he pulled me against him. "Fuck, I've been thinking about this nonstop." He kissed me gently.

It was nothing more than a tease since I knew there was so much more power waiting for me.

In his mouth.

In his hands.

Power that I now craved.

"What should we do all day?" I wrapped my arms around his neck and smiled. "Do you have any ideas?"

"Lots. In fact, I have every hour of the next eight planned."

"No?"

He pulled my lower lip into his mouth, gnawing across it. "Yes."

Before I could say another word, he led me across the hotel to the other side of the lobby and up a massive staircase. We crossed a catwalk, and once we were on the other side, I saw the sign for the spa.

"How does a massage sound?" His lips were close to my ear. The feel of his voice, the deepness of his tone, caused a tingle to shudder through me.

"Magical." I turned to face him. "But you know you didn't have to do that."

His arm went around my shoulders, and he kissed the side of my neck. "That's one of the things I really like about you, Sydney. You expect nothing and appreciate everything." His mouth stayed but moved higher toward my jaw. "I booked us for ninety minutes. Together."

I moaned, "You're too much."

He opened the door to the spa, and we were instantly greeted by name, the attendant telling us our room was ready and asking us to follow her.

I held Ford's hand as I walked with him down a hallway and through a doorway. The candlelight was the first thing I noticed when we stepped inside. The long, thick white pillars were everywhere, covering all the surfaces of the room. They were flickering, brightening the dark space, and on the floor were red rose petals.

I'd gotten plenty of massages before.

None of this was standard.

He'd arranged every bit of it.

"Ford"—I shook my head—"I can't believe you did this."

"Robes are against the back wall," the attendant said. I'd almost forgotten she was in here with us. "Your massage therapists will be in shortly."

The moment she was gone, he pulled me closer, cupping my face. "This vacation has been all about Eve. Now, it's your turn."

"But it's not supposed to be about me." I held the back of his hand. "We're celebrating her birthday, as we should be."

"My real intention for this trip was for Everly to experience us together—to feel our connection, our interactions, the way we work so well together—and then, on the way home, I'll tell her about us."

"You know I love that idea."

He kissed me, taking his time, breathing me in. "You're the most selfless person I know, Sydney. Let me spoil you. Let me show you what life with me will be like." His thumb rubbed across my lips. "Let me enjoy having you all to myself."

My body was on fire.

Not my heart.

That was beating so fast that I could barely breathe.

Every dream was coming true, and I continually had to tell myself that this was real.

That Ford was mine.

That he cared about me as deeply as I felt for him.

"Okay," I whispered, leaning into his hand. "I guess you can spoil me just this once."

"Let's get you naked."

He lifted the bottom of my shirt over my head and unhooked my bra. Once my breasts were loose, he worked on my jeans, lowering them down my legs along with my panties, and helped me out of my shoes.

I was suddenly standing before him, completely bare.

He stepped back, like he needed the distance to get a better look, and his gaze dropped down my body. "Damn it, I'm so fucking lucky," he moaned. "You're gorgeous."

Every time he said that, it felt like the first.

He captured me and pulled me against him, his lips devouring mine.

"*Mmm.*" I gripped the collar of his shirt when he pulled away. "I want more."

He growled, "If I give you more, I'm going to spread you over that massage table, and the only thing rubbing you will be my tongue."

"And there's something wrong with that?"

"My impatient girl." He kissed me again, his hand moving to my chin. "More will happen. You're just going to have to wait."

"That's not going to be easy."

He lifted his shirt off and tossed it onto the bench in the back. "For the next ninety minutes, I want you to think of all the ways I'm going to fuck you." After he took off his shoes and pants and placed our clothes together, he touched that spot. The one in between my legs that was pulsing. The one that made me gasp. "Fuck, you're wet."

"I told you ... I want you."

He sucked the wetness off his fingers and held my neck, his mouth hovering above mine. "And I told you, I'm going to take care of you once this massage is over." He bit that same lip again, harder this time. "Now, go get on your table unless you're looking to get spanked."

A type of pain I'd never had before Ford or realized how much I liked until he slapped my ass during sex.

I smiled, licking the spot he had just nipped. "And if I am?"

"Go."

I laughed as I headed for the table and slipped beneath the covers, getting lost in a sea of fluff and softness until I felt his hand. The tables were close, and his fingers had searched under the blanket until they found mine.

I glanced across the open space, meeting his grin.

My chest swelled, my throat tightening.

Some of the moments we spent together were so pure that they didn't need words.

They were raw, honest.

Full of emotion.

Like when he had walked into the pantry while I was presenting the birthday cake to Everly.

When we'd had dinner with his parents the night before we left and he held my hand under the table.

When I'd been on a call with Gabby while we were in Vegas and he took the phone from my hand, promising her he would keep me safe. That nothing would ever happen to me.

Like now.

The knock at the door pulled me out of my thoughts, and I heard Ford say, "Come in."

"Hello," one of the massage therapists said.

They closed the door behind them and washed their hands at the sink before they began to work on us. With fingers that were covered in oil, she started on my shoulders before running them up and down my spine.

I was lost.

Swallowed in a cloud of relaxation. The only thing that stayed constant was Ford's hand locked with mine.

The heat of his skin a reminder that he had me.

That he was never going to let go.

And while I clung to him, it felt like only minutes had passed before the therapist whispered, "Take your time in getting up. I've left some water for you in the back."

Once the door shut and I knew we were alone, I sat up and looked over at him. "I feel half dead." I tucked my hair behind my ears. "My God, that was amazing."

"I'm glad you enjoyed it." He swung his legs out and stood. "Put your robe on. I have another surprise."

I was curious why he hadn't told me to get dressed, but I didn't ask.

I just went over to where the robe was hanging and slipped my arms through the holes, tying the belt at my waist. My feet went into a pair of slippers, and I followed Ford through the room and out a door in the back.

"There's more?" I finally questioned, my voice dying as I saw the paradise waiting for us.

This time, it was a private garden that was decorated in more candles and rose petals. There were several lounge chairs across the space and a hot tub, filled and bubbling, built into the ground. Since we were outside, a wall blocked us from being seen, but the top gave just enough visibility that we could view the peak of the mountains.

"Ford ..." I swallowed, searching for words, overtaken by his gratitude. "This is absolutely stunning."

He stood behind me, his hands on my stomach, his face in my neck. "Are you hungry?"

I knew why he'd asked.

There was an entire spread that had been set up on a table with flutes of champagne, small sandwiches, fruit, salad, even dessert.

"Hungry?" I sighed. "More like blown away."

"This is nothing." He kissed up my shoulder, around my throat, and to my ear. "You have no idea the things I'm going to do for you."

I turned and wrapped my arms around him. "What made you think of this?"

He chuckled. "I saw you rubbing your neck while we were in Vegas. You do that whenever you sit for too long. I wanted to ease some of that pain."

My head shook from side to side. "You're observant."

"Just with you." He kissed me. "Because I can't take my fucking eyes off you."

There were times I felt that.

His stare so heated that I could sense every place he looked.

"Thank you." I pressed my nose to his. "For bringing me here. For putting this together. It's incredibly special."

"So are you." He held my face, keeping us close. "Once she knows, things are going to change. I'll be able to touch you whenever I want. Kiss you. Have you sleep in my bed. Not all at once, but eventually, as she gets used to us." He paused. "I want Everly to see what a relationship looks like. I don't want to hide it from her."

My heart took in his words; they circled through me, spun. And while I heard them repeat in my head, I took a moment to relish in his news. "Do you think she'll be okay with that —with us?"

"To be honest, she's never had to share me with anyone, but she loves you, Sydney. She emulates you in ways you probably don't even realize." He reached toward the table and grabbed the champagne, handing me a glass. "I suspect she's going to be thrilled." His hand slipped inside my robe, his fingers applying pressure on my breasts. "Now, it's time to celebrate you."

I gasped as he tugged on my nipple. He moved to the other side, rolling it between his fingers.

Pulling.

Flicking so gently.

"Ford ..."

He loosened the robe, and it fell from my shoulders, tingles instantly exploding inside me.

He dropped his robe and took me by the hand, escorting me down the three steps into the tub. The water was so hot that it took my breath away. He sat on the bench inside, the water landing in the middle of his chest, his arms resting across the edge.

I went to sit beside him, but he pulled me onto his lap.

Straddling him.

"Take a drink," he ordered.

Once I did, he set my glass outside the tub next to his.

With his hands free, he rubbed them over my body. "Fuck, you feel good." His lips landed on my collarbone, kissing down to my breast.

My eyes were starting to close when I felt something cold on my skin. Something almost electric. That was when I realized it was the champagne. He was pouring it on me, licking it off.

"Oh God." I quivered.

My nipples ached; they were so hard.

My body so wet that I was throbbing.

I moaned his name as I rose on his lap, giving him more space to pour.

To lap.

To bite.

I dived my fingers into his hair, leading him toward my nipple.

But the more I tried to direct him, the more he resisted.

Ford was the kind of man who was always in control.

He didn't take direction.

He gave orders instead.

And that was exactly what his eyes told me as he breathed across my nipple.

There was no touching.

Just air.

With feral, intense eyes, he asked, "Do you want more?"

"Yes."

"How badly?"

"Please," I pleaded, the need like a blast that required urgent attention. "Ford ... now."

He blew again, this time only a hairbreadth away from my nipple.

His tongue extended, but before it touched me, he pulled back.

"You're going to get everything you want," he told me. "But you're going to have to beg."

NINETEEN

FORD

I wanted her to beg.

Maybe it was the fact that I hadn't tasted her since we'd left LA, not risking the chance of Everly walking into Sydney's bedroom and seeing us.

Maybe it was because we were in a public setting and the thrill of that turned me the fuck on.

Maybe I just wanted to hear how badly she wanted me.

But as I had her positioned over me, her needs filled my ears.

One at a time.

"Please," she cried, her back arching.

I poured champagne over her shoulder, watching it dribble down her chest, pooling at the top of her nipple.

I licked the path, stopping when I neared her tit.

My mouth wasn't going there just yet.

She had to wait.

"Ford!"

I added more, this time to the center of her breasts. The

cold, bubbly liquid popped against her, telling me the carbonation was doing exactly what I wanted.

Tingling.

Urging.

"Oh God, touch me."

Words that were so fucking sexy.

But they weren't enough.

I covered more of her, every inch that wasn't beneath the water.

Slowly.

Meticulously.

Painting the champagne over her body, avoiding the spots that would give her any relief.

I wanted to see a build.

I wanted more begging.

"*Ahhh*! Please! Now!"

I didn't stop until both glasses were empty.

Instead of getting out to retrieve the bottle, I lifted her onto the edge of the tub and spread her legs across it. I moved in front of her, and her fingers raked through my hair, trying to pull me toward her pussy.

To give her the relief she'd been asking for.

I glanced up, my mouth inches from her pussy. "Is this what you want, Sydney?"

She nodded; her lips parted as she breathed through them.

"You want me to fucking eat you?"

She swallowed, nodding again. "Please."

"Tell me."

The oil they'd used to massage her made her skin slick, but that didn't stop me from gripping her. From holding her thighs where I wanted them.

From blowing strong, short bursts of air against her clit.

"Ford," she pleaded. "Oh God, please."

"Please what?"

This was where Sydney was timid. Where she didn't have much experience.

Where each time I slid into her pussy, it almost felt like I was taking her virginity.

"Please give me your tongue."

I moved closer, breathing harder so she felt every exhale. "Where do you want it?" I pressed the tip of my tongue against her thigh. "Here?" I gradually moved to the other side. "Here?"

"No."

"Where, Sydney?" I let my tongue settle. "Show me."

Her hand started at her nipple, pinching it, like she couldn't go another second without that sensation, and then she lowered. Down her ribs, past her navel, stopping at the top of her pussy.

"Here."

I licked the top of her fingers.

"On my clit."

That was what I'd wanted to hear.

"How do you want me to lick it?"

My cock throbbed as I waited for her to respond, the anticipation of eating her cunt almost too much to bear.

But I still didn't go directly to that spot.

I kissed around.

I nipped.

"Fast." She sucked in some air. "Hard."

I gazed up, our eyes locking. "To make you come?"

"Yes."

"Say it."

She was biting her lip, the sight making me fucking rabid.

"To make me come."

"That's it," I breathed, flattening my tongue to cover the entire length of her.

The width.

"*Yesss*," she sighed.

I dragged the tip up and down, grazing that perfect clit.

But before I really tasted, before I gave her what she'd asked for, I wanted to smell.

I wanted to bury myself in her scent.

I wedged my nose in between her lips and took a long, deep inhale.

"Fuck me," I moaned.

I was desperate to finger her, to cover myself in her wetness.

But I didn't.

I stayed there, breathing her in, moving my nose lower to press against her clit.

"*Ohhh*, yes."

She liked that, and I hadn't even started.

I dropped again, halfway down, my tongue giving her just the slightest bit of friction. It was enough that her legs began to close, her toes to bend, her hand to loosen in my hair.

I kept her thighs apart, holding them, pushing them as I dipped in once more.

This time to the entrance of her pussy.

My favorite fucking spot on her body.

The one that took me in.

That held me.

That fucking sucked the cum out of me.

I couldn't wait.

I needed to feel her.

Taste her.

My finger probed, and I immediately felt the tightness and wetness of her cunt.

"Goddamn it, Sydney," I moaned. "You're fucking perfect."

Her grip was back, flexing within the strands of my hair,

pulling me closer. With each tug, her head fell back farther, her hair dangling on the floor.

A trail of gorgeous skin led up to her face.

One that I couldn't see, but I still watched her.

The bounce in her throat as she moaned, "Ford." The rise in her chest as she brought in more air.

My finger went in deeper, aiming upward, giving her that arch I knew she desired. And while I pulled back to my nail and slowly slid in again, I dragged my tongue up her clit, stopping at the very top, where I gave it a quick swipe.

Her hips bucked.

"Oh God," she whispered. Her hand twisted within my locks. "Your tongue ... I can't even think of words."

That was how I wanted her.

Lost.

Because I was the same, mouth deep in her pussy, knowing even this wasn't enough.

I needed more of her.

My tongue flicked harder, staying in that same spot, my finger picking up speed.

And while I ate her, while I tapped my tongue back and forth, my dick grew.

It fucking ached to be inside her.

"Ford ..." She was tilting her head up, staring down at me with a hunger in her eyes and on her lips. "You're going to make me come."

I wanted to taste it.

To watch it.

To hear her scream.

To know I was the one giving her this feeling.

Rather than answer, I gave her more.

I twisted my wrist, my finger hitting her G-spot, rubbing across it.

"Oh fuck," she cried, her knees bending, her feet pushing onto the edge of the tub so she was rocking into me. "Yes!"

I could feel how close she was.

Her clit hardened, the wetness thickening on my skin.

God, she was fucking beautiful.

So was her pussy as it closed in around me, each breath a moan, each movement adding to her build.

I plunged.

I licked.

And within just a few of both, she was squirming.

"Ford!"

Ripples blasted across her stomach, and I watched each one, every burst of pleasure as it spread through her.

"Oh!" she gasped. "Yes!"

It happened quickly, wave after wave.

I could feel it on my finger.

I could see it move across her, the way her stomach shuddered, how her legs wanted to cave, how her pussy kept me sucked in, clenching as she moaned through each breath.

"My God!"

Stunning.

Always.

But when she came, when she turned her most vulnerable, now, that was a whole different look on her.

One I could stare at forever.

And I did as I licked through her orgasm, slowing only when she settled.

But I still stayed there, kissing, spreading her wetness, waiting for her to come back to me.

To push through that fog.

When she did, when her eyes refocused and fixed on mine, she panted, "What the hell was that?"

I tasted her on my lips. "What you asked for."

"I ..." Her voice trailed off as she tried to catch her breath. "Every time is unlike the others. It's never"—she shook her head—"felt like that before."

I kissed the inside of her thigh. "Do you want it again?"

I could spend all day with my face between her legs.

We were in no rush.

This room was ours until we left.

"Yes." She pulled at my hair, trying to lift me from the water. "But, no, I want you." She wrapped her legs around me. "Please, Ford. I need you."

And, damn it, I needed her.

I moved her to the very edge of the outer lip of the tub, and I stood from the steamy water, my dick so fucking hard that it was reaching for her.

My palm went around my shaft, pumping, readying myself.

I lifted her legs to my waist, feeling them lock behind me, holding the outside of her thighs while I teased her with my crown.

"Yes," she hissed. "Give it to me."

She was soaked.

Dripping over my tip.

And when I was only an inch in, she was already squeezing me.

"Sydney ..." I moaned, my head falling back, my mouth opening as I plunged into her. "Hell fucking yes."

I knew the feeling.

It greeted me every time.

But she had described it dead on—each time was different.

A tightness that instantly milked my cock.

A wetness that was sopping.

A heat that shocked the hell out of me, that I was never quite ready for.

"You feel so fucking good."

I buried my dick until my balls were slapping against her. Now that I was all the way in, I stilled, taking in the sensations, pressing our foreheads together so I could breathe in her air.

"Sydney ..." I kissed her, sucking the end of her tongue. "You make me fucking wild for you."

Her arms crossed behind my neck. "That's just how I want you."

She barely had the last word out before I reared my hips and dived back in—a movement that caused her to scream.

A sound I loved.

A sound I wanted to duplicate over and over.

"Fuck yes," I roared, sliding in, holding her ass.

Teasing that back hole.

A place I'd never entered.

Since there was no better lube than a woman's wetness, I added a finger into her pussy, soaking it while I also fucked her with my cock. Once my skin was slick enough, I pulled my hand away and moved it around to the back.

I started with just the tip of my finger, going in as far as my nail.

"Ah!" she released, and she leaned forward and took my lip into her mouth.

Her teeth came next.

Biting.

She began grinding as I went in deeper.

"Ford!" she shouted.

I waited to see if she was going to tell me to stop.

But she didn't.

That was her way of asking for more.

More was what I gave her.

My movements began to match. As I thrust into her pussy, my finger did the same to her ass.

Water splashed from the tub, and beads of sweat dripped from my face.

And Sydney couldn't stop moaning.

Especially as she bounced over me each time I sank into her, riding me as I was fucking her.

"Damn it," I breathed. "You're making me want to come."

"That's what I want." Her hand was suddenly on my balls, playing with them, circling them over her palm. "I want you to make me feel it."

That was a demand I couldn't refuse.

"You're coming with me," I growled. My hand left her ass, and I lifted her off the edge and brought her into the water, setting her on top of me as I sat on the bench inside. "Ride me." I gripped her cheeks, holding her face close. "Ride me like you want me to fucking come."

With her arms now around me, her knees bent at my sides, she lowered to my base and rose to my tip.

Taking it.

Working it.

Squeezing it.

She twisted her hips, dancing over my cock, the water making the temperature inside her pussy even hotter.

"Sydney ..." I reached behind her, finding that forbidden entrance once again and giving her my entire finger. "That's it; fuck me."

She froze for just a second, as though she was getting used to the feeling again, her ass forming its own wetness, and that was when I knew she was enjoying it. When she ground over me because she wanted me in deeper.

With each pump of her hips, my finger dived in and rotated, letting her feel the friction from all sides.

She was bringing me closer, and her sounds told me I was doing the same for her.

"*Ohhh,*" she released. "You have no idea how good you feel."

But I did.

Because I was there.

About to fucking blow.

I gripped her hip, holding her firmly.

But she didn't stop; she didn't slow.

She took control of me.

She glided up and down my shaft, stroking me with her tightness, pulling every sensation from my tip.

I clamped her face, holding her mouth above mine. "I'm going to come." The tingling was in my balls, moving through me. "I need you to fucking come with me." I arched my back, my cock giving her three quick, hard, relentless punches. And just as she started to pant, as her tone was getting higher, I ordered, "Come right fucking now."

She did.

Screaming.

And she turned louder when I scooped up more of her wetness and began to pound into her ass, adding another finger to fill her.

To drive that fucking orgasm straight through her.

"Oh God!" She sucked in a lungful of breath. "Yes!"

Her cunt was like a suction cup, a magnet for my cum.

And streams of it were shooting out of me, draining into her.

"Sydney!"

Sparks ignited within me, and I pulled her face to mine, closing the distance between us, and I kissed her through each shudder.

Both of us quivered at the same time, tightening as the orgasms ricocheted through our bodies.

"Ford! Yes!"

I held on, the feeling so overwhelming.

So fulfilling.

"Goddamn it," I barked. "Your fucking pussy."

Her movements were slow, and I had a feeling her pussy was sensitive, but she continued to ride me until I was empty.

Until she stilled on top of me, our arms grasped around one another.

Until there was nothing but breath between us.

I released her face, my fingers moving to her neck, my other hand sliding out of her ass. "Fuck me." I pressed my mouth softly against hers. "You are something else."

I kissed her again but hard this time, taking in her breath, her scent, her taste.

And then I took a few seconds to calm myself down and caught a quick glance of the table, of the food that hadn't been touched. "You didn't eat."

"I was more focused on you."

"Then, I need to properly feed you."

She smiled. "I feel like you just did."

TWENTY

SYDNEY

"I don't wanna go home." Everly pouted when we were twenty minutes into the return flight to LA.

She was sitting in the seat beside mine, coloring with me, while Ford was on his laptop, getting caught up on work.

I agreed with Eve.

This trip had been magical, where home was often so predictable.

Full of routine.

Sometimes, it just felt nice to escape those things, especially when there was scenery as beautiful as Colorado surrounding me.

I glanced over at Ford, smiling as I thought of the moments from this trip. The ones we'd spent with Everly and the ones alone.

He'd given me something I would never forget.

Freedom when it came to my body, acceptance when it came to my heart.

But there was something that still ate at me, even more so when we were home.

That was the lie I'd fed Ford when I went in to interview.

It felt like such a miniscule part of our journey in comparison to everything that had happened between us, yet it was big enough to filter into my mind.

To dwell on the different ways I could tell him the truth.

Like I was doing now.

And I still had no idea.

"I wanna go back," Everly said in a whiny voice. "I don't wanna go home," she repeated. She glanced up at me and banged her crayon hard enough that the tip broke and fell to the floor. Her meltdown was brewing as she yelled, "Syd, I don't want to go home! I wanna go back to Colorado! And ride horses!"

The tears were immediate.

Her bottom lip sticking out, her hands balled.

"I wanna go back to the hotel!"

I was holding the orange crayon to the sheet we were sharing, finishing up the stripes I'd been drawing across the tiger's body, and set it down.

She needed strength.

Comfort.

She was overtired and hungry since she hadn't eaten much earlier.

I unbuckled her seat belt and pulled her into my lap. "Come here, little muffin." I kissed the top of her head and rocked her, her tears dampening my shirt. "Do you know how much fun we're going to have when we get back?"

More crying erupted, her body shaking against me.

"How much baking we're going to do and how many hikes we're going to take?" I pushed her wisps off her forehead, which was getting sweaty from all the crying. "And we also have some gardening to do, Miss E. There're some basil and tomatoes that we planted before we left that need to be tended to."

"But I wanna go back."

"We will, one day soon," I told her. "And we're going to visit so many other places as well. Isn't that something to be excited about?"

"I gu-ess."

I lifted the curls off her neck, twisting them into a messy bun that I secured with an elastic from my wrist. "Remember that list of desserts we came up with that we want to try to re-create?"

"Y-esss."

"Well, think of all the desserts we had on this trip that we can add to that list." I leaned into her ear. "Like those straw-berry brownies with chocolate fudge. Remember those?" I wiped the wetness off her face.

She nodded, and after several seconds, she replied, "Yum-my."

"And the homemade ice cream we can make."

Her crying subsided, her little brows rising. "With M&M's?"

"Sure, we can try adding M&M's to our ice cream."

"*Mmm.*" Her eyes went so wide after she rubbed them with her hands. "And that stuff like cookies."

I wrapped my arm around her shoulders. "We can defi-nitely put some cookie dough in our ice cream too." I paused. "See? We're going to be so busy that all we're going to be doing is having fun. Right?"

When she nodded this time, her bun bounced, her cheeks turning a light pink.

"Sounds like someone had the best time on this trip," Ford piped in, looking up from his laptop.

"We both did," I added.

285

"Wicked vacation hangover," Everly said, now smiling.

I slapped my hand over my mouth. "Oh my God, she must have heard me when I said that on the phone with Gabby this morning." I held back my laugh and continued, "Everly! You're not supposed to repeat those things."

I tickled her sides, and she snorted.

"Listen," Ford said, joining her, "everything she said is accurate."

"But still ..." I groaned.

I knew nothing was safe around a child, but I hadn't thought she'd heard me on the phone.

He winked at his daughter and said, "You know what, Eve? Your dad has a vacation hangover too. But that just means it was a good time and we need to plan another trip very soon."

"Utah!"

He put his laptop away and replied, "Do you think Sydney would like Utah?"

"*Looove.*" She picked up my orange crayon and began to play with it. "It's so cool."

"Then, maybe that's where we'll bring her." He looked at me. "How does that sound?"

I couldn't hold back my smile. "I was ready before you even asked."

"Let's go now!"

I held her hand within mine, her tiny fingers so warm and semi-sticky. "We can't go now, silly. Your dad has to work, and we have a lot to get done at the house."

"Maybe we can go in a few weeks," he voiced. "Get in a couple trips before she starts school."

"Yay!"

I wrapped my arms around her belly and pulled her toward my chest. "Is that a yay about starting school? Or a yay about Utah?"

"Utah!"

I chuckled. "I thought so."

I glanced over at Ford, who was sitting across from us, and he mouthed, *It's time.*

Time to tell Everly about us.

I sucked in a deep breath and held it in.

I had known this was coming. Ford and I had discussed that this was the right moment. I was just anxious about how she was going to react.

If she was going to resent me.

Or if this was going to make Everly and me closer.

Ford patted his lap. "Eve, can you come over here for a second? I want to tell you something."

She climbed off me and moved across the space between our seats, maneuvering her petite body around the table of food, and she plopped down on Ford's lap.

I tucked my legs underneath me, wrapping my arms around my stomach, watching him place her where he wanted her.

Once she was settled, he held out his hand, and Everly placed her fingers on top of his large palm.

"Do you know how Uncle D and Kendall love each other very much?"

"Yes."

He folded his fingers over hers. "And you know how Uncle Jenner is engaged to Jo and she has that big diamond she wears on her finger and they're going to get married?"

"I tried it on." Her mouth formed an O. "*Sooo* pretty, Daddy."

"Do you understand how your uncles are dating Kendall and Jo and how your daddy is single? Do you understand the difference?"

She shrugged.

"When I say to you that Uncle D and Kendall are boyfriend and girlfriend, do you know what that means?"

I appreciated his patience, how he was trying to break this down in the best possible way.

Everly responded by shrugging again. "Gonna kiss like Anna and Kristoff?"

Of course she would recite the characters from *Frozen*, her favorite movie.

That was an adorable comparison.

"Possibly," he replied. "But it means that Uncle D cares about Kendall so much that he wants to be with her forever." He kissed her forehead. "That he spends all his time with her. That they have sleepovers every night."

She giggled. "Uncle D says I kick him when I sleep over."

He squeezed her cheeks. "Because you're a lion when you sleep." His hand dropped from her face. "Since you were born, it's always just been us, hasn't it?"

She nodded.

"Your dad hasn't had a Kendall or a Jo, has he?"

"You have me, Daddy."

"I do." He nuzzled into her neck. "But now, I have someone else who I want to spend time with as well. Someone who means a lot to me and someone who means a lot to you."

"You do?"

"Yes, Everly, I do."

"Who's gonna sleep over?"

He brought her hand up to his lips and kissed it. "She might sleep over on occasion. Would you be all right with that?"

She said nothing.

I was sure she was trying to process what all this meant.

"Everly"—he turned her butt, so the two of them now faced me—"the woman I care about very much is Sydney."

I didn't know my role in this conversation, but I felt the need to say something.

For her to hear my side even if she had a difficult time understanding.

"And I care about your dad just as much, just like I care about you, Everly."

"Syd's my friend, Daddy."

That made me smile, and I said, "I will always be your friend. That will never change. And I'm still your nanny. That won't change either."

"What do you think about that?" he asked her.

She was quiet for a moment and finally responded, "Will we still do fun things together?"

"Oh, sweetheart," I said so softly, "of course we will. We'll do all the things we've done before."

"Yay!"

I connected eyes with Ford before he leaned toward Everly.

"You understand that means that Sydney is now my girlfriend and she's going to be at the house a lot more?" He turned her face, locking their eyes. "We're still going to have our special time together—I want you to know that. But Sydney will join us during some of those occasions, and sometimes, you and I will be alone."

She said nothing.

And then, slowly, a devilish grin came across her face. "Daddy, are you gonna smooch Syd like Uncle D smooched Kendall at my birthday party?"

This kid.

I couldn't possibly adore her more.

And if that was how she defined our situation, if she saw love as affection, then that was perfectly acceptable to me.

"Yes, baby, I'm definitely going to smooch Syd the way Uncle D smooched Kendall."

"*Ewww.*"

"*Ewww*," he mocked, planting several wet ones on her cheek. "How can you say my kisses are *ewww?*"

"Daddy!" She laughed.

He waited until she calmed to say, "Are you happy Sydney's my girlfriend?"

She bobbed her head.

"How about you go give her a hug? I think she could use one."

The anxiety started to leave my chest as she wiggled off his lap and hurried over to mine. She wrapped her arms around my neck and squeezed.

I held her with all my strength.

I was so grateful for this moment, the way she had accepted me into their lives from the very beginning.

How she was accepting me now.

Those feelings only increased when I heard, "Love you, Syd."

Oh God.

My heart swelled to the point that my eyes squinted, fighting back the tears that wanted to form. "I love you too, Everly."

When I opened my lids, I looked across the seat at Ford.

It's okay, he mouthed.

He knew.

And for that, I was even more grateful.

TWENTY-ONE

FORD

"Ford, this is beyond," Sydney said, shaking her head as she gazed at me. "I can't believe you put this together." She glanced down at her plate as the emotion began to fill her eyes. "I can't believe you did it all for me."

As the ocean lapped in the background, the sun setting over us, I reached across the table and took her hand in mine. "I know how much you love desserts—we both do"—I grinned— "so if there's anyone who can enrich your dessert life, it's Gloria."

A woman who had been in our lives for as long as we'd known Brett.

That was because she was his mother.

Not only did she own a dessert shop in Miami, but she'd also opened one in Jo's newest hotel in Utah.

The moment I'd planned this evening, a date night that involved taking Sydney to my parents' house in Malibu, I'd called Gloria. My assistant then arranged her travel, sending the plane to pick her up in Florida and having a car service bring her straight here so she could start baking.

Craig had shared the kitchen with her, serving an extremely light dinner—nothing that would sit in our stomachs, preventing us from enjoying everything Gloria had prepared.

And that was five courses of dessert.

Each was a different kind of treat, ranging from airy to heavy, allowing us to experience varying layers of richness.

Over each course, Sydney spoke to Gloria about techniques and ingredients.

Most importantly, with each bite, I saw the happiness building on her face.

"Honestly"—she blushed—"I'm in total heaven. You couldn't have planned a better surprise." She licked some white chocolate off her spoon. "This is an experience I'll never forget." She glanced toward the ocean. "This view"—she looked back at me—"this house. Craig, Gloria. All of it." She squeezed my fingers. "Thank you."

She never stopped appreciating what I did for her.

She never took it for granted.

I didn't get the impression that anyone had ever taken care of Sydney. She was a giver, not a taker. But I wanted to be that person—to ensure she never wanted for anything, to fulfill her.

I wanted her to know what it felt like to be cared for.

"We can come back whenever you want." I released her fingers to take the last bite of my cake. A dense chocolate and raspberry creation that had fudge and syrup, a burst of tartness and a swirl of something achingly sweet. "My parents only come here about two weekends a month. The rest of the time, it's ours if we want it."

"I'd love that."

"After Utah or before?"

She set down her spoon, laughing. "Considering we're going to Utah next week, I'd say, after."

"You don't have to say that. Like I mentioned, the two of us can come whenever you want."

"What about Everly?"

I wiped my mouth with a napkin, drinking the last of my wine. "My parents are dying to have her more. Escaping for a night a week isn't out of the question, Sydney." I poured more wine into my glass and topped hers off. "Didn't you say that you forced the Turners to go out once a week?" I held the glass and leaned into the edge of the table.

"You're right." She sighed. "I guess it just feels different when you're living it rather than being on the outside."

"Time together is not something we're going to struggle with."

It was an issue with the other women I'd dated.

But it wasn't going to affect Sydney and me.

I would make sure of that.

She ran her spoon across her plate, dipping it in several different sauces. "I can't believe we're going to Utah." She brought the utensil up to her mouth, swiping something red across her lip.

She'd chosen my favorite one.

The sight made me fucking growl.

"I still can't believe I've never been," she continued. "It's funny; for some reason, the Turners never traveled to mountain states."

"You're going to love it. The air, the scenery, the hotel I've chosen for us." I smiled. "The fact that Gloria has a bakery inside the lobby."

"I die."

I chuckled. "You will."

Her face lit up under the setting sun. Her hair blew in the breeze. Her eyes turned warmer despite how icy they appeared.

God, she was gorgeous.

I would never stop thinking that.

I would never be able to get enough of her.

I cleared my mind with another swig of wine and said, "Once Everly starts school and gets settled, I'd like for just the two of us to get away. I want you to choose where we go."

She pointed at her chest. "You want me to pick the location?"

I nodded. "Anywhere."

"Oh, that's tough. There are so many beautiful places I'd like to see."

"We can go to all of them."

"Ford ..." She exhaled, and her head dropped. She stayed like that for a moment until she placed her napkin down and got up from her chair. She came over to my side of the table and sat on my lap, wrapping her arm around my neck. "I feel so undeserving of you," she whispered. "Like this is all a dream that I'm soon going to wake up from."

"Stop thinking that way." I rubbed down her spine and up her sides. "You're mine. Nothing is going to change that."

As my words resonated, her body stiffened. "I have to tell you something. I don't know if this will change things. If you're now going to look at me with disgust ..." Her voice trailed off as an eruption of pain deepened her expression. "I don't even know how to tell you this." She took in some air, holding it in. "I've wanted to. It just never felt like the right time." She swallowed, her chest rising and falling so fast.

"I know, Sydney."

She scanned my eyes, searching. "You ... know?"

I held her tighter, pressing her side against my chest. "Is this about the interview?"

She nodded.

"About Hannah telling you to apply for the job?"

She nodded again and said, "You really do know."

I held her cheek, rubbing my thumb across it. "Hannah told me at Everly's birthday party."

"I wish I had been the one to tell you." She tried to look down, and I wouldn't let her. "I wish I hadn't been such a coward."

"You're not a coward. You're far from that. Hannah told you not to tell me. That's an entirely different scenario. You were just doing what she'd asked."

She was quiet for several seconds. "But I should have been more loyal to you"—her hand went to my chest—"regardless if I promised Hannah or not."

"Hannah couldn't believe you didn't tell me. She's obviously trusted you from the very beginning. Now, I think she'd be willing to hand you the keys to her life." I kissed her, needing her to feel some affection.

"But I was wrong. I lied." Her brows lifted. "And, oh God, I can't even imagine what you're thinking. You must be wondering if there are other things I've lied about." Her voice was rising. "Ford, I know my word doesn't mean much right now, but I swear to you, on Everly's life, that you know everything. I've kept nothing else from you."

I grabbed her hand off my chest and brought it up to my mouth, kissing the back of each finger. "I don't think that at all. I trust you."

"I'm sorry—"

I hugged her against me, holding her as close as I could get her. "It's over. I don't want you to give it a second thought."

She rested into me, silence building between us until she broke it with, "Why didn't you ask me about it?"

"When Hannah told me, I was going to mention it to you. Discuss it in some way. And then life happened, and it slipped my mind."

"But ... did it really?"

I held her face, so she could look at me. "Listen to me. I've learned many things from my daughter and the way she was brought into my life. You can't judge a person for the decisions they make even if it's right or wrong in that moment. What matters is how they handle it." I softened my voice as I said, "You told me the truth, Sydney. Whether it took an hour or a day or a few months is insignificant. Time isn't always the deciding factor."

She gazed back and forth between my eyes. "Why are you so forgiving?"

Why?

Fuck, there were so many reasons for that.

Reasons I wasn't getting into now.

Since I knew we were both done with dessert, unable to fit in another bite, I lifted her off my lap and set her on the deck.

I linked our hands and said, "Come with me."

I brought her down the long stairway to the beach, where we left our shoes at the very bottom and sank our bare feet into the sand.

We were only a few paces into the waves when I heard the softness of her voice.

"This is so pretty."

I had known the feel of the water would help change her mood. The saltiness hitting her nose. The grittiness of the beach below her feet.

And she needed to feel my forgiveness, so I held her hand up to my mouth, keeping it there as I replied, "When I usually come here, I'm carrying bags and a cooler and toys and boards and towels—every goddamn thing a five-year-old uses." I glanced toward the ocean, the sun just starting to dip below the horizon. "I'm so busy riding the waves with her and building sandcastles that I never take a second to really look around."

"To realize how much you love it."

I stopped walking and turned toward her.

"How much I love it," I repeated.

Words that hit me.

Words that triggered a response.

I cupped her face, studying her eyes and cheeks, her lips that I was still so fucking obsessed with. "Sydney ..."

Her teeth ground into her lip, like she was anticipating what I was about to say.

I kissed her, just briefly, a brush of lips and air. "You know how wild I am about you."

Her arms circled my waist, gripping me. "And I'm so wild about you."

"But there's more."

She nodded. "For me too."

I lowered, keeping our lips inches apart, and I breathed in her coconut scent. An aroma that was stronger than the ocean. And I felt something that was deeper than anything I'd ever experienced with another woman.

"Fuck ..." I pressed our noses together, needing her to feel my words as I said, "I love you."

And then I kissed her.

Harder this time.

Emptying my chest.

Emotionally surrendering.

"I love you," she breathed back.

TWENTY-TWO

SYDNEY

I opened the backseat door of Ford's SUV and said to Everly, "Jump in, my little muffin."

She climbed into her high-back booster seat and got settled. "Syd, I'm pooped."

I laughed, adjusting her placement and securing her in, locking the seat belts in place. "That makes two of us, girlie." I checked to make sure it was all tight. "Comfy?"

"Yep." She yawned, and once Ford joined us in the doorway, she added, "Daddy, that hike was *haaard*."

"I was trying to tire you out. Did it work?"

I knocked him on the shoulder—for Everly and for me. "It worked. We're exhausted."

"*Exhauuusted*," Everly echoed.

I shut the door and giggled to Ford. "That kid," I said before I went over to the other side of the SUV and climbed into the passenger seat.

Ford started up the car and pulled out of the lot. "Are we stopping for ice cream? Or are my girls too tired?"

"Ice cream!"

"We're never too tired for that," I told him.

His hand went to my thigh, and I watched him look into the rearview mirror and ask Everly, "Are you all packed for Utah? As of this morning, there were two empty suitcases in your room and clothes everywhere."

"I need my pink dresses," she huffed.

I glanced over my shoulder at her. There were beads of sweat on her forehead, and her ponytail was slick in the front. Even her wisps were matted down. There was a smear of dirt on her cheek, and her hot-pink sunglasses were tilted on her face.

I reached back and fixed her frames, making them even. "Tell your dad we need time to pack. We're girls; we can't be rushed."

"We can't be rushed, Daddy."

He slowed for the red light, smiling at me. "We leave at seven tomorrow morning. That isn't much time."

As I faced the front, I wrapped my fingers around his. "Don't worry. We'll get it done. We just need to feel out each outfit and decide if we'll be in the mood to wear it on our trip. It's called options, *Dad*. Get with it."

"Get with it, Dad," Everly repeated.

You're going to get it, he mouthed at me, joking.

I winked at him and turned toward Everly. "After ice cream and a bath, we're on it. Aren't we, little lady?"

"Yep!"

As I faced the windshield, something flashed across my vision.

A swirl of black.

And a sound followed, one I couldn't quite distinguish.

But then it hit me.

It was brakes.

Screeching.

From the car that was coming right for us.

My eyes widened.

My mouth opened.

"Ford!" I pushed my back against the seat. "The car!"

It didn't matter that it tried to slow.

It was moving fast.

Too fast.

There was no way out of this.

It was going to hit us.

"Ford!" I shouted again.

But he was already reacting, yanking the steering wheel to the right, sending us toward the side of the road.

"Hold on!" he yelled.

Our SUV veered.

There was another screech of tires.

I didn't know if it had come from us or the other driver.

And there was screaming, but that was all I heard.

"Oh my God!" I filled my lungs.

"Daddy!" Everly shouted.

I couldn't reach for her. I couldn't move.

And her voice was the last thing I heard before the crunch exploded in my eardrums.

The impact sent me to the door, and then I flew forward, where the airbag hit me in the face, stopping me from nailing the dashboard. I bounced against the seat, ricocheting forward and back until I could finally stop myself.

"Ford!" I couldn't breathe. I couldn't see. Everything in my head was ringing. "I smell smoke."

"It's the airbags," he said. His tone immediately rose as he said, "Everly! Everly, baby, are you okay?" When she didn't answer, he said again, "Everly! I need you to talk to me. I need to hear that you're all right."

She made a sound that I couldn't understand.

"Sydney," he said, distraught, "are you okay?"

I swallowed air down my throat, trying to move the airbag out of my way to free myself. "I don't know ..." I couldn't feel my body. When I rubbed my fingers together, they were all there. My toes wiggled. I could lift my legs. "I think so."

"Everly," Ford said, frantically trying to undo his seat belt to get to her. "Everly, baby girl, answer Daddy. Are you all right?"

Except he couldn't get out. The car that had hit us had crushed half of his door and half of Everly's—that whole side of the SUV jammed up.

I turned around and looked at Eve.

Her head was slumped forward.

Her hands limp.

"Oh God, Everly!"

There were noises outside.

More sounds that I couldn't process.

Shouting.

A horn that wouldn't stop blaring.

"Everly!"

I needed her to lift her head.

I needed to hear her voice.

I needed her to respond.

Why is she silent?

Why is her head down?

I reached for my seat belt, every bone aching as I got it undone. "Everly!"

Ford was holding his left arm in the air while he was trying to get his door open. "Everly, answer us. Talk to Daddy; tell me you're not hurt." His wrist was bent in an awkward direction, telling me something was seriously wrong with it. "Everly, talk to me."

"Stay there," I told him. "Your arm is broken. I've got her." I freed myself and got onto my knees, turning toward the backseat. I grabbed her leg, shaking it, trying to gain her attention. "Everly, look at me, baby." I waited. "Are you okay?"

As she lifted her head, her expression stabbed me in the chest.

A blast of concern now bubbling inside me.

Pain was etched across her face.

Her skin was pale, ghostly.

She took in a breath, her lips slowly parting, her eyes filling. "Daddy ..." The first tear dripped, followed by many more. "It hurts." And then, "Help ... Daddy."

"I can't open"—Ford slammed his fist into the door, shaking the SUV—"the fucking door. Get me the fuck out of this car!"

"You're going to hurt yourself even worse," I cried out to him.

"I don't give a fuck. I need to get to my daughter."

"I'm climbing back there right now." I slid through the small opening between our seats and landed on the seat beside Everly's. "Tell me where it hurts." I gently touched one leg and said, "Here?"

She didn't answer.

She just looked at me, confusion filling her eyes.

"How about here—"

"Ow!" she shouted when I reached her belly.

"What's going on, Sydney?! Tell me what's wrong!"

I lifted her shirt; a large bruise was forming on her abdomen.

"Oh God, Ford, there's a bruise on her side."

What does that mean?

I touched her forehead.

She was sweaty.

Not like when she'd been hiking.

This was clamminess that was growing across her face, seeping through her arms and legs.

As the tears fell from her eyes, she glanced toward the window, the glass cracked like a giant spiderweb. "Daddy ... where am I?"

My heart catapulted into the back of my throat. "You don't know where you are?"

"Everly, tell me what's wrong, baby," Ford said. "Tell me what you're seeing."

She looked at me, dazed.

"Everly?" I said.

"Daddy ... head hurts." She lifted her hand to her eye and winced.

Fuck.

"Ford, she looks confused."

My fingers shook as I touched her.

My stomach churned.

"Ford—"

"Something's wrong!" he yelled. "Something's fucking wrong!"

I didn't realize he had turned around and was leaning across the opening I'd climbed through, his hand on Everly's thigh.

"She needs a doctor," I told him. "Call 911."

I couldn't stay calm.

I couldn't stop the worry.

As I stared at him, his arm dangling, the position of it even worse now, he reached for the door again and tried to pry it off. "Open the fuck up!"

The movement shook Everly, and I screamed, "Ford, stop!"

"I need out. I need to get a fucking doctor."

He was stuck.

That only left me.

When I turned toward my door, someone was opening it.

"Is everyone all right in here?"

"No!" I gasped. "Call 911!" I pushed myself off the seat, rushing past the person who had opened my door, and yelled, "I need a doctor!"

My ears buzzed, and my eyes blinked as I took in all the chaos.

People.

Cars.

Everywhere.

A mix of voices, a jumble of words I could barely make out.

But enough that I heard, "Call 911."

"Break the fucking window."

"Shouldn't we wait until the ambulance arrives?"

"What if she dies?"

"They're on their way. Two minutes out."

I put my hands over my ears, trying to block out everything everyone was saying.

But the moment I had them secured like earmuffs, there was a hand on my arm, shaking me, forcing my attention toward them.

It was a woman.

She was now holding my shoulders and said, "Help is on the way. We called 911."

I clung to her arms. "She needs help," I panted. "Everly needs help."

"Don't worry, honey; they're close. Can't you hear them?"

I shook my head. "Hear them?"

I tried to listen.

But there was too much noise.

Too many people.

Too much movement.

Ford.

Oh my God, Ford.

I let the woman go and turned toward the car, leaning into the opening. "Ford, the ambulance is on the way." I dropped onto the seat, my hand going to her cheek. "Eve."

Her face was becoming paler.

Her skin damper.

"They need to hurry!" I yelled out the door.

Questions then came from behind me.

Voices.

More than one.

"Is everyone all right?"

"Does anyone besides the little girl need help?"

"I think your arm is broken, buddy."

I ignored them and rubbed Everly's cheek, up to her forehead, whispering, "You're going to be okay." I then looked at Ford and added, "She's going to be okay."

Her little sounds were what bothered me.

The whimpers of pain.

The way she appeared so delirious.

And the way Ford's arm was angled, the way his hand was hanging.

"Paramedics here. Can you let us in?"

Paramedics?

I turned around, and there were two men at the base of the door, dressed in black.

"Sydney, let them in!" Ford shouted. He then addressed the paramedics and said, "Help my daughter right now!"

I slid off the seat and backed up as one of the men reached inside the SUV.

"She's going to be okay, honey."

I turned toward the voice.

It was a woman.

Was it the one from before?

I didn't know.

But she continued, "The paramedics are going to fix her right up," she said.

She was holding my shoulders.

She was staring me in the eyes.

"She's not good," I whispered. "Her skin ..." I swallowed. "She's so pale."

"Don't you worry." She nodded behind me. "Look, they've got her now, and they're going to help her."

I turned around, and Everly was being carried out of the SUV and placed on a stretcher.

"Daddy," Everly cried. "I want my daddy!"

I didn't know if the tears had been in my eyes this whole time or if seeing Everly on a stretcher had caused them, but they were streaming, and they wouldn't stop.

"Be careful with her!" I shouted.

As they started to wheel her away, Ford climbed into the backseat and came out the door.

I threw my arm around his back. "Are you okay?"

"I just need to be with her."

"Your arm—"

"It's fine, Sydney."

"It's not fine," a woman said, stopping us before we even took a step. Her uniform told me she was also a paramedic. She held his arm with gloved hands. "It's definitely broken."

He pulled his arm away from her and said, "I need to be with my daughter."

"Then, I'll look at it when we get in the ambulance." Her gaze moved over to me. "Were you in the car with them?"

I nodded. "Yes."

"Do you need to get checked out as well?"

"No, I'm okay."

"You two, follow me," she said.

As I held Ford, we hurried behind the paramedic, weaving around the people who had pulled over to watch or help along with the firemen and police.

When we arrived at the back of the ambulance, a paramedic was standing there, gripping the doors.

He asked, "Who's going with her?"

"I am," Ford replied. He looked at me. "Meet us at the hospital."

The hospital.

I tried to find my breath, my chest pounding. "How? What hospital?"

"Cedars-Sinai," the paramedic replied.

He helped Ford into the back of the ambulance, and the doors shut, the vehicle pulling away.

I couldn't take a deep breath.

The flashing lights were now blurred from the wetness filling my eyes.

"The hospital," I exhaled. "Will someone take me?"

"I will," I heard.

I didn't know I had even asked the question out loud.

I didn't know who had agreed.

But when I turned toward the voice, there was the woman.

"Come on. My car is right over here. We'll follow the ambulance."

I said nothing as her arm moved around my back, taking some of my weight, helping me to her car. She opened the passenger door and set me inside, closing it once my feet were in.

Once she got in the driver's seat, she wasted no time, pulling out and catching up to the ambulance.

"Oh God," I cried as the rear lights flashed across my face.

"I can't believe this happened." My chest felt like it was going to cave. "We were just on our way to get ice cream."

A hand was on my back, rubbing circles over me. "She's going to be all right."

My brain was spiraling.

Fear was filling it.

In a way that was almost paralyzing, causing a wave of nausea to rush up my throat.

I wrapped my arms around my stomach, rocking back and forth.

"Is there someone you should call?" she asked.

I looked at her.

"Your parents? Your husband's parents? So they can meet you at the hospital?"

She was right.

I needed to call his family.

I needed to let them know what had happened.

"Yes." I forced the bile down. "Yes, I'll do it right now."

I reached into my back pocket, where I always kept my phone.

Thank God it was there, that the accident hadn't caused it to fall out.

I stared at the screen, telling myself to pull up my Contacts.

I needed to phone his family.

They all needed to know.

But who should I call first?

His mother was the first number I came across, and I held the phone to my face, listening to it ring.

Please answer.

Please.

"Hello, Sydney—"

"There's been an accident." I flattened my hand against my

chest, holding it there. Pushing. "A car hit us, and Everly and Ford are on their way to the hospital."

"What?" Her voice rose as she said, "Are they injured? Are you hurt?"

"I'm fine." I leaned into the door, needing something to hold me. "Something is wrong with Ford's arm. I think it's broken and ..." My throat tightened, my face soaked with tears. They dripped onto my lips as I said, "I don't know about Everly. They took her away on a stretcher. Something isn't right."

"Oh God," she gasped. "What hospital?"

"Cedars-Sinai."

"I'm on my way. You don't have to notify the boys. I'll tell them. I'll see you as soon as I can."

I nodded even though she couldn't see me, and I hung up.

The phone dropped onto my lap.

And I kept my eyes on the ambulance, only closing them to wipe my face, until we were pulling up to the Emergency Department. The ambulance went to the left, around the building, and the woman drove me to the right.

She stopped by the front doors.

"Thank you," I said to her.

"Go be with your husband and daughter."

I couldn't correct her.

I could only say, "Okay."

I looked down and grabbed my phone.

I didn't have a purse.

I didn't have any money.

"I don't have anything to give you," I said. "Money or—"

"Nonsense. Go inside. Go help them."

I didn't know why, but I threw my arms around her neck, and I squeezed her.

So tightly.

And she squeezed me back.

I cried, "Thank you," again.

The second we released each other, I rushed out the door and into the hospital.

"Everly," I panted to the nurse at the front desk. "Everly Dalton. She's in the ambulance."

"I need you to calm down and catch your breath, so I can understand what you're saying," she replied.

I tried to swallow.

I tried to breathe.

And once there was enough air in me, I explained the situation to her.

"Come with me," she said, and she led me to a private room. "Wait here. Someone will be in shortly."

I didn't have time to reply before the door shut.

And I was alone.

The room was all white.

Except for the door. That was brown.

And my hands. Those were brown too.

Covered in dirt.

Somehow.

I paced the small space, my hiking boots squeaking on the floor.

Back and forth.

I checked my phone, the screen showing me nothing, and I shoved it back into my pocket.

I didn't know how many passes I'd made, but when I heard the door open, I froze mid-step and turned toward it.

Ford was walking in.

His arm in a sling, a bandage on his forehead, another on his neck.

I threw my arms around him. "You're okay." I pressed my cheek against his chest. "Thank God you're okay." I finally pulled my head back and reached up to his face, holding it, taking him all in. "How is she?"

He wrapped his uninjured arm around me and said nothing for a few seconds. "I don't know. They took her somewhere, and they won't tell me anything."

"I called your mom. She's on her way here. She's going to get in touch with your brothers."

Silence built between us as we stared at each other.

An aching quietness that I felt in my gut.

"That car"—his head dropped, his hand rubbing across the top of his hair—"it came out of fucking nowhere. I didn't have time. I couldn't ..."

"Ford"—I gripped his good arm, shaking him, making him look at me—"this isn't your fault."

"But she's back there. All by her-fucking-self. And she's hurt. And that's my fucking fault."

"No, it's not, do you hear me?" I squeezed him, trying to make him listen. "You did everything you could to help her. There's nothing you could have done to stop that car from hitting us."

"Fuck, Sydney!"

He got out of my hold and paced toward the chairs in the back of the room. When he reached them, he stood over the set, staring down at the metal and cushions. "She fucking needs me, and I can't be with her." One-handed, he lifted a chair into the air, held it over his head, and smashed it against the wall.

"Ford—"

"I'm supposed to fucking protect her." The hinges that held the metal together snapped, sending the cushions across the room. "I promised her I would always protect her." He lifted the second chair, but when he had it up, he didn't smash it like the first one. He held it against his chest and then lowered it, gripping the armrest. "When I looked at her on that stretcher, she was so fucking tiny." The emotion in his voice was thick, the tears in his eyes heavy. "She was in so much pain, enough that it made her pass out." He looked up, our eyes connecting. "Oh God, what if she doesn't make it?" His chest heaved. "What if she doesn't survive?" He fell into the seat that he'd just been holding, his arm resting on his knee, his palm holding his forehead. "I can't live in a world that Everly's not in."

I rushed to his side, falling to the floor in front of him, hugging his legs.

"She has to be okay, Sydney. She has to be."

I clung to him even harder, pressing my face against his knee. "She will be." I swallowed, my own tears dropping. "She's going to be just fine."

I didn't move off the floor.

I stayed just like that, wrapped around him, giving him my comfort.

But it didn't help.

Because with each breath that he took, the emotion continued to build on his face. The anger as well as he squeezed his fingers into a fist. The angst in his inhales every time he sucked in air.

The only time it all stopped was when the door opened, Ford's mom and dad rushing into the room. Dominick and Jenner were right behind. Jo and Kendall too.

Ford's mom pulled him into a hug.

"Mom, they have my baby girl."

The sound of him, the pain, it caused me to cry even harder, and Dominick wrapped his arms around me.

"Everything's going to be okay," Dominick said, not letting me go.

More arms circled me.

More words were said.

I heard Ford speak. I heard him give answers.

I heard his family's encouragement that was supposed to make us feel better.

But it didn't.

The unknown was too much.

I just wanted one thing—we all did.

While we waited, I couldn't look at my phone.

I couldn't take a deep breath.

Not until the door opened one final time, a nurse walking into the room, who said, "Which one of you is Ford Dalton?"

"That's me," Ford said, taking several steps forward. "Where's Everly? What's happening to her?"

A stabbing pain shot through my stomach, and I gripped it with both hands, my fingers shaking so badly that I was almost hitting my ribs.

The nurse said, "Everly's in surgery. She has a ruptured spleen, multiple broken ribs. A concussion. But she's a little fighter, and we anticipate a full recovery."

The entire room sighed.

"However, she's lost a great deal of blood. We need to do a blood transfusion." She continued to look at Ford, adding, "We've had quite a few emergencies today, and we're running low on O positive. I came out to ask if you'll donate blood to your daughter."

He stared at her.

He said nothing.

And after several seconds passed, he took a few steps toward the remaining chair and back to the door.

He was pacing again.

What is he doing?

Why isn't he rushing out the door to donate his blood?

"Ford?" I said.

He looked at me, and then he glanced at the nurse. "I can't donate to her. I'm not O positive. I'm AB."

"AB?" The nurse paused, confusion filling her face. "In my thirty-two years as a pediatric nurse, I've never seen or heard of a child having O positive if one of their parents is AB."

He took a breath, holding it in. "That's because I'm not her biological father."

TWENTY-THREE

FORD

Silence penetrated the room. It was so quiet that I could have heard a fucking pin drop.

I knew the bomb I'd just detonated. I knew it would affect them tremendously, but I couldn't worry about that now.

"I'm—"

"What did you just say?" my father voiced, cutting me off as I was about to address the nurse. "You're not Everly's biological father? But how?"

I continued looking at the nurse, ignoring my father as I tried again to say, "I'm happy to give AB, but I know that won't be of any help."

She shook her head. "It won't."

"I can donate," Sydney said from behind me.

I turned to face her as she was pushing herself off the wall, walking toward the nurse and me.

"I happen to be O positive," she added.

I glanced at the nurse as she asked, "Are you all right with this? Her blood will be tested before it's given to Everly."

"Yes," I replied. "Of course."

The nurse held the door open a little wider and voiced, "Please come with me," to Sydney.

As they disappeared and the door shut, I felt everyone's eyes on me.

Still, I didn't worry about them.

They weren't important at the moment.

I needed my baby out of surgery.

I needed her safely in my arms.

Where she belonged.

I didn't know what her recovery was going to look like, how long it would take her to heal, but I knew I wasn't going to leave her side until she was back to being the little girl she'd been before this fucking nightmare.

"Ford ..." The sound of my father speaking my name didn't come as a surprise.

I had known it was only a matter of seconds before he pressed his questions.

With my family behind me, I said over my shoulder, "Not now."

"Not now, honey?" My mom walked over and placed her hands on my shoulders. "I just found out my granddaughter isn't yours by blood, and you don't want to talk about it?" Her bottom eyelids were dark and heavy, as though the weight of today was dragging through her. "Please, Ford. At least say something." She waited. "I understand today's been a tragedy—we're all a mess over it—but the nurse said she's going to be all right, and so are you once her surgery is over and you let them take an X-ray of your arm."

Even though the pain was almost debilitating, my arm was the last thing on my mind.

I hadn't even let them do more than give me a sling when I arrived at the ER.

My only focus was on my baby girl.

And Everly's story was one I never intended on telling.

I was going to go to the grave with that truth.

In my mind, it was no one's business.

Goddamn it, she was mine.

That was all that mattered.

But as I looked at my mother, I knew she needed something to satisfy her.

Something that jarred my patience.

"Fuck," I gritted through my teeth. When I finally glanced up, I felt all the eyes on me. "What do you want to know?"

"What do we want to know?" my mother asked. "How about everything?"

"We're all a bit flabbergasted right now," Dominick said.

Kendall nodded.

So did Jenner, and he asked, "Why didn't you tell us?" His eyes narrowed. "Have you known this whole time?"

I felt like I was standing in front of a firing squad.

I needed time to get my thoughts straight before I opened up and told this story. So, after I paced several times, I found the nearest wall, and I pushed my back against it.

I breathed.

And the moment Sydney walked through the door, a Band-Aid over the crease of her elbow, an expression I couldn't quite read on her face, I knew it was time.

She shut the door behind her and walked over to me. "She's still in surgery. The nurse thinks it'll be about forty-five minutes until you can see her." She ran her fingers over my arm. "Are you okay?"

I didn't reply.

I just looked up at the group.

If I gave them pieces of Everly's past, they would only ask for more.

They'd want the joints, the filler.

The timeline.

The legal process.

In this room, I'd be put on trial.

The only way to share this tale was to start at the beginning.

I pressed my foot against the wall and shifted my gaze across each of their faces. "From the very beginning, I knew something was off. Aside from you all asking if I'd gotten a paternity test, it went deeper than that. It was a feeling I just can't explain, something that wasn't sitting right, so I went and got the test done." I took a breath, the exhale burning through my nose as I remembered when I'd read the results and how, even though I'd had my suspicions, the news had stabbed me in the darkest places. "As you know now, it proved I wasn't her father. But I couldn't let it rest. I needed the truth. Since I wasn't able to find Rebecca, I hired Jefferson, our in-house PI, and he tracked her down. While Mom watched Eve, thinking I was on a work trip, I flew to where Rebecca was living, and she confessed and signed the paperwork I had drafted."

Silence ticked.

The only thing I heard was their breathing, the sound of Jenner moving against the wall, Sydney's hand as it traveled up and down my arm.

"I need to understand this," my mother finally said. "I thought she gave you paperwork when she left Everly with you?"

"She did," I replied. "Those papers were generated under the presumption that I was Everly's biological father. They were legal documents that contained false information." I stilled, breathing. "She knew I wasn't the father."

"That doesn't make any sense," my dad said. "Why did she give you a child who wasn't yours?"

"Everly's father was a criminal. A son of a bitch who had

quite the rap sheet. Rebecca knew he wouldn't provide." My hands fucking shook as Rebecca's words echoed in my head, causing my arm to throb. "Aside from the father's lack of interest in childrearing, Rebecca didn't want to be a mother. What she had told me the night she gave Everly to me—the abortion attempt, the adoption arrangement—that was all true."

"So, she devised a plan," Dominick said.

I looked at my oldest brother and nodded. "Once she found out she was pregnant"—I lifted my uninjured arm, pressing my palm onto the top of my head—"I was the lucky guy who walked into the bar at just the right time."

"You're well dressed," Jenner said. "You opened a tab with a black card. She asked a few questions, found out you're a lawyer, where you live—she had her man." He shook his head. "She probably got you so drunk that you wouldn't remember if you'd put on a condom."

That was the way he saw it.

Probably the way all of them did.

Not me.

I wasn't the sucker who'd walked into the bar that night.

I was the man who'd eventually become Everly's father.

I didn't care that I'd gotten hustled.

I didn't care that I'd gotten lied to.

She wasn't a fucking burden.

She was the biggest blessing of my life.

I looked at Sydney, who hadn't known any of this. Who had apologized endlessly for lying when there was something I was holding back from her.

Something I'd like to think I would have eventually told her, but I didn't know if that was true.

And as I stared into her eyes, I said, "She wanted her daughter to have a better life. Better than hers. Better than growing up in foster homes, like she had, apparently. So, she gambled on me." I looked at my family. "She chose the right man."

"I told you not to trust that woman," my father said. "The moment we rushed over to your house the night you got her, we asked you if you were positive the baby was yours."

I came from a family of lawyers. I'd been trained at birth not to trust anyone.

But this wasn't about trust.

This was about love.

This was about Everly.

"And I told you she was my daughter," I shot back. "Because, despite how fucking stressed and overwhelmed I was, I wasn't going to give her up." I clenched my fingers together, the same way Everly's tiny hand had gripped my finger that night. "She was mine."

More silence spread across the room.

"I can't fathom why you wouldn't tell us," my mother said.

"Why?" I took my time glancing at each of their faces. "Would you have loved her any differently?"

"You still should have told us," my father said.

"What would it have changed?" I challenged. "The way you looked at her? The way you treated her? Nah. It wouldn't have made a difference. That little girl is my daughter." I looked at my parents. "She's your granddaughter." I glanced at my brothers. "She's your niece. Period."

Dominick's expression told me he agreed.

Jenner's too.

"But what if, legally, you lose all parental rights?" Dominick asked. "What if Rebecca comes back and takes her from you?"

"She can't, Dominick. Give me more credit than that, asshole." My voice lowered as I added, "Her parental rights were terminated. I legally adopted Everly."

It didn't matter that she'd just turned five and she'd legally been mine for almost as many years; saying those words came with such relief.

"What about the father?" Jenner asked. "You haven't mentioned anything about his rights. Does he not know she's his? Or that he has a daughter? What if he comes back and wants her?"

I glanced at the floor, a path that I'd paced several times today. "He's dead."

Another fact Jefferson had found during the legal process.

A copy of his death certificate was even in my safe.

"Ford ..." Sydney's voice cut through the quiet room, her fingers still tightly linked with mine. "I know Rebecca has no contact with Everly, but does she have any desire to?"

"No," I replied. "Every year, on Everly's birthday, I send her a photo. I just want her to see her. I ..." My voice trailed off as I exhaled, trying to come up with a way to describe my motivation. "I don't know. I guess I just want her to know she's well cared for and loved. That there's someone in this world who's a part of her." I took in Sydney's eyes, their softness, gentleness. "She's never once acknowledged the photos or reached out."

"You're a good man, Ford."

I glanced at Dominick just as he finished speaking. "I wouldn't say that, Dom. I'm just a father who loves his daughter with every fiber of his being. When Rebecca handed over that little girl, when I held her, when I smelled her, she was mine. No one and nothing would ever take her from me."

"I still wish you had told us," my mother said.

I gazed at her.

And I tried to put myself in her position, to process what it would feel like to be hit with this news.

"Mom, I can understand how shocking this is, especially to find out this way, but I want you to remember something.

Everly is half me. The moment Rebecca set her in my arms, my duty was to protect her. One day, I'm going to have to tell that little girl this same story, and she deserves to hear it from me. That was the main reason I didn't tell anyone." My stare shifted between each family member. "What matters, what's most important, is that she's a Dalton, whether she has our blood or not."

The moment the words left my mouth, there was a knock on the door, the same nurse walking in as before.

She glanced around the room until she found me and said, "Everly's in recovery. You're more than welcome to go see her now."

Without any hesitation, I pushed myself off the wall, continuing to hold Sydney's hand. We walked out of the room and followed the nurse down the hallway.

I needed Sydney with me.

I didn't know what we would be walking into, how banged up Everly would be.

But I needed Sydney's strength.

She held my fingers with both of her hands, keeping up with my pace as we passed several corridors, finally arriving at post-op.

Once we got to Everly's bed, my chest ached.

There were pads stuck to her chest, machines beeping as they monitored her, a needle taped to the crease of her elbow, which was attached to a full IV stand.

My baby.

She was so tiny in the bed, her head so small as it sank into the pillow.

I looked at the nurse as she said, "She's going to be a bit out of it from the anesthesia. Don't worry; we've got all eyes on her, and we'll be handling her pain."

I thanked her and moved to Everly's side, sitting on the bed next to her. I pressed my lips against her forehead, my eyes closing as I breathed her in. "My princess. I love you so much."

As I pulled my mouth away, her eyes fluttered open.

And as she stared at me, I saw the recognition in her eyes.

"Daddy ... where am I?"

I held back the emotion—she didn't need to see that—and kissed her cheek. "We were in a car accident, and the doctors had to fix you up, but you're going to be okay, baby girl." I held her hand and brought it up to my face. Her skin, usually so warm, was cold, the scent nothing like I was used to. "You've been such a big girl, my Eve. You fought so hard today and did so well."

There was movement on the other side of Everly as Sydney took a seat next to her.

Everly's lips were so dry as they parted. "Hi, Syd."

"Eve," Sydney whispered, "my little muffin." She rubbed Everly's leg over the blanket. "You're the strongest girl I know."

Everly's eyes got heavy, and they closed.

I didn't panic.

I knew she would go in and out until the anesthesia wore off.

But just because she was sleeping didn't mean I was going to leave her side.

I wasn't going anywhere.

I'd continue listening to the beep of the machines. I'd watch her chest rise and fall.

And I'd think about how grateful I was that her injuries were treatable, that she would make a full recovery.

I rubbed my hand over her forehead, sinking my fingers into her curls, my thumb reaching down to brush her cheeks. "My ever and ever, my little Everly."

"Ford ..."

My eyes shifted to Sydney.

"Is that how you came up with her name?"

I was sure she had other questions.

I was sure the conversation I'd had in the waiting room was far from over.

But I nodded and replied, "When Rebecca placed her in my arms and I finally made my way inside my house and it all hit me"—I swallowed and tried to take a breath, the emotion returning—"I knew only one thing. Ever and ever—that was how long she'd be mine."

TWENTY-FOUR

SYDNEY

"How are the patients doing today?" Gabby asked as I set my phone on speaker mode, placing it on the counter in my bathroom.

Even though Ford had told me to take all the time I needed, I'd given myself thirty minutes to shower and get dressed and return to his side of the house.

I didn't want to take a second longer.

Because even though he didn't want to put any pressure on me, he needed me.

Everly did too.

And in my heart, there was no better feeling.

"Eve is much better," I told her as I rubbed lotion over my skin. "But her ribs are still so sore. Every time she moves, she winces."

"Oh God, can't they give her something to make this go away? That poor little girl has been through enough. This pain needs to stop already."

"You're telling me." I put the lotion away and applied some

deodorant along with adding serum and moisturizer to my face before I took a seat on the bench in the back of the bathroom, waiting for the slickness on my skin to dry. "It's just going to take time. But we're icing and giving her Motrin—that's really all we can do."

"And Ford? How's he doing after surgery?"

My pillar of strength, who hadn't even acknowledged anything was wrong with his arm until I forced him to get it looked at. Of course, that was after Everly got out of surgery and was in her hospital room and I promised him, along with his mom, that we wouldn't leave her side while he was gone.

The way his arm had broken wouldn't heal with just a cast. He'd needed a three-hour surgery and the insertion of several screws and a plate. He'd be wearing a cast for up to twelve weeks.

"I can see the pain all over his face even though he won't admit it." I sighed. "He's far too worried about Everly to give himself any thought. At least he's somewhat following the surgeon's orders and taking it easy."

"You've got your hands full, woman."

I looked at myself in the mirror above the sinks. My wet hair was wrapped in a towel, pulling my forehead high. My skin dewy, giving me that perfect glow.

But underneath all this stretching and lotion were dark bags under my eyes and probably some heavy crow's-feet.

The last week had been an emotional tornado.

My worry shifted from Everly to Ford, depending on the hour. Sometimes, I was equally sick with worry over the both of them.

They were going to be fine—I knew that.

But that didn't mean my concern just vanished.

It also didn't mean the accident was behind us.

Constant reminders consistently popped up, like the police who had come to the hospital to take our statements. The insurance company that Ford had to deal with to handle his totaled SUV. The news reports that had been aired across every location station since the accident was so large that it had shut down the entire road for hours.

And then there was the poor old man who had fallen asleep behind the wheel—the cause for all of this.

Nothing premeditated, nothing malicious.

Just an unfortunate mishap that could have happened to any of us.

But it'd resulted in something we would never forget.

"I do have my hands full," I finally replied. "But as long as I can see them both and be with them, that's all that matters."

"Syd ..."

I continued to stare at my reflection, pulling the towel tighter around me. "Yes?"

"Are you okay? I feel like no one's asked you that question, nor have you even taken the time to think about what your answer would be. You've just been so focused on Eve and Ford."

I'd been in this bathroom for almost twenty minutes, making myself smell better than I had in days, and I hadn't thought once about whether I was okay.

I hadn't even thought about myself.

I'd thought about Ford and Eve.

If they needed anything while I was gone.

What I would do for them once I returned.

"I don't know," I answered. "I think so. I'm sore still."

"Sydney, I know you better than you know yourself." She paused. "And I know you're not okay. I can hear it in your voice."

I couldn't hide it.

I didn't know why I was even trying to.

But now that it was out there, I couldn't seem to rein the emotion back in.

"Gabs," I whispered as the first tear fell, reaching toward the counter for a tissue and my phone, holding both to my face, "it was so scary."

"I know."

Once the first tear dripped down my cheek, there were so many behind it. My lips quivered; my chest pounded.

"The noise from the accident, the metal on metal, and then seeing Everly being carried away on a stretcher and Ford injured, and then the explosion of him throwing the chair and ..." I didn't tell her that Ford wasn't Eve's biological father—that wasn't my news to share—but there was that too. I took a breath, my lungs so tight. "I honestly think it's going to be a while before those images are out of my head."

"I don't think they'll ever leave you, babe."

When I glanced at my reflection, I didn't see someone who was weak.

I saw someone who was surviving.

And as I cried to my best friend in my bathroom, the heaviness inside my chest started to break away.

"You're probably right," I told her.

"But do you know what will come out of this? You and Ford and Everly are going to be stronger, the three of you—together."

I dabbed the tissue under my eyes. "You're probably right about that too."

"I know I'm right. Now, do you need anything? Booze? Chocolate? An escape car? A trip to Cancun? Name it, and it's yours."

I laughed.

It felt so good and was so needed.

"No, you've already done so much."

She'd sent two massive bouquets, which were sitting in Ford's kitchen, one entirely made of pink flowers. She'd had multiple meals delivered to me in the hospital. Not to mention, she'd sat with me and his family during Ford's surgery.

"Um, hello? That's what besties are for, which reminds me. I'm coming over tomorrow night for drinks. I don't care if I have to sit with you and Ford and Eve on the couch or snuggle between you guys in bed. I'm there. I'm bringing multiple bottles of wine. I'm staying the night. And we're drinking *alll* of it."

I exhaled the largest breath of air. "I can't wait."

"Then, I'll see you tomorrow. I love your ass."

"I love you more."

We hung up, and I quickly threw on some clothes and braided my hair, so I wouldn't have to dry it. My face was a mess from crying, so I lathered on some concealer and blush, a little mascara, and I made my way across the garage into the house.

The smell of Craig's cooking instantly hit me.

He'd arrived while I was gone, and I'd forgotten he was even coming.

"Chicken soup?" I asked as I walked into the kitchen.

Craig stood at the stove, stirring the large pot.

My mouth watered as I got closer, the scent becoming stronger.

"The one and only," he replied. "It cures everything."

I smiled. "Then, we'll each take double servings."

"You got it."

I continued into the living room, where Ford and Everly were spread across the couch, an animal show playing on the TV.

"How are my favorites doing?" I asked, sitting on the small

bit of cushion between their heads, running my hands through their hair.

"Syd, you're missing the lions." She reached up and played with the end of my braid. "They're roaring all over the place."

I kissed her forehead. "I'm here now, so I can get all caught up."

Ford tilted his head back to look at me, staring for several seconds before he said, "You were only gone for twenty-five minutes."

"I told you I just needed to shower."

"And I told you to take your time."

I winked. "I did. I even shaved."

He laughed. "I guess that's a good thing since Malorie is on her way over."

"Who?"

"The massage therapist my mother uses. She's coming to give you a two-hour massage."

My chest felt tight again, but for an entirely different reason. "You're kidding ..."

"And then you're having dinner with Kendall and Jo and Hannah tonight. They wanted to surprise you, but I figured you'd want a little time to get ready."

The tears were threatening to return to my eyes. "But what if you guys need me—"

"Dominick and Jenner are coming with them, and they're going to stay here while you're gone. In their words, they're going to play nurse—whatever the fuck that means."

"Daddy! Bad word! You put a dollar in the swear jar!"

"Fudge. Whatever the fudge that means."

I ran my hand across his beard. It had grown so much thicker; it hadn't been groomed since the accident. "I don't know what to say ..."

He pushed himself up and kissed me.

"*Ewww*, Daddy! Enough smoochin'."

I laughed as we separated and said to Ford, "I love you." And then I pressed my lips to Everly's cheek and whispered, "I *looove* you."

TWENTY-FIVE

FORD

I was just finishing a set of curls when Everly came running into my home gym, shouting, "*Bye, Daaaddy!*"

Her hair, which was getting so long, bounced like the top of a mop, her glittery shoes squeaking across the rubber flooring.

"No running."

She only slowed when she reached me. "Oopsie. Too late." She raised her arms in the air.

I placed the weights down and lifted her up, holding her against my chest, and noticed Sydney standing in the doorway. Her hand was wrapped around the handle of Eve's pink suitcase. "Looks like you have everything packed for Mimi and Papa's house."

"Yep." She made a face. "You're sweaty."

I laughed. "Are you going to be a big girl and not kick Mimi in the face when you sleep with her and Papa tonight?"

She giggled. "Daddy, I don't do it on 'urpose."

I used my weaker arm to tickle her and roared into her neck, "You don't do it on *puuurpose.*"

"Daddy, you sound like a cat, *puuuring.*"

This kid.

I cuddled her into me. "I'm going to miss you tonight." I kissed her cheek. "I love you."

She giggled, still feeling the tickles, and said, "More than all the stars in the sky."

Every time she'd said that since the accident, it was more meaningful.

It had been sixteen weeks, and I would never know that girl had experienced a single second of pain.

But we talked about it. We kept the communication open. The last thing I wanted was there to be emotional triggers that had a lasting effect.

"Be good," I told her. "Listen to your grandparents and don't stay up too late." I gave her another kiss and set her down. "And don't run. There are too many things in here that you can trip on."

"*Okaaay*, Daddy." She joined Sydney in the doorway.

"Your mom will be here any second," Sydney said. "I'm going to walk her out."

Damn it, I was grateful my family had accepted the way Everly had come into my life, and although many conversations were had with my parents and brothers, nothing had changed between them and my daughter.

I watched her and Sydney disappear and picked up the weights, slowly working through another set.

Since the cast had come off my arm, I'd hired a trainer and physical therapist to come to my home several times a week, the two of them working together to ensure I made a full recovery. On the days they weren't here, like today, I worked out without them.

I wanted my arm to be as strong as it had been before.

And in the short time since my cast had been taken off, I could already feel a huge difference.

I finished the set and pulled off my T-shirt, using it to wipe the sweat from my body. Once I was done, I tossed it on a bench and started some triceps extensions. I was only halfway through my count when Sydney came in.

She'd changed into a pair of yoga pants and a sports bra, not the jeans and tank top she'd been wearing only a few minutes before.

"Care if I join you?"

I smiled. "Please do."

Even though I knew I wouldn't be able to take my eyes off her fucking body.

That she would be the biggest distraction.

That I was certain I'd lose count during every set.

She grabbed the twenty-pound free weights from the rack, and while she watched herself in the mirror, she started doing shoulder presses.

Since she'd moved into the apartment above the garage, she used the gym almost every day. Her body had been fucking incredible before. Toned, curvy—everything I wanted in a woman.

But with her constant workouts, her arms were becoming more sculpted, her legs a little more muscular. She still had that soft, gentle frame, but now with a bit more punch.

I grabbed the thirty-pound free weights and went over to the decline bench.

"Need a spotter?" she asked.

I knew I could handle it.

These weights were light compared to what I used to lift before the accident.

I just wanted her close.

"If you don't mind," I replied.

She moved behind me, standing close to my head. "How many are you doing?"

"Eighteen reps, three sets."

"You've got this."

I chuckled. "All right, Coach Summers."

As I pushed the weights up from my chest, Sydney's hands hovered next to mine. They never touched me; they never grabbed for the weights. They just stayed there in case I needed her.

And although I was focused on my form, I couldn't ignore the view.

From this angle, her pussy wasn't far from my face. With her pants so tight, they were outlining one of my favorite parts of her, showing the dips of her lips, the gap between her thighs.

Teasing me.

Fucking taunting me.

"Twelve more," she said.

Past the waist of her pants was her bare stomach.

Flat.

Perfect.

The sports bra enhanced her cleavage, the tops of those gorgeous tits bulging from the material.

"Nine," she continued.

If I inhaled deep enough, I could smell the coconut.

My eyes briefly closed as I imagined what that flavor would taste like on her skin.

How it would roll across my tongue as I licked her.

How it would swirl down my throat as I swallowed her.

My dick was hard and throbbing as she said, "Three more."

I needed her.

"Great job," she added and placed her hands near mine. "I'm going to take these. You need to rest before your next set." She turned and set the weights on the floor.

Goddamn it, that fucking ass.

"Sydney ..."

She rose and turned around, looking at me. "Yes?"

Those pouty lips.

Those eyes that induced the naughtiest thoughts in my head.

There was no way I could do another set without tasting her. Without having her wetness on me.

My dick was too hard for me to focus on anything but her.

"Come here," I hissed, my stare dipping down her body. "Now."

She smiled.

She knew exactly where this was going.

She bit her bottom lip. "I'm distracting you, aren't I?"

And now, I knew she'd done it on purpose.

"It's far past that." I reached for her waist behind my head and guided her over until she was straddling the bench. As she went to sit on top of me, I stopped her and said, "No. Stand."

My grip lowered to the base of her pants.

There would be too many steps involved for her to take them off.

I didn't want to wait.

I needed her right now.

I positioned my hands at the crotch of her stretch pants and pulled until the cotton ripped.

"Ford!"

"I'll buy you ten more pairs." I created a sizable hole and demanded, "Get over here. Sit on my fucking face."

She moved past my waist and up to my chest, stopping at my neck with only a few inches to go.

I leaned up and placed my nose at the base of the hole I'd shredded, inhaling her scent. "Fuck me, Sydney." Our eyes connected, and my mouth watered for her. "I need you."

Her fingers dived into my hair, pulling me toward her pussy as she took her final steps, closing the gap between us.

The moment she was over my face, I didn't waste any time.

Nor did I lick slowly.

My tongue slid through the opening of her pants and flicked across her clit.

Fuck, she tasted good.

"Oh God!"

I tore an even larger hole to fit my face and focused on the very top of her pussy, swiping back and forth over that sensitive spot. My finger probed her wetness.

Twisting.

Turning.

A rhythm that was making her scream, "Ford!"

She ground her hips over me, causing my tongue to move faster.

Harder.

I added another finger, filling her with two, arching my wrist to give her G-spot more friction.

When I glanced up, she was staring down at me, eyes that were animalistic, lips that were parted and hungry.

"Sydney, ride my fucking face."

As she balanced on my shoulders, her head tilted back, her tits high in the air, her fingers stabbed me.

She rocked.

Back and forth.

And each time, my tongue swiped her.

"Faster," I barked.

Even though I couldn't get enough of her taste.

Even though I could have her in this position all day.

I wanted her to come.

"Oh, yes!"

She was close.

Her body was giving me every sign—her clit hardening, her pussy tightening around my fingers.

And she was fucking dripping.

But she needed just a little more.

A final push that would make her shudder.

So, I increased my speed. I thrust my fingers in and out of her, and I waited until her breaths ended in moans before I barked, "Come on my fucking face." I connected eyes with her. "Right now."

Within a few more licks, she was shuddering. "Ford!" She inhaled a deep breath, gasping, "Oh my God!"

I sucked on her clit, flicking the end with the tip of my tongue, watching the beat of the orgasm burst through her.

"*Yesss,*" she cried.

Nothing was hotter or more satisfying than owning Sydney's movements.

Then watching the pleasure spread across her.

Then having her turn so sensitive that even my tongue was too much.

She lifted her pussy off my mouth, so I could no longer reach her, and she backed up.

I swallowed her delicious taste down my throat and said, "Now, fucking ride me."

A grin came across her mouth as she shimmied down the rest of my body. "I need something first." She started to tug off my shorts and boxer briefs, eyeing my cock the second it sprang free.

Desire was etched across her face, and I knew where this was going.

What she wanted.

What she was about to give me.

Goddamn, this girl.

She surrounded my crown and began to bob down my shaft.

"Oh fuck." I banged the back of my head onto the bench, taking in the sensation of her throat. "Yes. Suck it."

This girl knew how to give head.

She used her hands, twisting her fingers around my shaft until she reached the base, rising to the center, where her fist met her lips.

That pattern repeated.

And with each dip, my hips drove up, and my fingers tightened around her hair.

"Fuck, Sydney ..."

I was paralyzed on this bench.

Drowning in pleasure.

I wanted to shoot my load into her mouth.

But I wasn't going to do that.

I was going to fill her pussy instead.

Except she was gripping her fingers around me, taking me deeper into her mouth.

Sucking her cheeks against me.

Swirling her tongue around me.

Urging my fucking orgasm.

Bringing me dangerously close.

I was seconds away from losing it when I barked, "Ride me."

When she didn't move, when it seemed like she couldn't get enough of my cock, I leaned up and pulled her mouth away, walking her body toward my tip.

"Jesus, Sydney. That fucking mouth of yours."

She smiled, wiping her lips as she positioned herself over me. "I can't get enough of you."

"And I can't wait to feel how fucking wet you are."

She lowered. "God, yes!"

The intensity was immediate.

As hard as her lips had drawn me in, this was the same.

But with her cunt.

"You're so tight," I moaned. So much so that she wasn't letting me go. "Fuck."

After a few more dips, I was lost.

The only thing I knew was that I needed to touch her.

To bite her.

I lifted the sports bra over her head and took her nipple into my mouth.

I tugged.

I licked.

I bit the very end.

And each time I moved my mouth, her fingers dived into my hair. "Ford, yes."

She was lifting, dropping, circling her hips, moving me inside her.

I needed the control, I needed to stop what was building in me, so I wrapped my arm around her waist, taking her weight, and I switched to her other nipple.

This time, I only used my teeth.

I scraped across the edge, pulling.

Flicking.

And right before I surrounded the back of her nipple, she increased her speed, causing me to moan, "Sydney."

She didn't slow as I squeezed her or as I tried to stop her.

She was taking what she wanted.

At this moment, it was my cock, and she was fucking me like she wanted to come.

Bringing me to that place I wouldn't be able to return from.

If I was going to fucking lose it, then so was she.

I licked my fingers and reached down to the top of her clit, and while her pussy stroked me, I rubbed back and forth.

"Yes!" she screamed, her hips bucking. "*Yesss!*"

She was narrowing.

She was getting even wetter.

She was close again.

I took one of her nipples into my mouth and released it, only to say, "Now, fuck me as hard as you can," before I bit down on it. I let go of her waist and reared my hand back, slapping her across the ass. "That's it, Sydney. Harder."

Her head fell back.

Her pussy clenched around me, keeping me in.

I arched my hips forward, giving her every inch I had.

And she took it.

"Faster," I growled.

I needed to see her come.

I needed to feel her quivers.

I needed her cunt to milk me.

"Ford!"

And there it was—that tightness, that wetness that flooded over me.

"Fucking come," I ordered, skimming my fingers across her clit like she was a guitar.

She gripped my shoulders and held on.

After only a couple more plunges, she mashed our lips together.

And she lost control. "Ford!"

Her body was overcome with shudders, ripples.

"Oh God!" she shouted. "I'm coming!"

It was fucking gorgeous to see her in that state.

And I was about to join her.

My fingers gripped her, stabbing. "Sydney! Fuck!"

She was dragging the orgasm out of me, pulling the cum from my cock.

The explosion moved fast, through my balls, through my dick.

I held it in for just a second.

And then I shot my first load into her pussy. "Yes!"

She was gliding back and forth, her moans telling me that the waves were just starting to calm in her body, and I was moving up and down, pumping, filling her.

"Fuck!" I propelled upward, burying myself. "Hell yes."

And she sank over me, taking my dick, swallowing everything I gave her.

I didn't stop until I was drained.

Until I was empty.

Until there was nothing left to give her.

Our movements halted, and she fell against my chest, her face in my neck.

That was where she stayed.

Breathing.

Cuddling.

But when she finally leaned back, her hands surrounded my cheeks, and her lips softly pressed to mine.

I couldn't get enough.

Of that coconut scent.

Of the feel of her.

Of the heat from her mouth enveloping me.

I separated us, and a swell moved through me.

One that made everything in my body tingle.

"Sydney ..." I hovered over her lips, tasting her in the air, my cock growing, hardening inside her. "I want you to fuck me again."

EPILOGUE

FORD

There were some things that looked extra stunning on Sydney. One of those was the sun. That was a reason—among many—that I'd taken her to Bali, a place she'd never been.

A place I knew where she could completely unplug.

A place I knew she would fall in love with.

Since she had eight weeks off until she started her fourth semester of college, finishing the last three on the Dean's List, we had plenty of time to play.

To celebrate.

I couldn't be fucking prouder of her.

She had a dream, and nothing was stopping her from achieving it. Not the seven classes she was taking a semester, doubling up to graduate early. Not the credits she had snuck in during her Christmas break. Not being Everly's nanny.

Not even me.

A man who had planned to be the single dad forever.

But Sydney had blown into my life and altered those plans.

And of course, things had changed at home since her first

day of school. She now lived in the main house. She had her own side in my large closet, the sink on the right in our en suite.

She also had half my heart.

The only person she had to share it with was Everly.

But for this trip—as far as Sydney knew—it was only going to be us.

When I'd told her that my parents were going to be watching Everly while we were gone for the two-week vacation, she had been disappointed.

She wanted Eve to experience Bali.

She wanted to create a picture book.

She wanted memories.

With the three of us.

Together.

The two of them had a special bond.

It had started before the accident, but the crash had only made them stronger. There was a unique level of trust between them.

A friendship.

My daughter soaked up every minute.

She finally had a woman in her life who wasn't a grandmother or an aunt or a cousin.

Sydney had crossed that mother border.

It was the most beautiful thing to watch.

Just as beautiful as seeing Sydney in a bikini.

She was next to me, spread across the lounge chair, her hair splayed over the top of the towel, a drink balanced in her hand.

The ocean lapped the sand only feet from where we lay, creating the perfect soundtrack.

I reached across the small space between us, tracing her stomach.

Bare.

Flat.

Curves I knew so well that I could draw them with my eyes closed.

"God, you're gorgeous."

She'd been staring at the water, but she slowly looked over at me. "Every time you say that …" Her voice trailed off as she gazed into my eyes, really taking me in. "It feels like the first time all over again."

I surrounded her fingers and brought them up to my mouth. I kept them there, kissing across her knuckles, breathing her in. "Come take a walk with me."

She kicked her legs over the lounge chair and stood in front of me, keeping our fingers locked.

She didn't question.

She just trusted me.

I led her a few paces into the ocean, so the waves crashed against our shins.

My arm rested across her shoulders, hers wrapped around my waist as we walked. The height difference allowed me to press my lips into the top of her head.

Inhaling her.

Kissing her.

"Paradise," she said softly, her sound almost getting carried into the wind. "I can't believe we have another week here." She gazed up at me, smiling. "At first, I thought two weeks was a little much to be away from our girl. But you're right; Bali can't be done in just seven days."

I stopped moving, positioning her right where I needed her to be, and I held her chin, tilting it up.

Lost in her eyes.

Her presence.

And then I kissed her.

Just briefly.

My lips brushing hers, my hand holding her steady.

And when I pulled my mouth away, I glanced over Sydney's shoulder, making sure she didn't see what I did.

The plan I'd put in place.

The one I wanted to keep as a surprise for just a few more seconds.

Holding her face with both hands, I said, "What if I told you we're only going to spend a few more days here, and then we're going to fly to Sydney and on to Melbourne and a stop in Auckland before heading home?"

"Are you serious?"

I nodded.

"Then, there's no way we'll only be gone for another week."

I grinned. "No ..." I gnawed on her bottom lip before I released it to say, "It'll be closer to three weeks total."

She sucked in a breath. "Ford, that would be so incredible, like beyond words."

As she paused, I waved my hand behind Sydney's back, giving the signal. "But ..." I said to her.

She continued to gaze at me, her chest rising as she said, "But what about Everly—"

"Syd! *Daaaddy*," I heard Everly shout.

Sydney processed the sound, and she turned around to where Everly was running down the beach.

"Oh my God," Sydney sang as Eve got closer.

My baby, all grown up in my eyes, was dressed in a pink bathing suit and a straw hat, looking so mature and still adorable.

An outfit I was sure Jo and Kendall had picked out.

"What are you doing here?" Sydney said as Everly fell into her arms.

I rubbed Everly's back, hugging the both of them against my chest.

"I came with Uncle D and Uncle Jenner."

"You did?" Sydney asked, looking at me.

"She sure did," I said to Sydney.

I pulled Sydney's face closer and kissed her.

"Did you plan this?" she asked the second we separated.

I didn't answer.

I just shifted my eyes to my daughter and said, "Everly, I think you have something you want to say to Sydney, don't you?"

She nodded so hard that her hat almost fell off. But she held it on tightly and said, "Syd, Daddy and I want you to be our ever and ever."

She held out her hand, and a diamond ring was on her thumb.

One that had taken weeks to design.

I'd wanted it to be everything I imagined for my future wife, everything that resembled Sydney's personality.

The round stone was surrounded by two diamonds.

My Everly and I came as a pair.

Sydney's fingers went over her mouth, her eyes wide and teary as she looked at me.

She hadn't realized I'd gotten on my knee.

That I was holding out my hand.

That I was asking, "Be my wife?"

"And my mommy," Everly chimed in.

I slipped my other arm around Everly, glancing at my daughter as I added, "Be ours."

I took the ring from Everly, and I positioned it over Sydney's finger.

Waiting.

It took only seconds for Sydney to reply, "Yes." Once the ring was on her finger, she bent down and threw her arms around us. "Forever and ever."

Interested in reading the other books in the Dalton Family Series

...

The Lawyer
The Billionaire
The Intern
The Bachelor
Or check out Signed, which stars Brett Young

ACKNOWLEDGMENTS

Nina Grinstead, every time I reach this section, it's hard for me to put into words what our journey has looked like over the last few months. Each book is so different, each process unlike the previous. This one is definitely no exception. You helped me overcome my fears. You held me when I wasn't sure I could go on. And you pushed me to reach goals and dreams I never thought were ever possible. We're in this together until the very end—and I'm talking about walkers, not words. *Love you* doesn't even come close to cutting it. Team B forever.

Jovana Shirley, there are very few people in my life who I could hand my child to and know that when it returns to me, it's going to be better than before. There are very few people who understand the creative process and how our minds work. And there are very few people who can help you polish your craft by showing rather than telling. But, Jovana, that's you. You've made me a better writer, you've encouraged me to tap into creative places I didn't know existed, and you've guided me in ways I'll always be grateful for. I'm never doing this without you. Never, ever. Love you so, so hard.

Hang Le, my unicorn, you are just incredible in every way.

Judy Zweifel, as always, thank you for being so wonderful to work with and for taking such good care of my words and for always squeezing me in last minute. <3

Chanpreet Singh, thank you for always holding me together and for helping me in every way and for being such a huge resource—this book needed you, and so did I. Adore you, lady. XO.

Kaitie Reister, I love you, girl. Thanks for being you.

Nikki Terrill, my soul sister. This one ... OMG, this one. You were my rock in every possible way. Every tear, vent, virtual hug, life chaos, workout—you've been there through it all. I could never do this without you, and I would never want to. Love you hard.

Sarah Symonds, my friend, you are the biggest blessing. I remember the beginning, the early conversations. The meetups at signings. The hugs—oh gosh, the hugs. And I think to where we are now, the constant help you give me, the love you share, and having you as my partner in crime through this wild, wild ride. I wouldn't want to do this without you. Ever.

Ratula Roy, thank you for the countless conversations, the brainstorming, for celebrating every bit of happiness with me, and for helping me through every patch of tears. I always say, you have my back, my heart, and my love—and it couldn't be truer. Love you.

Kimmi Street, my sister from another mister. We'll never forget this one, will we? ;) Thank you from the bottom of my heart. You saved me. You inspired me. You kept me standing in so many different ways. I love you more than love.

Sarah Norris, you were such a tremendous help and such a huge asset for this book. Thank you endlessly. I appreciate you so much.

Extra-special love goes to Valentine PR, Kelley Beckham, Kayti McGee, Tracey Waggaman, Elizabeth Kelley, Jennifer Porpora, Pat Mann, and my group of Sarasota girls, whom I love more than anything. I'm so grateful for all of you.

Mom and Dad, thanks for your unwavering belief in me and your constant encouragement. It means more than you'll ever know.

Brian, my words could never dent the love I feel for you. Trust me when I say, I love you more.

My Midnighters, you are such a supportive, loving, motivating group. Thanks for being such an inspiration, for holding my hand when I need it, and for always begging for more words. I love you all.

To all the bloggers who read, review, share, post, tweet, Instagram—Thank you, thank you, thank you will never be enough. You do so much for our writing community, and we're so appreciative.

To my readers—I cherish each and every one of you. I'm so grateful for all the love you show my books, for taking the time to reach out to me, and for your passion and enthusiasm. I love, love, love you.

MARNI'S MIDNIGHTERS

Getting to know my readers is one of my favorite parts about being an author. In Marni's Midnighters, my private Facebook group, I post covers before they're revealed to the public and excerpts of the projects I'm currently working on, and team members qualify for exclusive giveaways.

To join Marni's Midnighters, click HERE.

ABOUT THE AUTHOR

USA Today best-selling author Marni Mann knew she was going to be a writer since middle school. While other girls her age were daydreaming about teenage pop stars, Marni was fantasizing about penning her first novel. She crafts sexy, titillating stories that weave together her love of darkness, mystery, passion, and human emotions. A New Englander at heart, she now lives in Sarasota, Florida, with her husband and their yellow Lab. When she's not nose deep in her laptop, working on her next novel, she's scouring for chocolate, sipping wine, traveling, or devouring fabulous books.

Want to get in touch? Visit Marni at ...
www.marnismann.com
MarniMannBooks@gmail.com

ALSO BY MARNI MANN

STAND-ALONE NOVELS

Even If It Hurts (Contemporary Romance)

Before You (Contemporary Romance)

The Assistant (Psychological Thriller)

THE DALTON FAMILY SERIES—EROTIC ROMANCE

The Lawyer

The Billionaire

The Single Dad

The Intern

The Bachelor

THE AGENCY SERIES—EROTIC ROMANCE

Signed

Endorsed

Contracted

Negotiated

THE BEARDED SAVAGES SERIES—EROTIC ROMANCE

The Unblocked Collection

Wild Aces

MOMENTS IN BOSTON SERIES—CONTEMPORARY ROMANCE

When Ashes Fall

When We Met

When Darkness Ends

THE PRISONED SERIES—DARK EROTIC THRILLER

Prisoned

Animal

Monster

THE SHADOWS DUET—EROTIC ROMANCE

Seductive Shadows

Seductive Secrecy

THE BAR HARBOR DUET—NEW ADULT

Pulled Beneath

Pulled Within

THE MEMOIR SERIES—DARK MAINSTREAM FICTION

Memoirs Aren't Fairytales

Scars from a Memoir

NOVELS COWRITTEN WITH GIA RILEY

Lover (Erotic Romance)

Drowning (Contemporary Romance)